THE WOMAN IN THE WOODS

and Other North American Stories

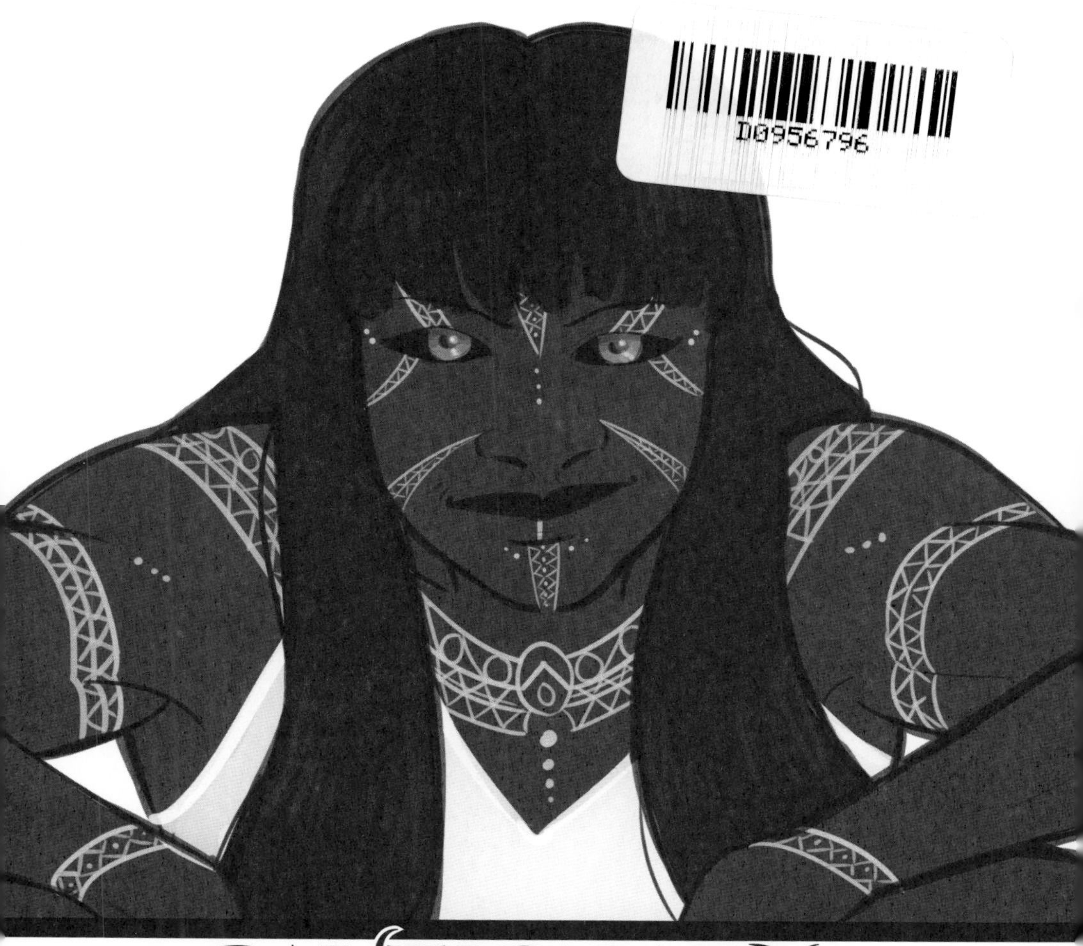

A CAUTIONARY FABLES & FAIRYTALES Book

editors
Kel McDonald, Kate Ashwin & Alina Pete

cover artist
Alina Pete

publisher
C. Spike Trotman

art director
Matt Sheridan

print technician & book design
Beth Scorzato

proofreader
Abby Lerkhe

published by
Iron Circus Comics
329 West 18th Street, Suite 604
Chicago, IL 60616
ironcircus.com

first edition: April 2022

ISBN: 978-1-945820-97-7

10 9 8 7 6 5 4 3 2 1

Printed in United States

strange and amazing

inquiry@ironcircus.com www.ironcircus.com

The Woman in the Woods and other North American Stories

Publisher's Cataloging-In-Publication Data
(Prepared by The Donohue Group, Inc.)

Names: McDonald, Kel, editor. | Ashwin, Kate, editor. | Pete, Alina, editor.
Title: The woman in the woods : and other North American stories / [editors, Kel McDonald, Kate Ashwin & Alina Pete].
Other Titles: Cautionary fables & fairytales (Series) ; 5.
Description: First edition. | Chicago, IL : Iron Circus Comics, 2022. | Interest age level: 010-012. | Summary: "A comics anthology featuring updated takes on ancient stories from tribes spanning the North American continent"--Provided by publisher.
Identifiers: ISBN 9781945820977 (trade paperback)
Subjects: LCSH: Indians of North America--Folklore--Comic books, strips, etc. | Fairy tales--North America--Comic books, strips, etc. | CYAC: Indians of North America--Folklore--Fiction. | Fairy tales--North America--Fiction. | LCGFT: Folk tales. | Fairy tales. | Fables. | Graphic novels.
Classification: LCC PZ7.7 .W66 2022 | DDC [Fic] 398.2097--dc23

TABLE OF CONTENTS

As It Was Told To Me *(Odawa)*
Elijah Forbes..5

chokfi *(Chickasaw)*
Jordaan Arledge & Mekala Nava 16

White Horse Plains *(Métis/Cree)*
Rhael McGregor..34

The Rougarou *(Métis)*
Maija Ambrose Plamondon & Milo Applejohn......................49

Agonjin In The Water *(Ojibwe)*
Alice RL...79

The Woman In The Woods *(Taino)*
Mercedes Acosta 99

Into The Darkness *(Navajo)*
Izzy Roberts & Aubrie Warner 107

By The Light Of The Moon *(S'Kallam)*
Jeffrey Veregge & Alina Pete 126

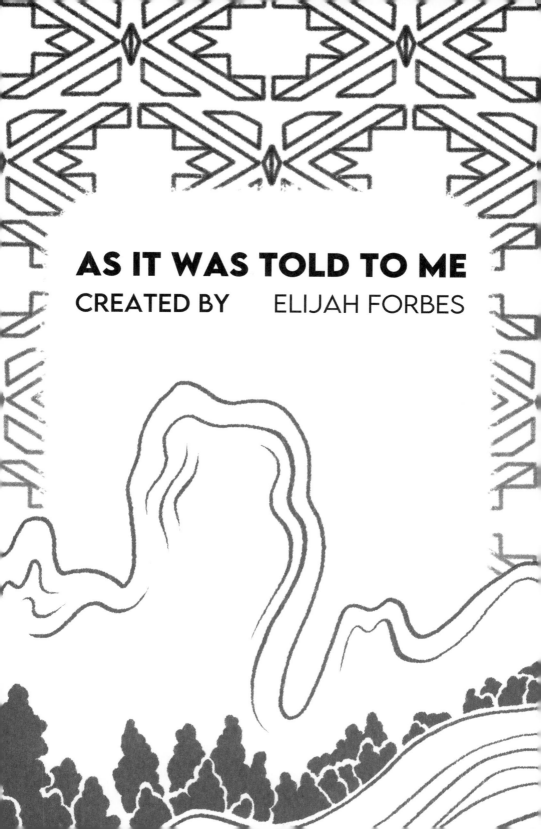

AS IT WAS TOLD TO ME
CREATED BY   ELIJAH FORBES

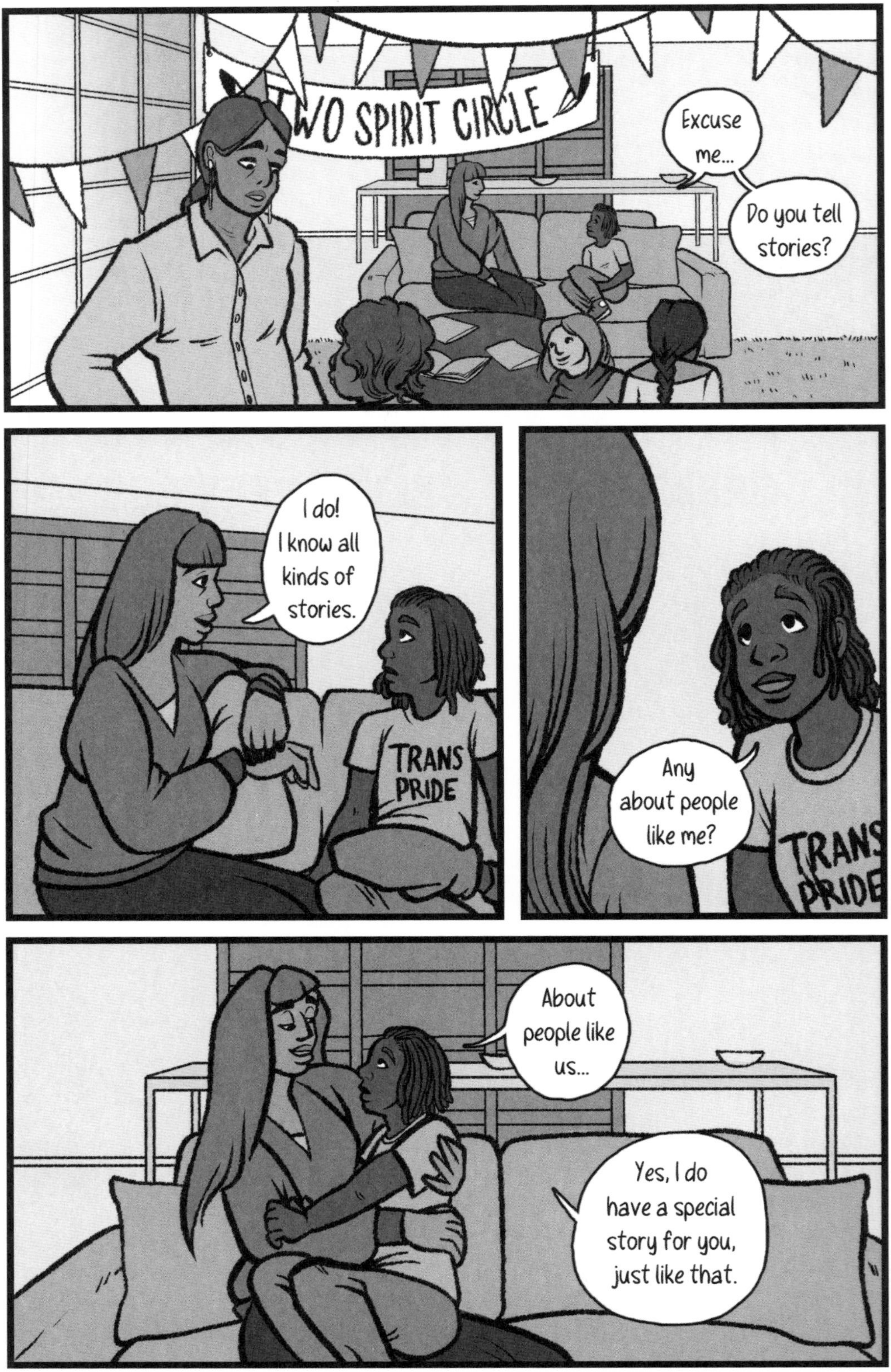
TWO SPIRIT CIRCLE
Excuse me...
Do you tell stories?
I do! I know all kinds of stories.
TRANS PRIDE
Any about people like me?
TRANS PRIDE
About people like us...
Yes, I do have a special story for you, just like that.

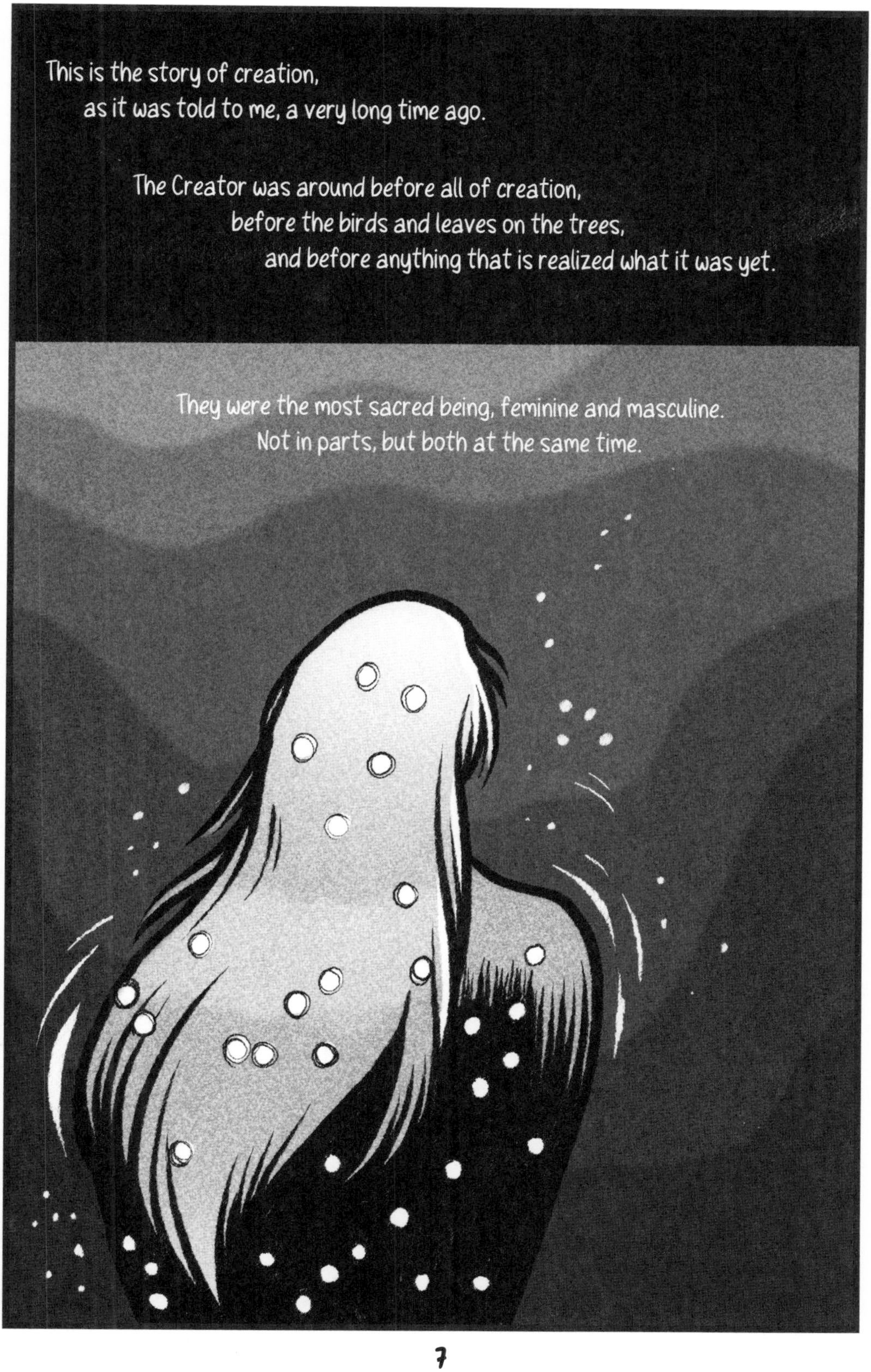
This is the story of creation,
as it was told to me, a very long time ago.
The Creator was around before all of creation,
before the birds and leaves on the trees,
and before anything that is realized what it was yet.
They were the most sacred being, feminine and masculine.
Not in parts, but both at the same time.

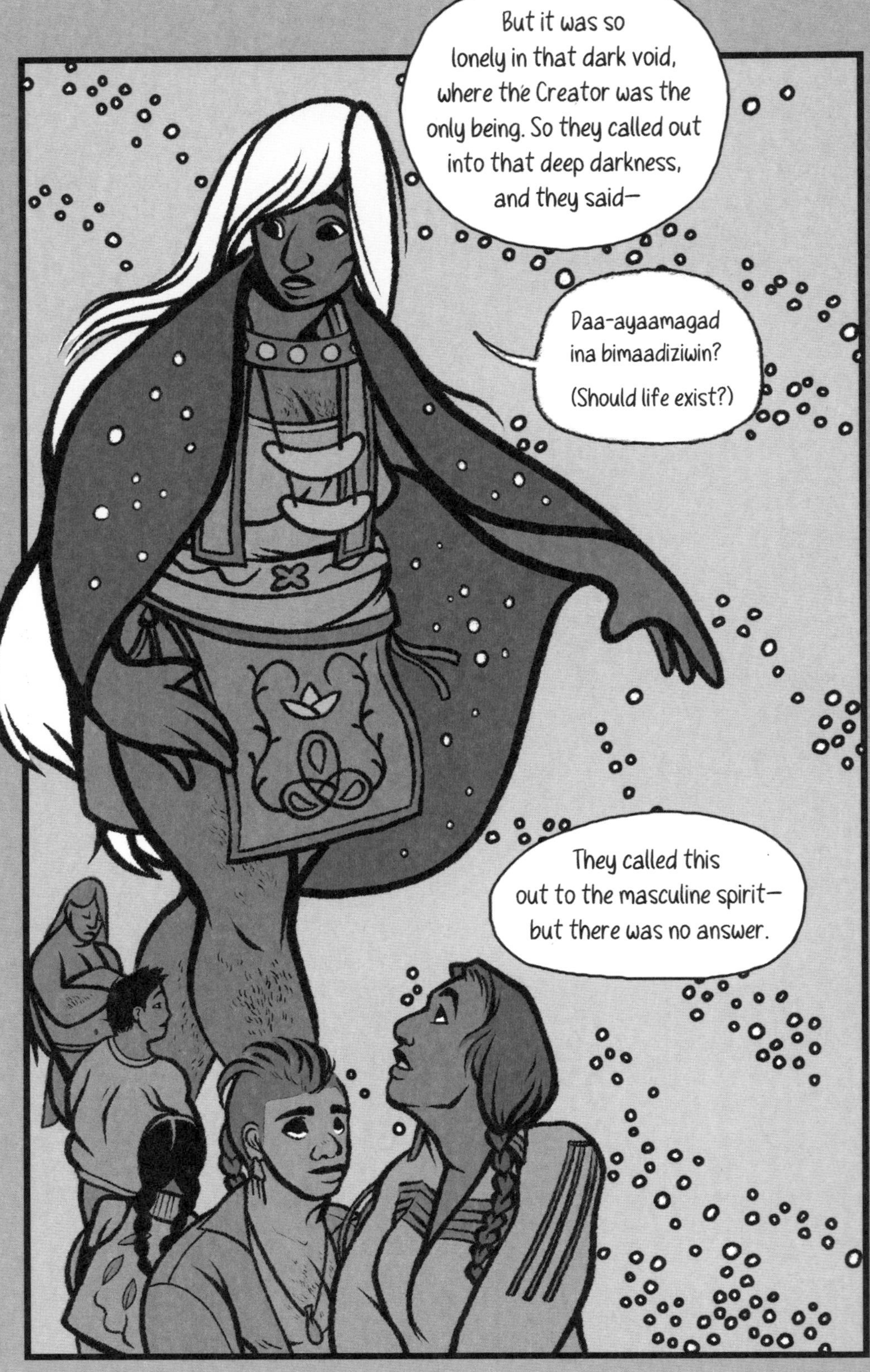
But it was so lonely in that dark void, where the Creator was the only being. So they called out into that deep darkness, and they said—
Daa-ayaamagad ina bimaadiziwin?
(Should life exist?)
They called this out to the masculine spirit— but there was no answer.

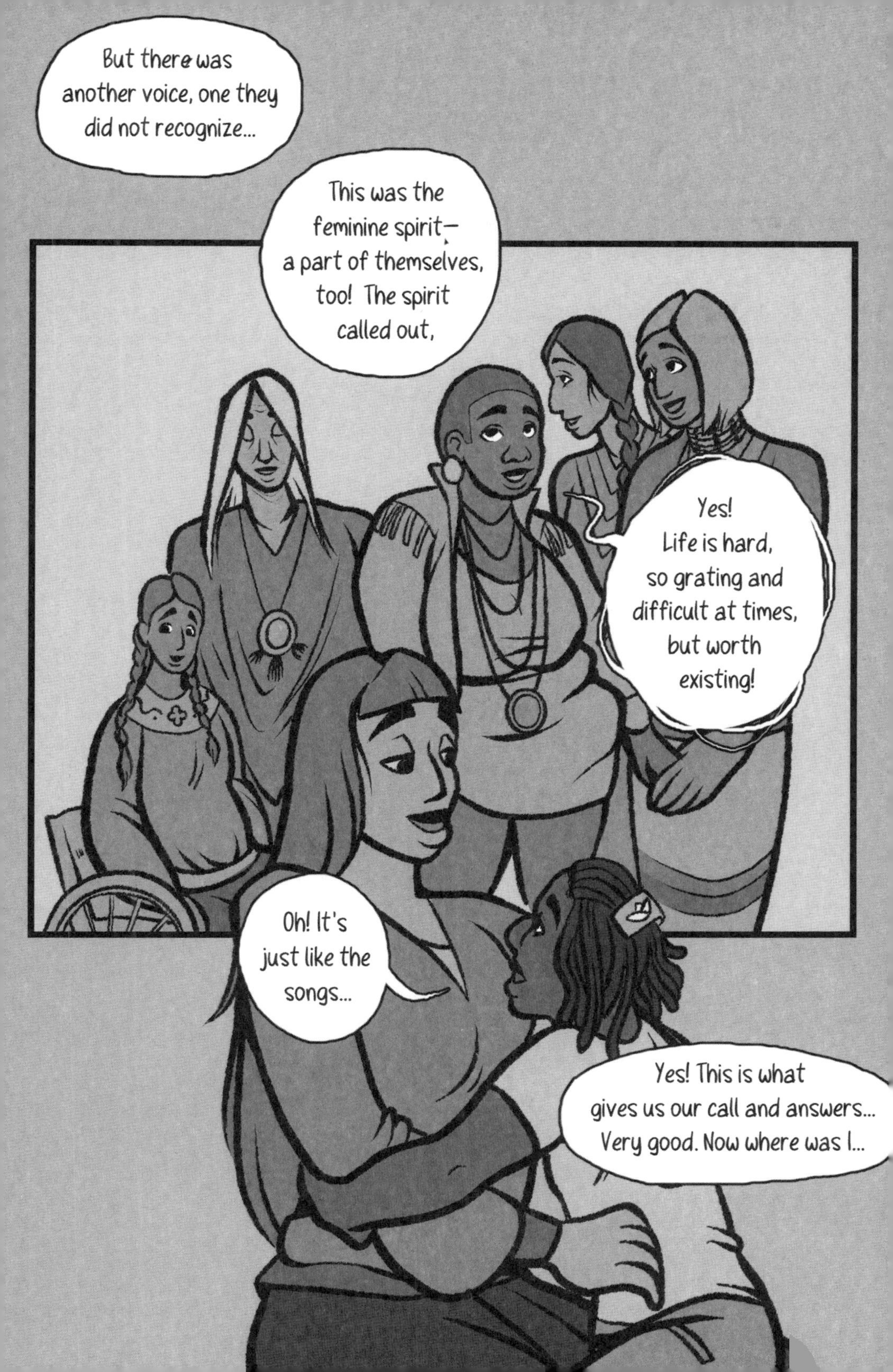
But there was another voice, one they did not recognize...
This was the feminine spirit— a part of themselves, too! The spirit called out,
Yes! Life is hard, so grating and difficult at times, but worth existing!
Oh! It's just like the songs...
Yes! This is what gives us our call and answers... Very good. Now where was I...

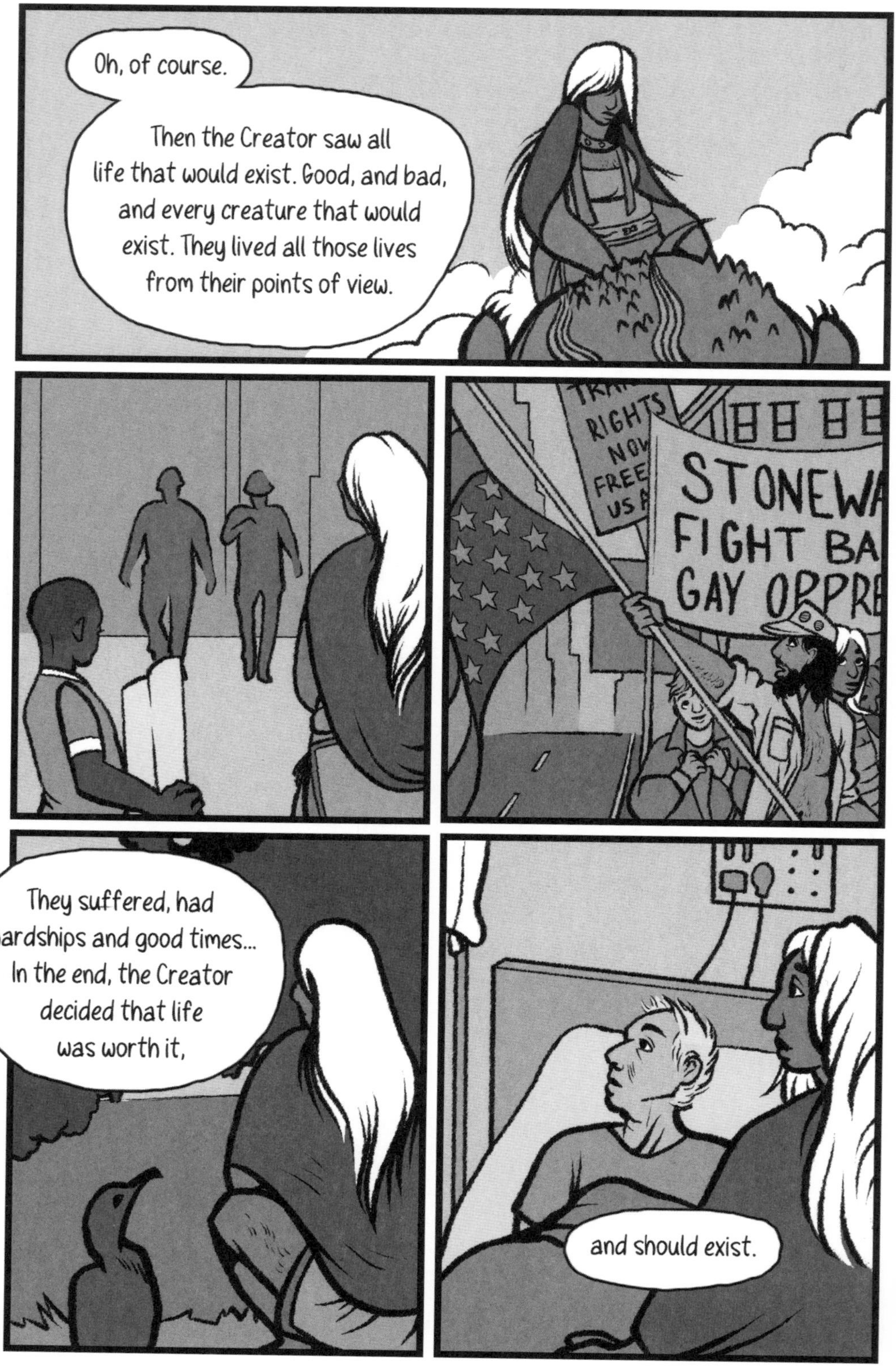
Oh, of course.
Then the Creator saw all life that would exist. Good, and bad, and every creature that would exist. They lived all those lives from their points of view.
RIGHTS NOW FREE US
STONEWA FIGHT BA GAY OPPRE
They suffered, had hardships and good times... In the end, the Creator decided that life was worth it,
and should exist.

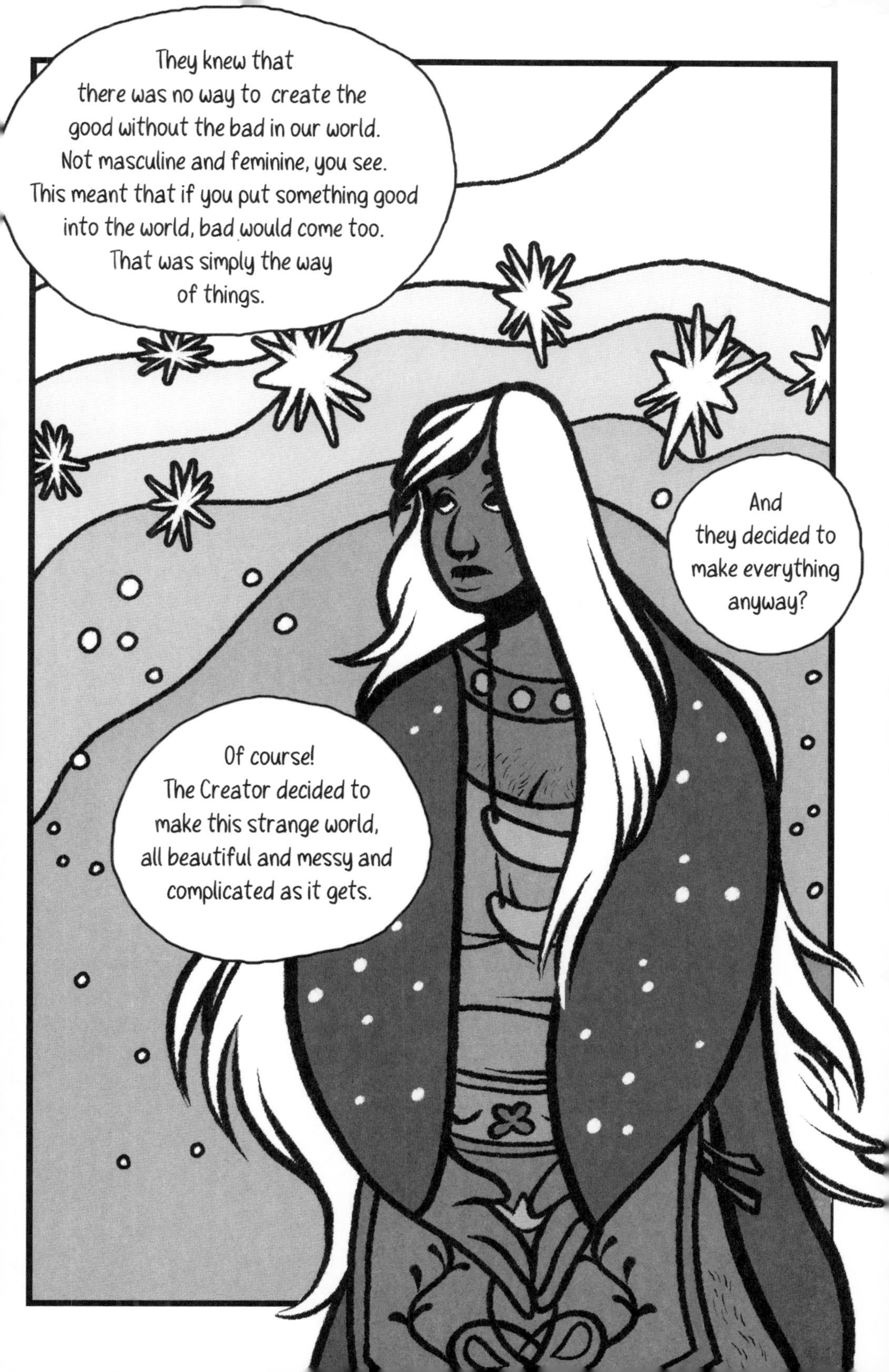
They knew that there was no way to create the good without the bad in our world. Not masculine and feminine, you see. This meant that if you put something good into the world, bad would come too. That was simply the way of things.
And they decided to make everything anyway?
Of course! The Creator decided to make this strange world, all beautiful and messy and complicated as it gets.

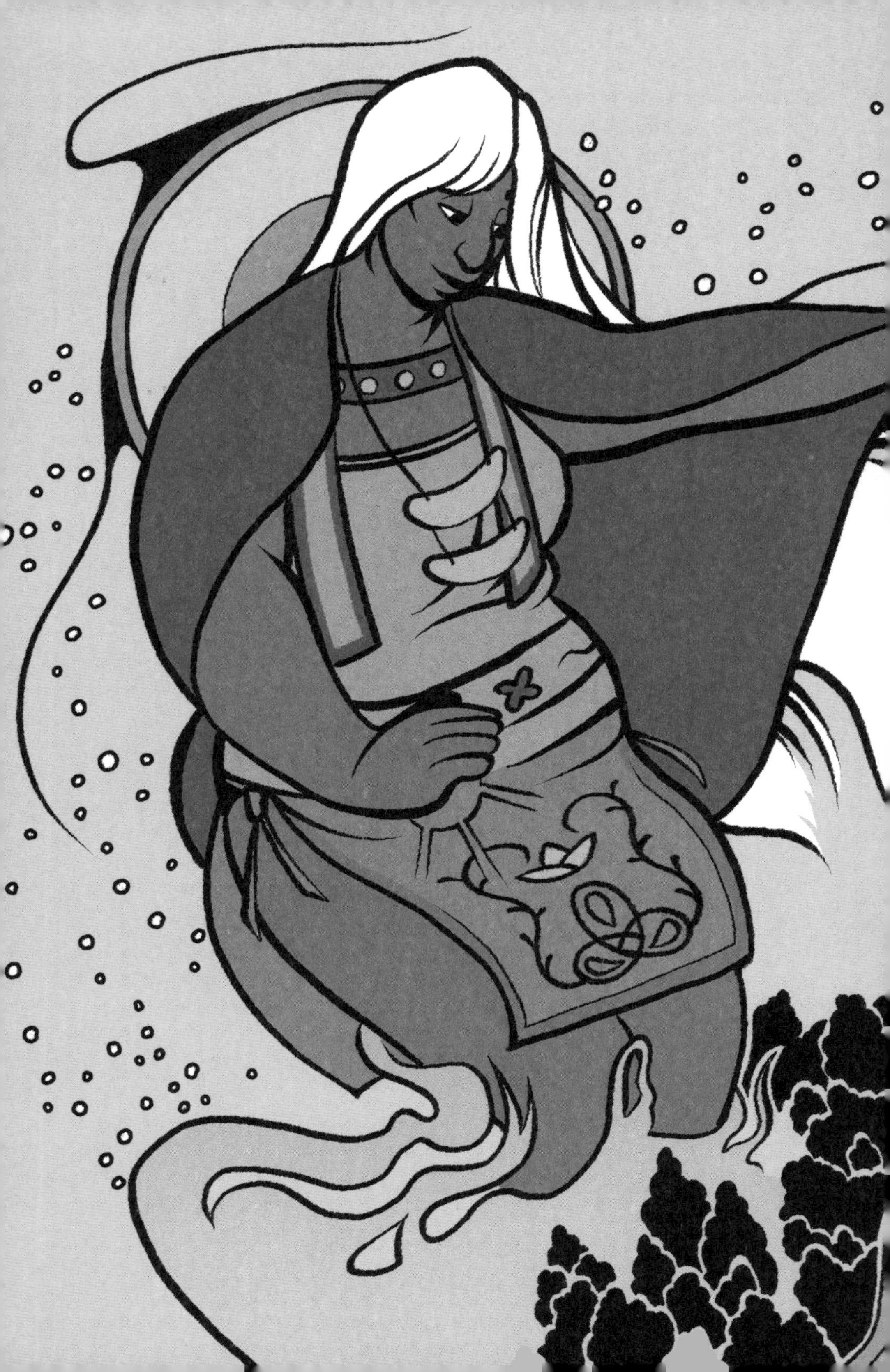

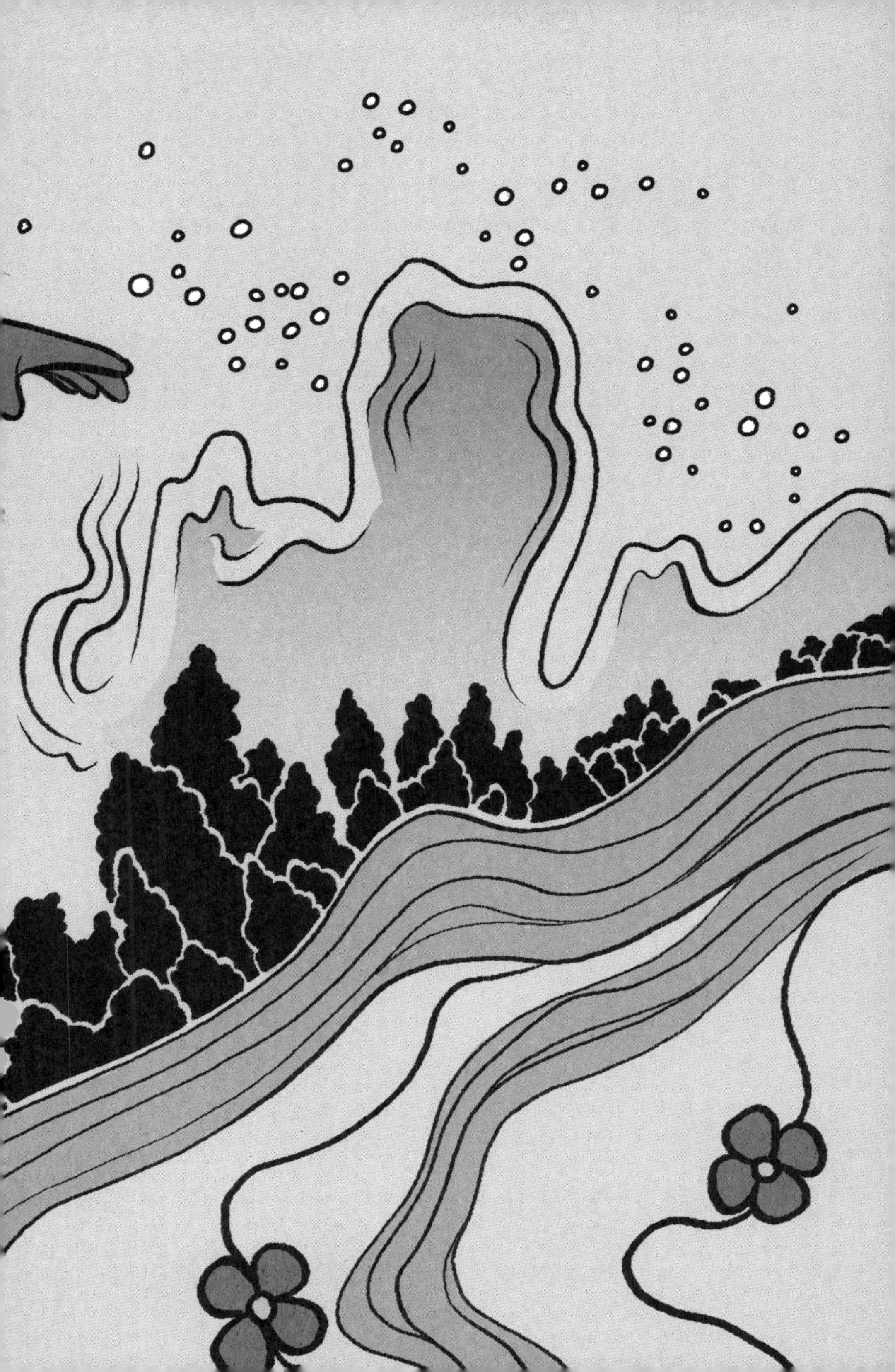

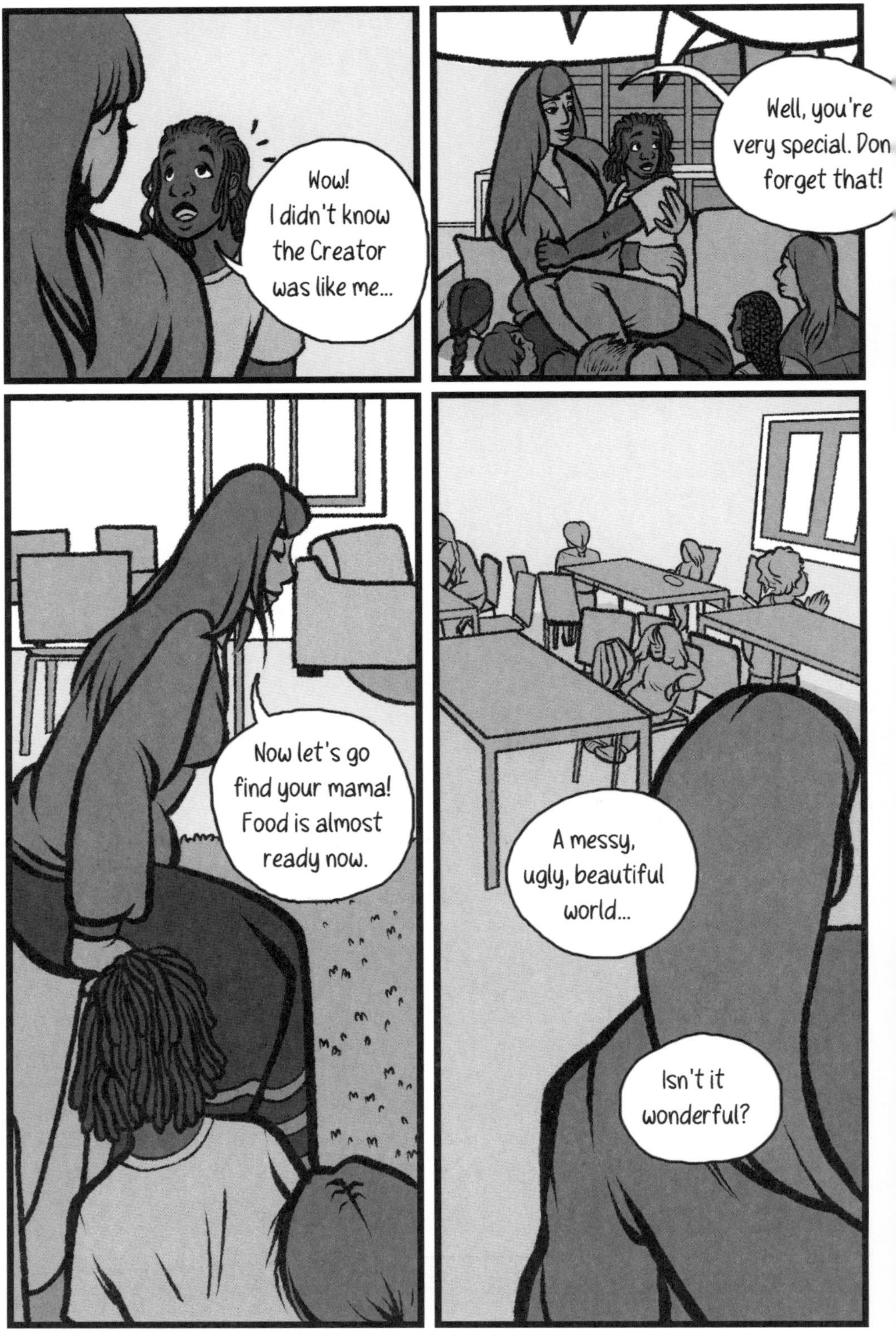
Wow! I didn't know the Creator was like me...
Well, you're very special. Don forget that!
Now let's go find your mama! Food is almost ready now.
A messy, ugly, beautiful world...
Isn't it wonderful?

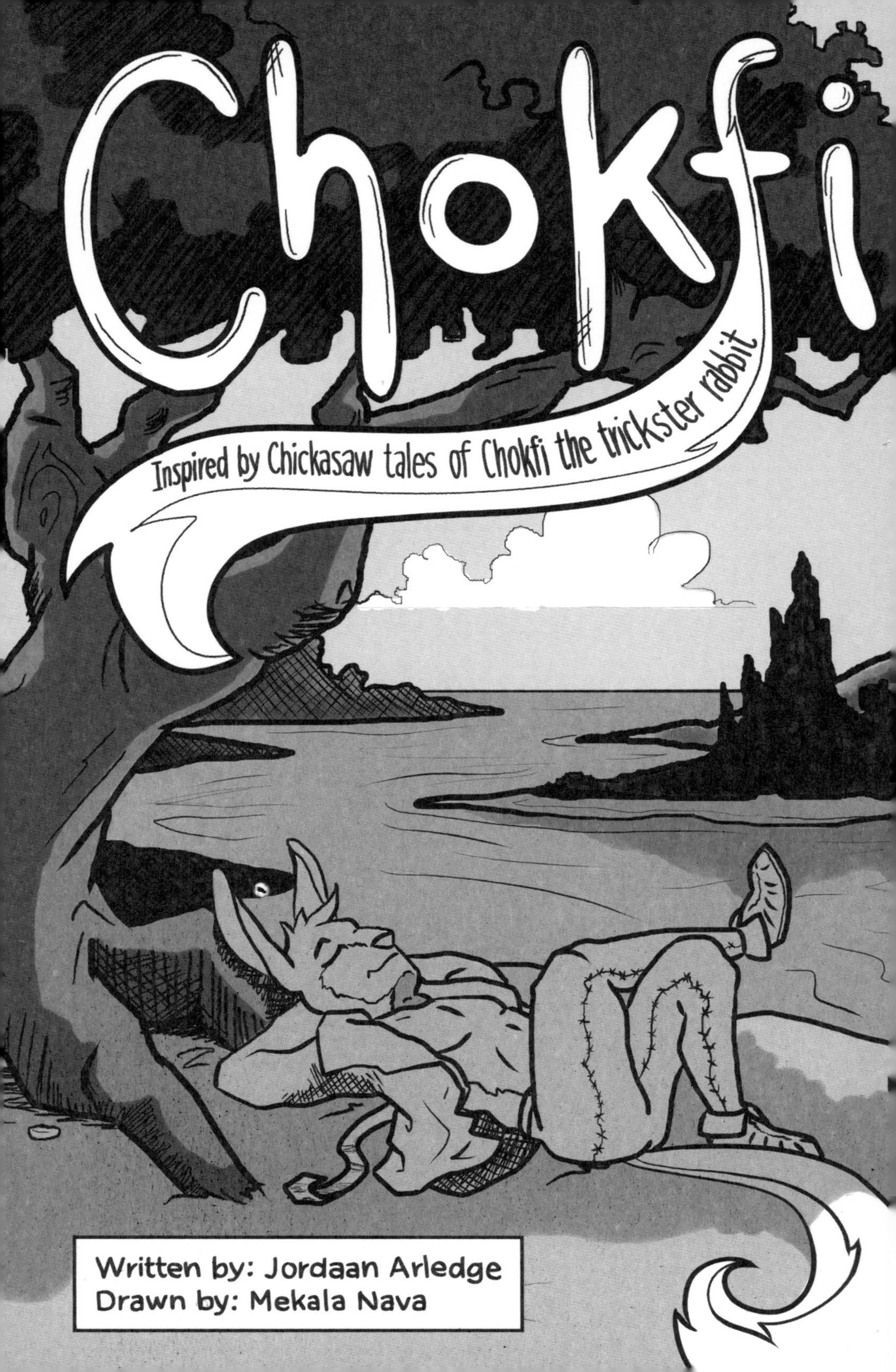
Chokfi
Inspired by Chickasaw tales of Chokfi the trickster rabbit
Written by: Jordaan Arledge
Drawn by: Mekala Nava

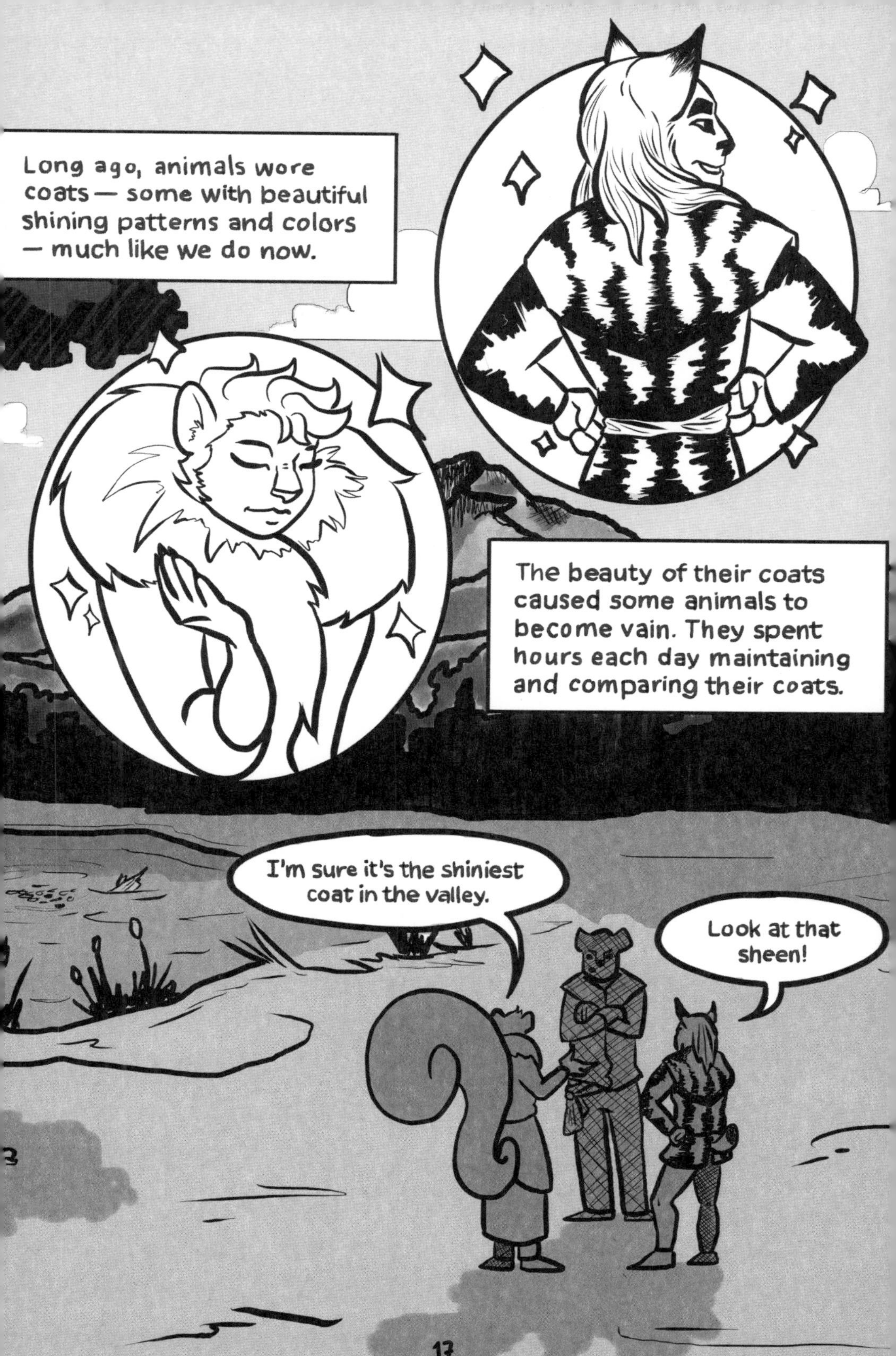

Long ago, animals wore coats — some with beautiful shining patterns and colors — much like we do now.
The beauty of their coats caused some animals to become vain. They spent hours each day maintaining and comparing their coats.
I'm sure it's the shiniest coat in the valley.
Look at that sheen!

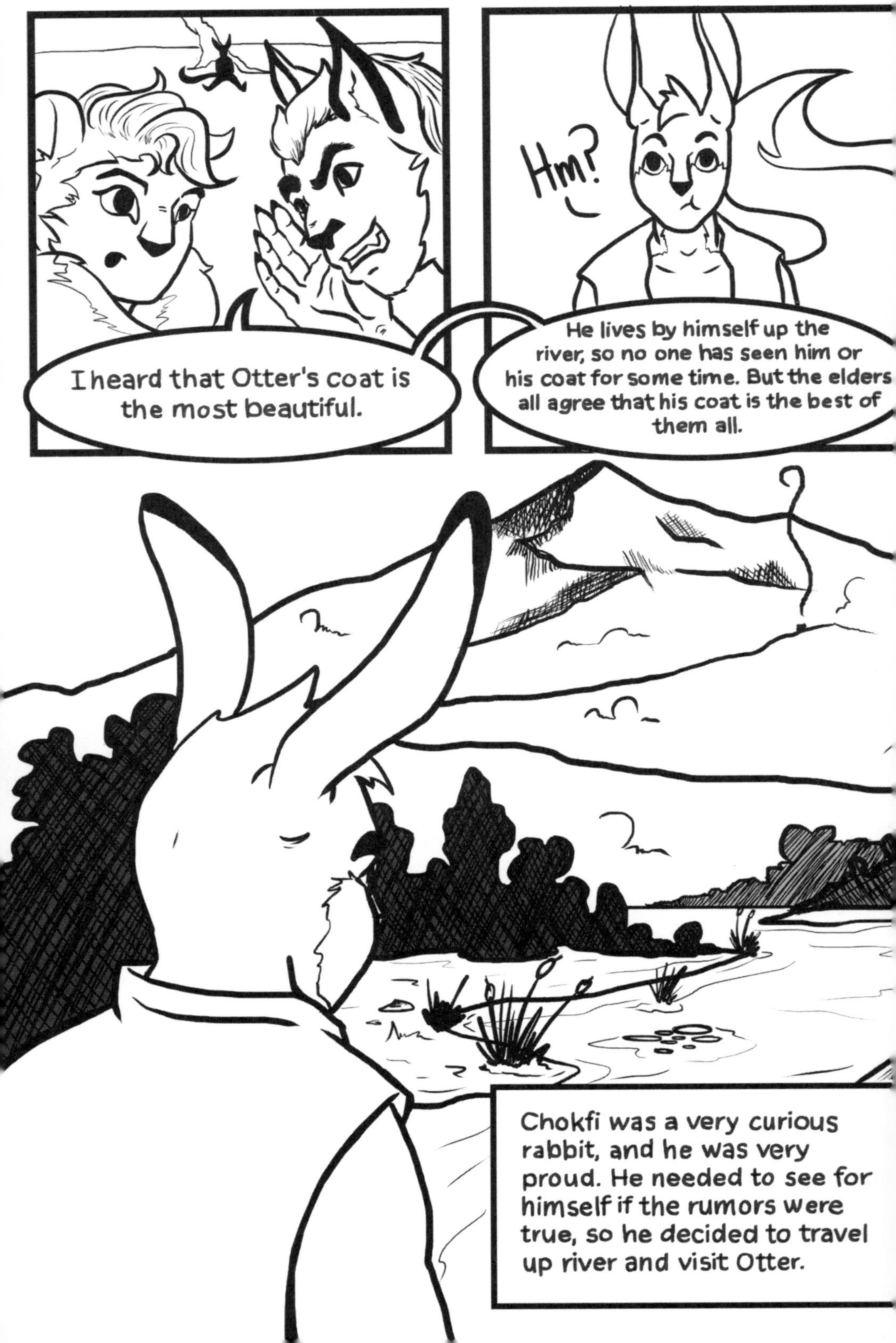

I heard that Otter's coat is the most beautiful.
Hm?
He lives by himself up the river, so no one has seen him or his coat for some time. But the elders all agree that his coat is the best of them all.
Chokfi was a very curious rabbit, and he was very proud. He needed to see for himself if the rumors were true, so he decided to travel up river and visit Otter.

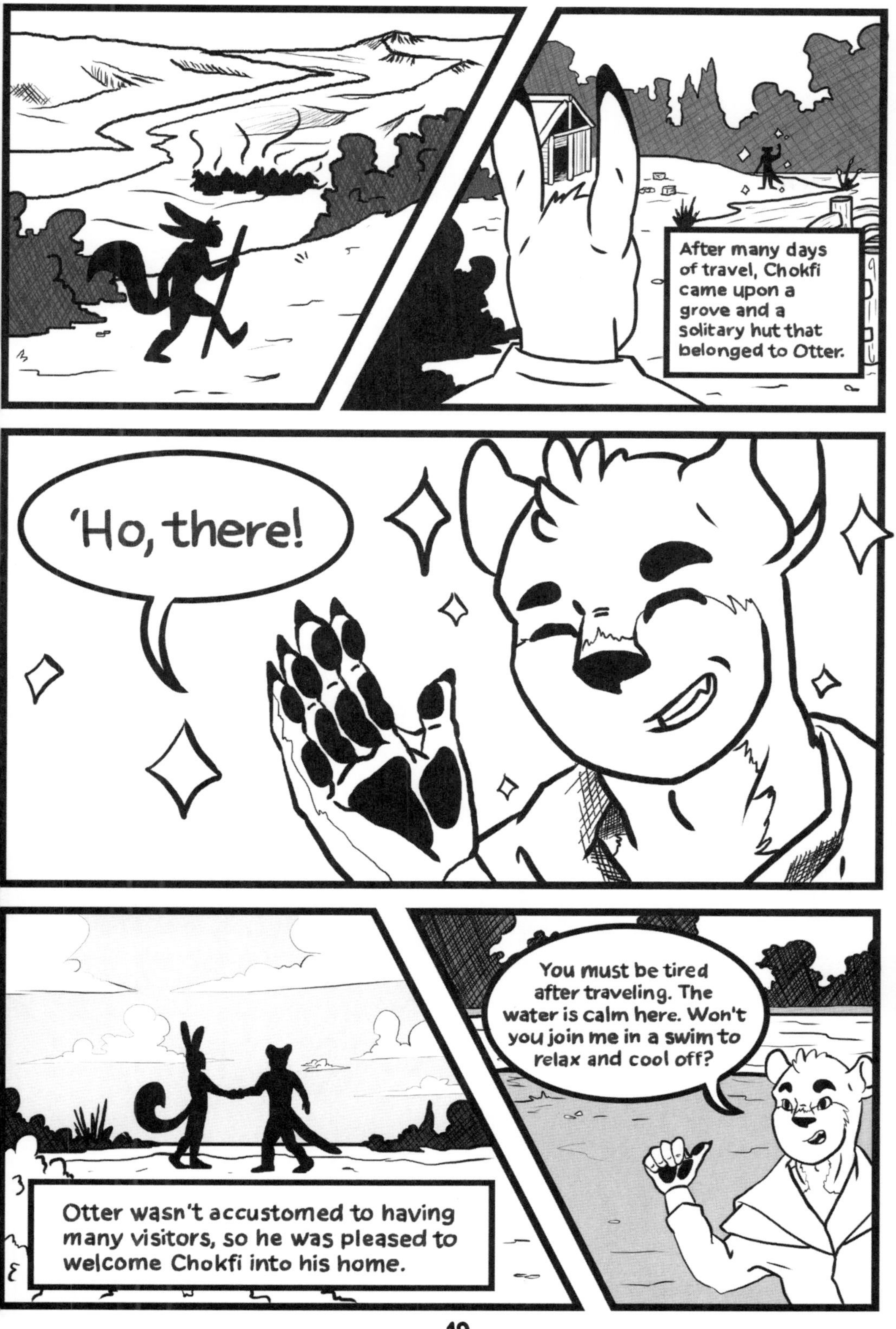
After many days of travel, Chokfi came upon a grove and a solitary hut that belonged to Otter.
'Ho, there!
Otter wasn't accustomed to having many visitors, so he was pleased to welcome Chokfi into his home.
You must be tired after traveling. The water is calm here. Won't you join me in a swim to relax and cool off?

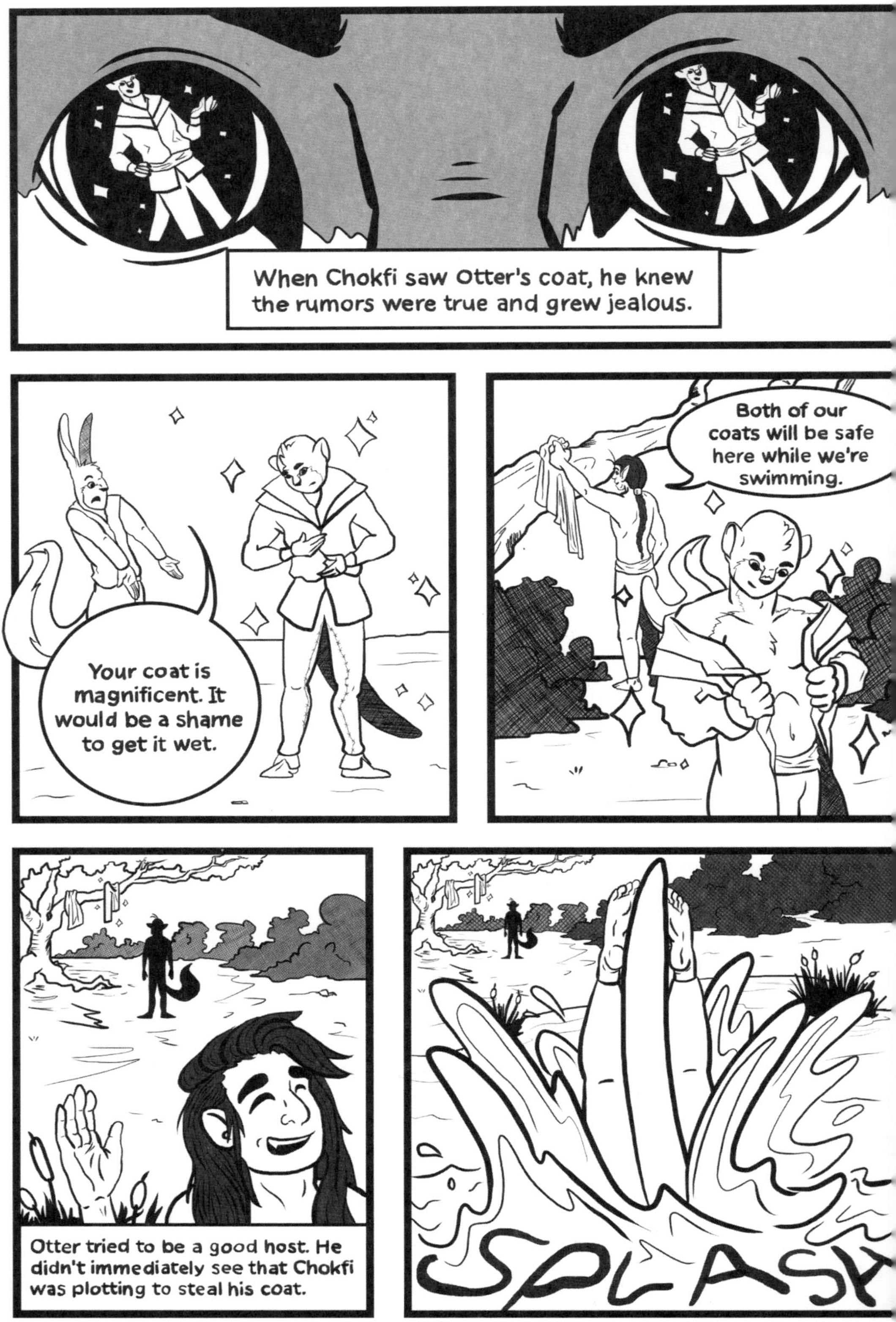
When Chokfi saw Otter's coat, he knew the rumors were true and grew jealous.
Your coat is magnificent. It would be a shame to get it wet.
Both of our coats will be safe here while we're swimming.
Otter tried to be a good host. He didn't immediately see that Chokfi was plotting to steal his coat.
SPLASH

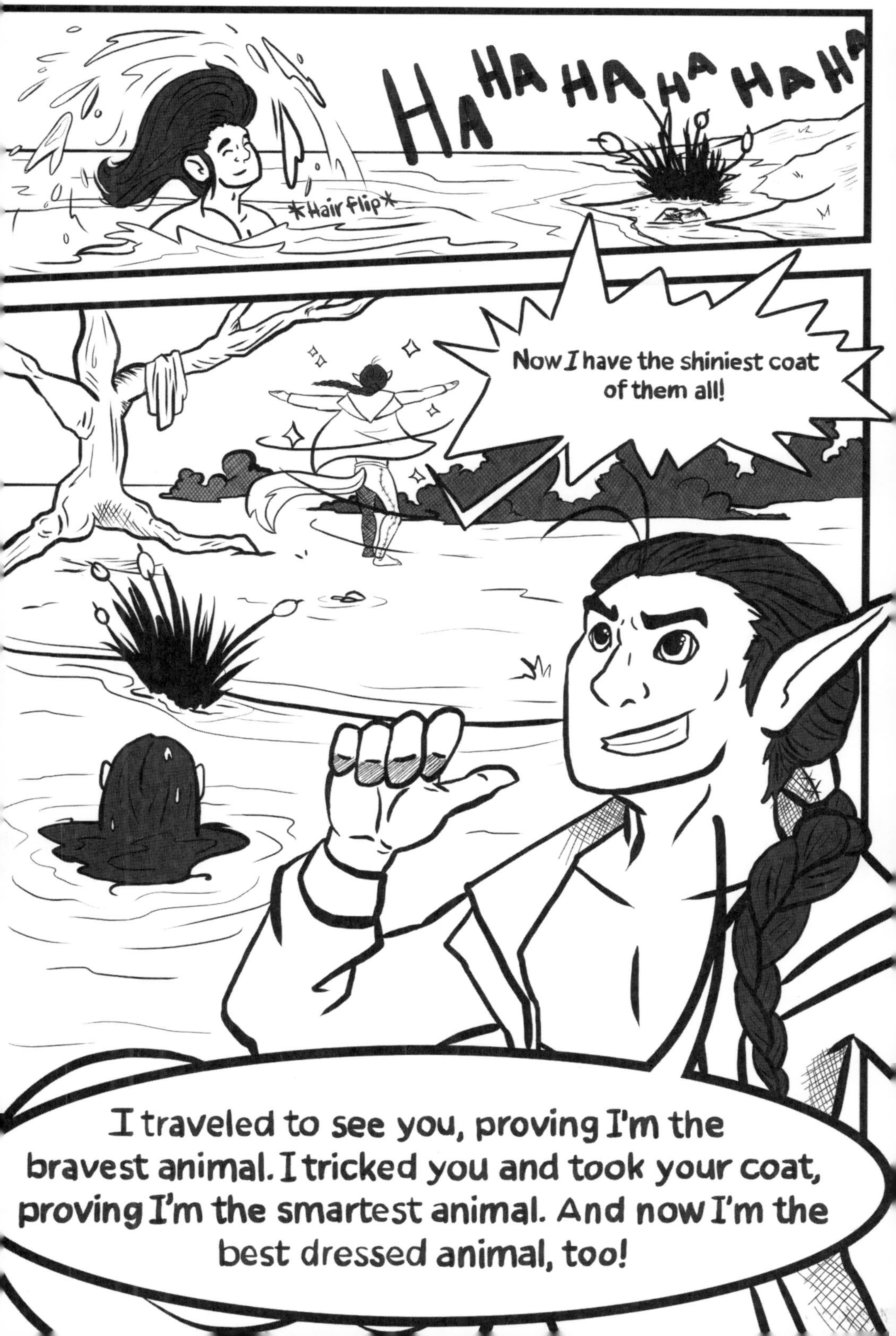
Hair flip
HA HA HA HA HA HA HA HA
Now I have the shiniest coat of them all!
I traveled to see you, proving I'm the bravest animal. I tricked you and took your coat, proving I'm the smartest animal. And now I'm the best dressed animal, too!

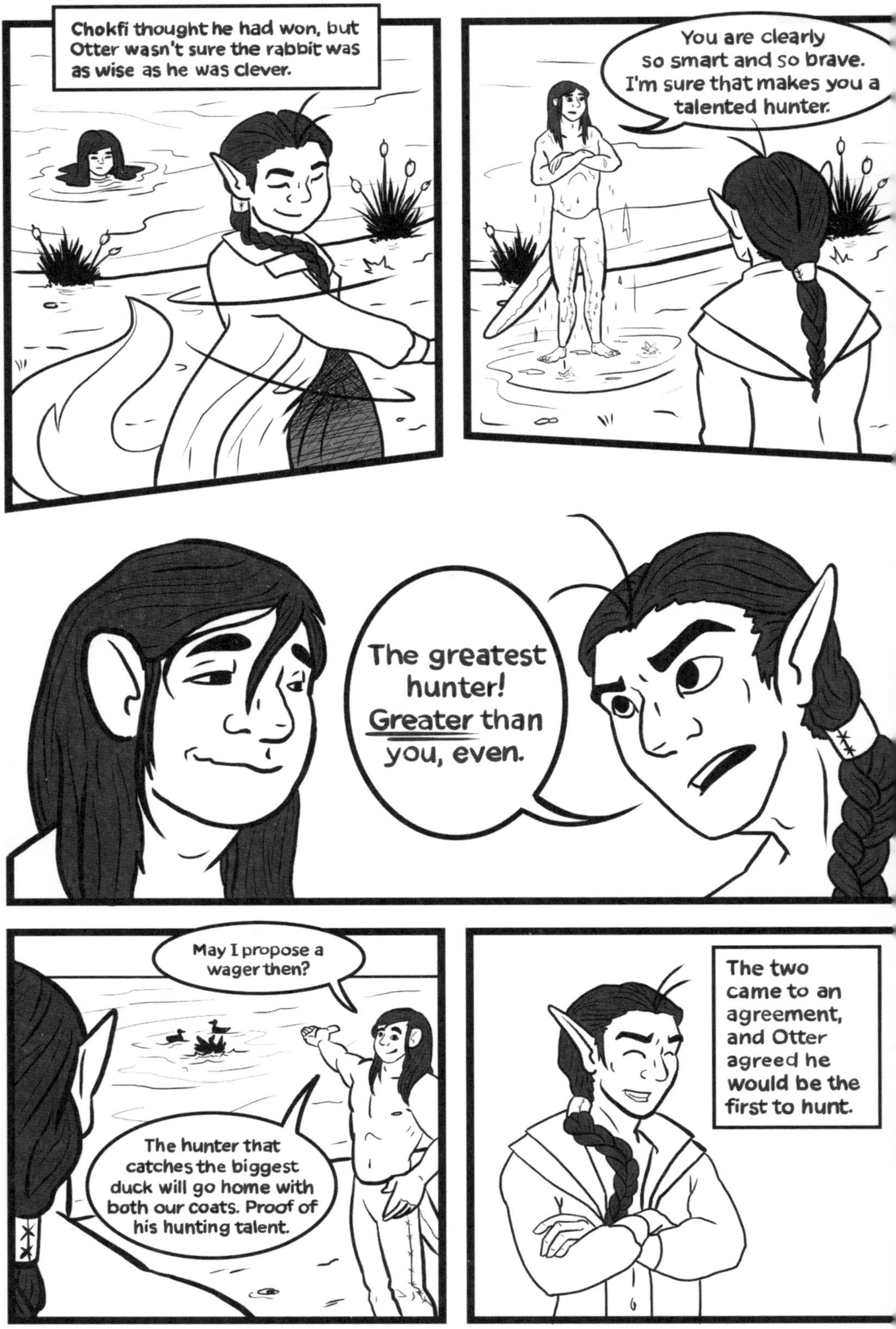
Chokfi thought he had won, but Otter wasn't sure the rabbit was as wise as he was clever.
You are clearly so smart and so brave. I'm sure that makes you a talented hunter.
The greatest hunter! Greater than you, even.
May I propose a wager then?
The hunter that catches the biggest duck will go home with both our coats. Proof of his hunting talent.
The two came to an agreement, and Otter agreed he would be the first to hunt.

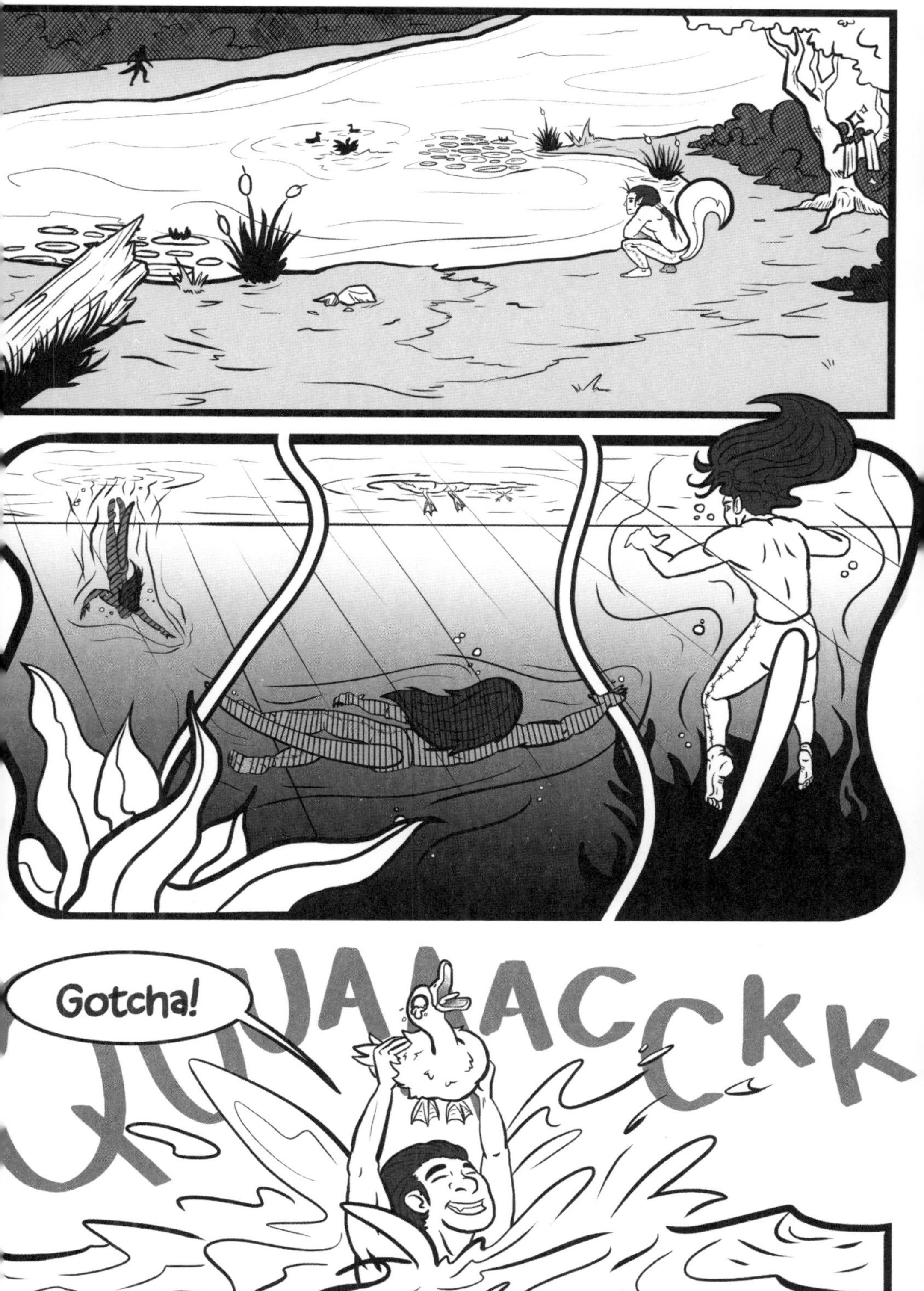
Gotcha!
QUUAAACCKK

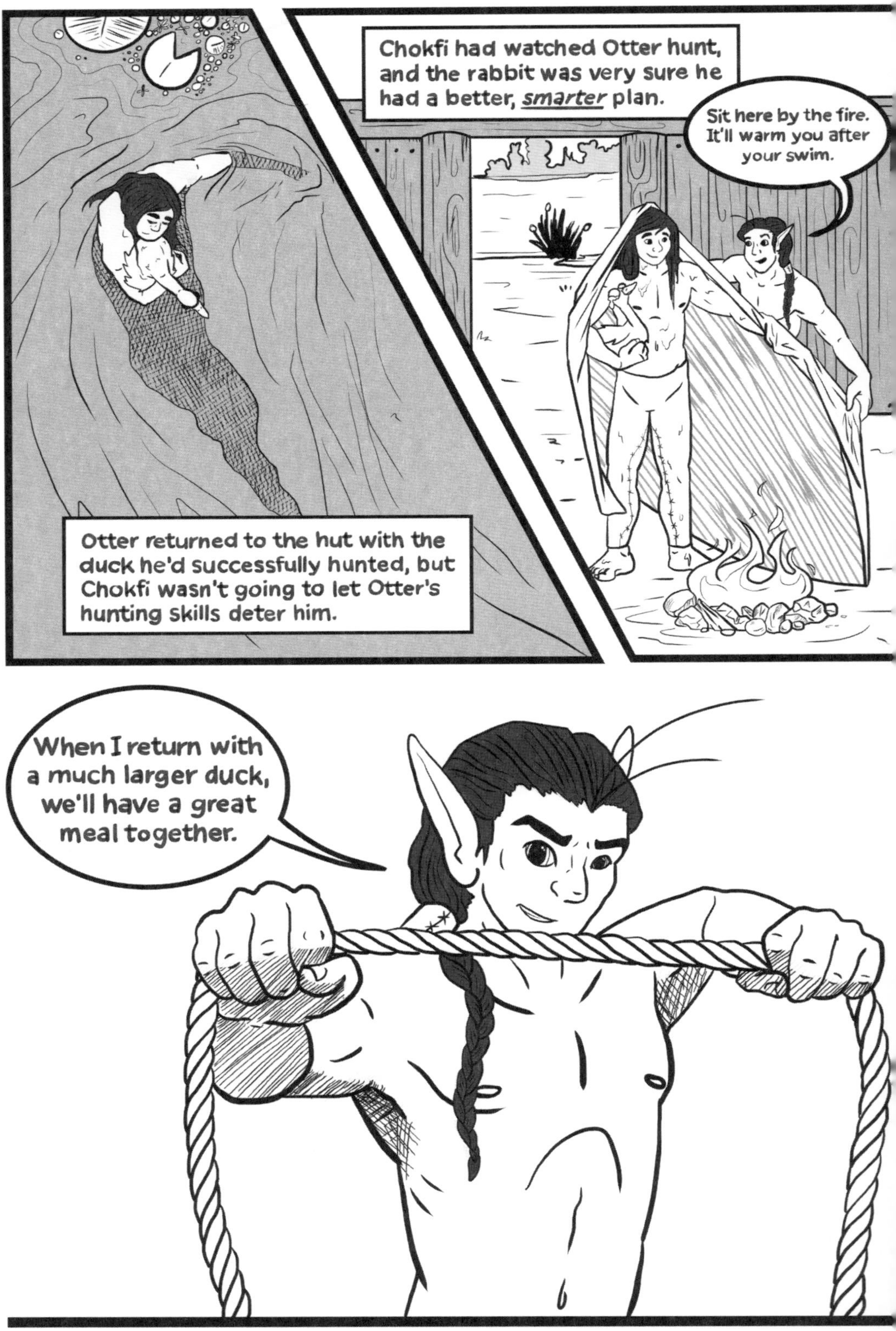
Otter returned to the hut with the duck he'd successfully hunted, but Chokfi wasn't going to let Otter's hunting skills deter him.
Chokfi had watched Otter hunt, and the rabbit was very sure he had a better, *smarter* plan.
Sit here by the fire. It'll warm you after your swim.
When I return with a much larger duck, we'll have a great meal together.

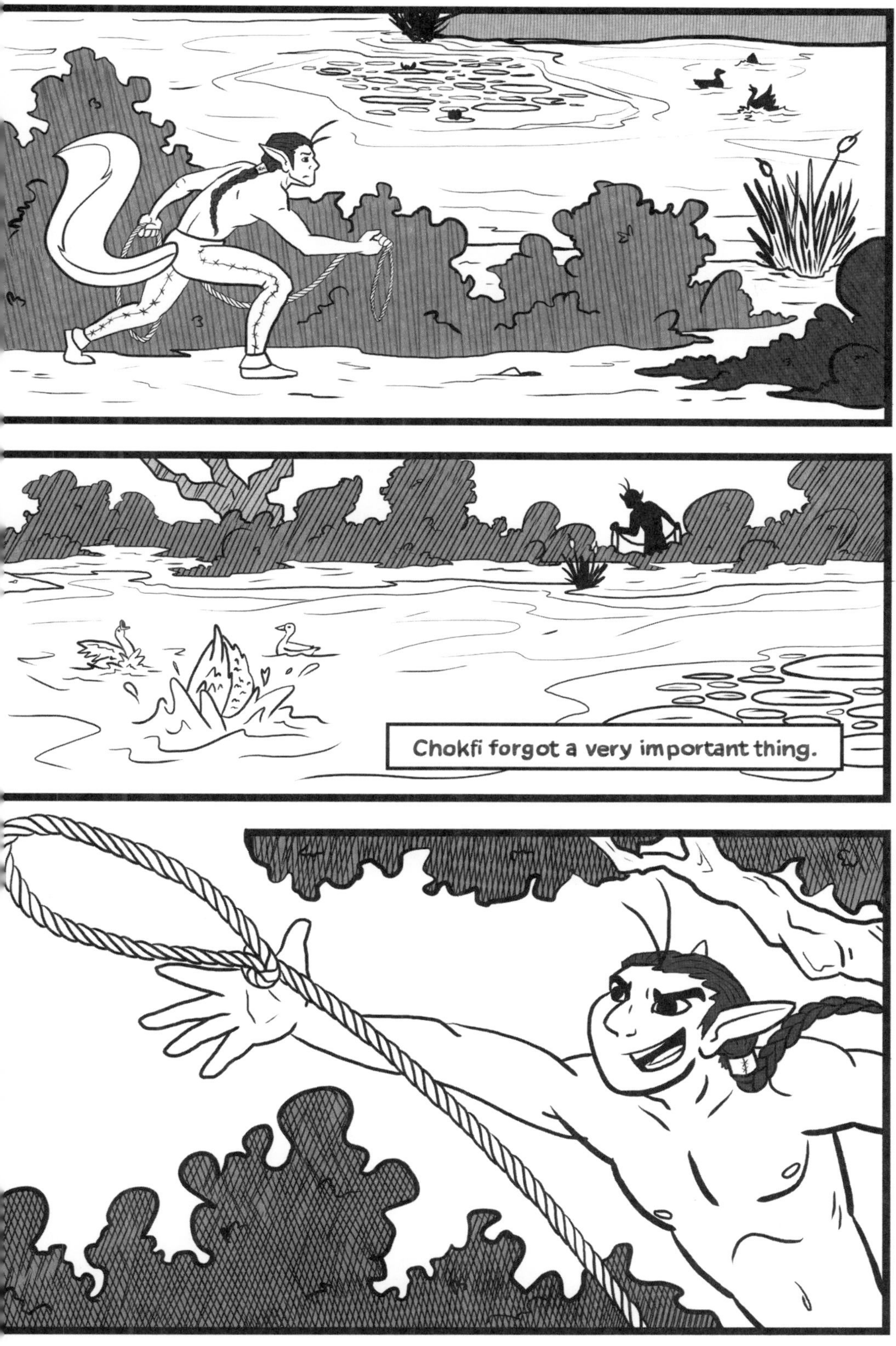
Chokfi forgot a very important thing.

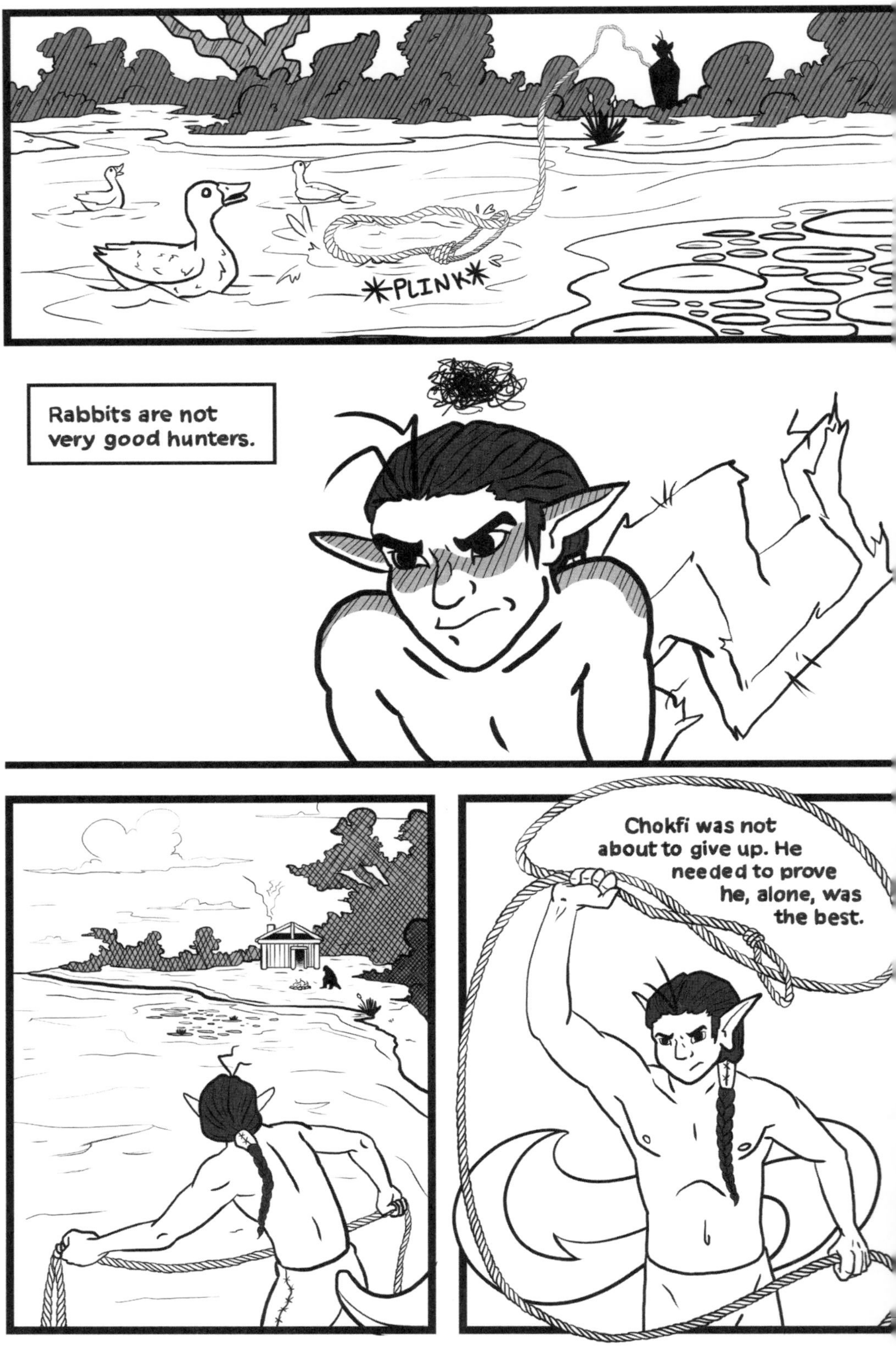
PLINK
Rabbits are not very good hunters.
Chokfi was not about to give up. He needed to prove he, alone, was the best.

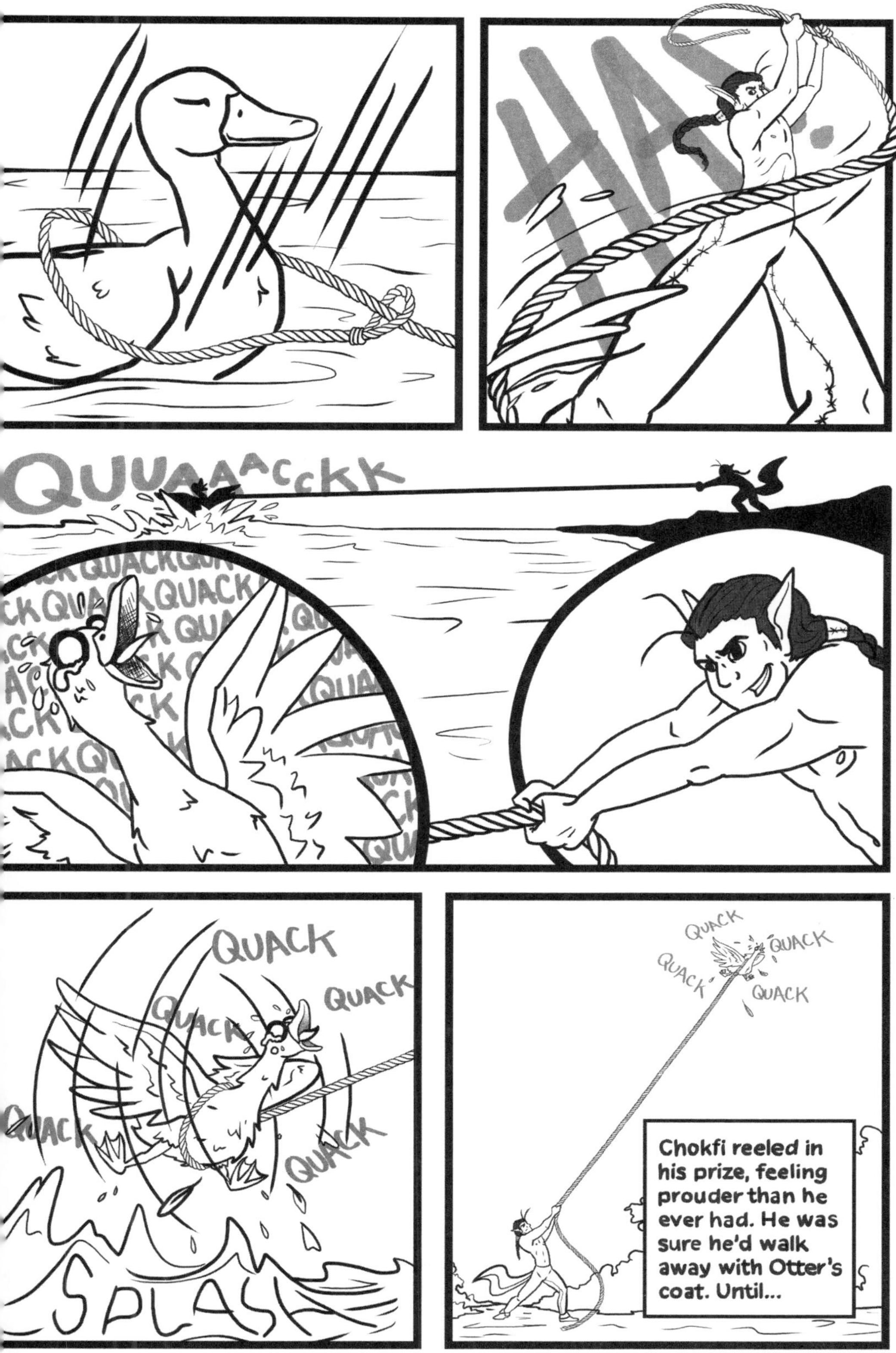
HA!
QUUAAACCKK
QUACK QUACK QUACK
QUACK
QUACK
QUACK
QUACK
QUACK
SPLASH
QUACK
QUACK
QUACK
QUACK
Chokfi reeled in his prize, feeling prouder than he ever had. He was sure he'd walk away with Otter's coat. Until...

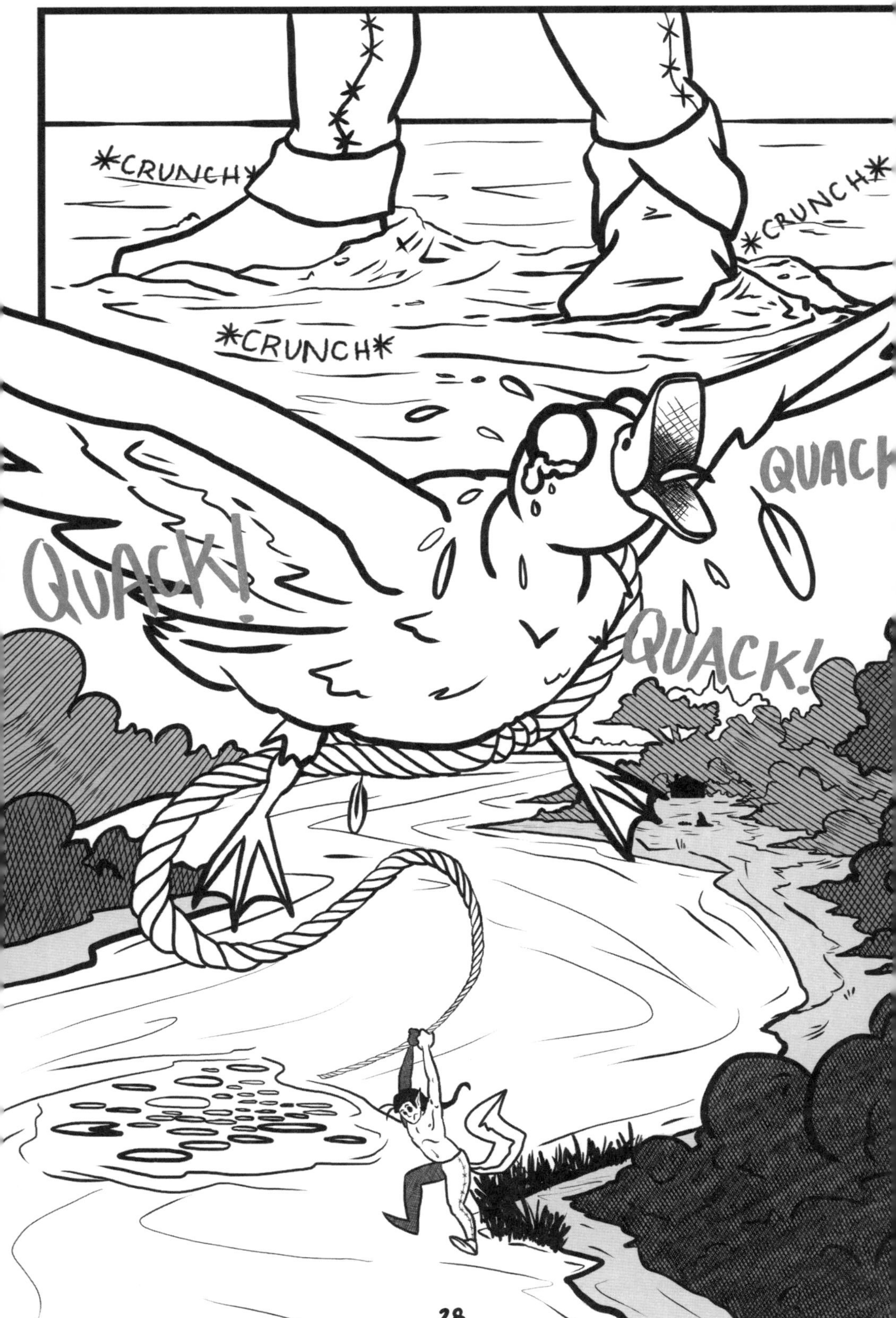
CRUNCH
CRUNCH
CRUNCH
QUACK!
QUACK!
QUACK!

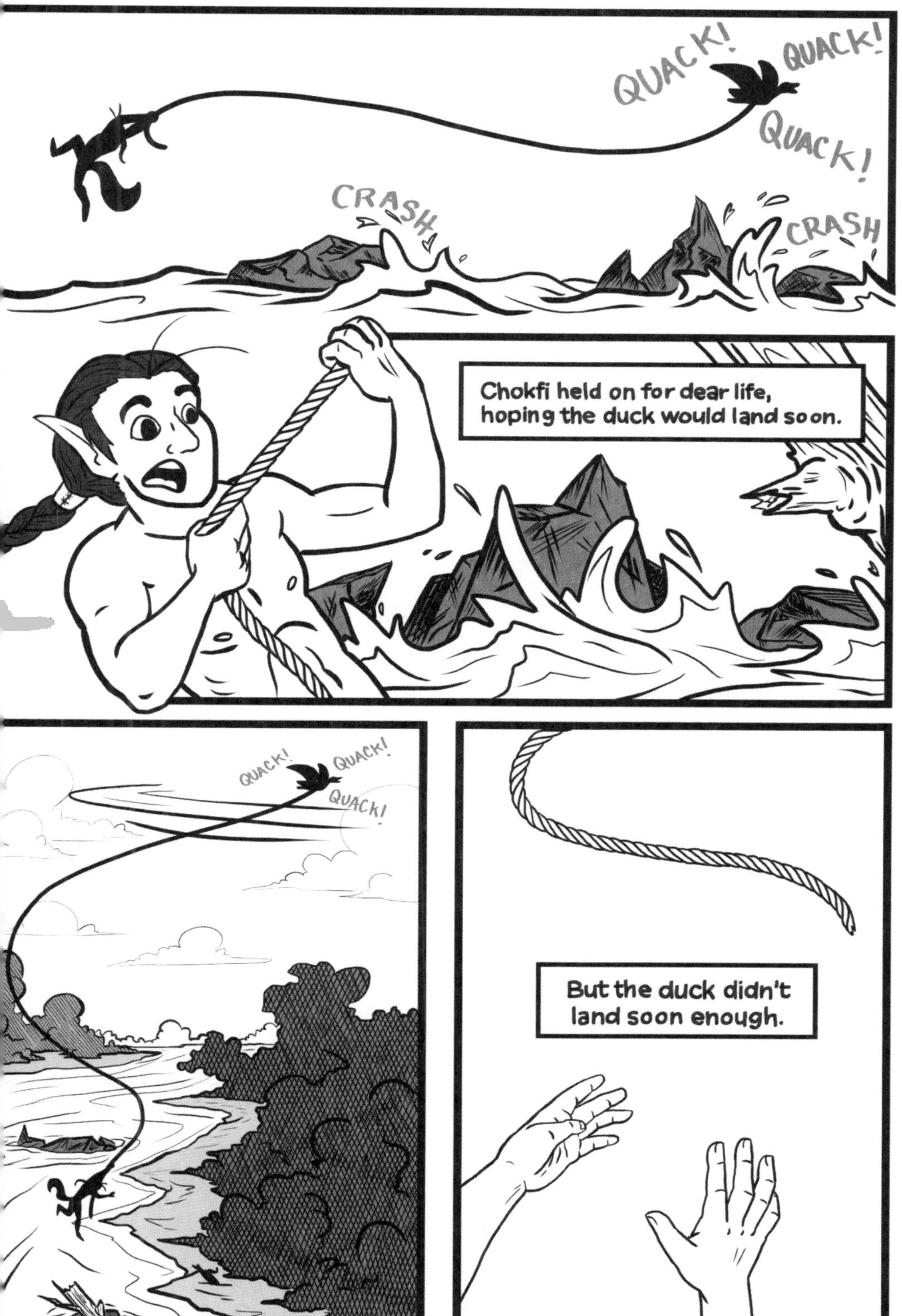
QUACK!
QUACK!
QUACK!
CRASH
CRASH
Chokfi held on for dear life, hoping the duck would land soon.
QUACK!
QUACK!
QUACK!
But the duck didn't land soon enough.

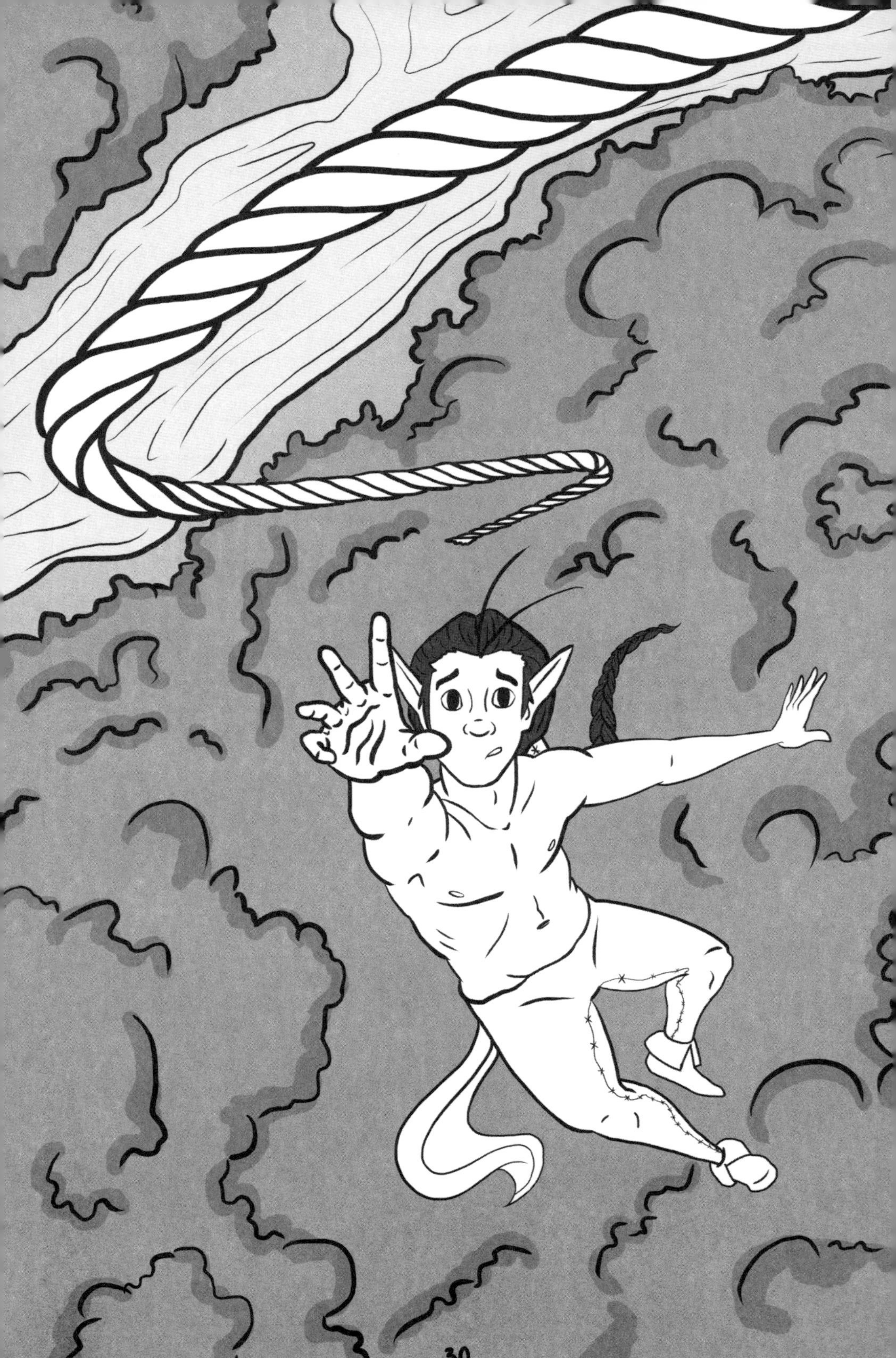

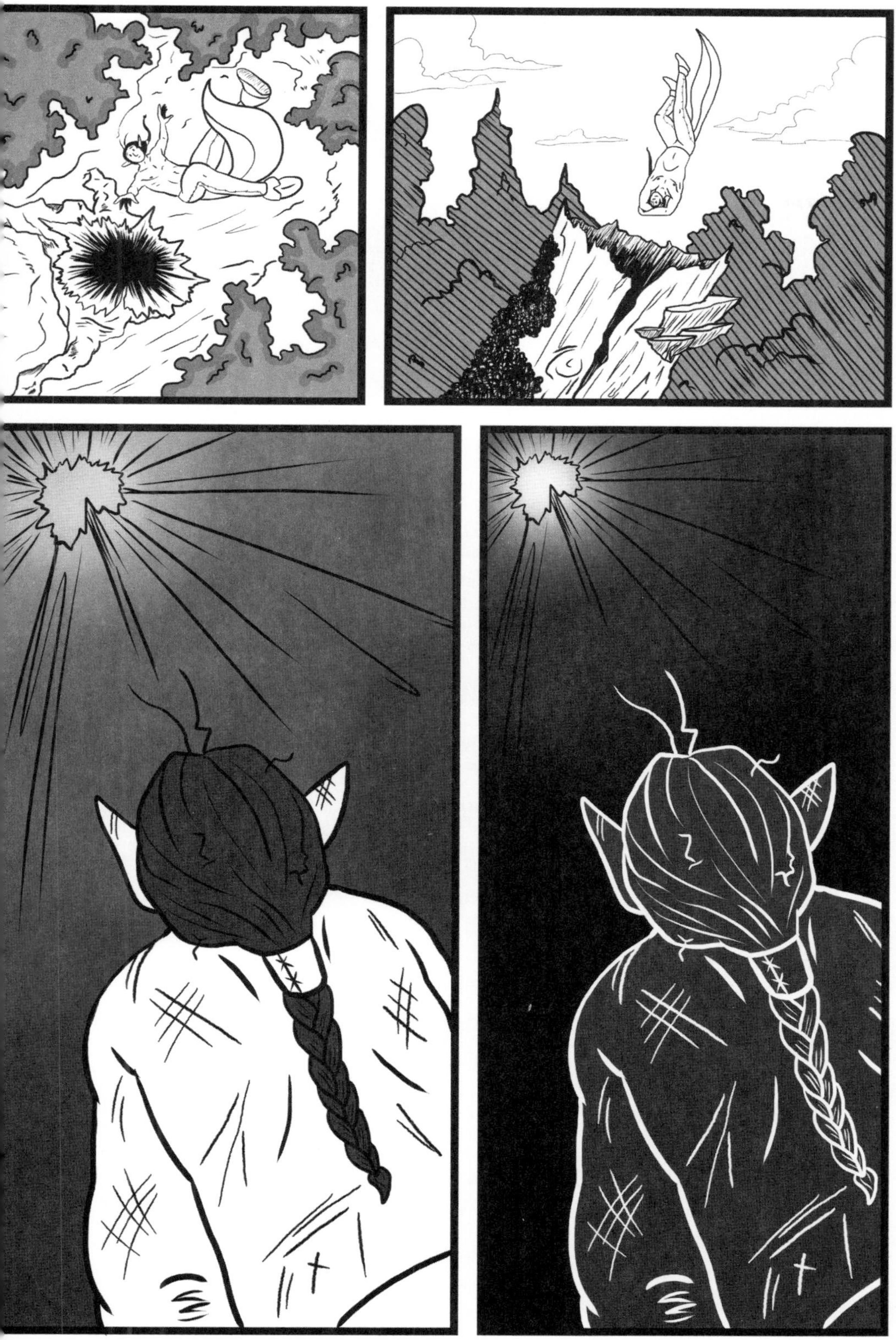

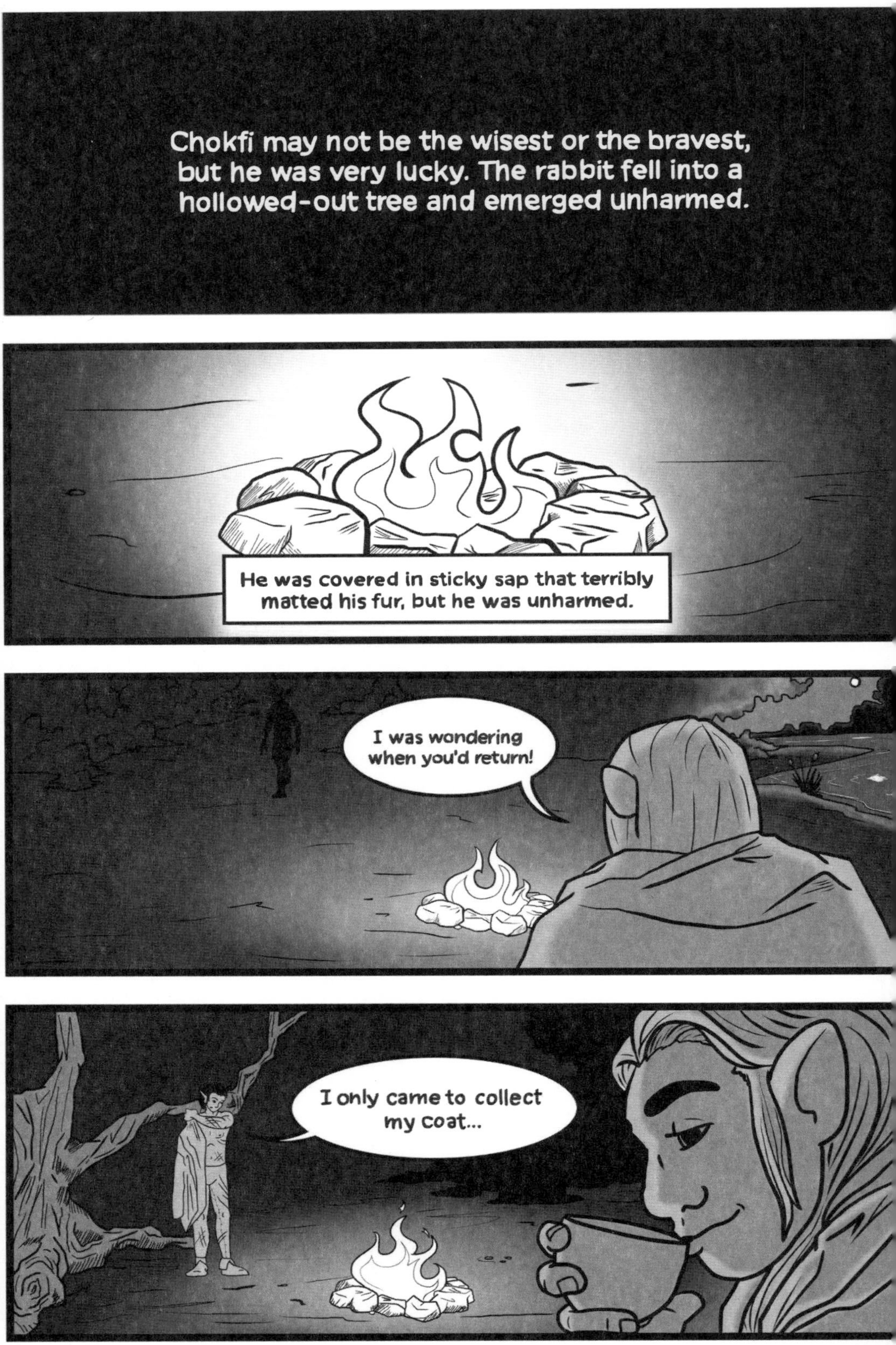
Chokfi may not be the wisest or the bravest, but he was very lucky. The rabbit fell into a hollowed-out tree and emerged unharmed.
He was covered in sticky sap that terribly matted his fur, but he was unharmed.
I was wondering when you'd return!
I only came to collect my coat...

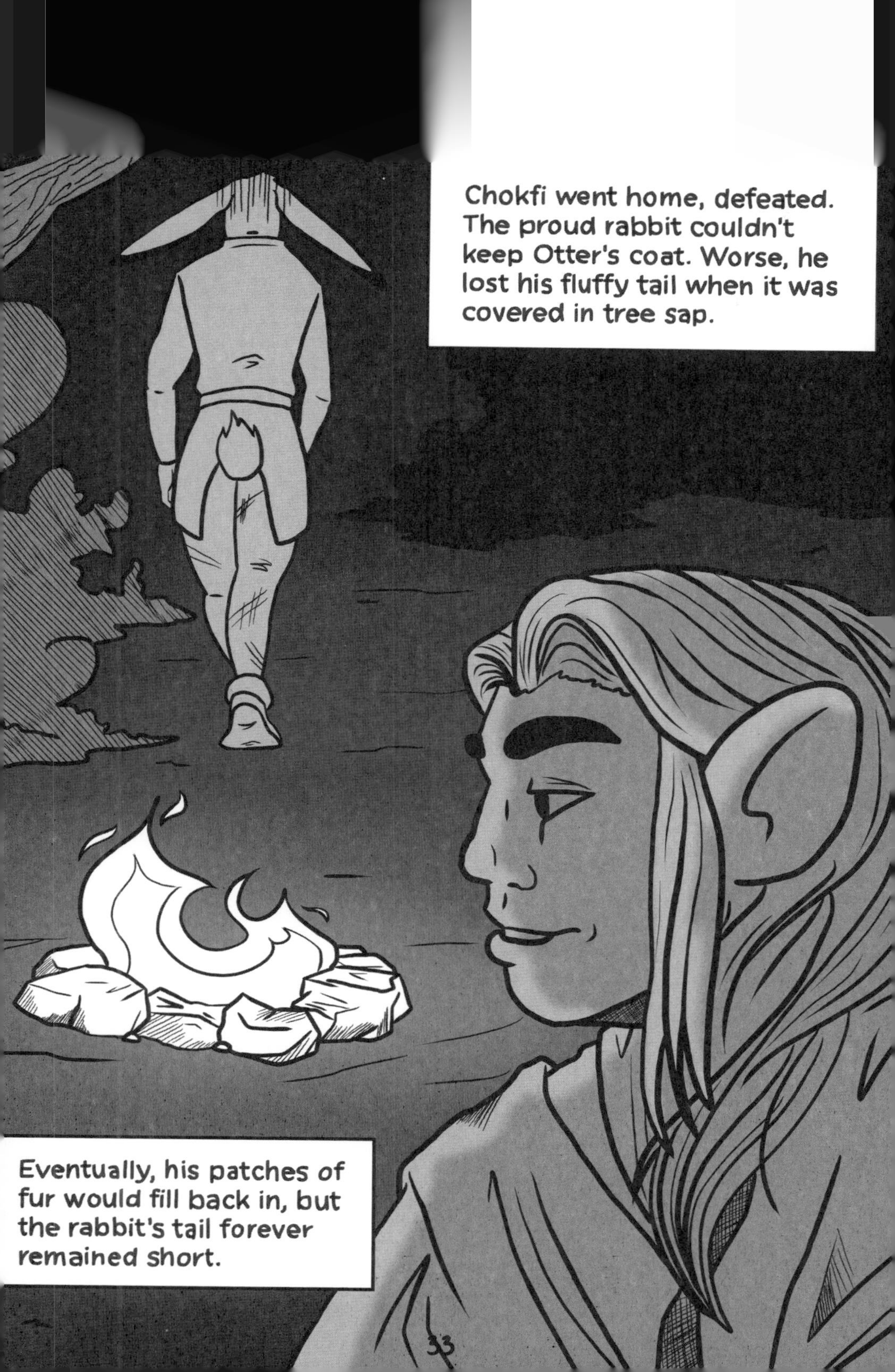
Chokfi went home, defeated. The proud rabbit couldn't keep Otter's coat. Worse, he lost his fluffy tail when it was covered in tree sap.
Eventually, his patches of fur would fill back in, but the rabbit's tail forever remained short.

WHITE HORSE PLAINS

DRAWN BY:
RHAEL MCGREGOR

STORY CONSULT:
SYLVIA BOYER

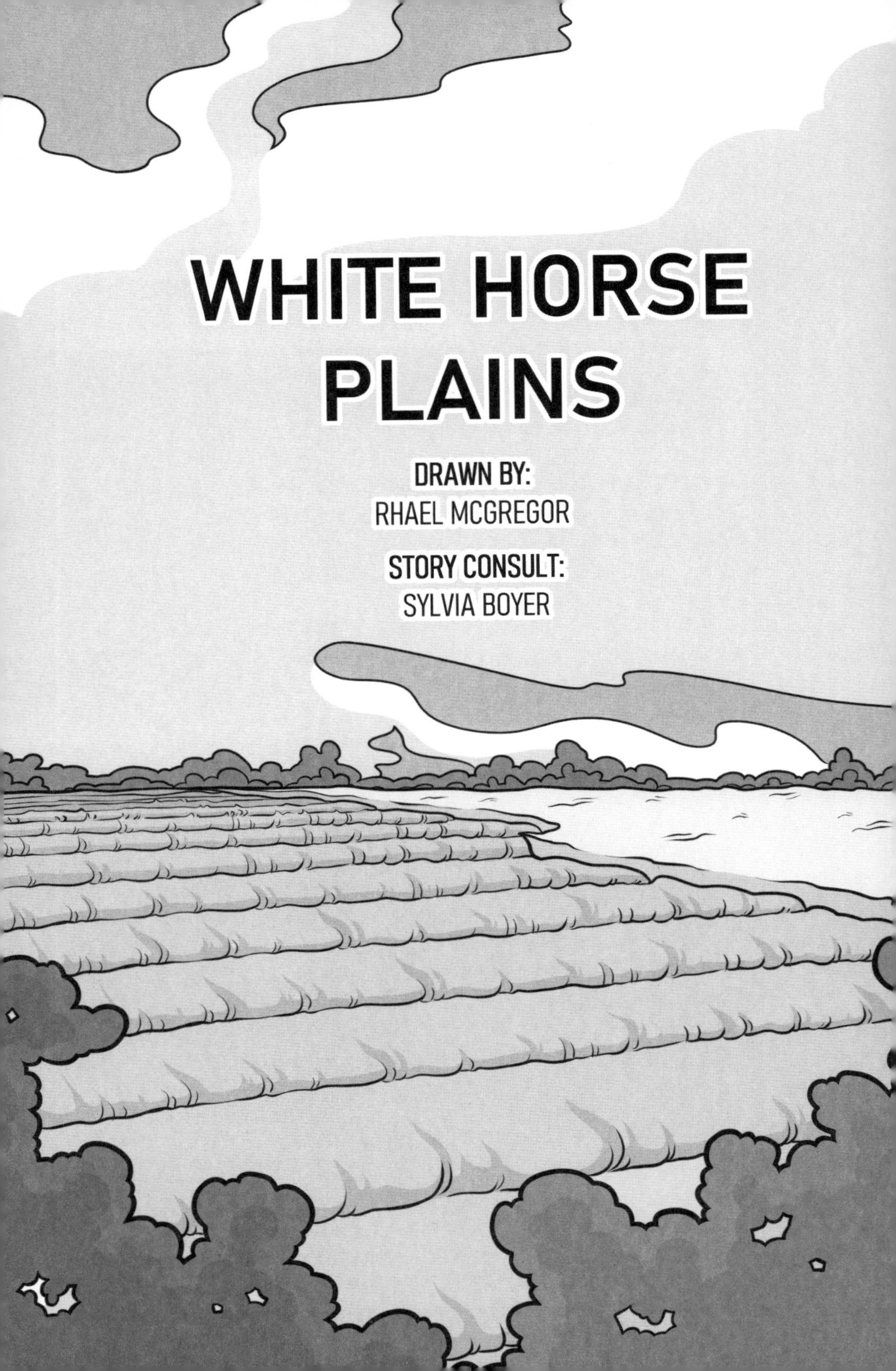

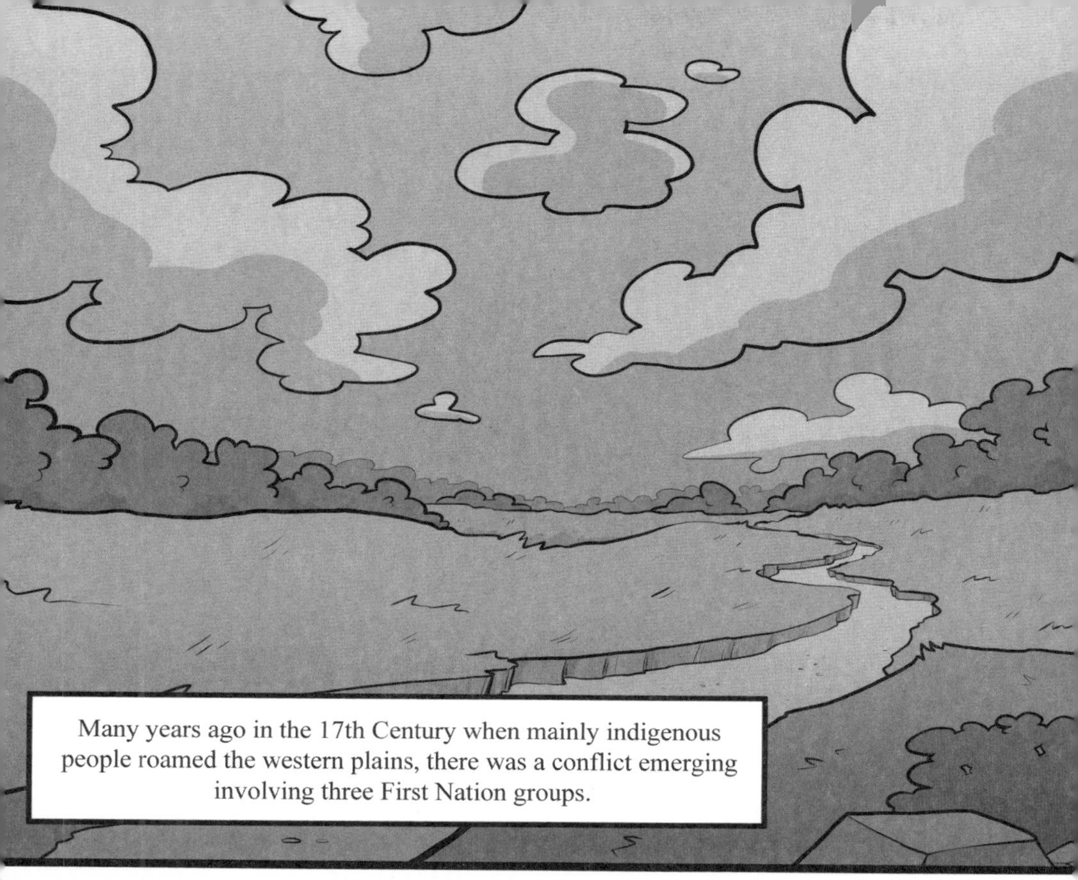

Many years ago in the 17th Century when mainly indigenous people roamed the western plains, there was a conflict emerging involving three First Nation groups.

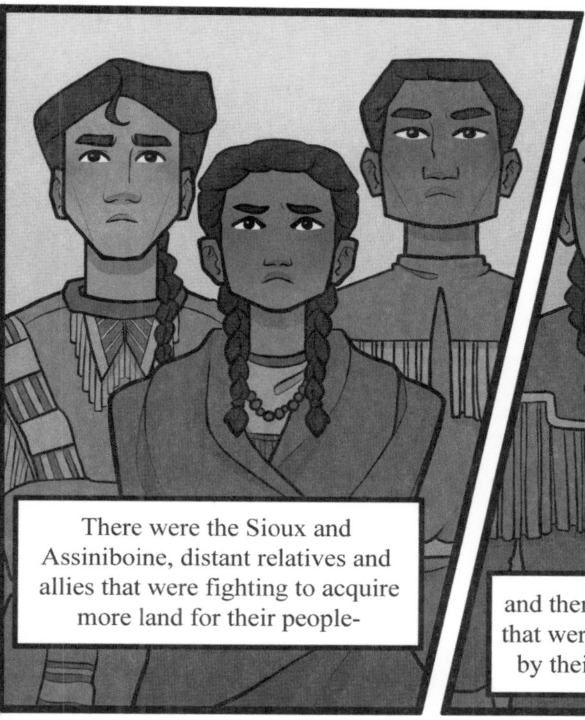

There were the Sioux and Assiniboine, distant relatives and allies that were fighting to acquire more land for their people-

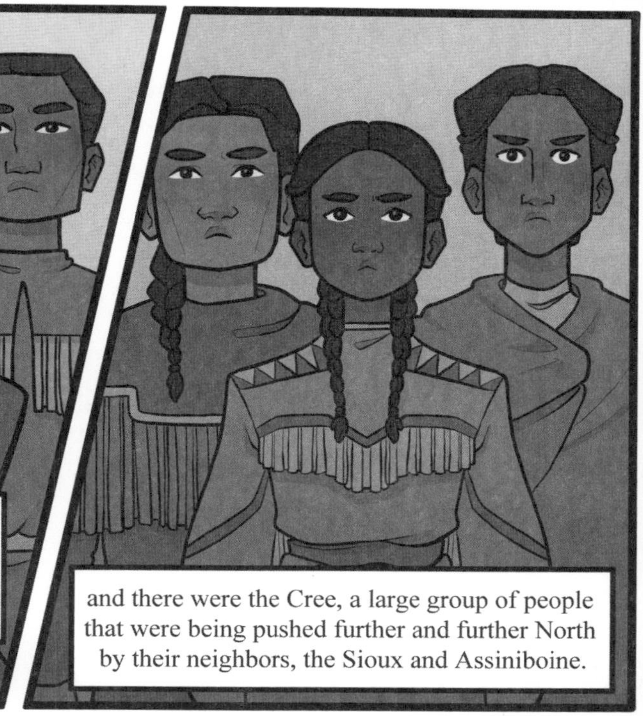

and there were the Cree, a large group of people that were being pushed further and further North by their neighbors, the Sioux and Assiniboine.

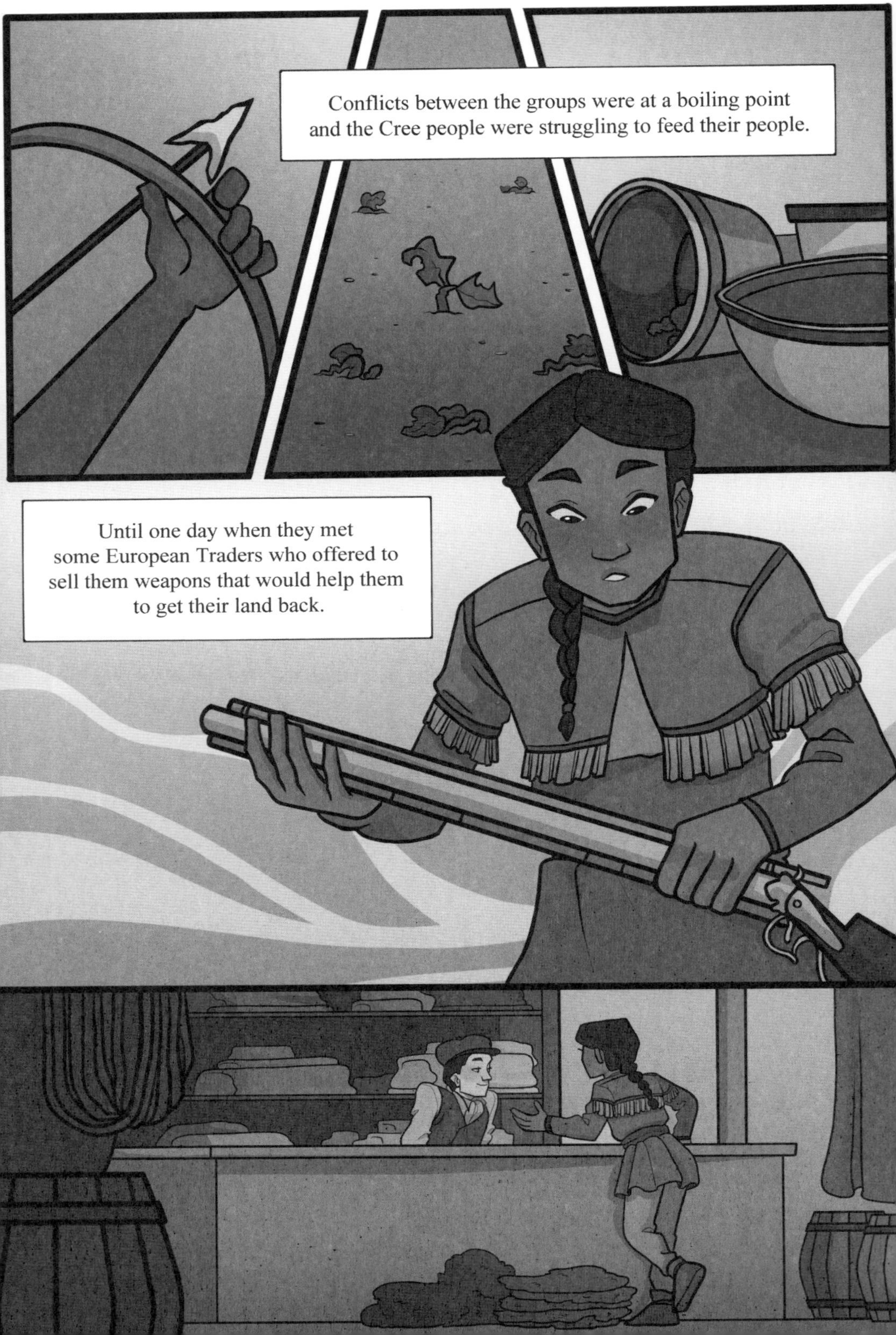
Conflicts between the groups were at a boiling point and the Cree people were struggling to feed their people.
Until one day when they met some European Traders who offered to sell them weapons that would help them to get their land back.

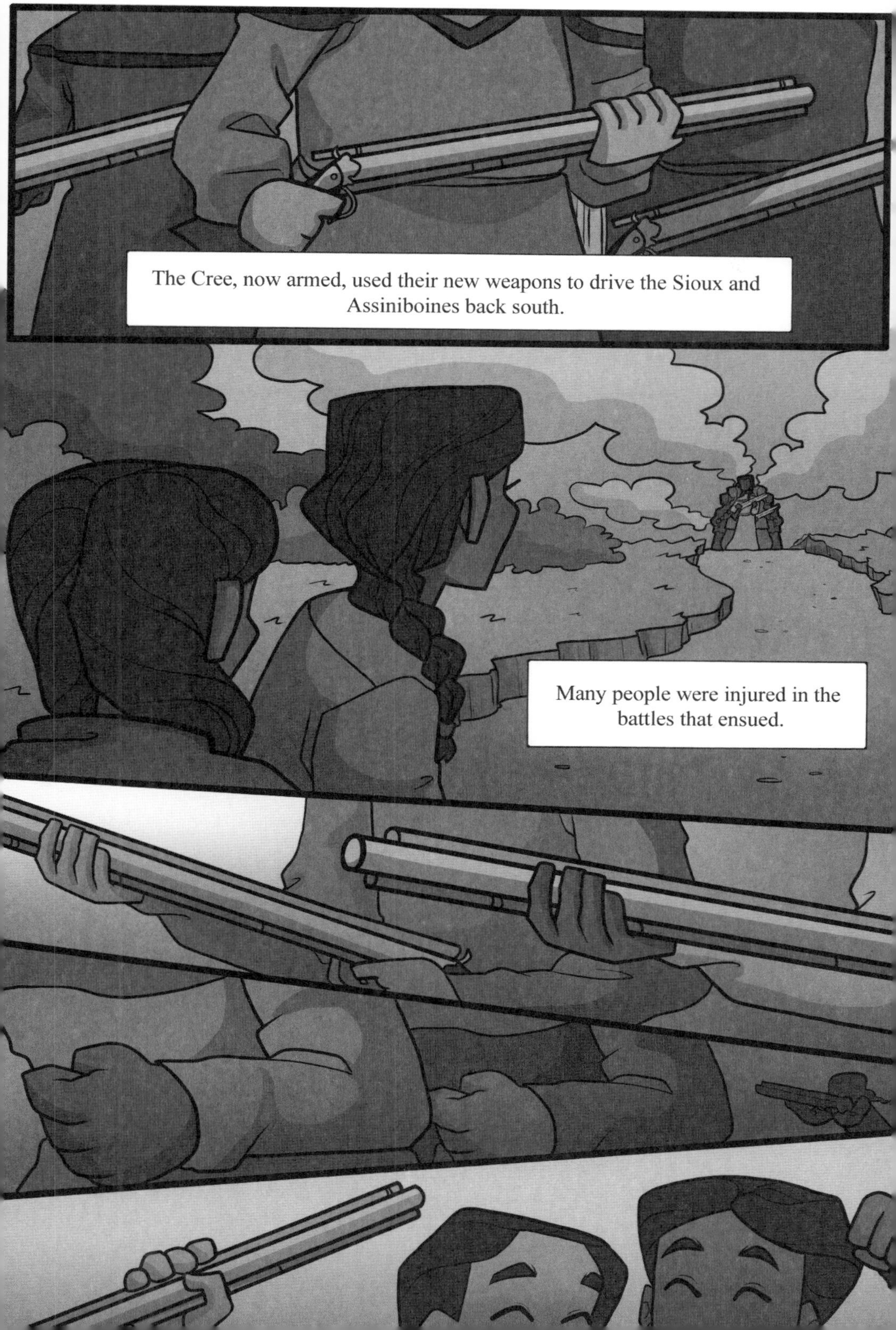
The Cree, now armed, used their new weapons to drive the Sioux and Assiniboines back south.
Many people were injured in the battles that ensued.

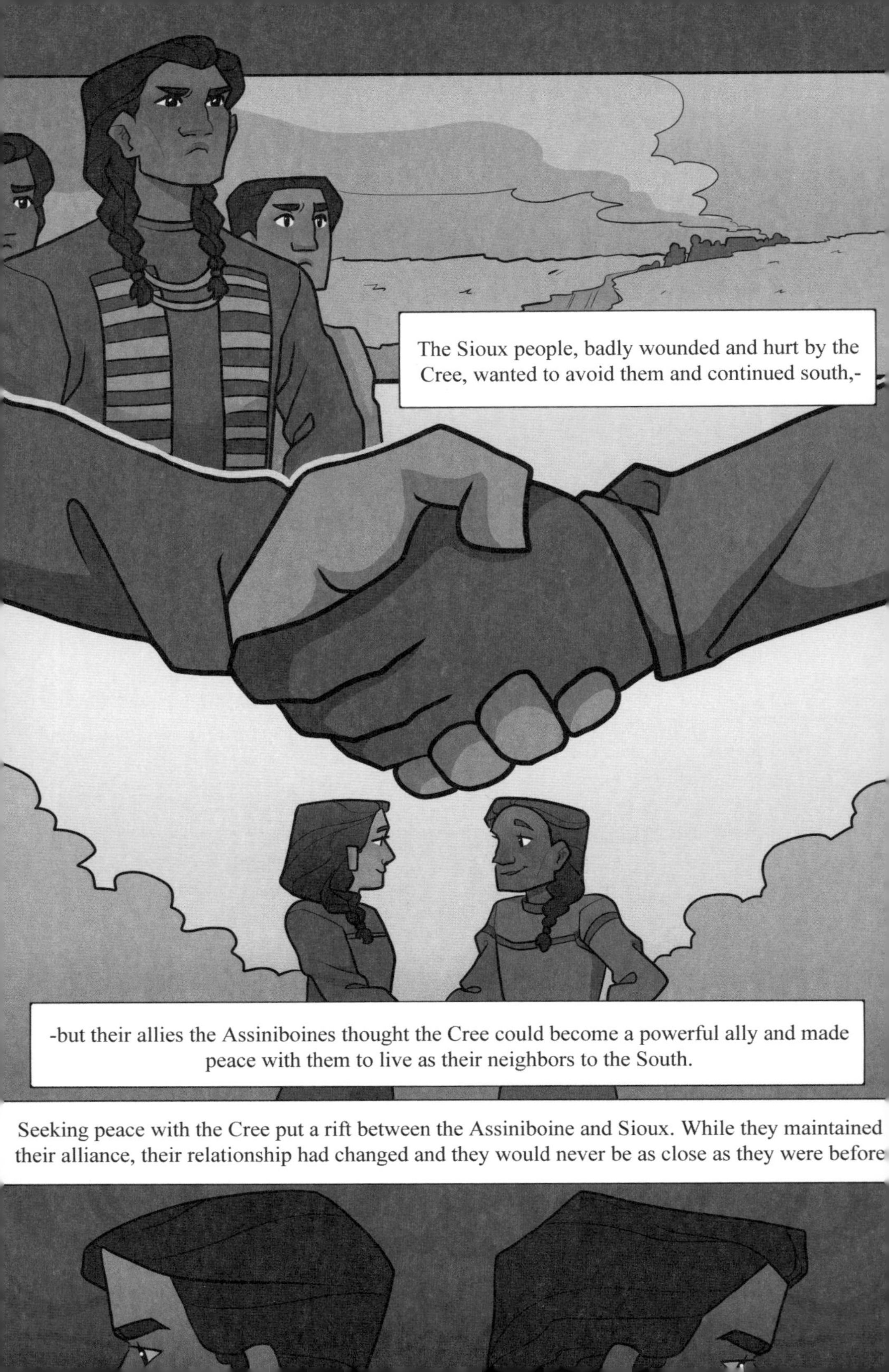
The Sioux people, badly wounded and hurt by the Cree, wanted to avoid them and continued south,-
-but their allies the Assiniboines thought the Cree could become a powerful ally and made peace with them to live as their neighbors to the South.
Seeking peace with the Cree put a rift between the Assiniboine and Sioux. While they maintained their alliance, their relationship had changed and they would never be as close as they were before

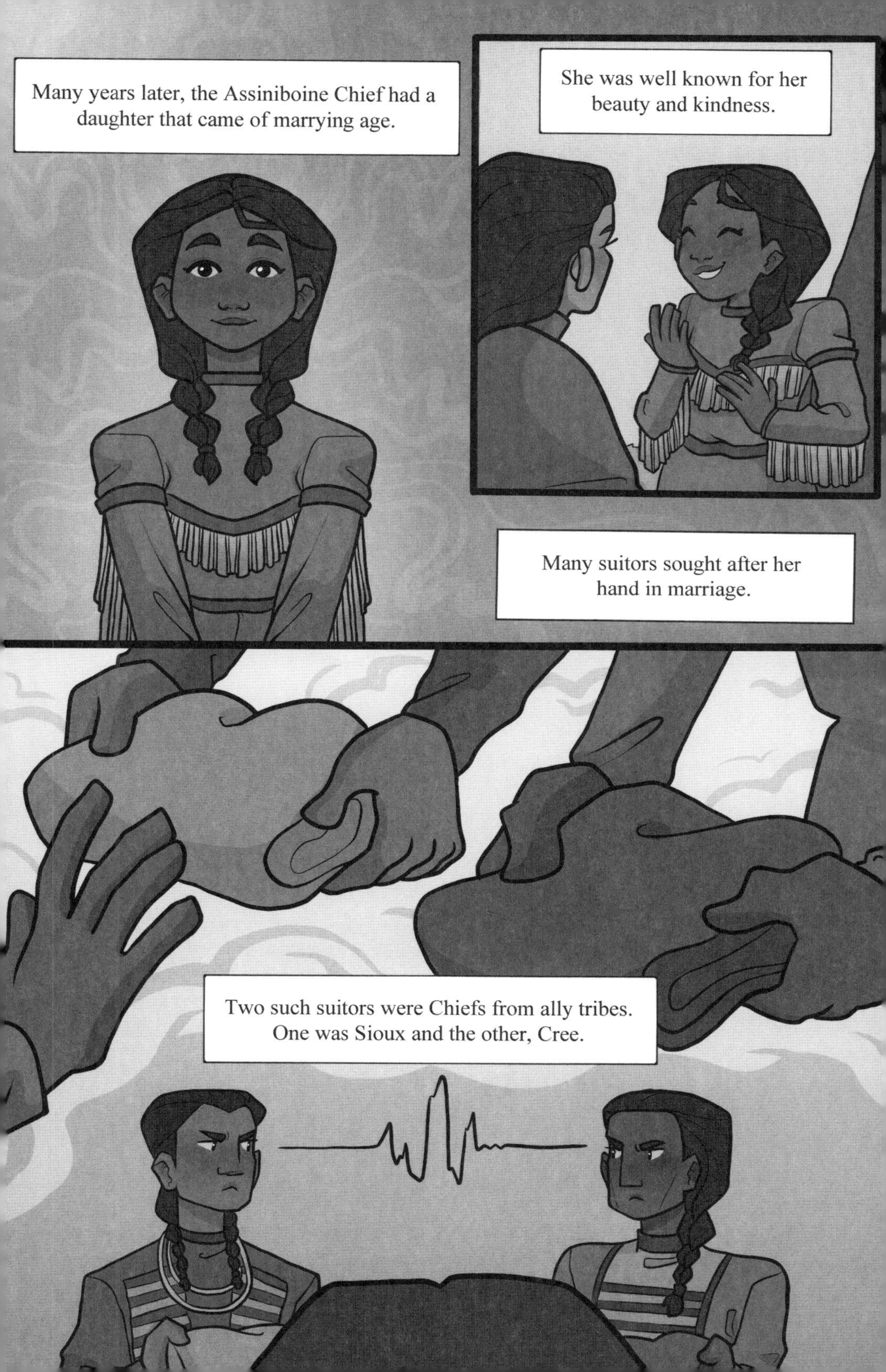
Many years later, the Assiniboine Chief had a daughter that came of marrying age.
She was well known for her beauty and kindness.
Many suitors sought after her hand in marriage.
Two such suitors were Chiefs from ally tribes. One was Sioux and the other, Cree.

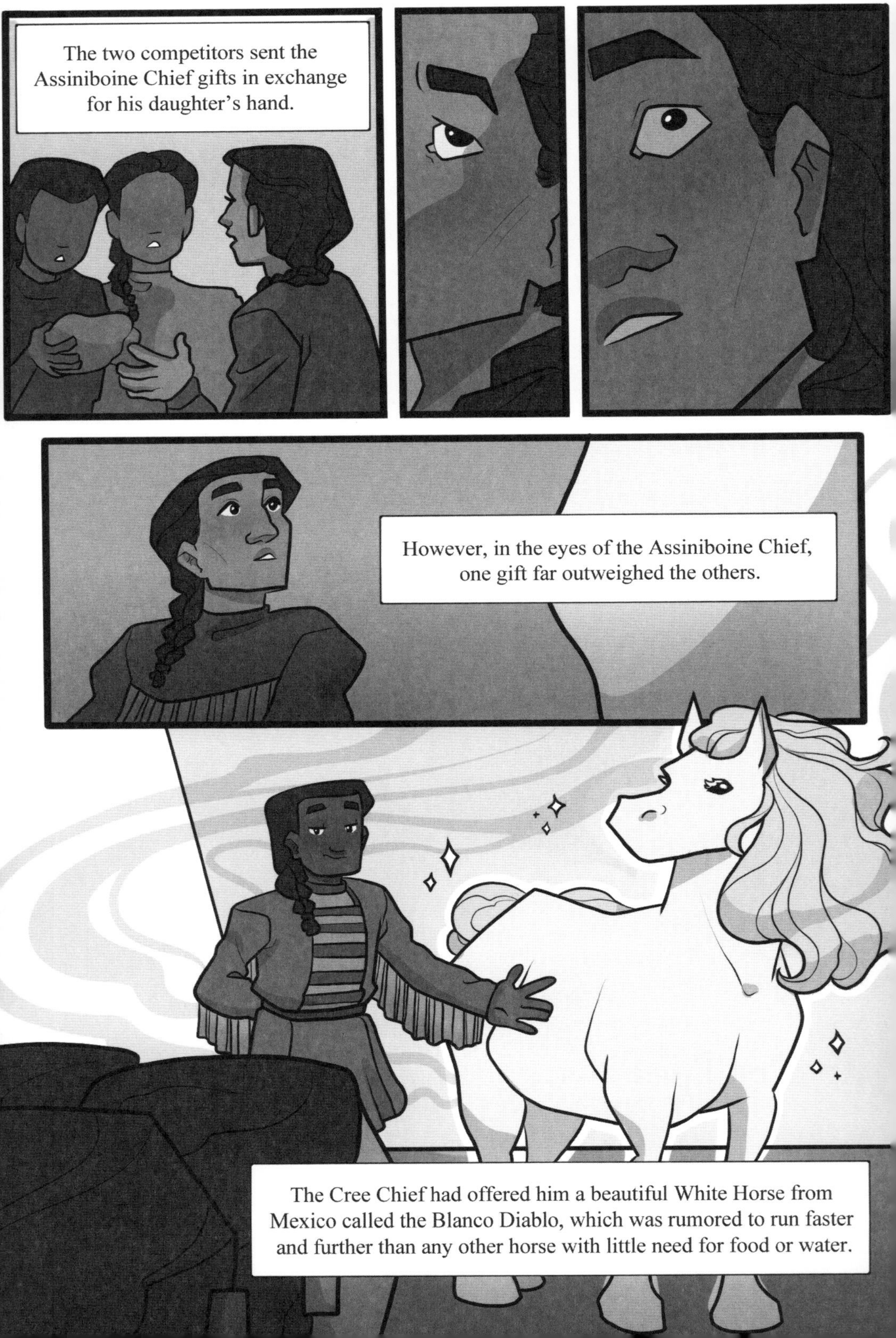
The two competitors sent the Assiniboine Chief gifts in exchange for his daughter's hand.
However, in the eyes of the Assiniboine Chief, one gift far outweighed the others.
The Cree Chief had offered him a beautiful White Horse from Mexico called the Blanco Diablo, which was rumored to run faster and further than any other horse with little need for food or water.

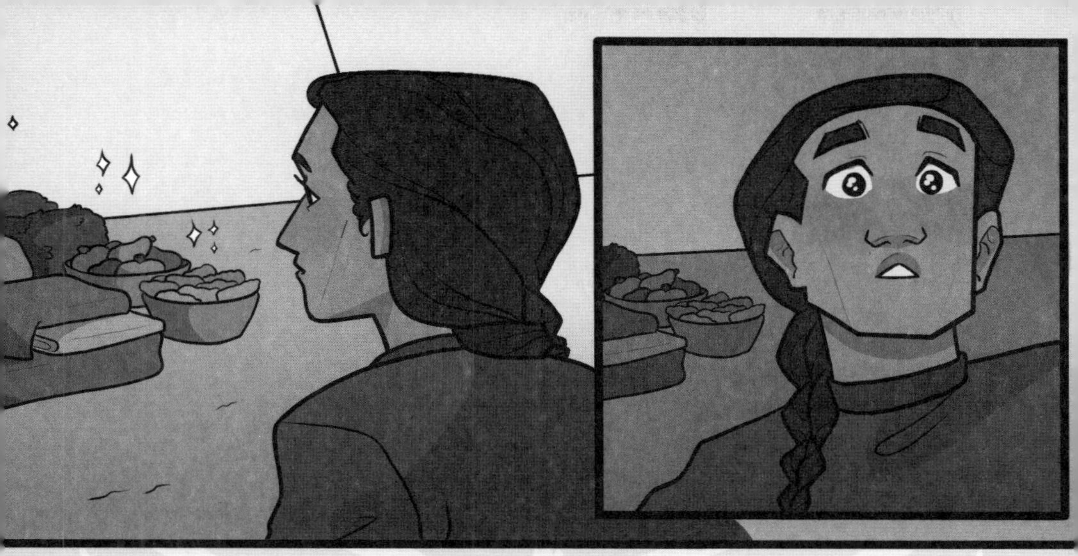

While the Assiniboine Chief had originally favored the Sioux Chief to take his daughter's hand because of their long-standing alliance and blood ties, he could not resist the temptation of the powerful gift from the Cree. So, he agreed for his daughter to marry the Cree Chief instead. The two lovers were to be wed when the Sioux Chief would be travelling, so there would be no interference at the celebration.

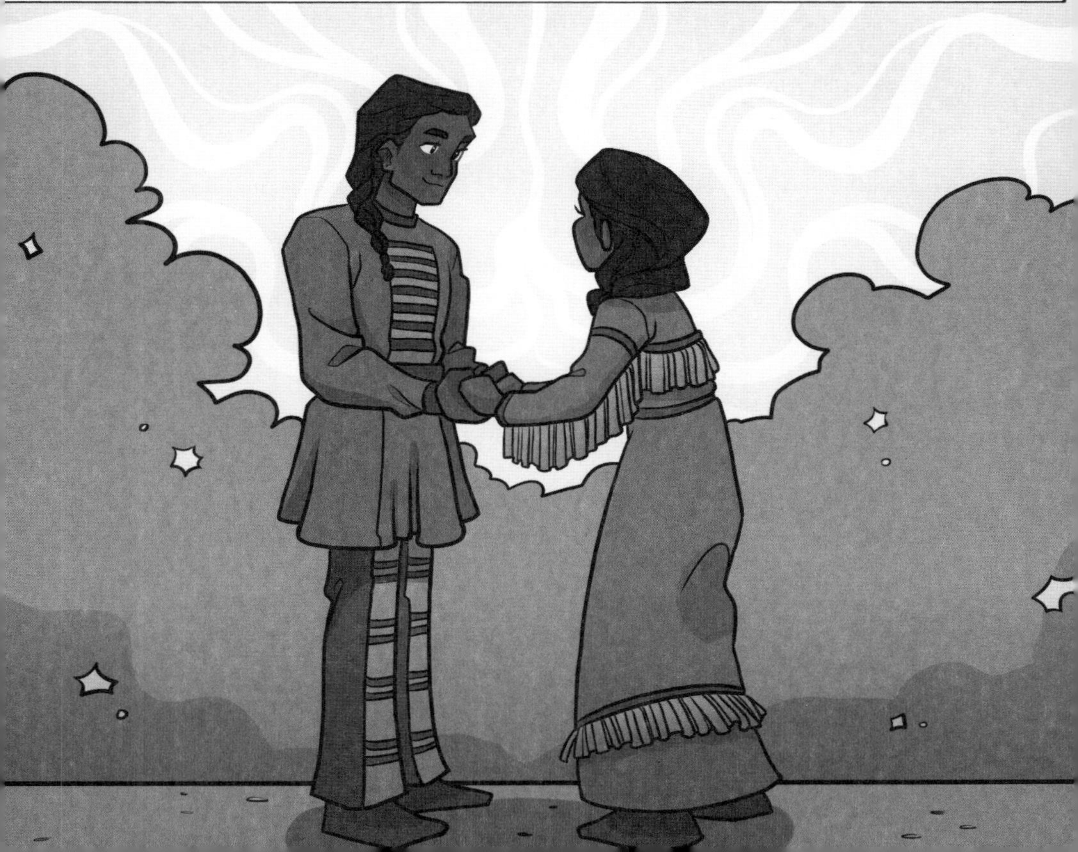

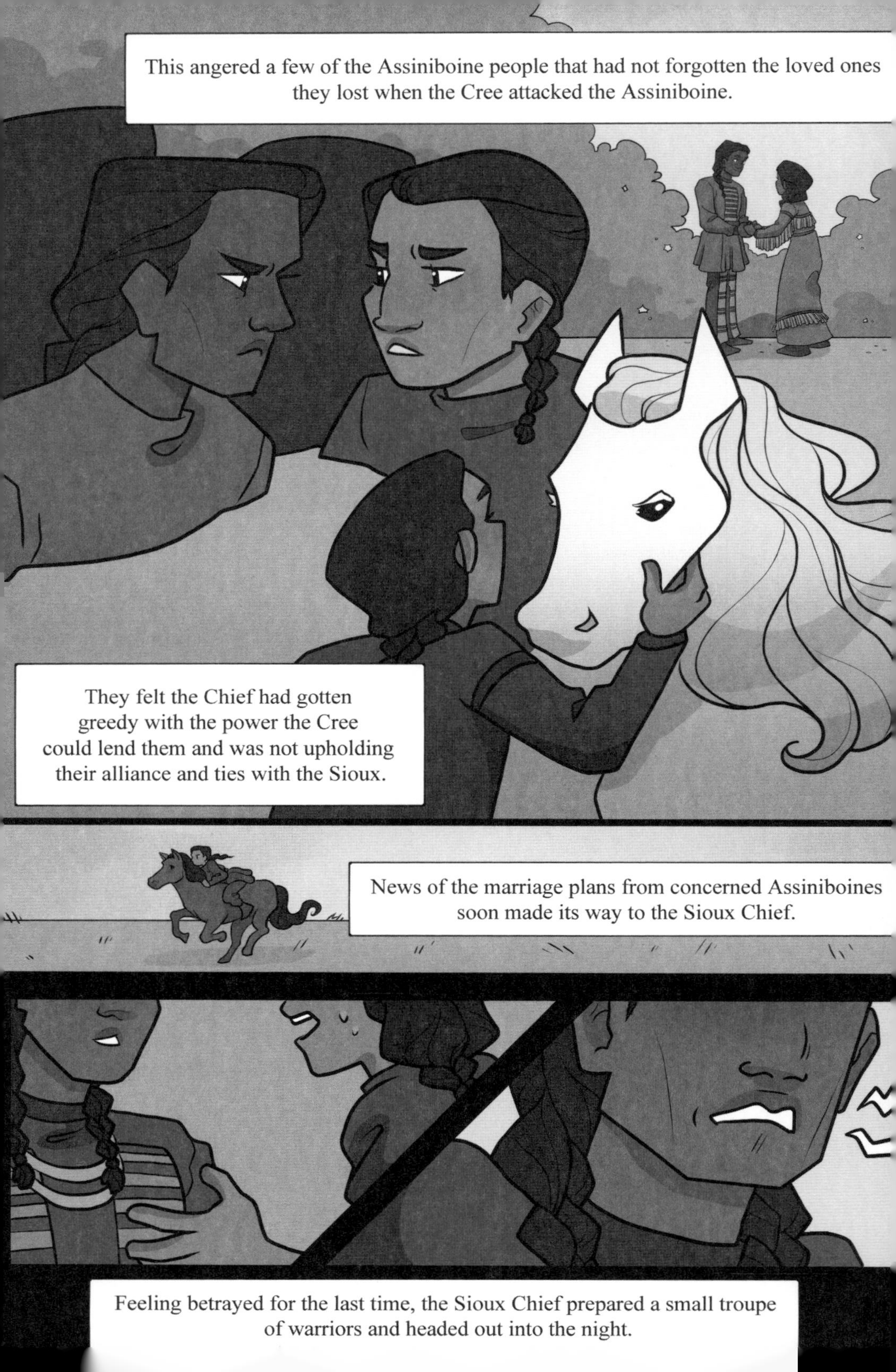
This angered a few of the Assiniboine people that had not forgotten the loved ones they lost when the Cree attacked the Assiniboine.
They felt the Chief had gotten greedy with the power the Cree could lend them and was not upholding their alliance and ties with the Sioux.
News of the marriage plans from concerned Assiniboines soon made its way to the Sioux Chief.
Feeling betrayed for the last time, the Sioux Chief prepared a small troupe of warriors and headed out into the night.

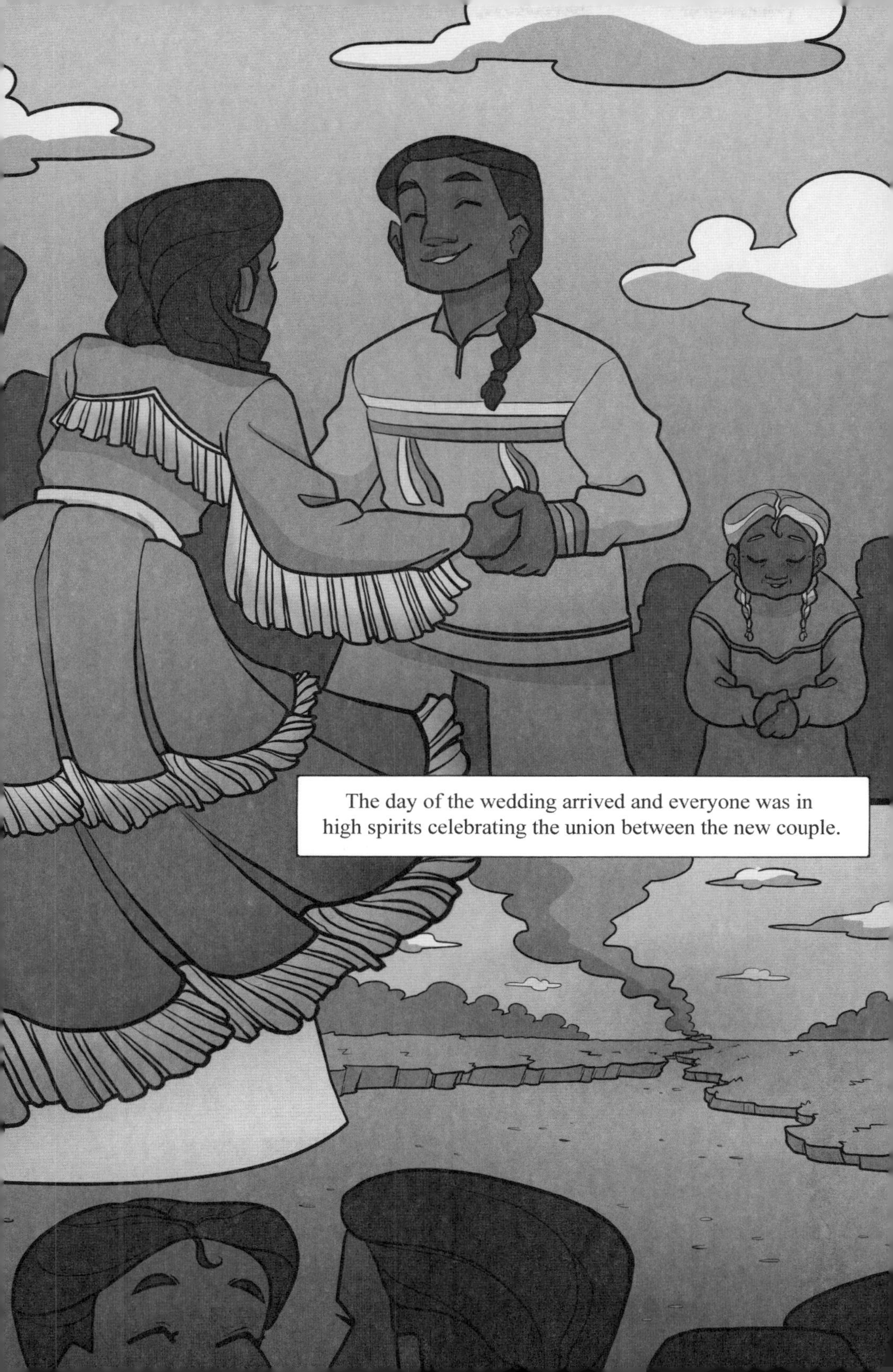
The day of the wedding arrived and everyone was in high spirits celebrating the union between the new couple.

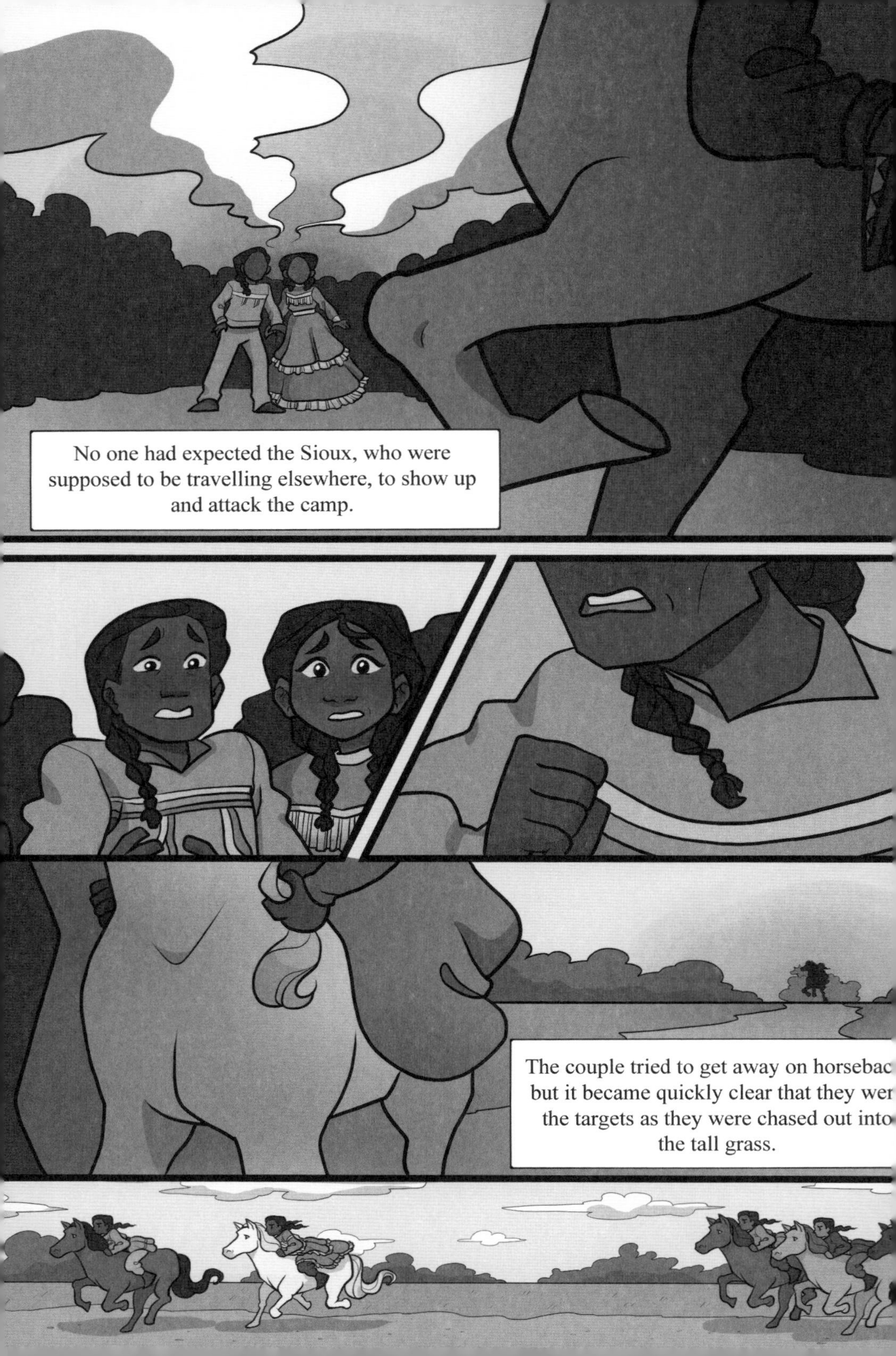
No one had expected the Sioux, who were supposed to be travelling elsewhere, to show up and attack the camp.
The couple tried to get away on horsebac but it became quickly clear that they wer the targets as they were chased out into the tall grass.

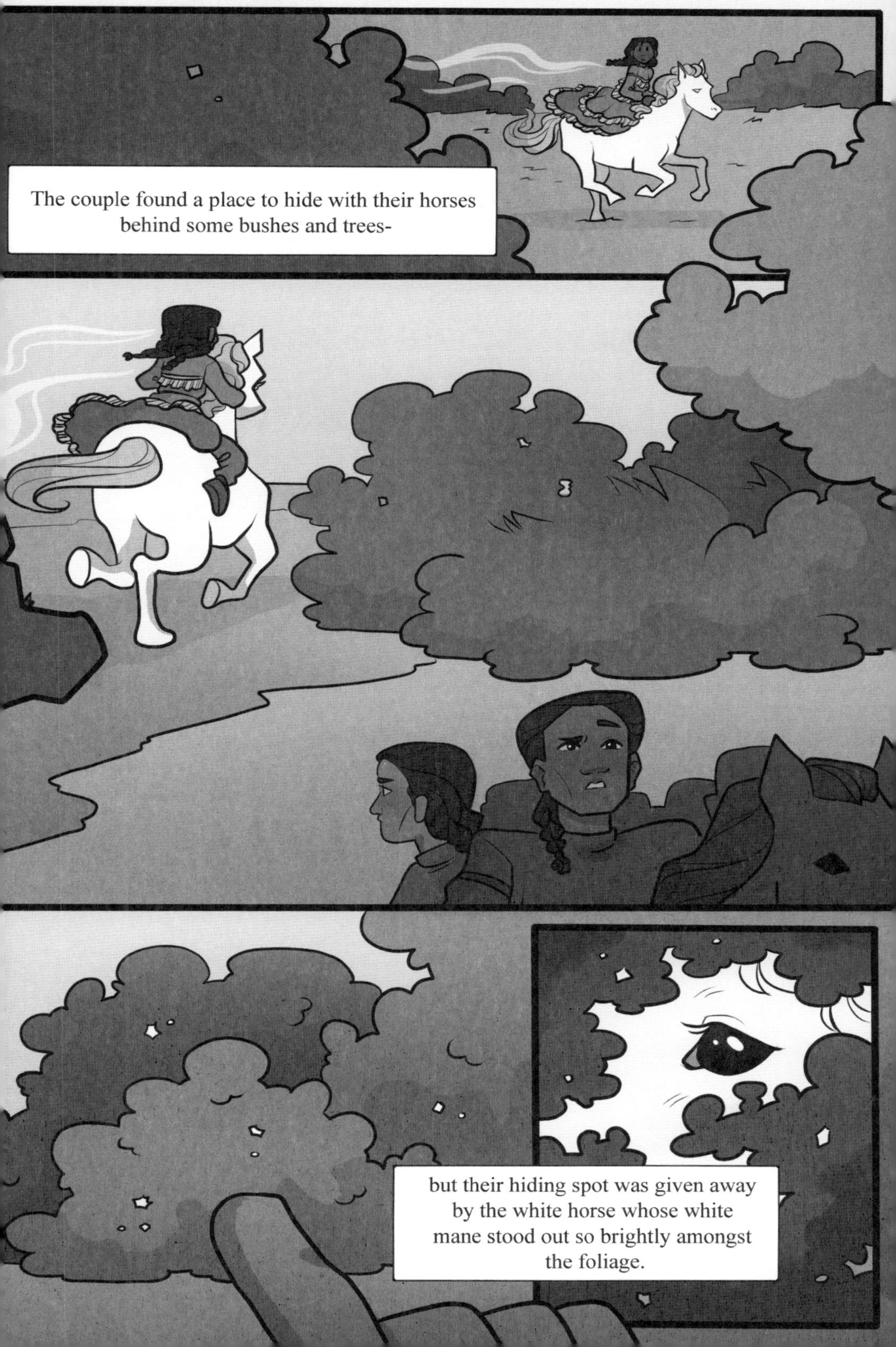
The couple found a place to hide with their horses behind some bushes and trees-
but their hiding spot was given away by the white horse whose white mane stood out so brightly amongst the foliage.

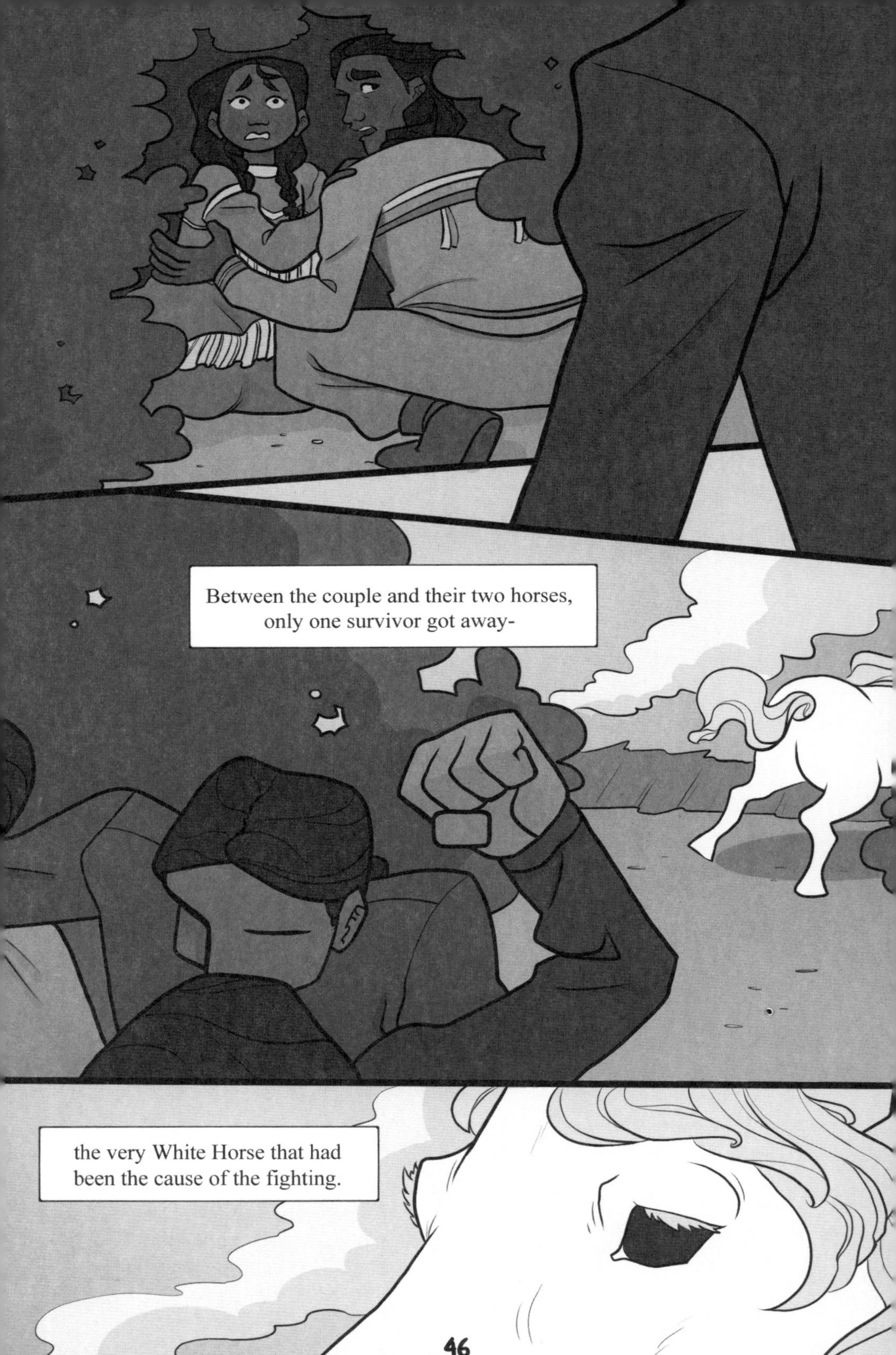
Between the couple and their two horses, only one survivor got away-
the very White Horse that had been the cause of the fighting.

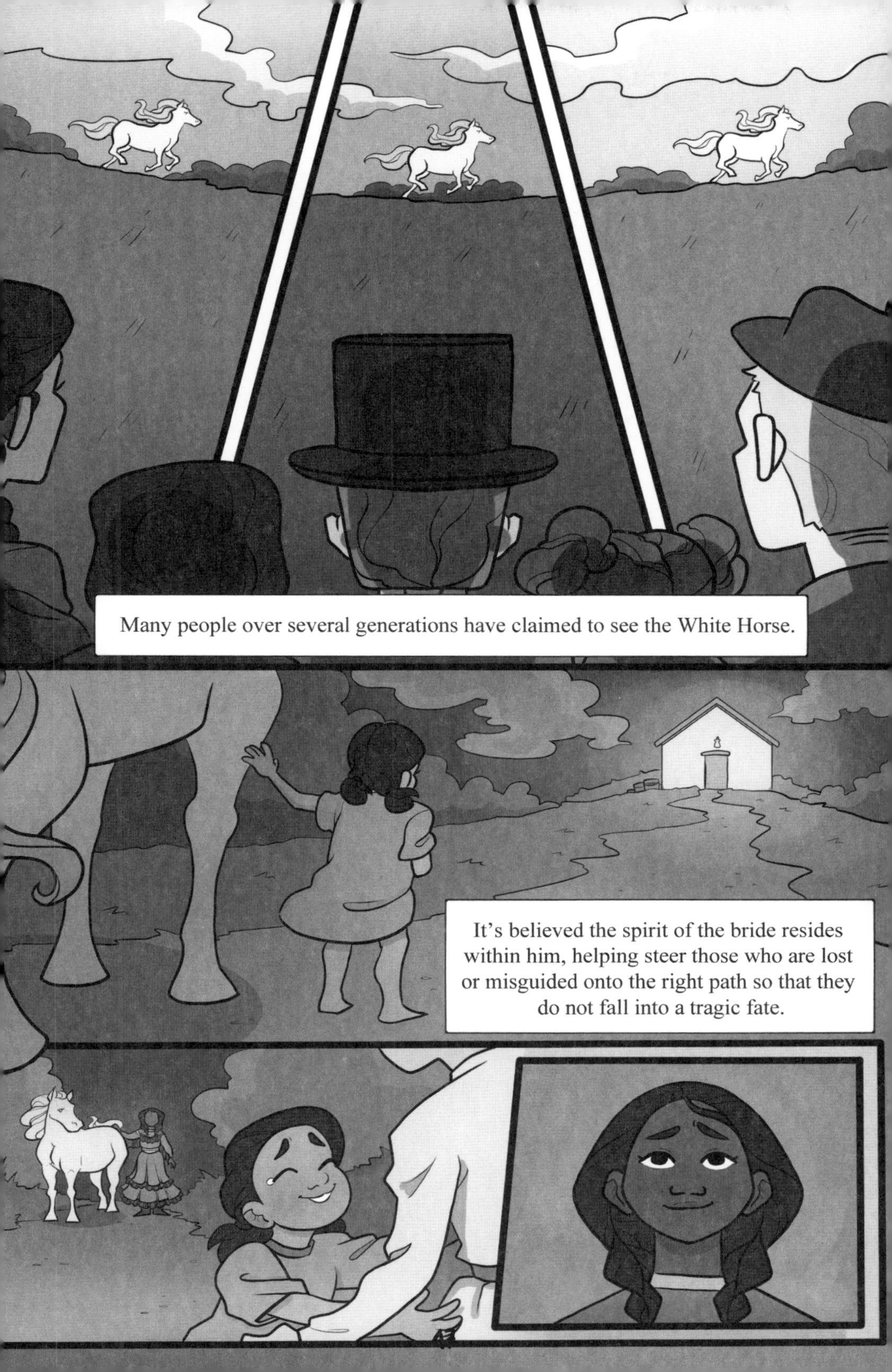
Many people over several generations have claimed to see the White Horse.
It's believed the spirit of the bride resides within him, helping steer those who are lost or misguided onto the right path so that they do not fall into a tragic fate.

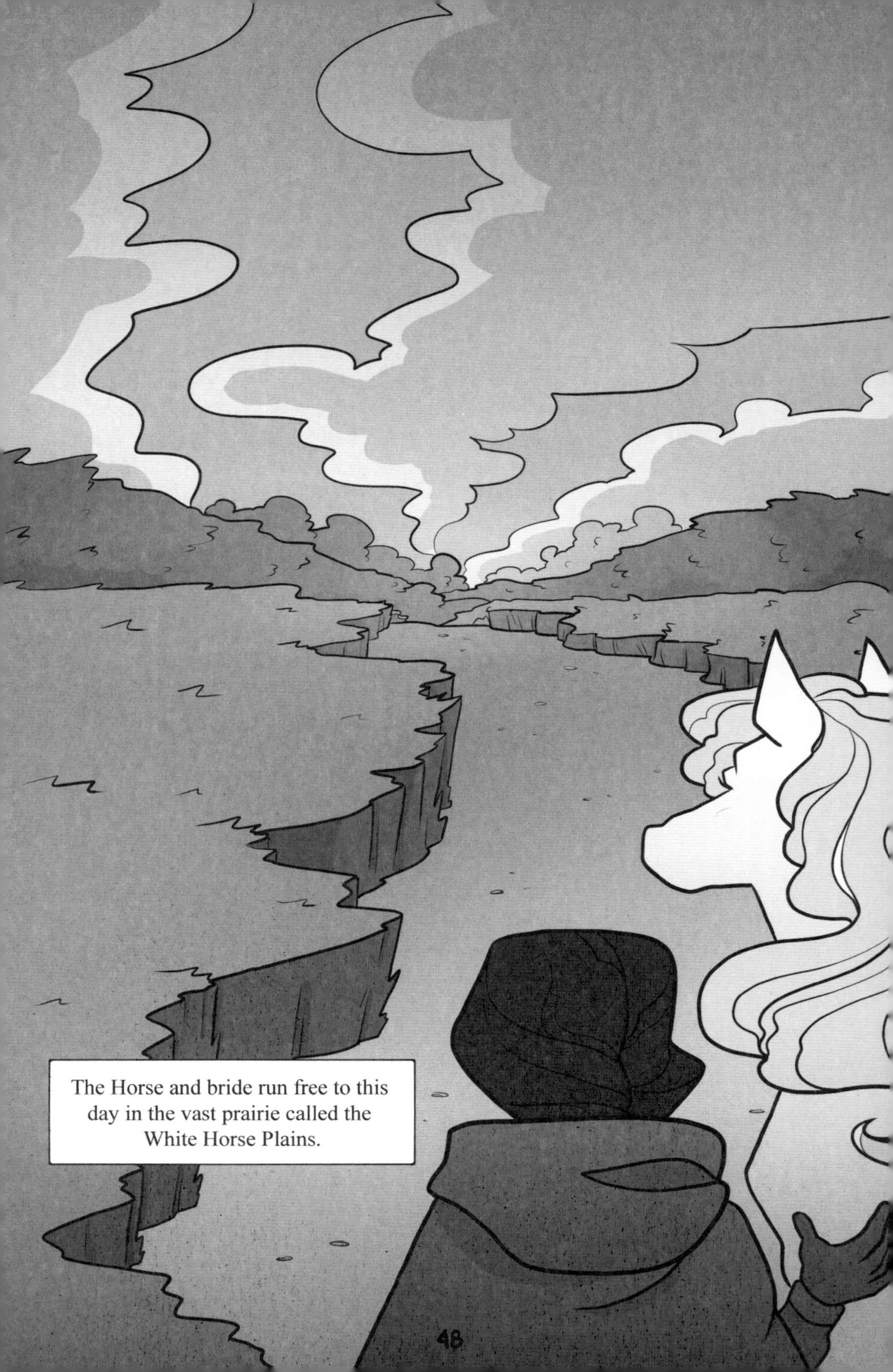
The Horse and bride run free to this day in the vast prairie called the White Horse Plains.

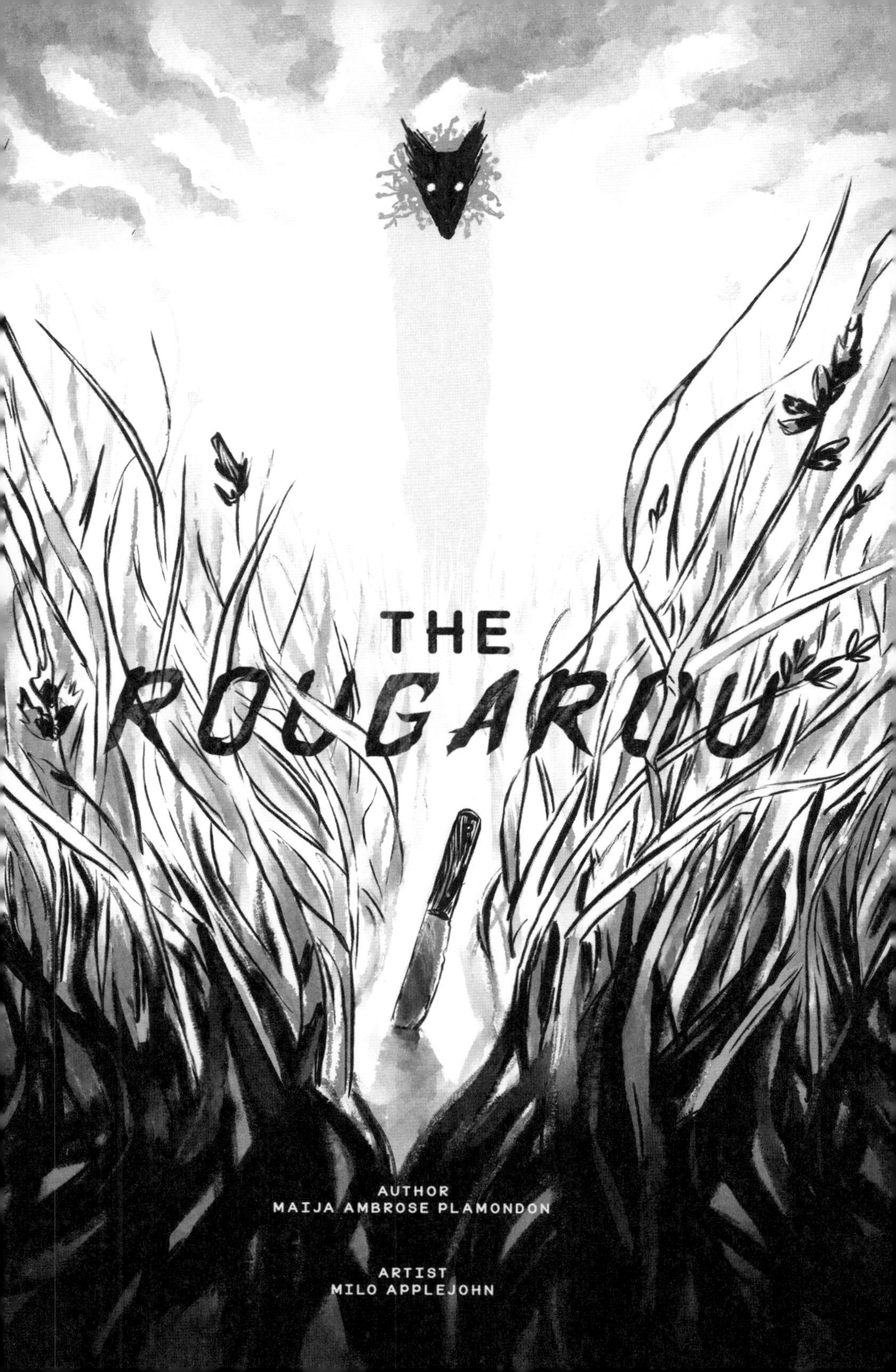
THE
ROUGAROU
AUTHOR
MAIJA AMBROSE PLAMONDON
ARTIST
MILO APPLEJOHN

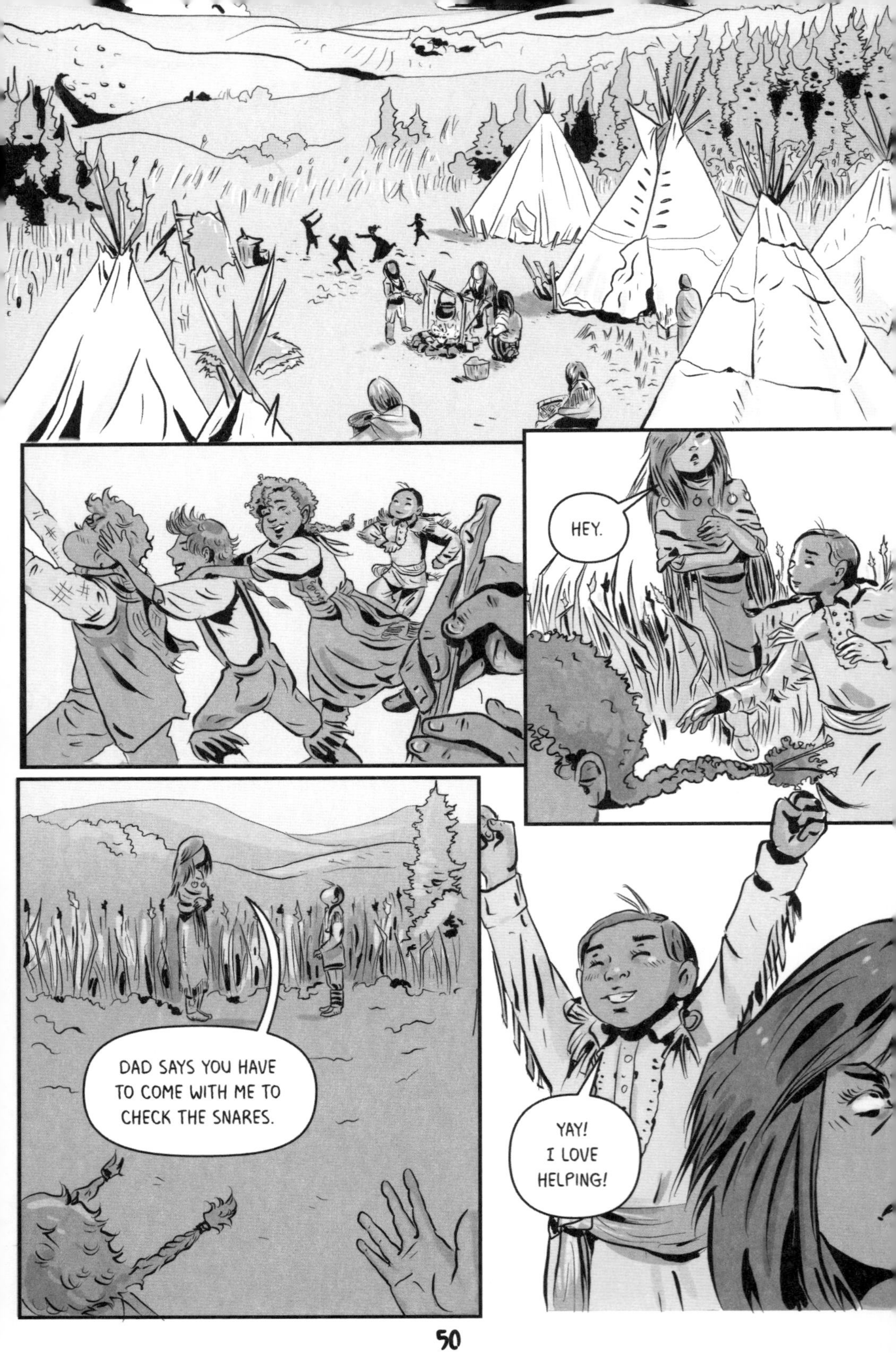
HEY.
DAD SAYS YOU HAVE TO COME WITH ME TO CHECK THE SNARES.
YAY! I LOVE HELPING!

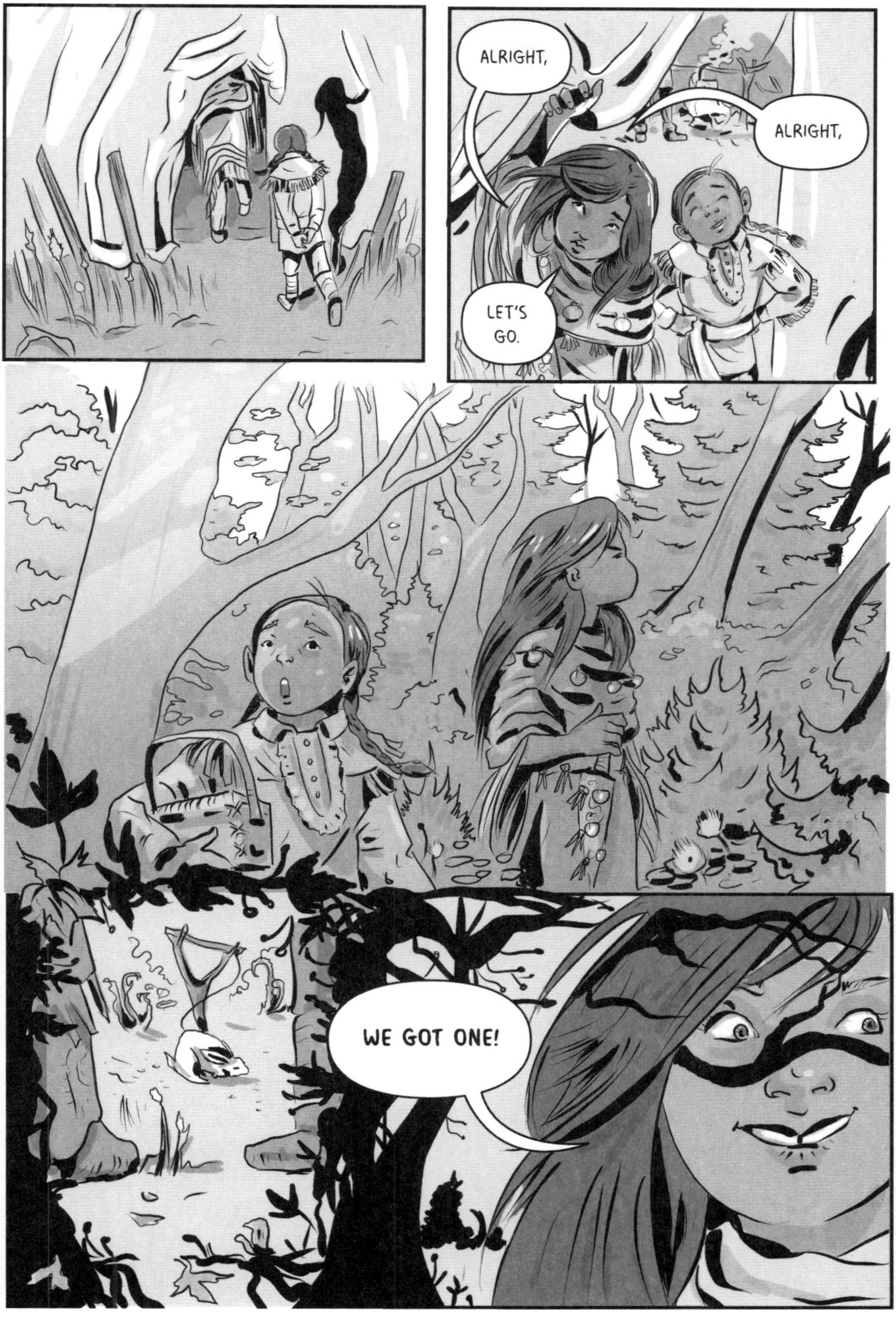
ALRIGHT,
ALRIGHT,
LET'S GO.
WE GOT ONE!

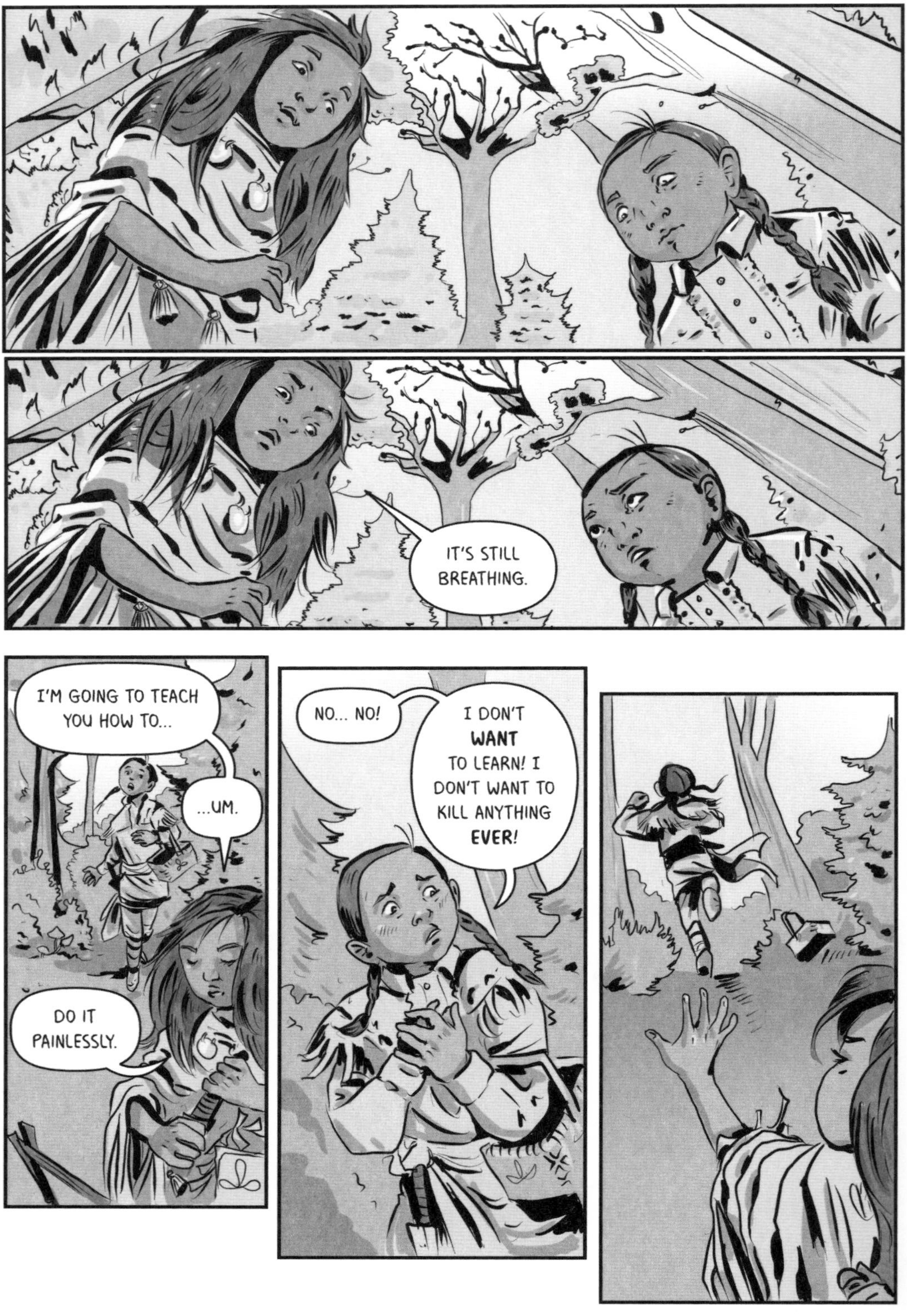
IT'S STILL BREATHING.
I'M GOING TO TEACH YOU HOW TO...
...UM.
DO IT PAINLESSLY.
NO... NO!
I DON'T **WANT** TO LEARN! I DON'T WANT TO KILL ANYTHING **EVER**!

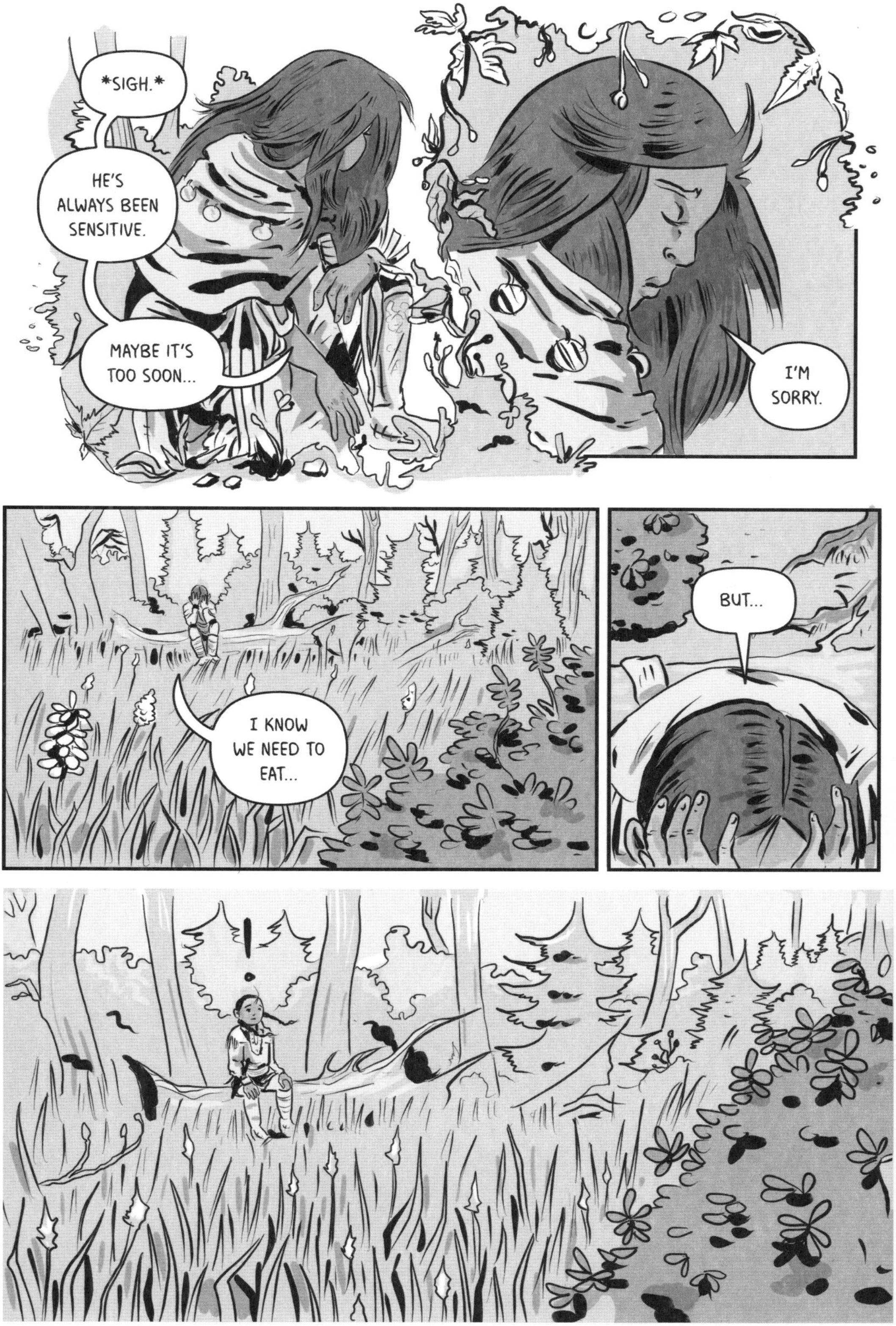
SIGH.
HE'S ALWAYS BEEN SENSITIVE.
MAYBE IT'S TOO SOON...
I'M SORRY.
I KNOW WE NEED TO EAT...
BUT...
!

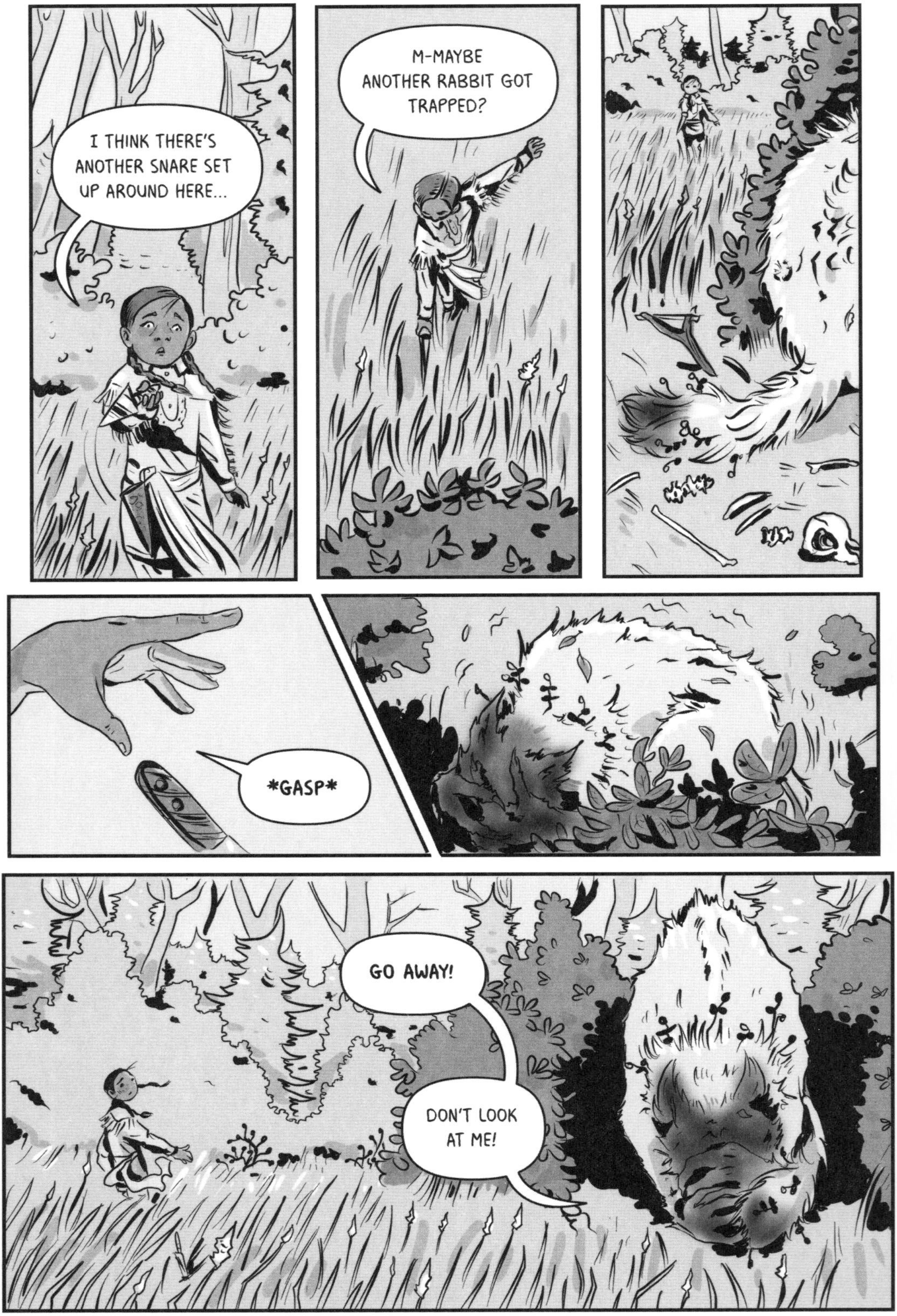
I THINK THERE'S ANOTHER SNARE SET UP AROUND HERE...
M-MAYBE ANOTHER RABBIT GOT TRAPPED?
GASP
GO AWAY!
DON'T LOOK AT ME!

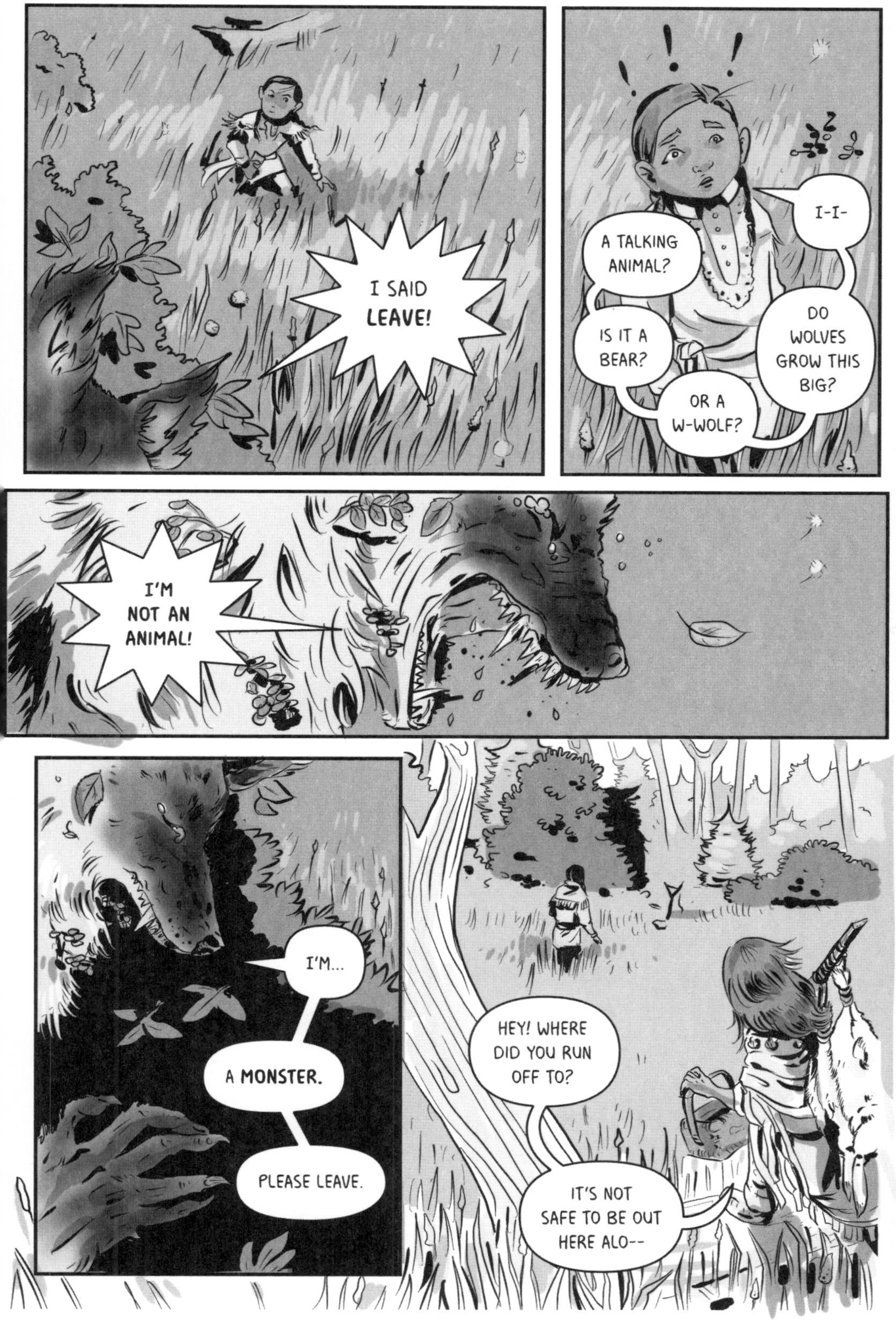
I SAID **LEAVE!**
!!
A TALKING ANIMAL?
IS IT A BEAR?
OR A W-WOLF?
I-I-
DO WOLVES GROW THIS BIG?
I'M NOT AN ANIMAL!
I'M...
A **MONSTER.**
PLEASE LEAVE.
HEY! WHERE DID YOU RUN OFF TO?
IT'S NOT SAFE TO BE OUT HERE ALO--

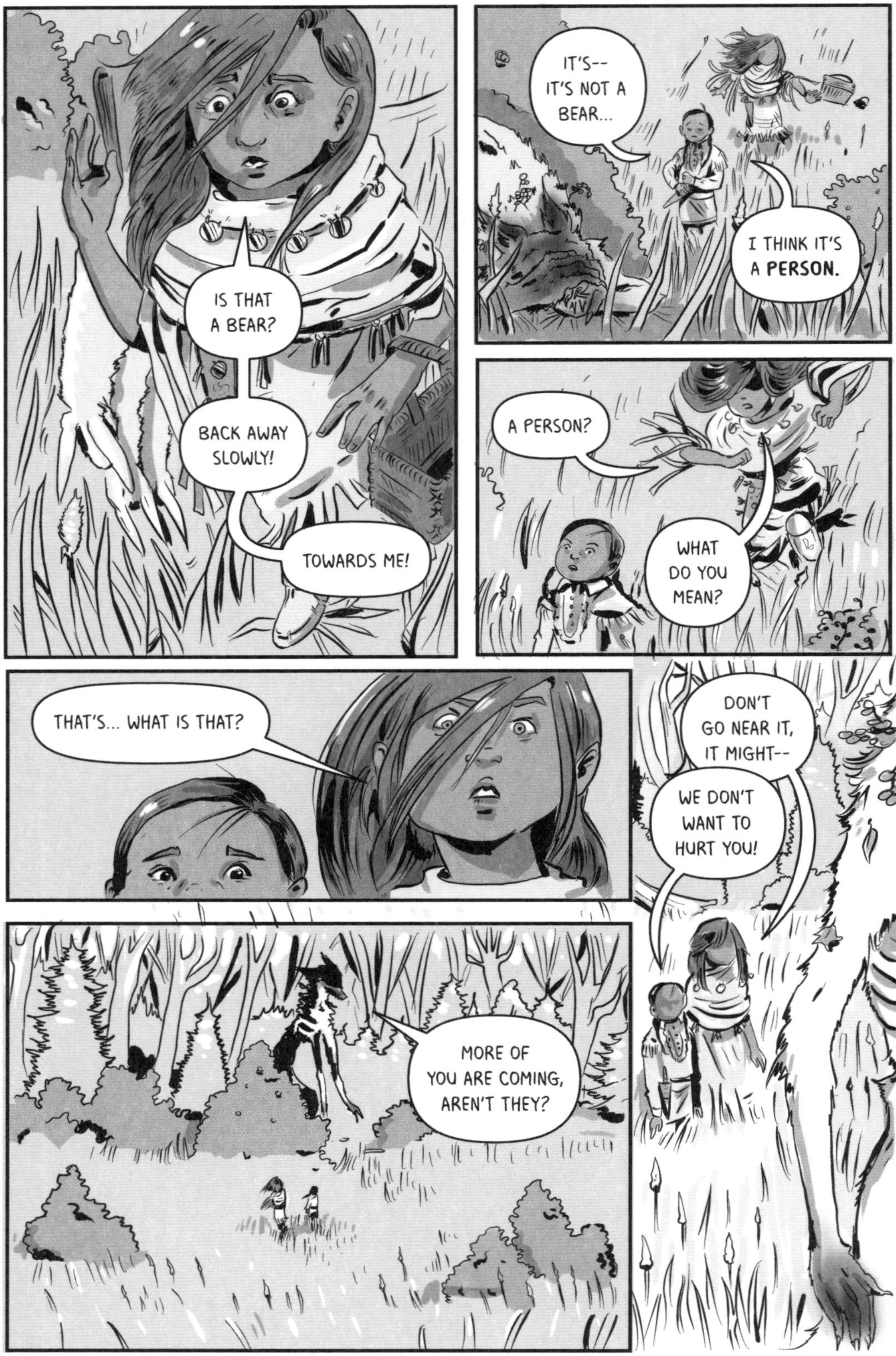
IS THAT A BEAR?
BACK AWAY SLOWLY!
TOWARDS ME!
IT'S-- IT'S NOT A BEAR...
I THINK IT'S A **PERSON.**
A PERSON?
WHAT DO YOU MEAN?
THAT'S... WHAT IS THAT?
DON'T GO NEAR IT, IT MIGHT--
WE DON'T WANT TO HURT YOU!
MORE OF YOU ARE COMING, AREN'T THEY?

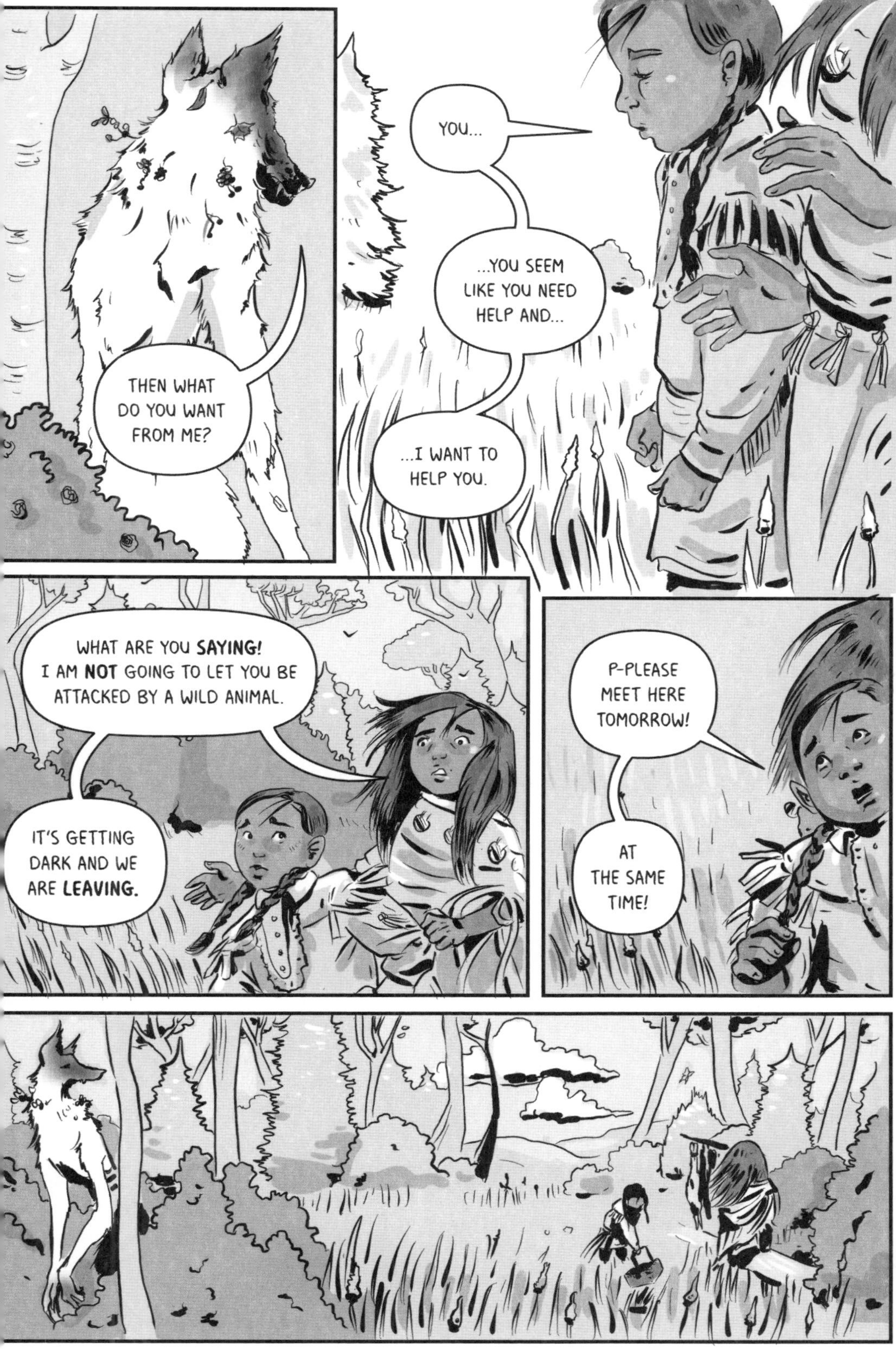
THEN WHAT DO YOU WANT FROM ME?
YOU...
...YOU SEEM LIKE YOU NEED HELP AND...
...I WANT TO HELP YOU.
WHAT ARE YOU SAYING! I AM NOT GOING TO LET YOU BE ATTACKED BY A WILD ANIMAL.
IT'S GETTING DARK AND WE ARE LEAVING.
P-PLEASE MEET HERE TOMORROW!
AT THE SAME TIME!

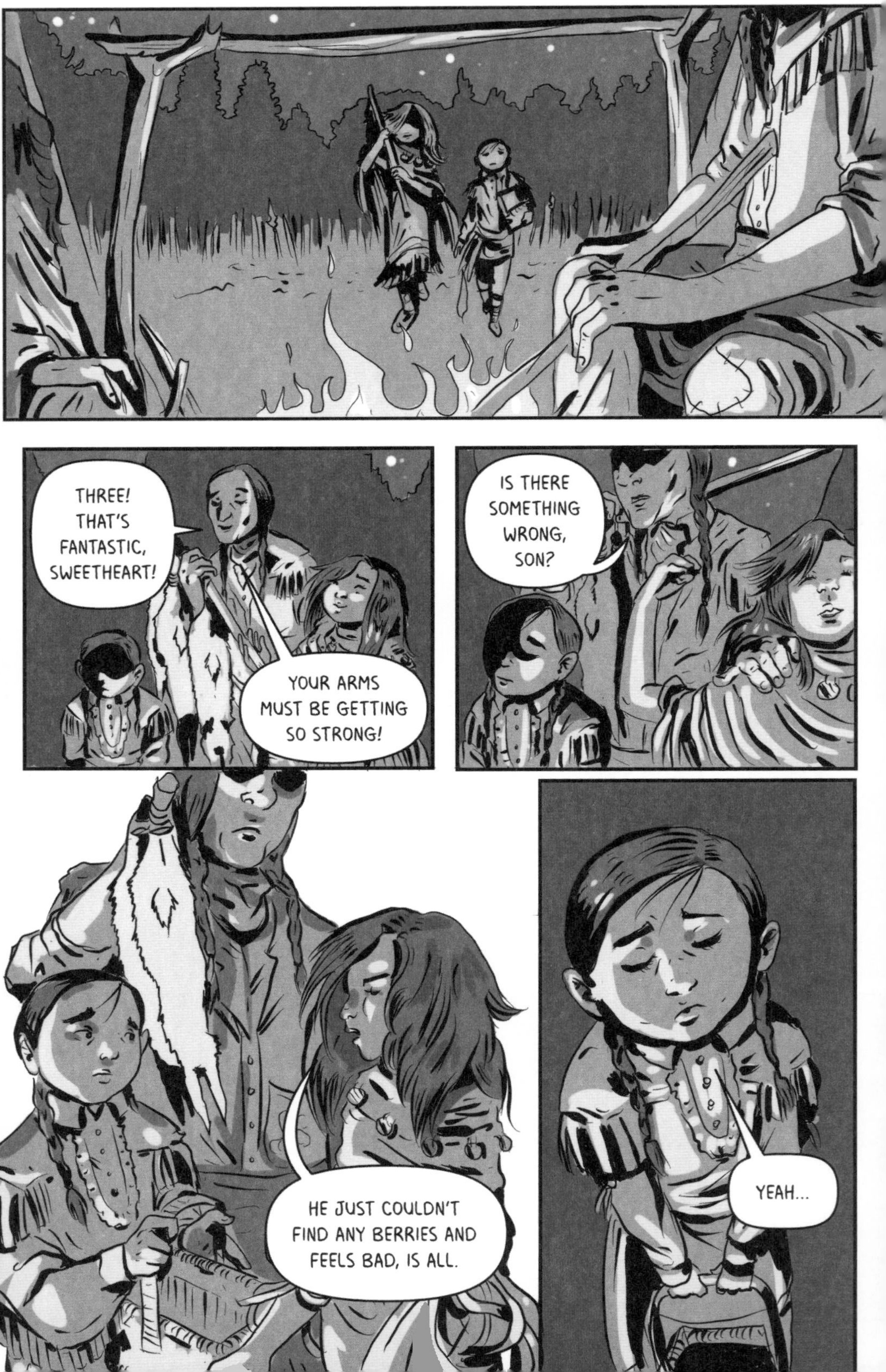
THREE! THAT'S FANTASTIC, SWEETHEART!
YOUR ARMS MUST BE GETTING SO STRONG!
IS THERE SOMETHING WRONG, SON?
HE JUST COULDN'T FIND ANY BERRIES AND FEELS BAD, IS ALL.
YEAH...

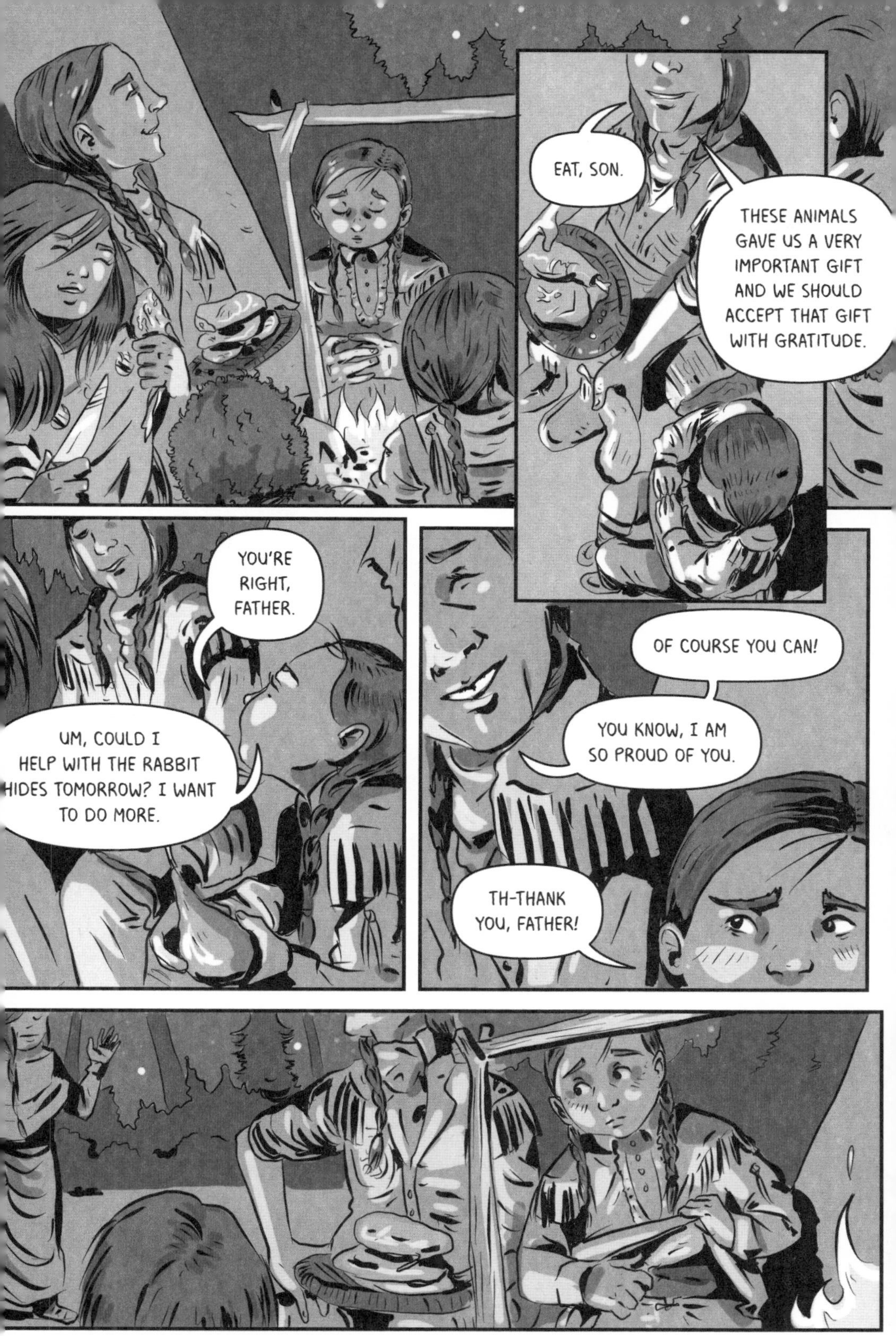
EAT, SON.
THESE ANIMALS GAVE US A VERY IMPORTANT GIFT AND WE SHOULD ACCEPT THAT GIFT WITH GRATITUDE.
YOU'RE RIGHT, FATHER.
UM, COULD I HELP WITH THE RABBIT HIDES TOMORROW? I WANT TO DO MORE.
OF COURSE YOU CAN!
YOU KNOW, I AM SO PROUD OF YOU.
TH-THANK YOU, FATHER!

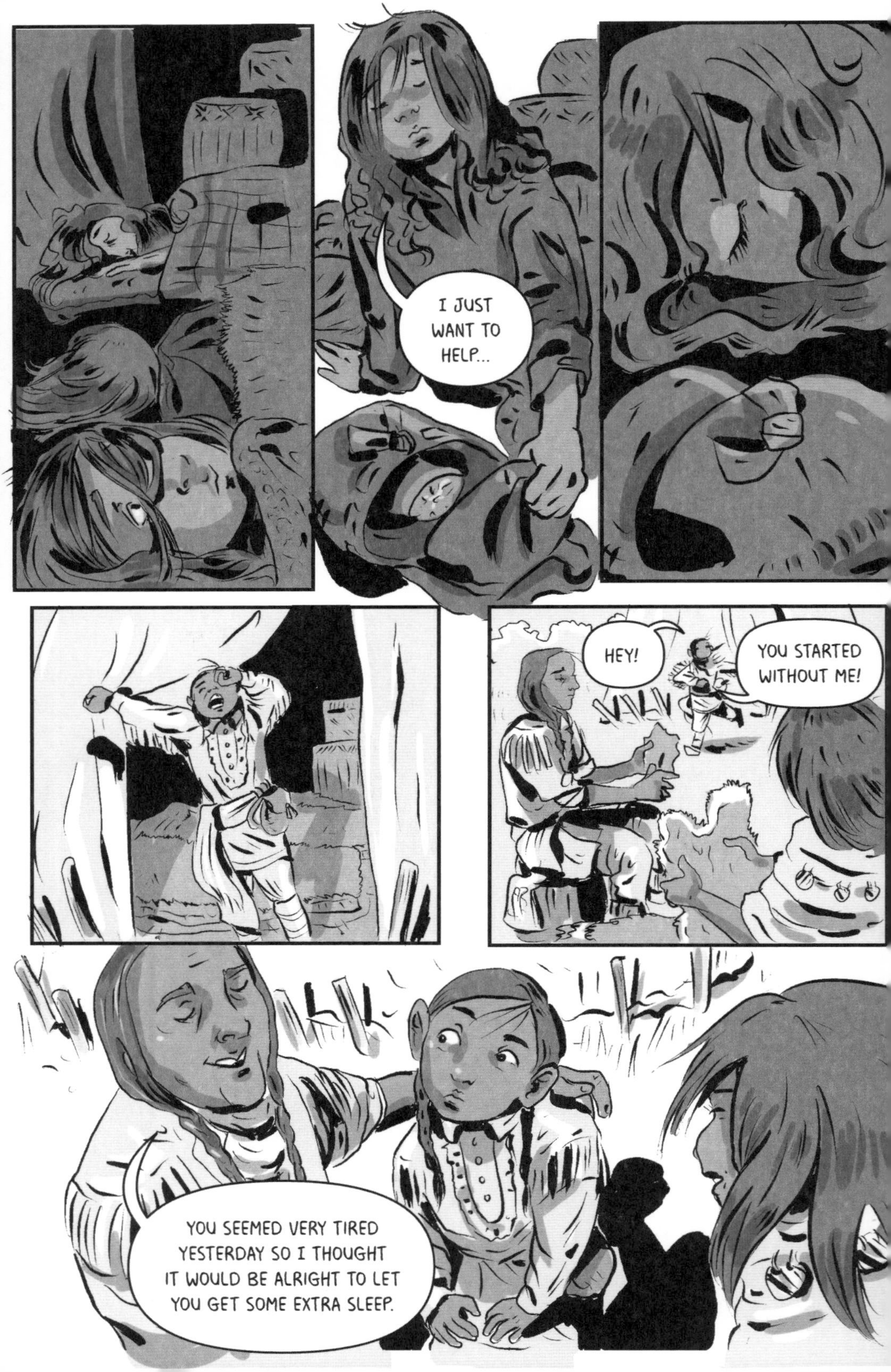
I JUST WANT TO HELP...
HEY!
YOU STARTED WITHOUT ME!
YOU SEEMED VERY TIRED YESTERDAY SO I THOUGHT IT WOULD BE ALRIGHT TO LET YOU GET SOME EXTRA SLEEP.

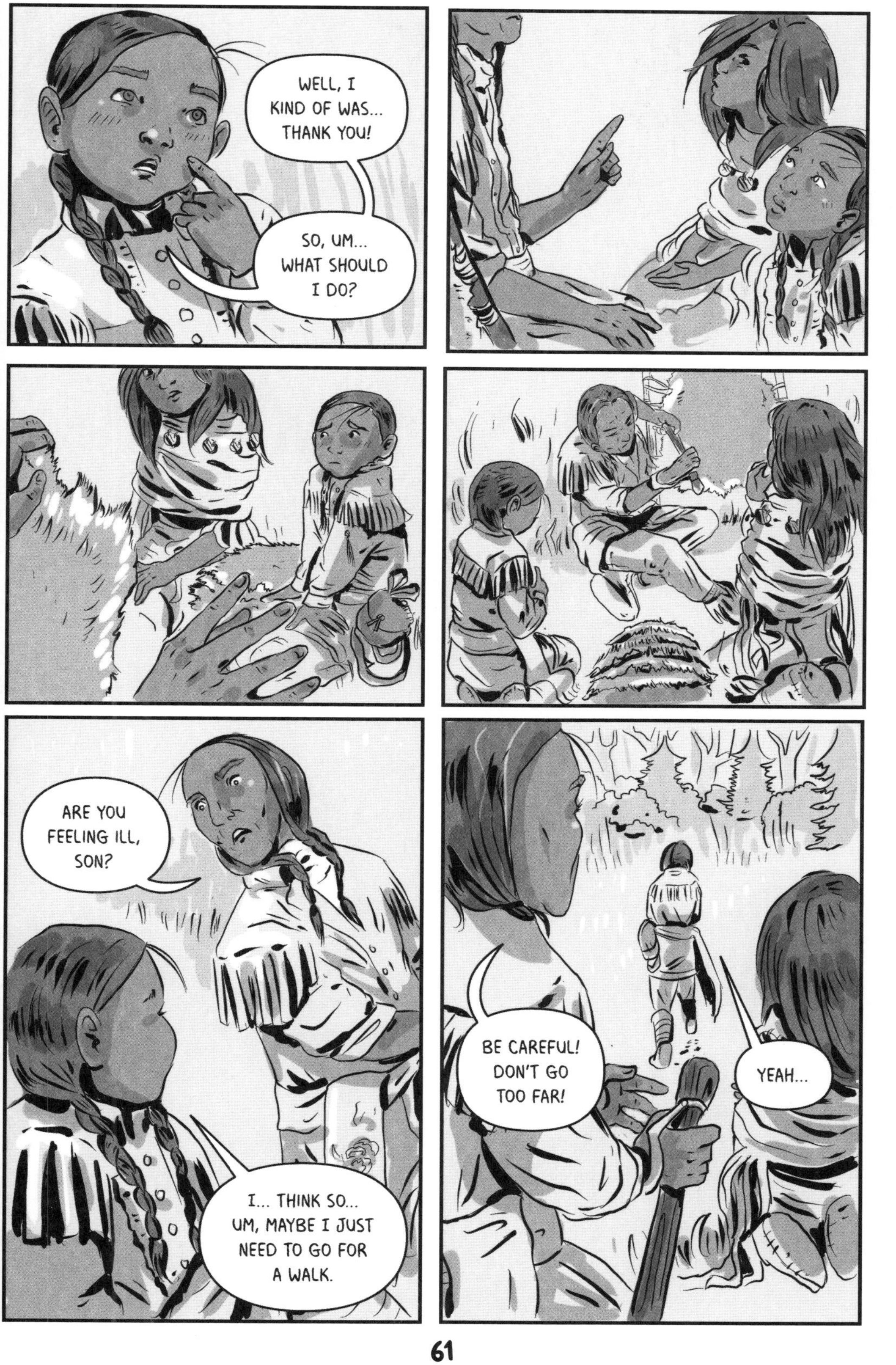
WELL, I KIND OF WAS... THANK YOU!
SO, UM... WHAT SHOULD I DO?
ARE YOU FEELING ILL, SON?
I... THINK SO... UM, MAYBE I JUST NEED TO GO FOR A WALK.
BE CAREFUL! DON'T GO TOO FAR!
YEAH...

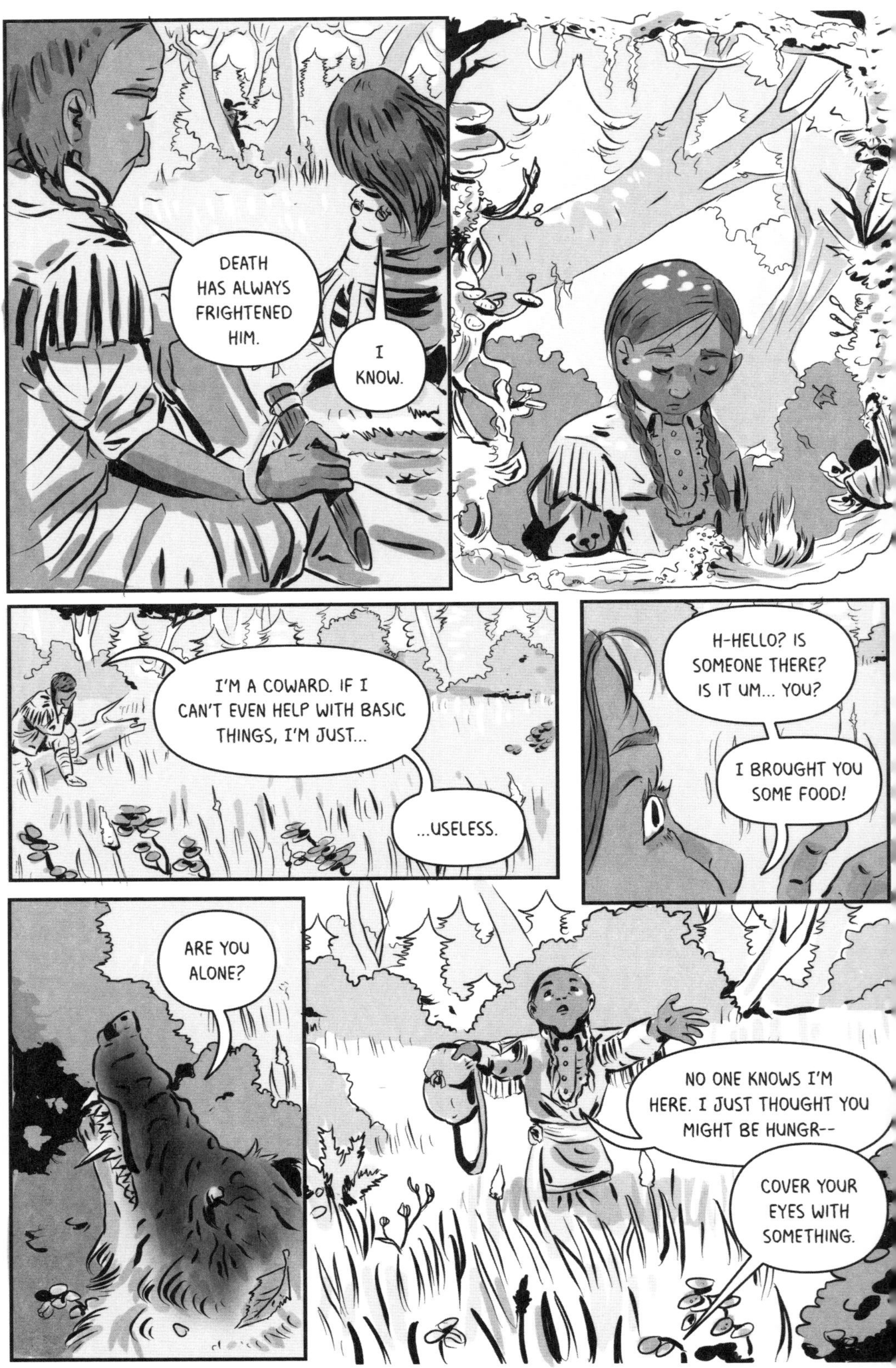
DEATH HAS ALWAYS FRIGHTENED HIM.
I KNOW.
I'M A COWARD. IF I CAN'T EVEN HELP WITH BASIC THINGS, I'M JUST...
...USELESS.
H-HELLO? IS SOMEONE THERE? IS IT UM... YOU?
I BROUGHT YOU SOME FOOD!
ARE YOU ALONE?
NO ONE KNOWS I'M HERE. I JUST THOUGHT YOU MIGHT BE HUNGR--
COVER YOUR EYES WITH SOMETHING.

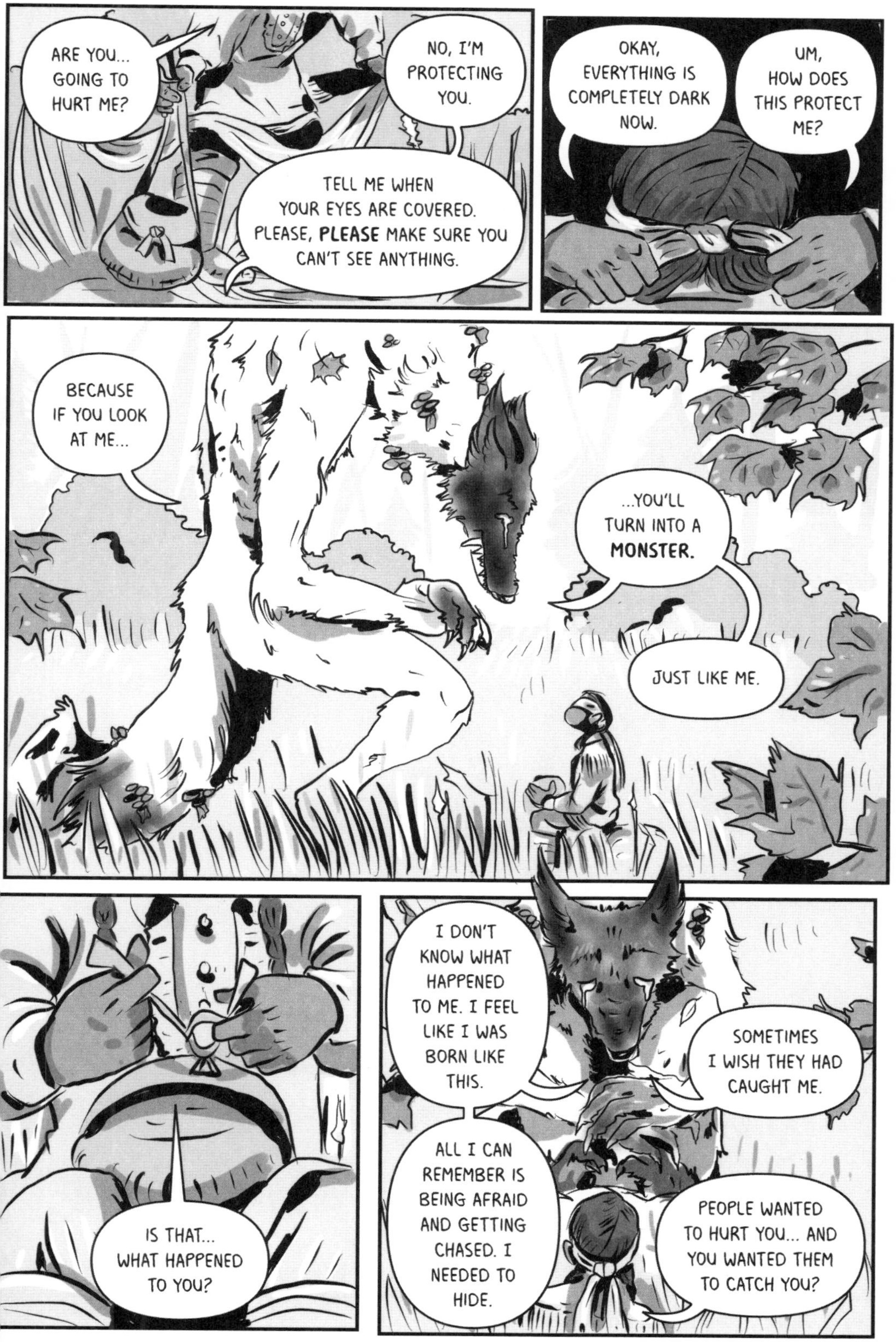
ARE YOU... GOING TO HURT ME?
NO, I'M PROTECTING YOU.
TELL ME WHEN YOUR EYES ARE COVERED. PLEASE, **PLEASE** MAKE SURE YOU CAN'T SEE ANYTHING.
OKAY, EVERYTHING IS COMPLETELY DARK NOW.
UM, HOW DOES THIS PROTECT ME?
BECAUSE IF YOU LOOK AT ME...
...YOU'LL TURN INTO A **MONSTER.**
JUST LIKE ME.
IS THAT... WHAT HAPPENED TO YOU?
I DON'T KNOW WHAT HAPPENED TO ME. I FEEL LIKE I WAS BORN LIKE THIS.
ALL I CAN REMEMBER IS BEING AFRAID AND GETTING CHASED. I NEEDED TO HIDE.
SOMETIMES I WISH THEY HAD CAUGHT ME.
PEOPLE WANTED TO HURT YOU... AND YOU WANTED THEM TO CATCH YOU?

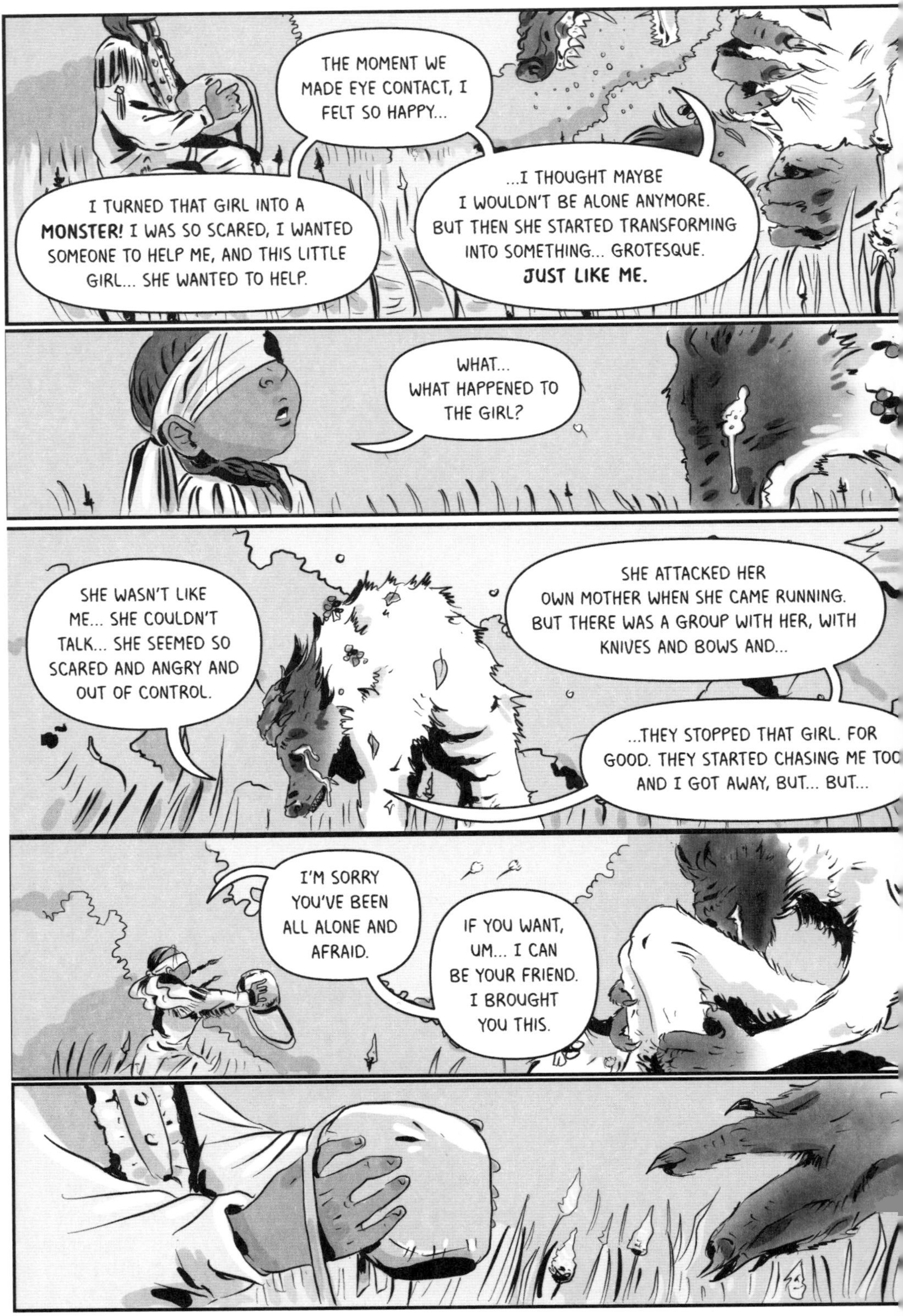
THE MOMENT WE MADE EYE CONTACT, I FELT SO HAPPY...
I TURNED THAT GIRL INTO A MONSTER! I WAS SO SCARED, I WANTED SOMEONE TO HELP ME, AND THIS LITTLE GIRL... SHE WANTED TO HELP.
...I THOUGHT MAYBE I WOULDN'T BE ALONE ANYMORE. BUT THEN SHE STARTED TRANSFORMING INTO SOMETHING... GROTESQUE. JUST LIKE ME.
WHAT... WHAT HAPPENED TO THE GIRL?
SHE WASN'T LIKE ME... SHE COULDN'T TALK... SHE SEEMED SO SCARED AND ANGRY AND OUT OF CONTROL.
SHE ATTACKED HER OWN MOTHER WHEN SHE CAME RUNNING. BUT THERE WAS A GROUP WITH HER, WITH KNIVES AND BOWS AND...
...THEY STOPPED THAT GIRL. FOR GOOD. THEY STARTED CHASING ME TOO AND I GOT AWAY, BUT... BUT...
I'M SORRY YOU'VE BEEN ALL ALONE AND AFRAID.
IF YOU WANT, UM... I CAN BE YOUR FRIEND. I BROUGHT YOU THIS.

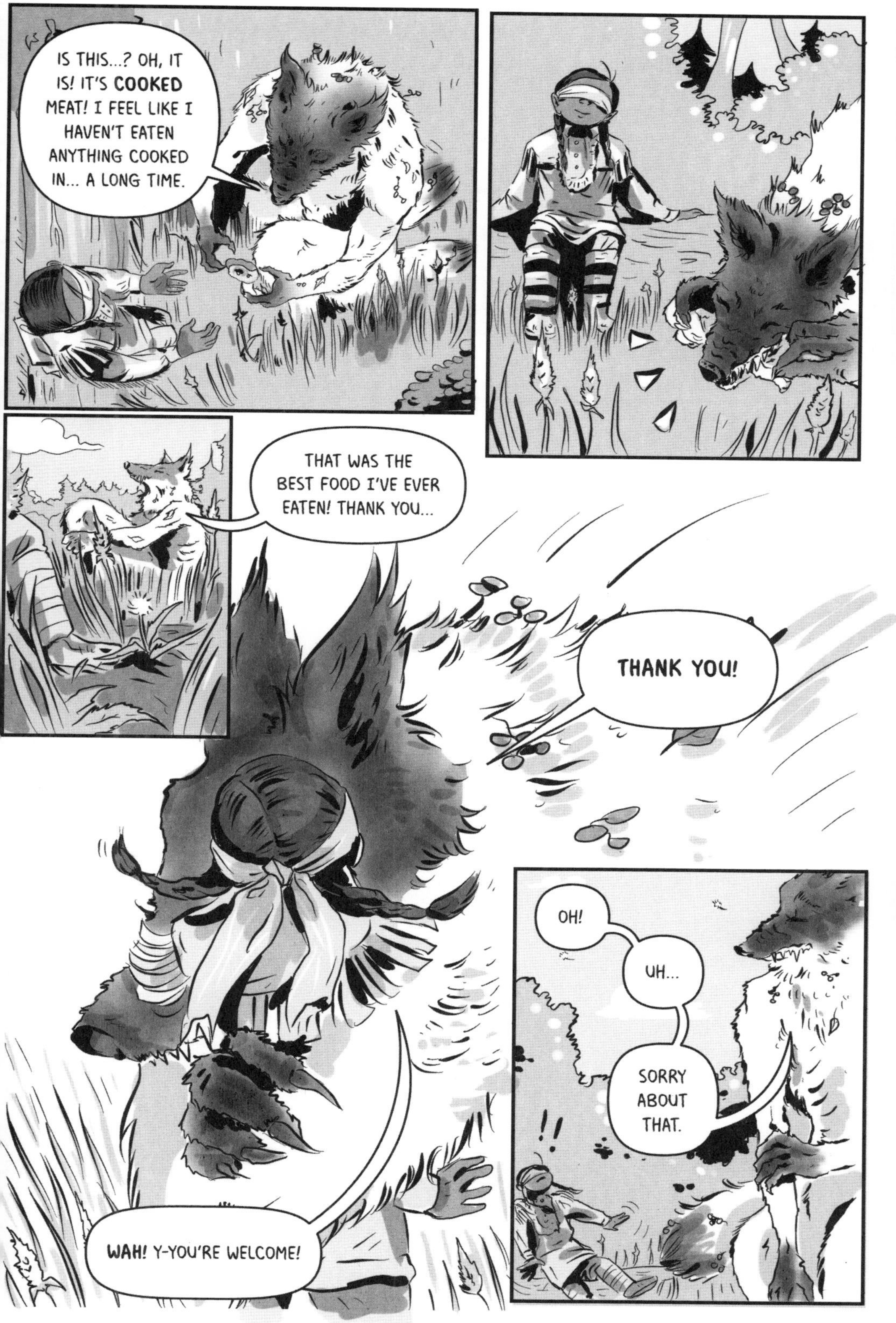
IS THIS...? OH, IT IS! IT'S **COOKED** MEAT! I FEEL LIKE I HAVEN'T EATEN ANYTHING COOKED IN... A LONG TIME.
THAT WAS THE BEST FOOD I'VE EVER EATEN! THANK YOU...
THANK YOU!
WAH! Y-YOU'RE WELCOME!
OH!
UH...
SORRY ABOUT THAT.
!!

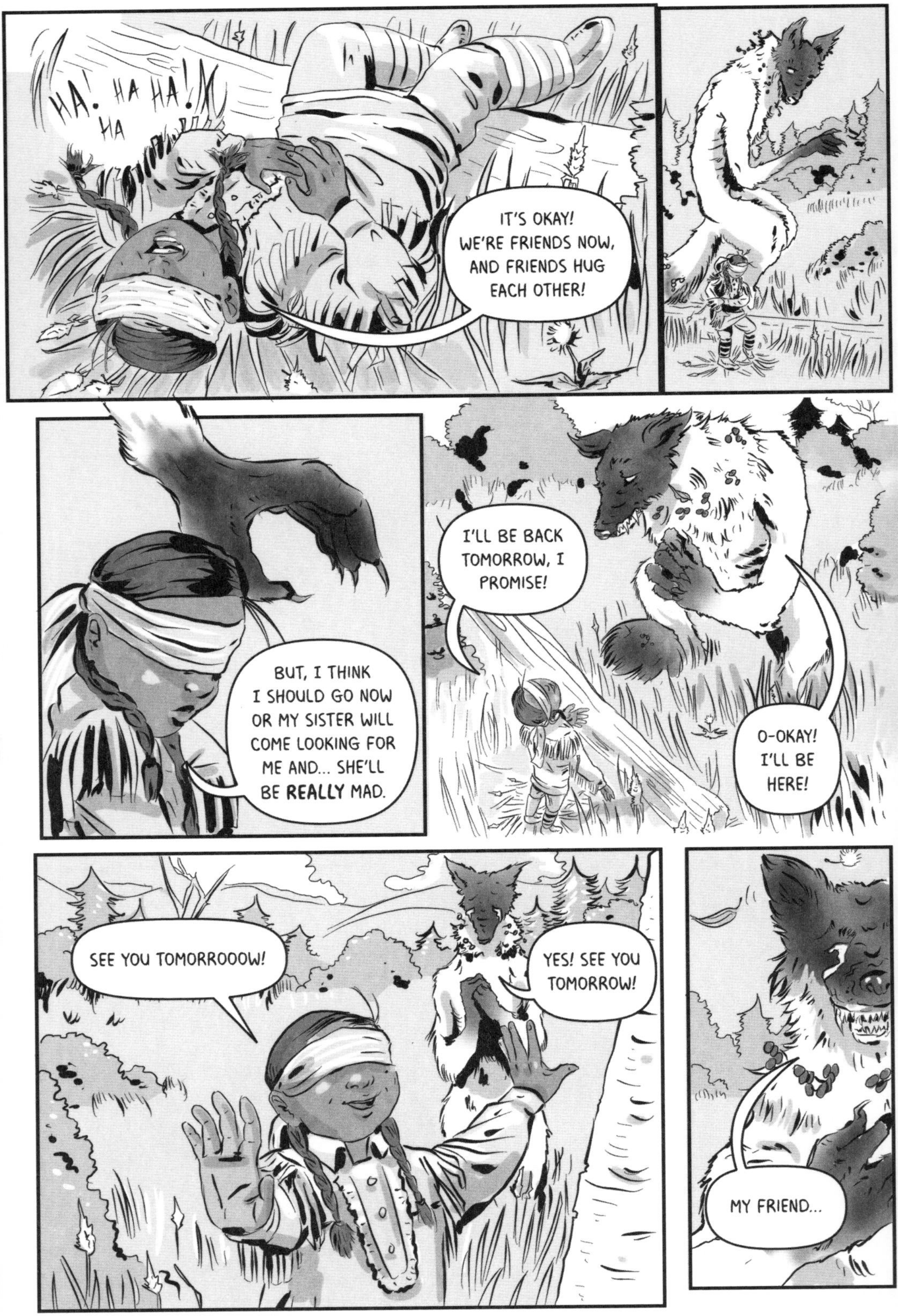
HA! HA HA! HA
IT'S OKAY! WE'RE FRIENDS NOW, AND FRIENDS HUG EACH OTHER!
BUT, I THINK I SHOULD GO NOW OR MY SISTER WILL COME LOOKING FOR ME AND... SHE'LL BE **REALLY** MAD.
I'LL BE BACK TOMORROW, I PROMISE!
O-OKAY! I'LL BE HERE!
SEE YOU TOMORROOOW!
YES! SEE YOU TOMORROW!
MY FRIEND...

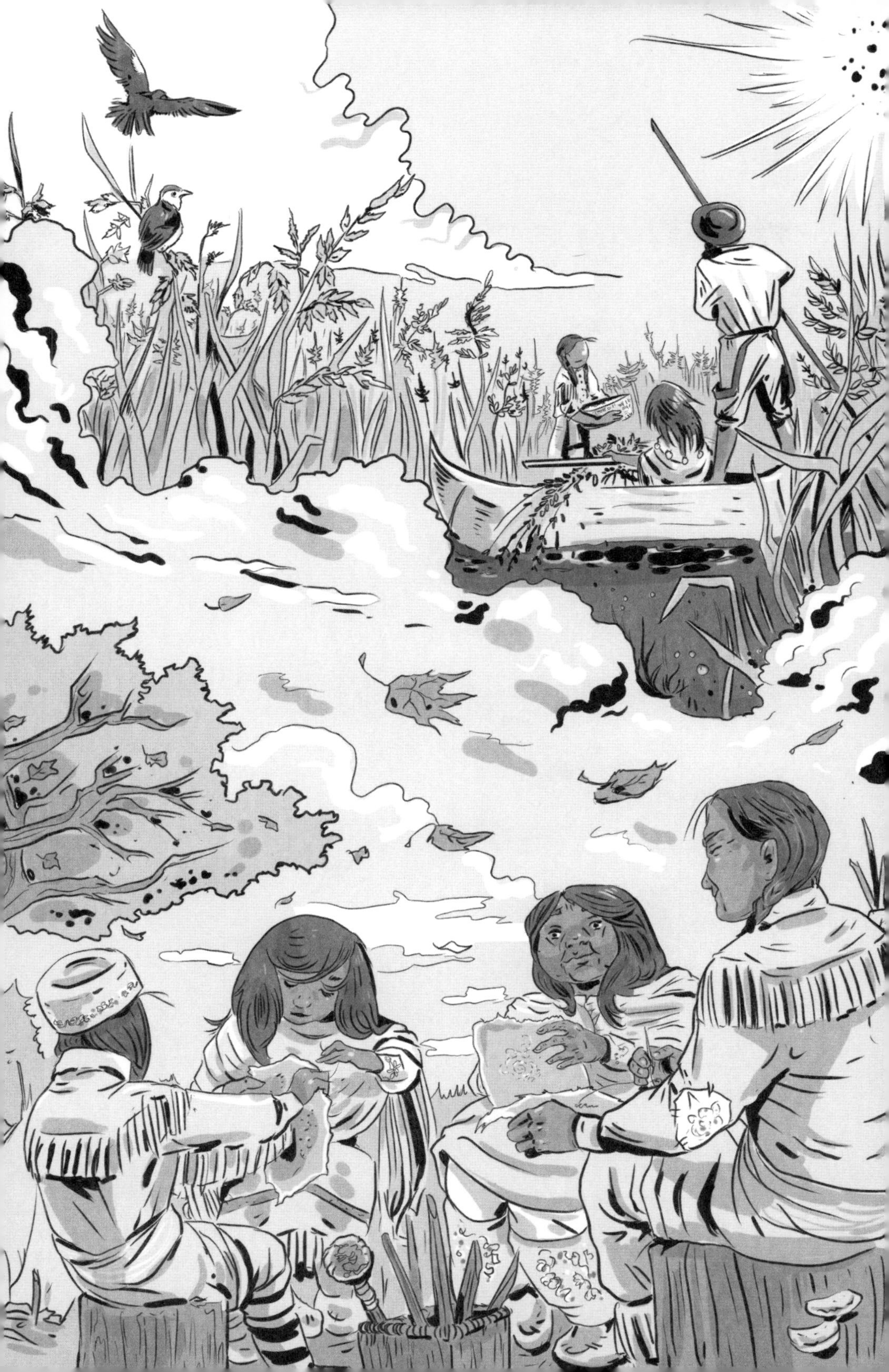

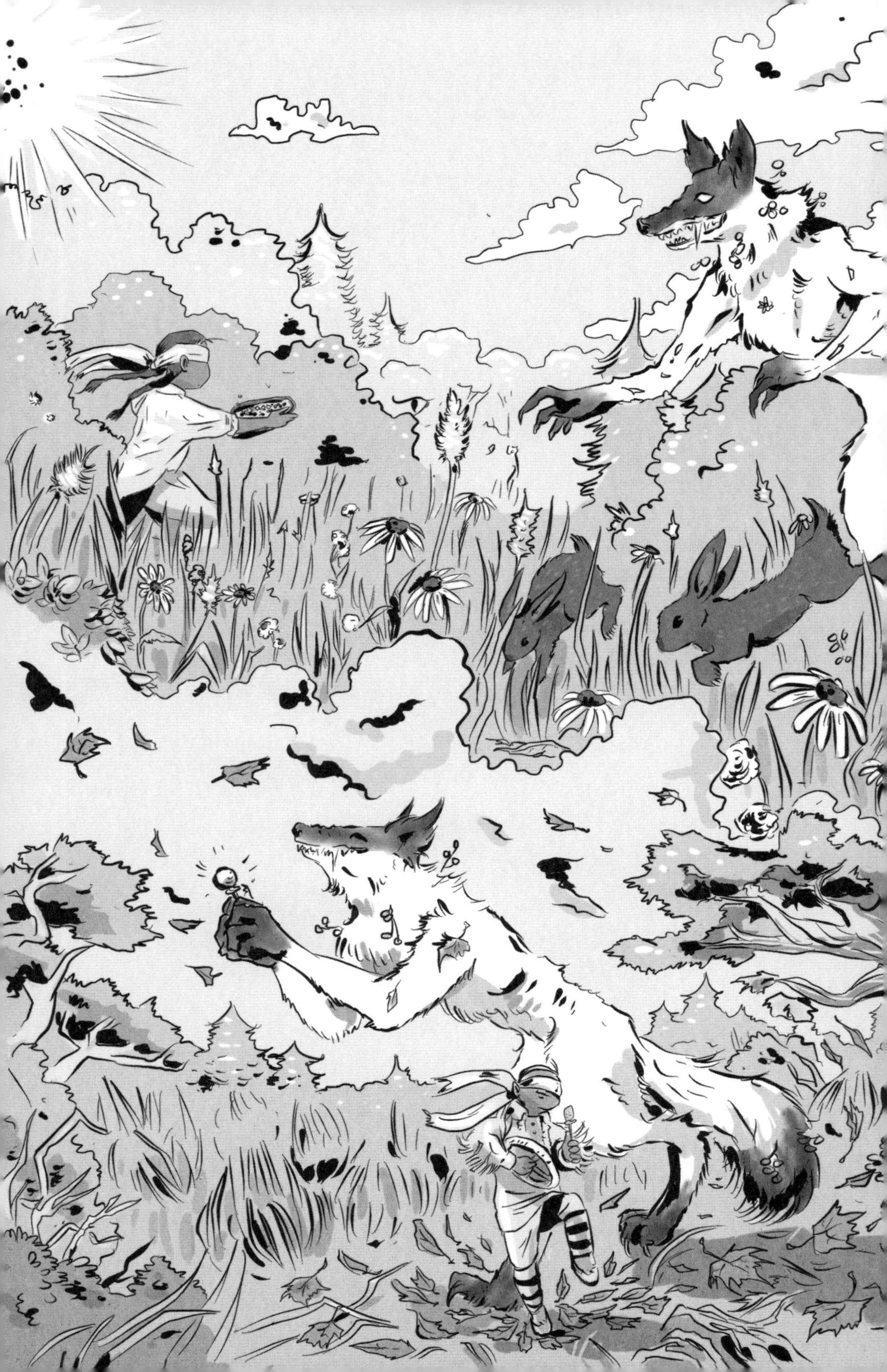

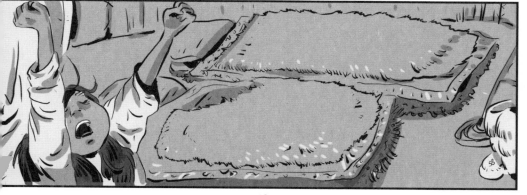

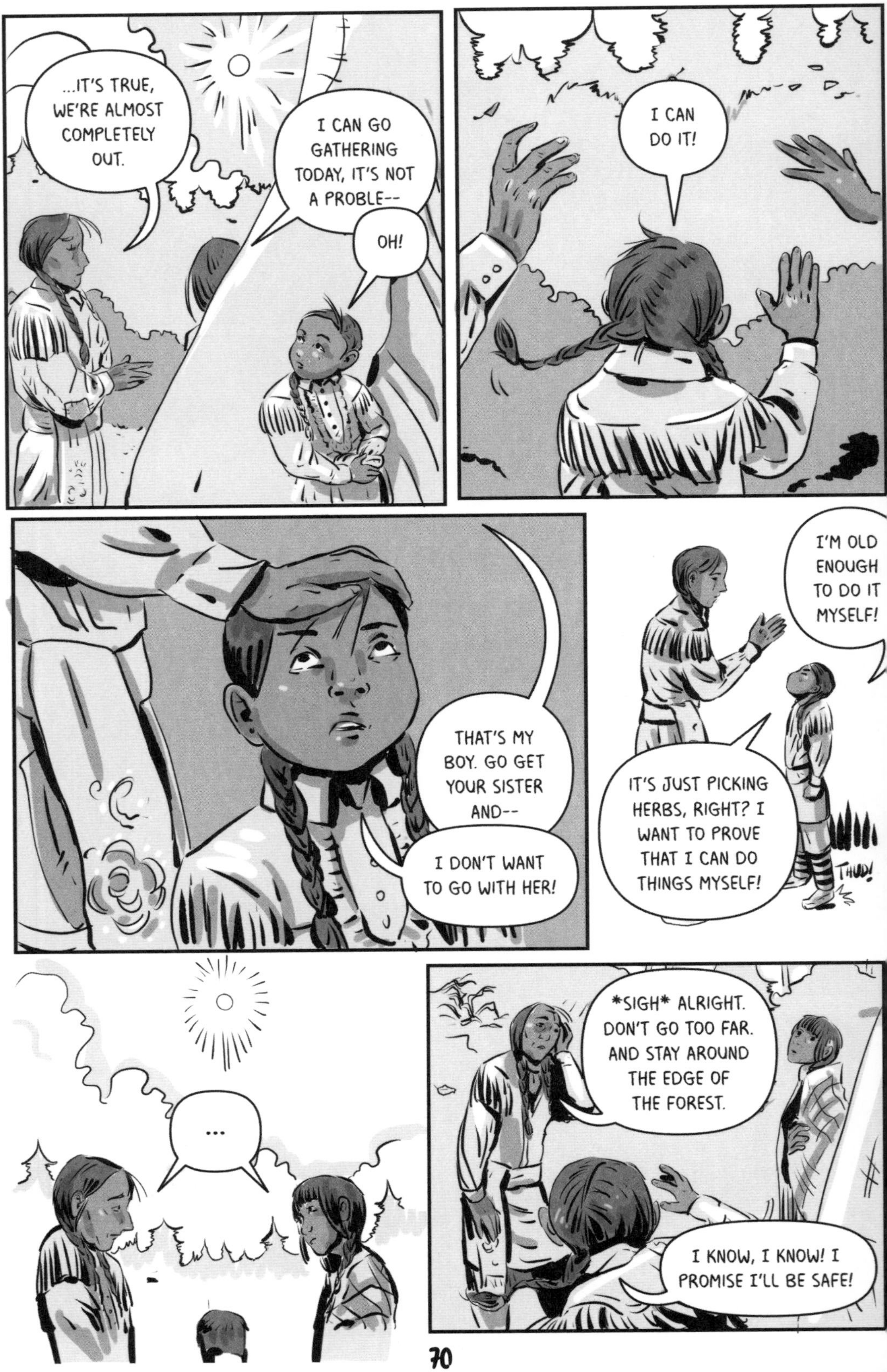
...IT'S TRUE, WE'RE ALMOST COMPLETELY OUT.
I CAN GO GATHERING TODAY, IT'S NOT A PROBLE--
OH!
I CAN DO IT!
THAT'S MY BOY. GO GET YOUR SISTER AND--
I DON'T WANT TO GO WITH HER!
I'M OLD ENOUGH TO DO IT MYSELF!
IT'S JUST PICKING HERBS, RIGHT? I WANT TO PROVE THAT I CAN DO THINGS MYSELF!
THUD!
...
SIGH ALRIGHT. DON'T GO TOO FAR. AND STAY AROUND THE EDGE OF THE FOREST.
I KNOW, I KNOW! I PROMISE I'LL BE SAFE!

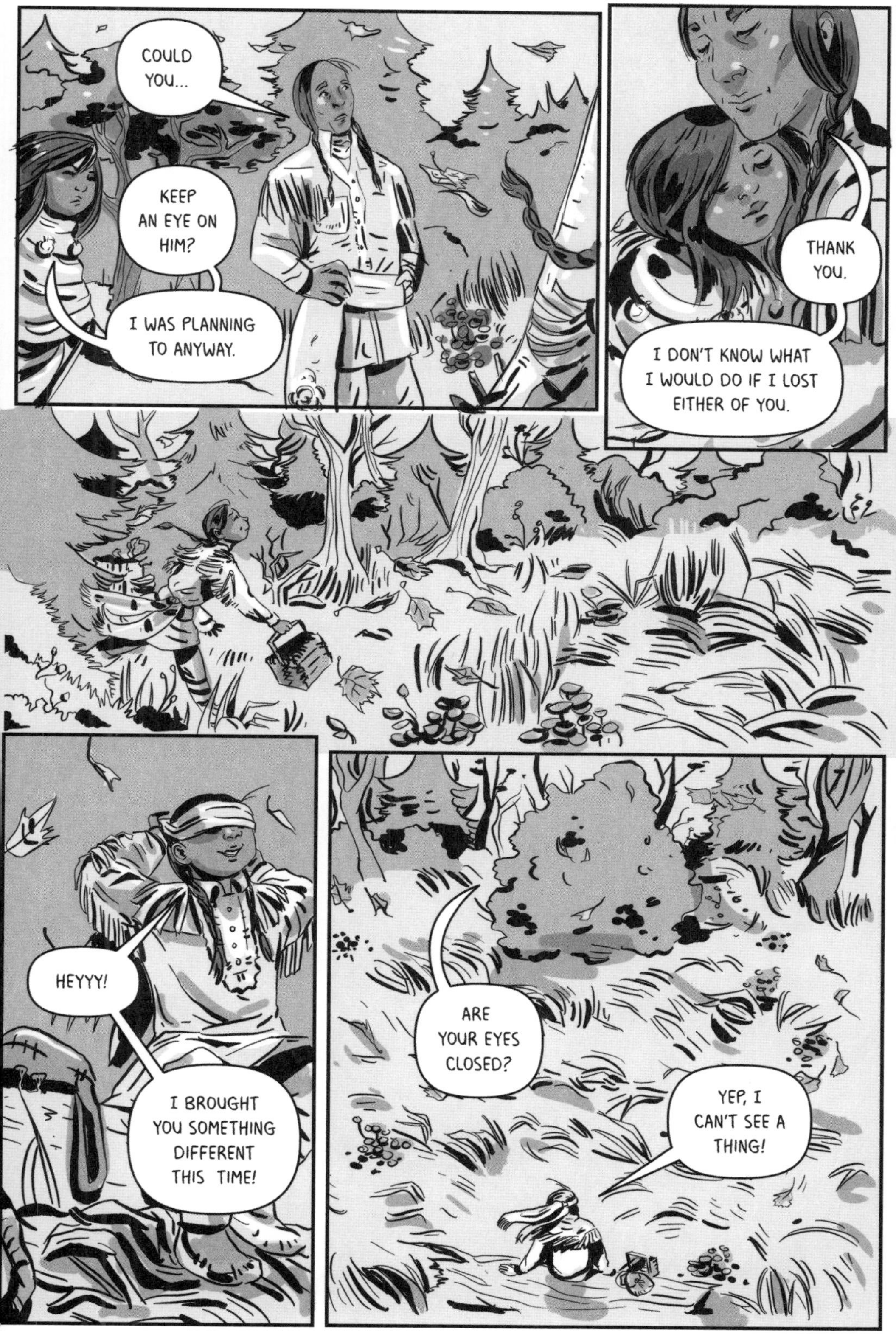
COULD YOU...
KEEP AN EYE ON HIM?
I WAS PLANNING TO ANYWAY.
THANK YOU.
I DON'T KNOW WHAT I WOULD DO IF I LOST EITHER OF YOU.
HEYYY!
I BROUGHT YOU SOMETHING DIFFERENT THIS TIME!
ARE YOUR EYES CLOSED?
YEP, I CAN'T SEE A THING!

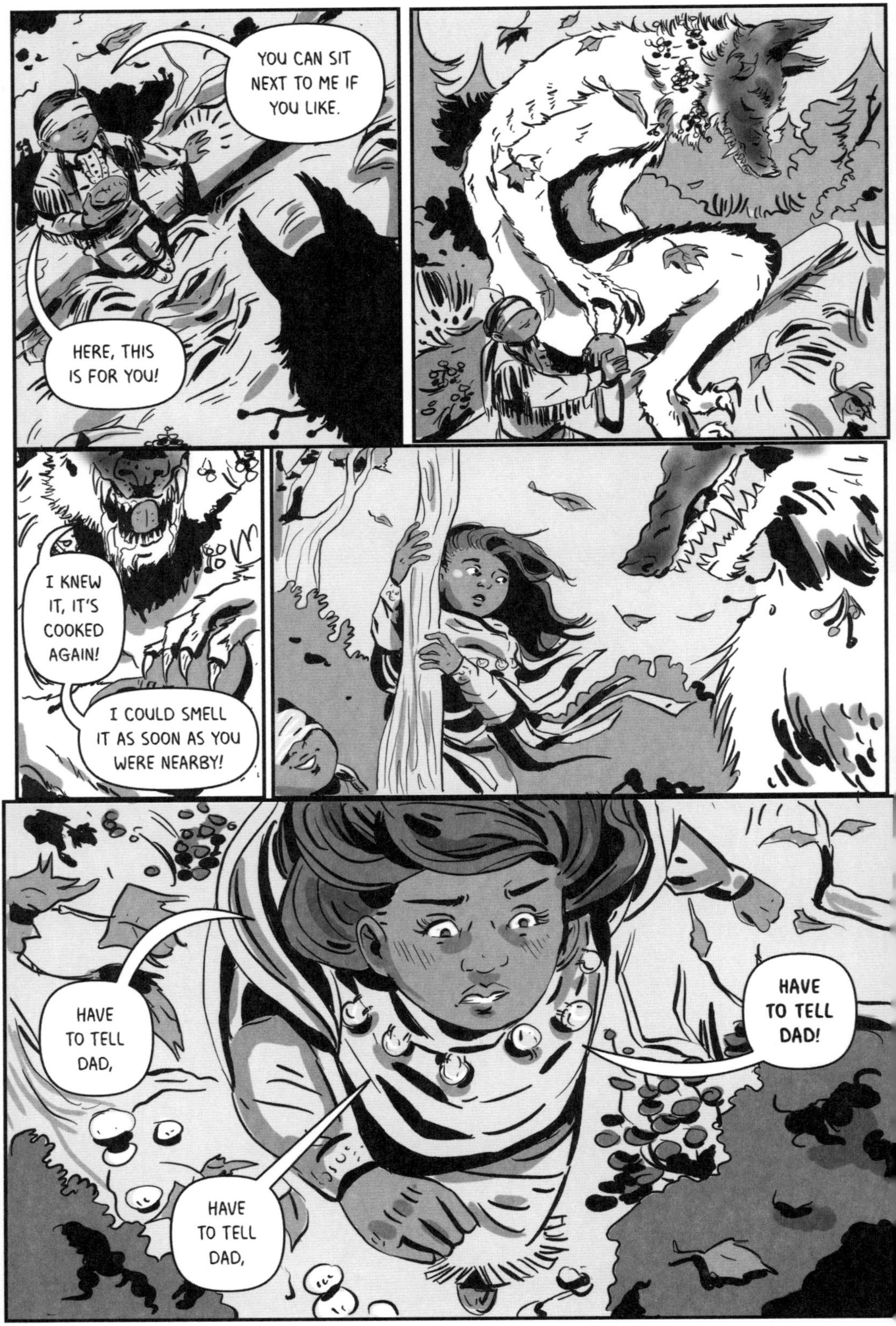

YOU CAN SIT NEXT TO ME IF YOU LIKE.
HERE, THIS IS FOR YOU!
I KNEW IT, IT'S COOKED AGAIN!
I COULD SMELL IT AS SOON AS YOU WERE NEARBY!
HAVE TO TELL DAD,
HAVE TO TELL DAD,
HAVE TO TELL DAD!

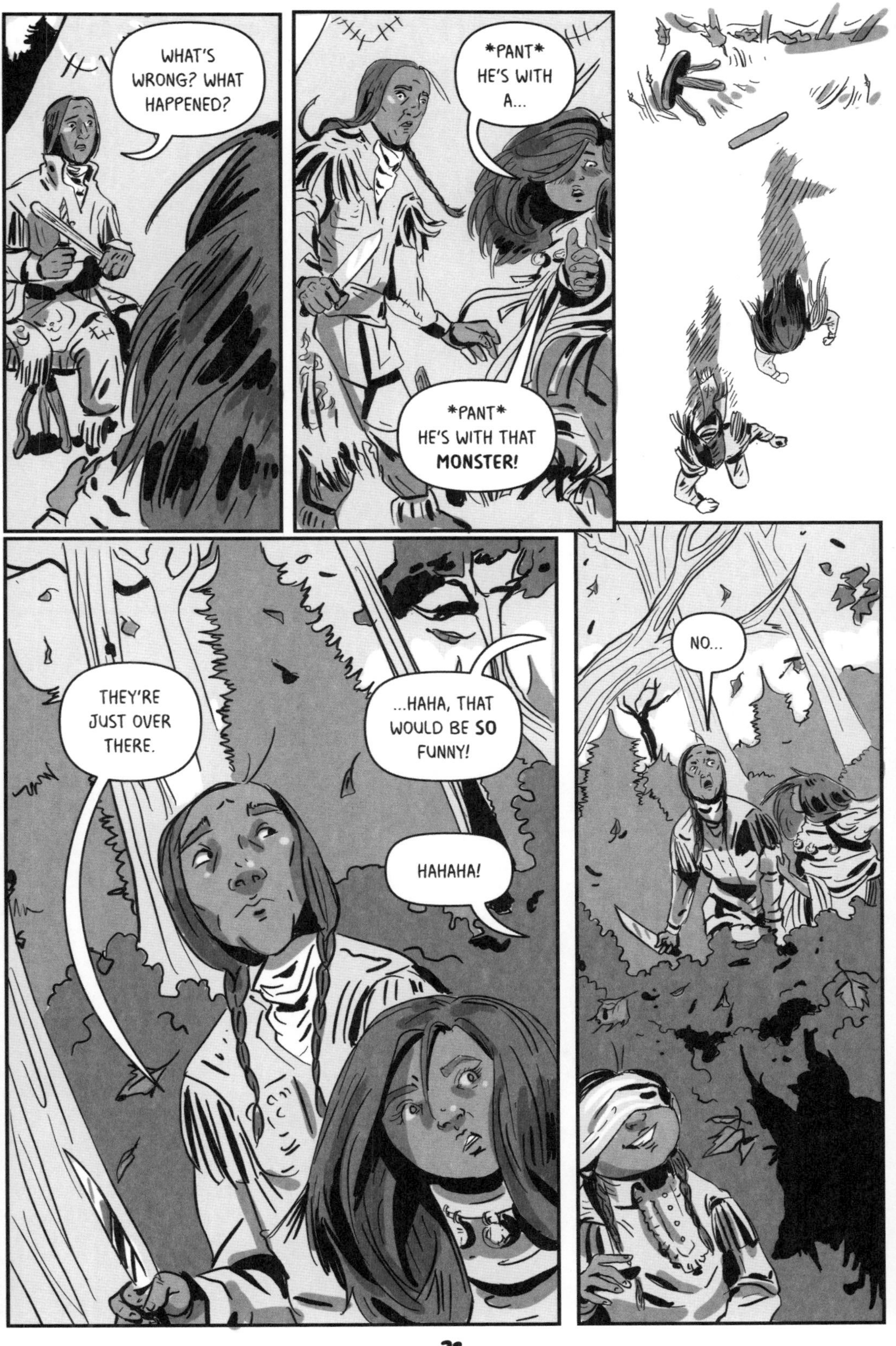
WHAT'S WRONG? WHAT HAPPENED?
PANT HE'S WITH A...
PANT HE'S WITH THAT **MONSTER!**
THEY'RE JUST OVER THERE.
...HAHA, THAT WOULD BE **SO** FUNNY!
HAHAHA!
NO...

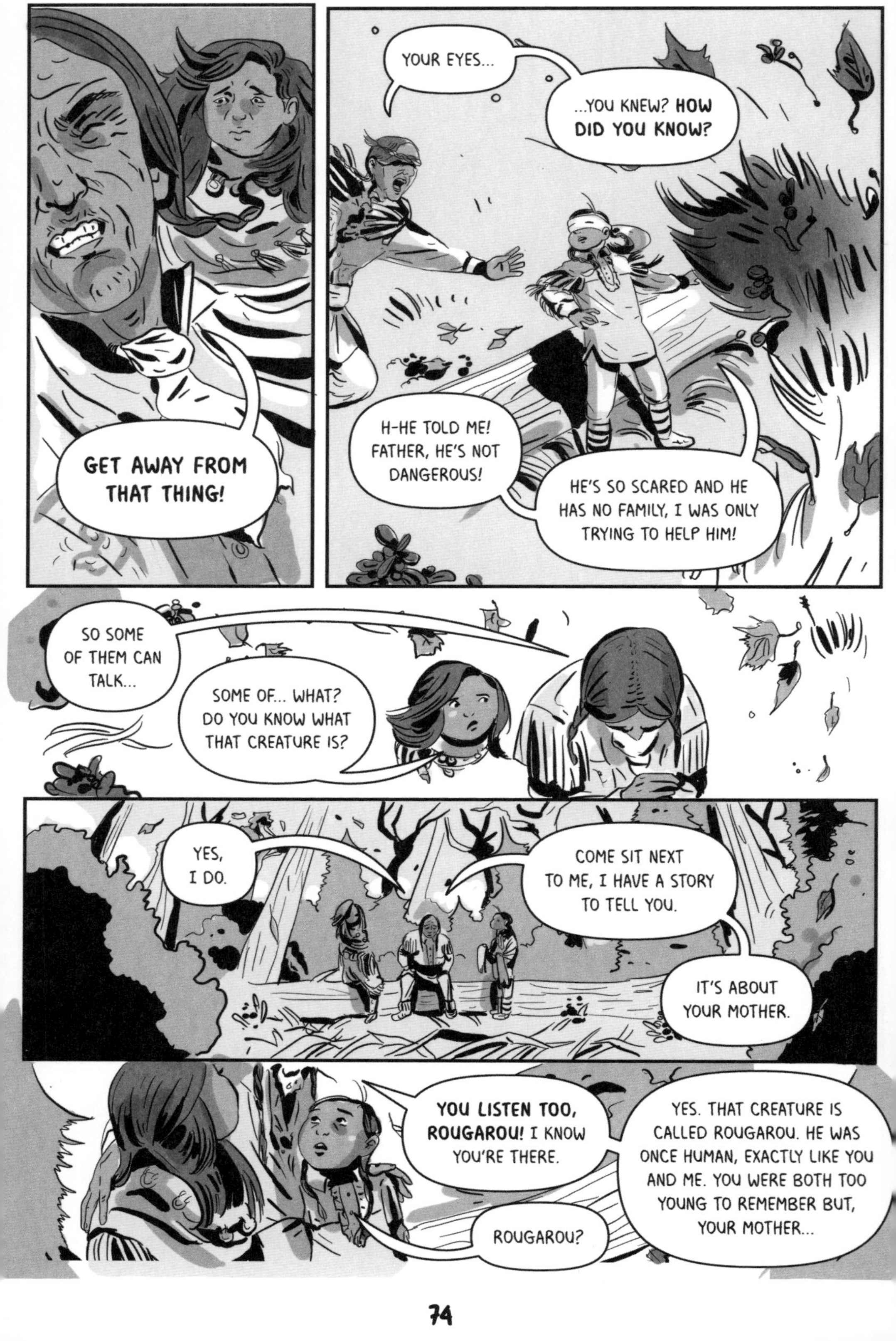
GET AWAY FROM THAT THING!
YOUR EYES...
...YOU KNEW? **HOW DID YOU KNOW?**
H-HE TOLD ME! FATHER, HE'S NOT DANGEROUS!
HE'S SO SCARED AND HE HAS NO FAMILY, I WAS ONLY TRYING TO HELP HIM!
SO SOME OF THEM CAN TALK...
SOME OF... WHAT? DO YOU KNOW WHAT THAT CREATURE IS?
YES, I DO.
COME SIT NEXT TO ME, I HAVE A STORY TO TELL YOU.
IT'S ABOUT YOUR MOTHER.
YOU LISTEN TOO, ROUGAROU! I KNOW YOU'RE THERE.
ROUGAROU?
YES. THAT CREATURE IS CALLED ROUGAROU. HE WAS ONCE HUMAN, EXACTLY LIKE YOU AND ME. YOU WERE BOTH TOO YOUNG TO REMEMBER BUT, YOUR MOTHER...

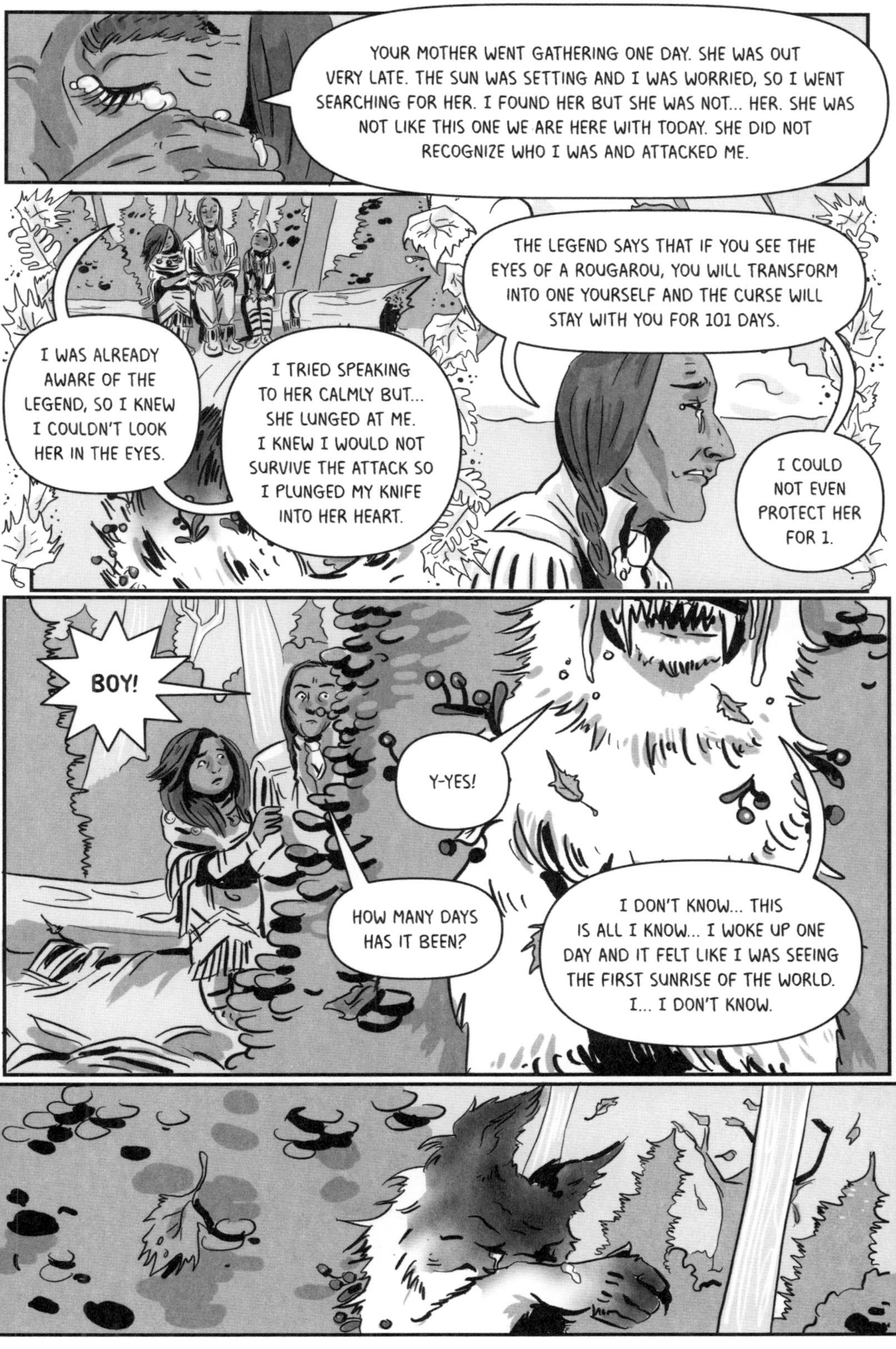
YOUR MOTHER WENT GATHERING ONE DAY. SHE WAS OUT VERY LATE. THE SUN WAS SETTING AND I WAS WORRIED, SO I WENT SEARCHING FOR HER. I FOUND HER BUT SHE WAS NOT... HER. SHE WAS NOT LIKE THIS ONE WE ARE HERE WITH TODAY. SHE DID NOT RECOGNIZE WHO I WAS AND ATTACKED ME.
I WAS ALREADY AWARE OF THE LEGEND, SO I KNEW I COULDN'T LOOK HER IN THE EYES.
I TRIED SPEAKING TO HER CALMLY BUT... SHE LUNGED AT ME. I KNEW I WOULD NOT SURVIVE THE ATTACK SO I PLUNGED MY KNIFE INTO HER HEART.
THE LEGEND SAYS THAT IF YOU SEE THE EYES OF A ROUGAROU, YOU WILL TRANSFORM INTO ONE YOURSELF AND THE CURSE WILL STAY WITH YOU FOR 101 DAYS.
I COULD NOT EVEN PROTECT HER FOR 1.
BOY!
Y-YES!
HOW MANY DAYS HAS IT BEEN?
I DON'T KNOW... THIS IS ALL I KNOW... I WOKE UP ONE DAY AND IT FELT LIKE I WAS SEEING THE FIRST SUNRISE OF THE WORLD. I... I DON'T KNOW.

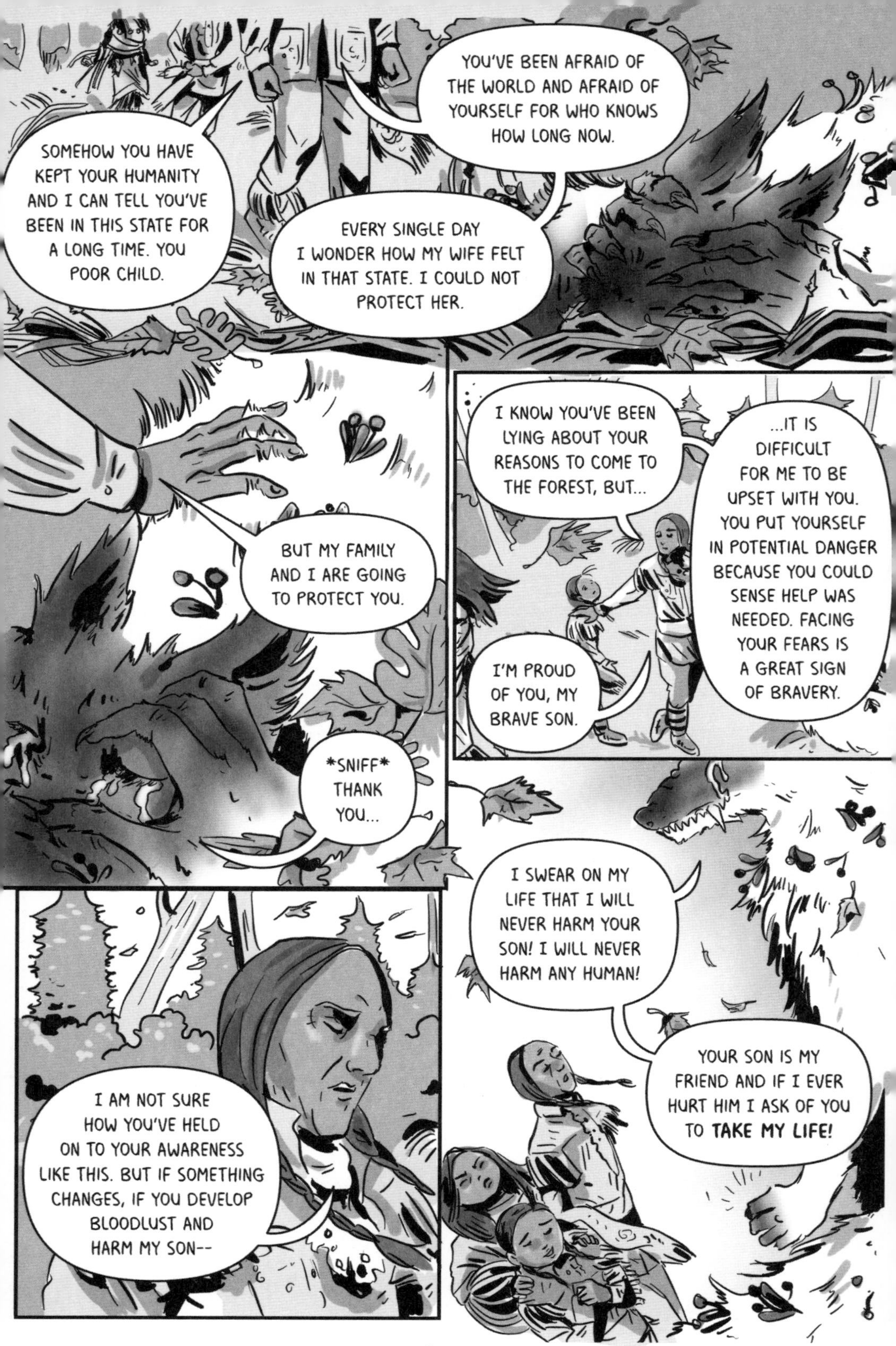
SOMEHOW YOU HAVE KEPT YOUR HUMANITY AND I CAN TELL YOU'VE BEEN IN THIS STATE FOR A LONG TIME. YOU POOR CHILD.
YOU'VE BEEN AFRAID OF THE WORLD AND AFRAID OF YOURSELF FOR WHO KNOWS HOW LONG NOW.
EVERY SINGLE DAY I WONDER HOW MY WIFE FELT IN THAT STATE. I COULD NOT PROTECT HER.
BUT MY FAMILY AND I ARE GOING TO PROTECT YOU.
SNIFF THANK YOU...
I KNOW YOU'VE BEEN LYING ABOUT YOUR REASONS TO COME TO THE FOREST, BUT...
...IT IS DIFFICULT FOR ME TO BE UPSET WITH YOU. YOU PUT YOURSELF IN POTENTIAL DANGER BECAUSE YOU COULD SENSE HELP WAS NEEDED. FACING YOUR FEARS IS A GREAT SIGN OF BRAVERY.
I'M PROUD OF YOU, MY BRAVE SON.
I AM NOT SURE HOW YOU'VE HELD ON TO YOUR AWARENESS LIKE THIS. BUT IF SOMETHING CHANGES, IF YOU DEVELOP BLOODLUST AND HARM MY SON--
I SWEAR ON MY LIFE THAT I WILL NEVER HARM YOUR SON! I WILL NEVER HARM ANY HUMAN!
YOUR SON IS MY FRIEND AND IF I EVER HURT HIM I ASK OF YOU TO TAKE MY LIFE!

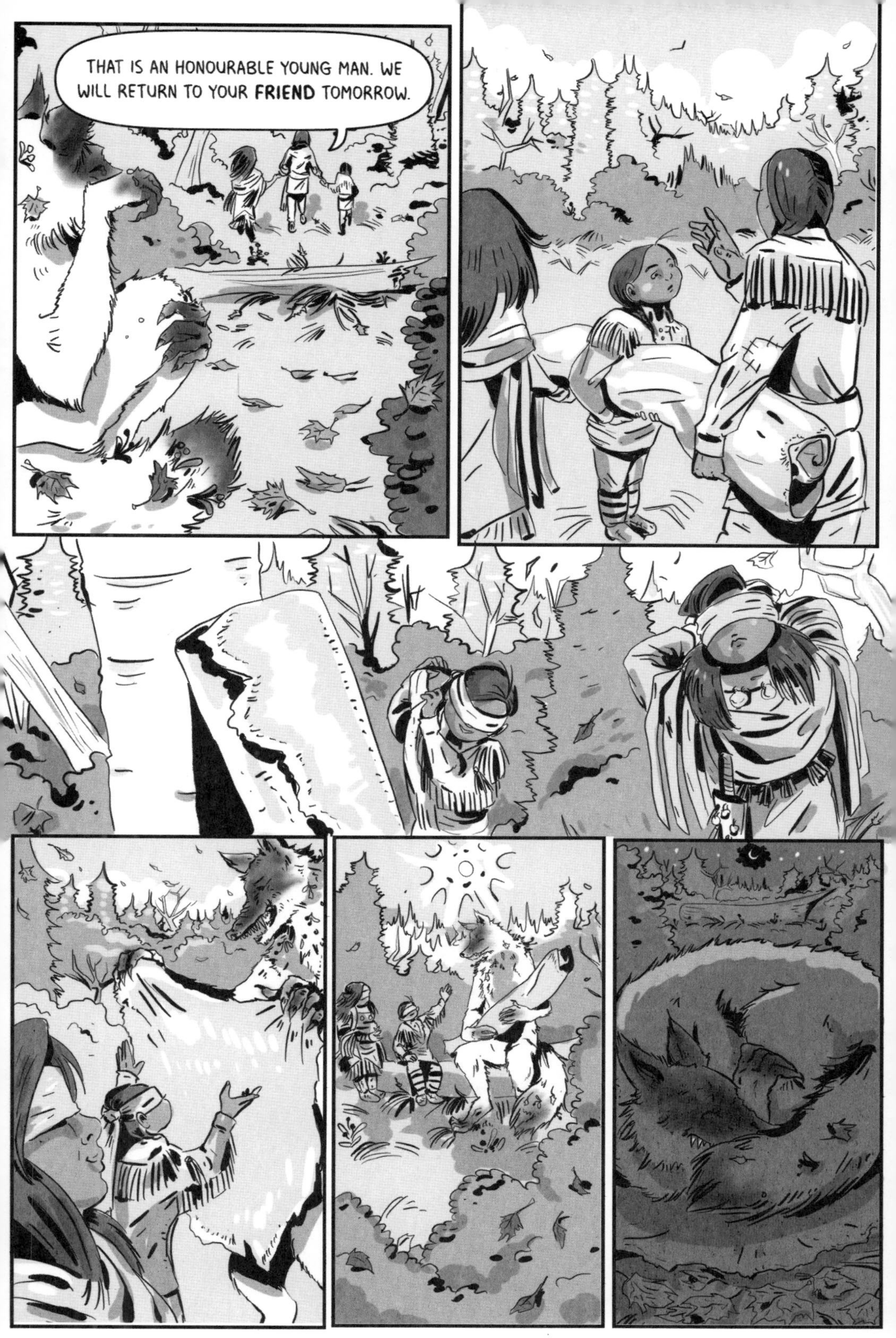

THAT IS AN HONOURABLE YOUNG MAN. WE WILL RETURN TO YOUR **FRIEND** TOMORROW.

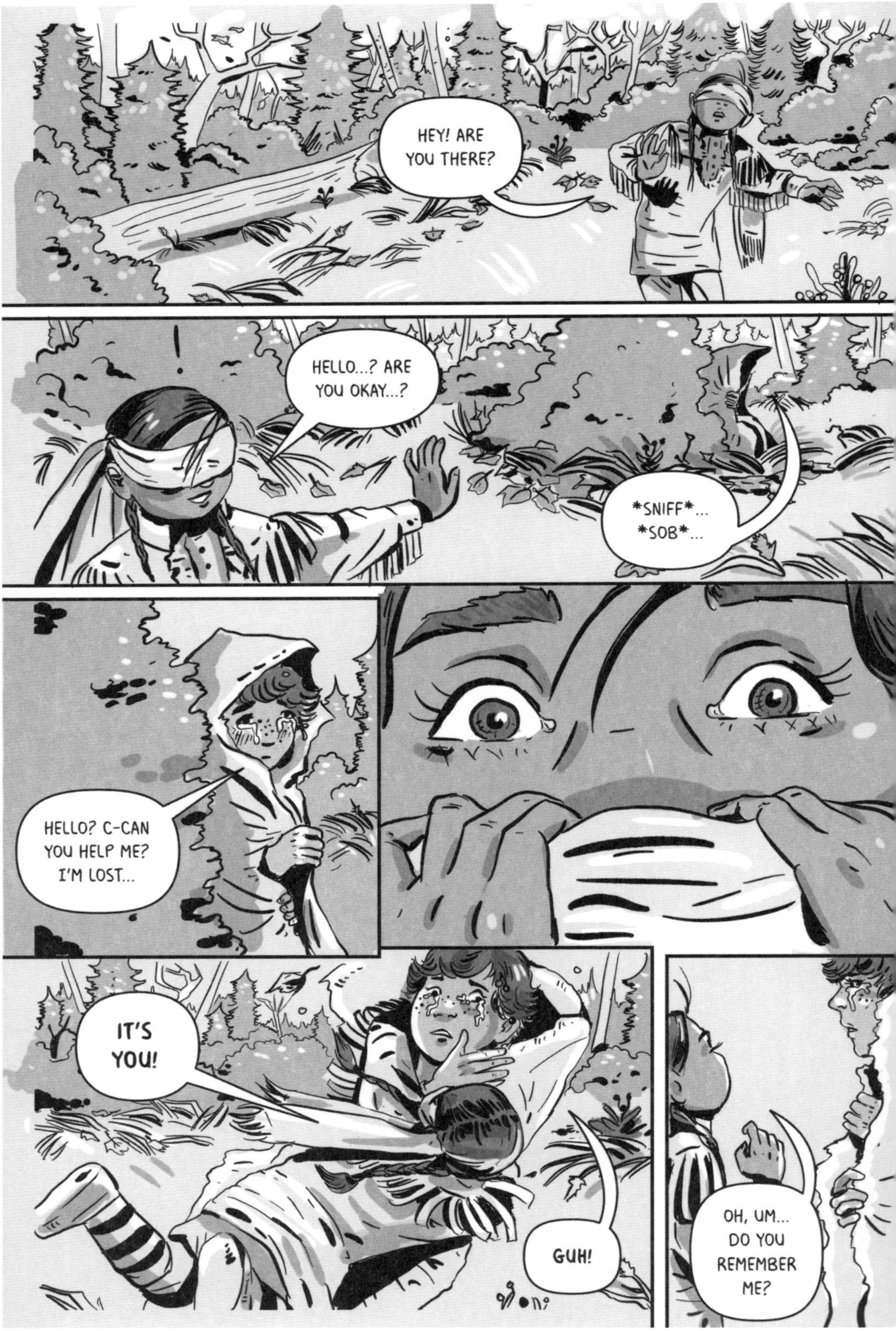
HEY! ARE YOU THERE?
!
HELLO...? ARE YOU OKAY...?
SNIFF... *SOB*...
HELLO? C-CAN YOU HELP ME? I'M LOST...
IT'S YOU!
GUH!
OH, UM... DO YOU REMEMBER ME?

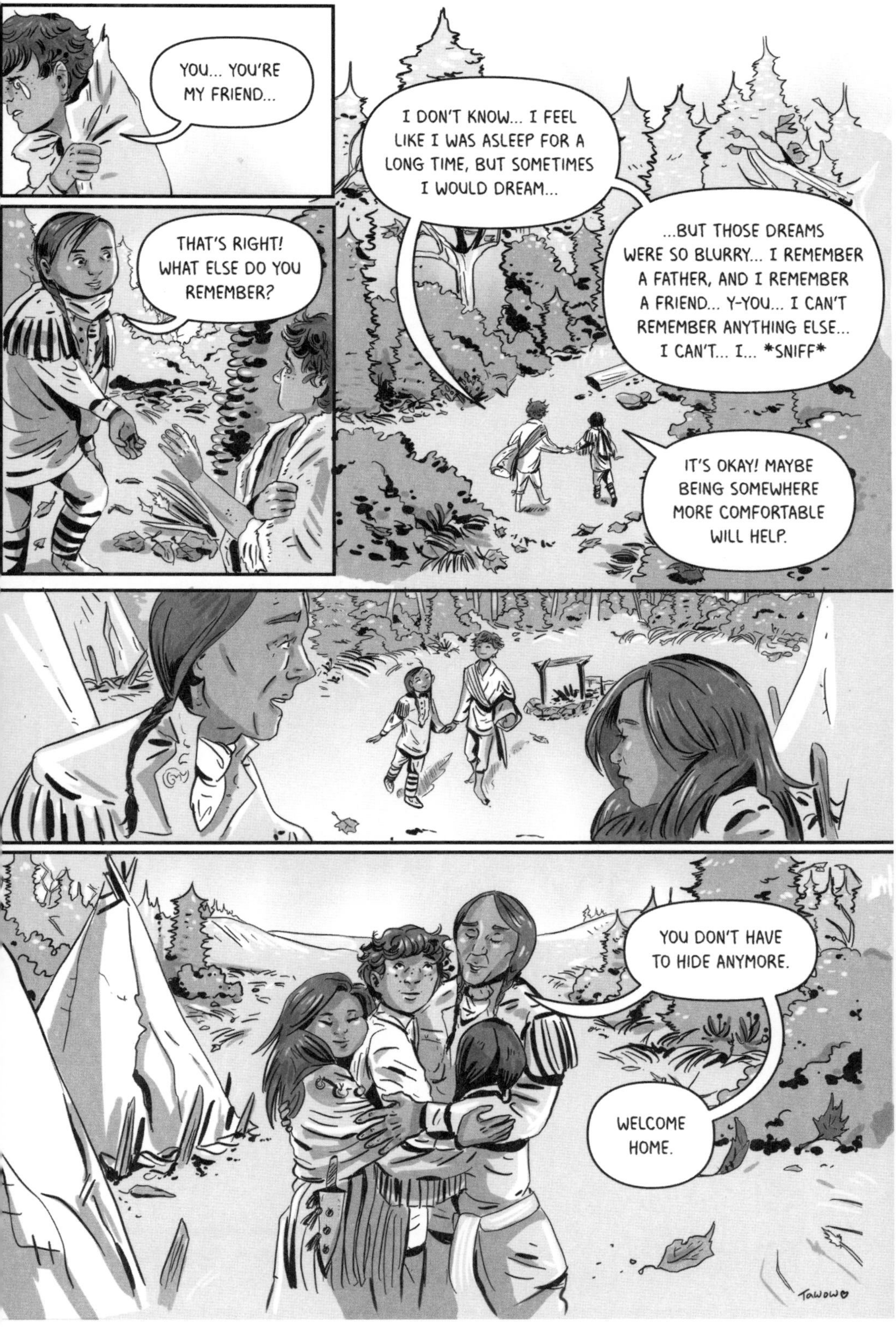

YOU... YOU'RE MY FRIEND...
THAT'S RIGHT! WHAT ELSE DO YOU REMEMBER?
I DON'T KNOW... I FEEL LIKE I WAS ASLEEP FOR A LONG TIME, BUT SOMETIMES I WOULD DREAM...
...BUT THOSE DREAMS WERE SO BLURRY... I REMEMBER A FATHER, AND I REMEMBER A FRIEND... Y-YOU... I CAN'T REMEMBER ANYTHING ELSE... I CAN'T... I... *SNIFF*
IT'S OKAY! MAYBE BEING SOMEWHERE MORE COMFORTABLE WILL HELP.
YOU DON'T HAVE TO HIDE ANYMORE.
WELCOME HOME.

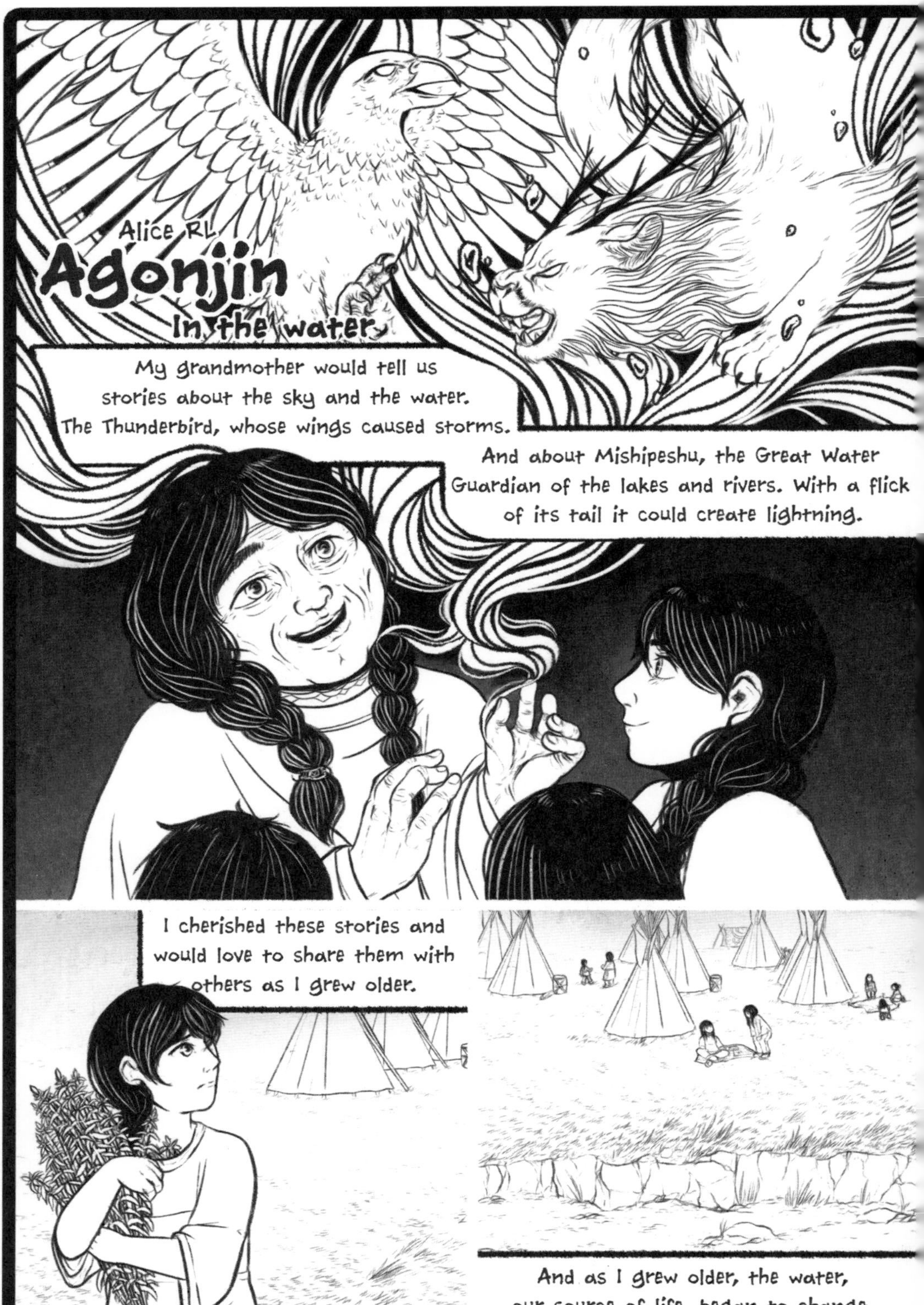
Alice RL
Agonjin
In the water
My grandmother would tell us stories about the sky and the water. The Thunderbird, whose wings caused storms.
And about Mishipeshu, the Great Water Guardian of the lakes and rivers. With a flick of its tail it could create lightning.
I cherished these stories and would love to share them with others as I grew older.
And as I grew older, the water, our source of life, began to change.

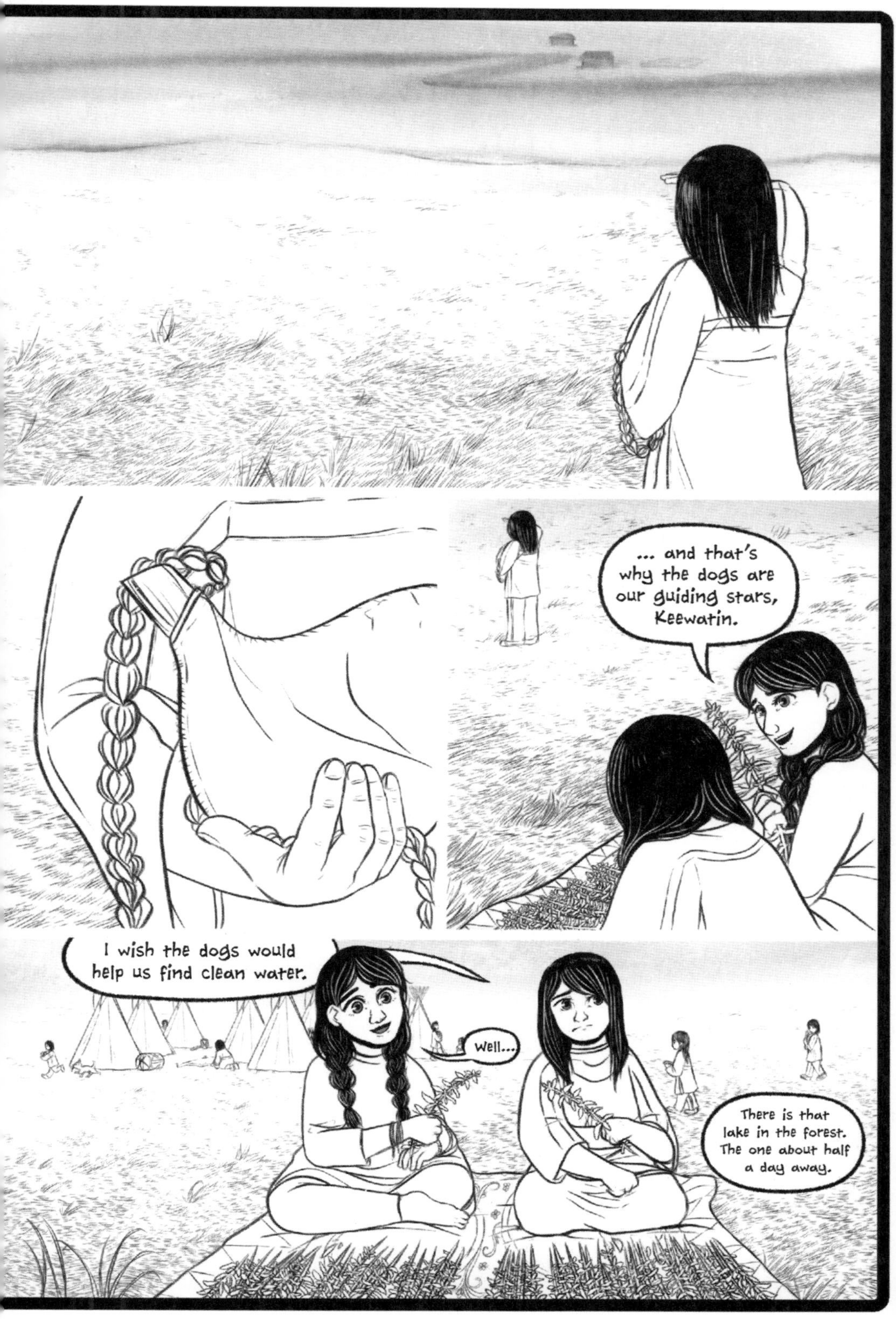
... and that's why the dogs are our guiding stars, Keewatin.
I wish the dogs would help us find clean water.
Well...
There is that lake in the forest. The one about half a day away.

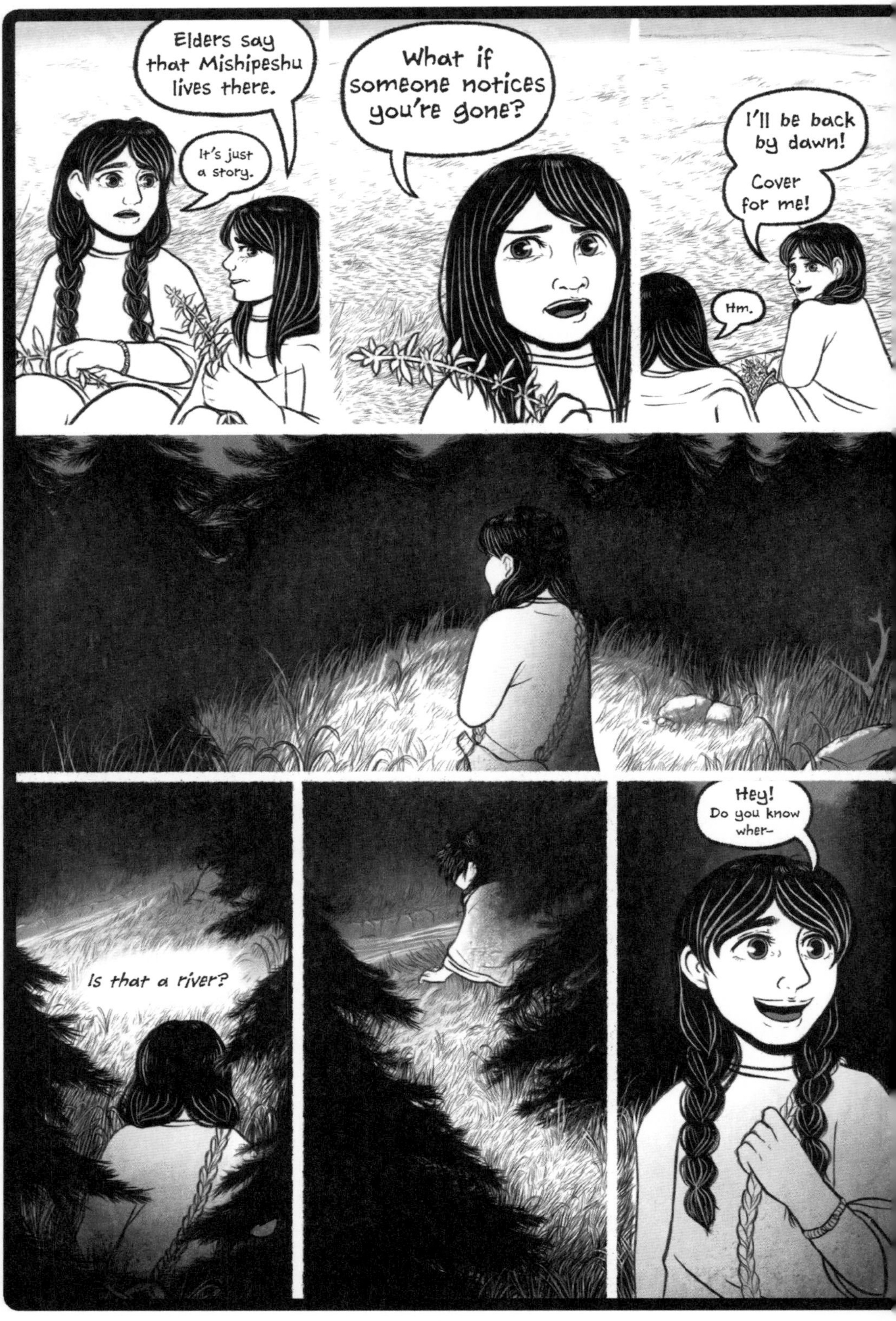

Elders say that Mishipeshu lives there.
It's just a story.
What if someone notices you're gone?
I'll be back by dawn!
Cover for me!
Hm.
Is that a river?
Hey! Do you know wher–

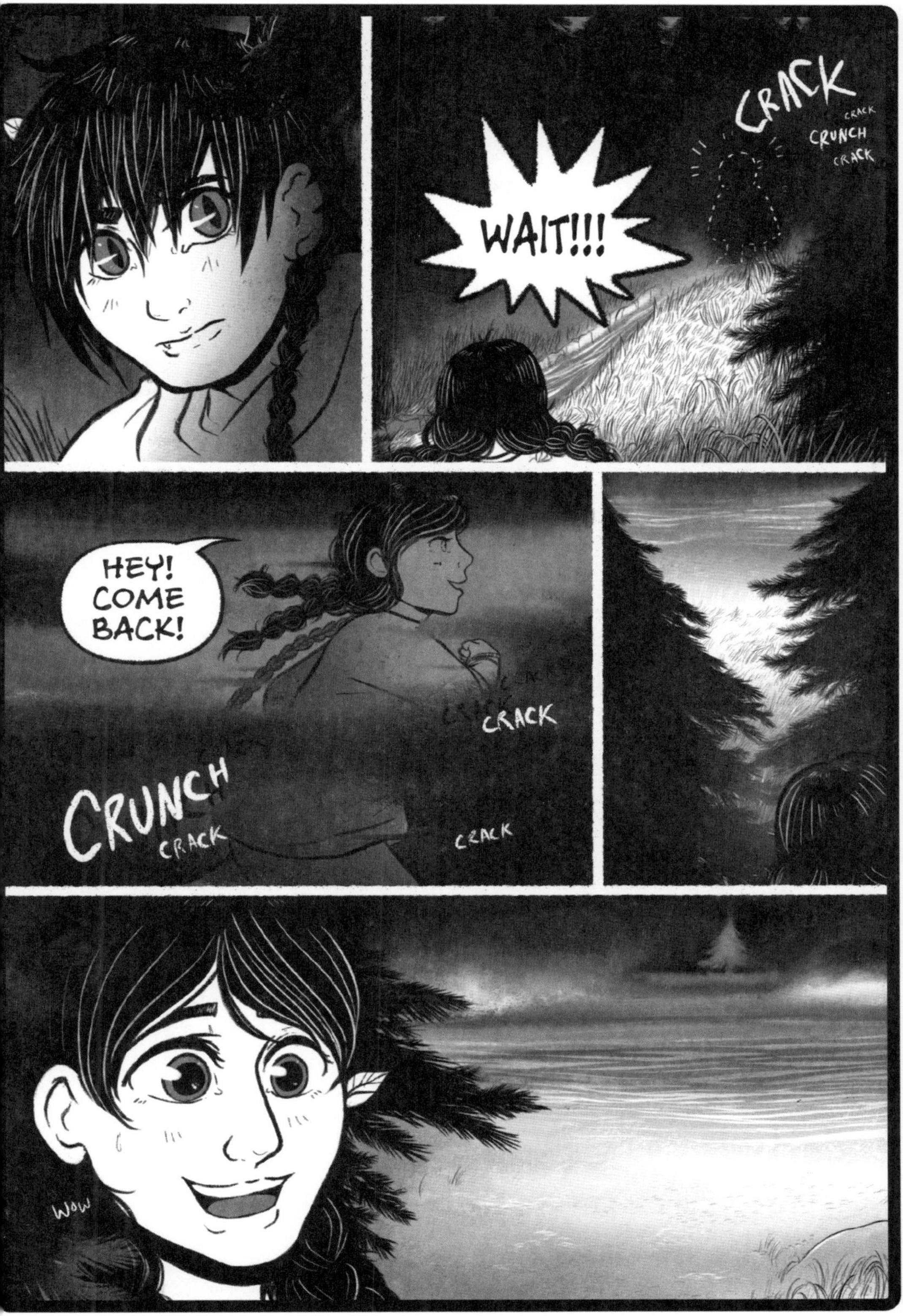
WAIT!!!
CRACK
CRACK
CRUNCH
CRACK
HEY! COME BACK!
CRACK
CRUNCH
CRACK
CRACK
WOW

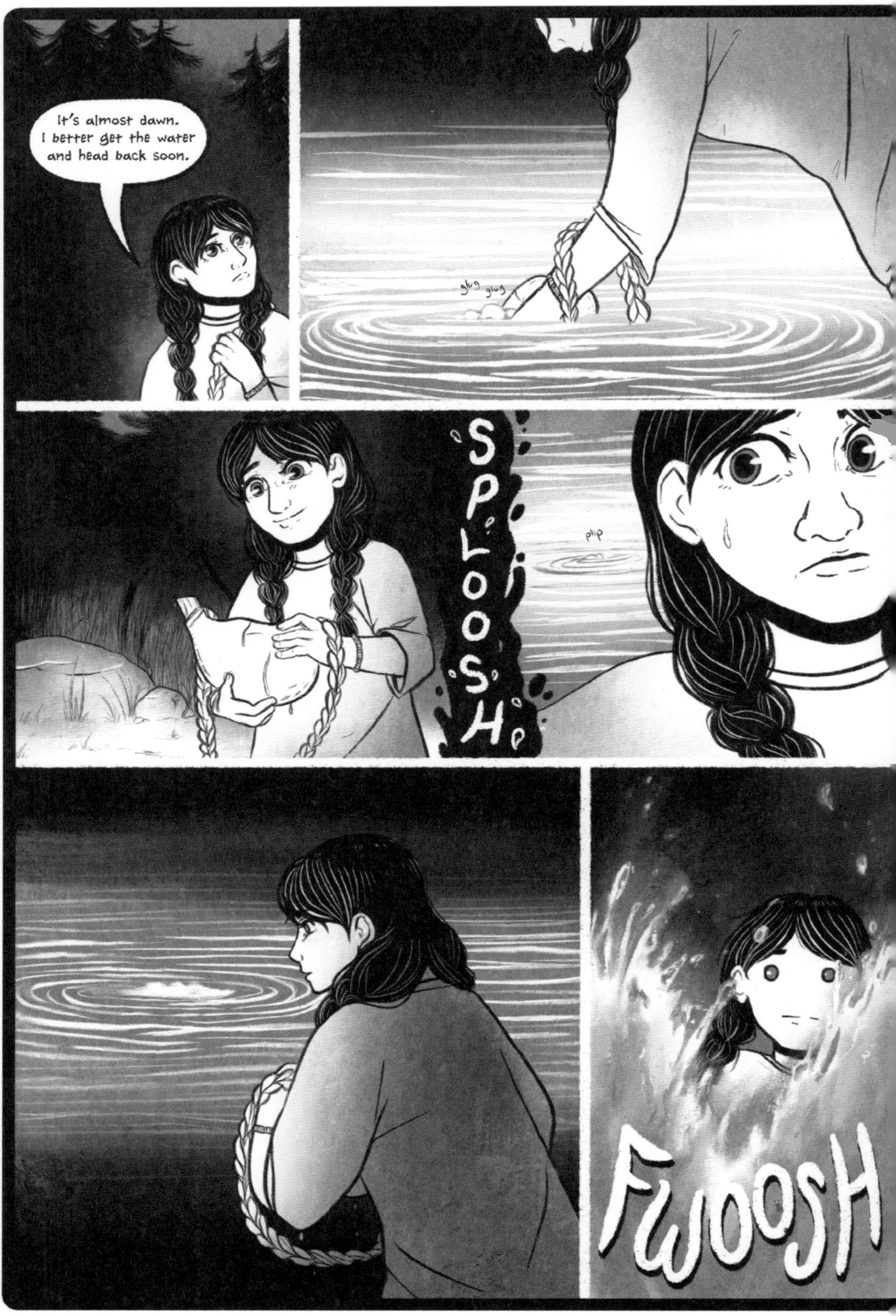
It's almost dawn. I better get the water and head back soon.
glug glug
SPLOOSH
plip
FWOOSH

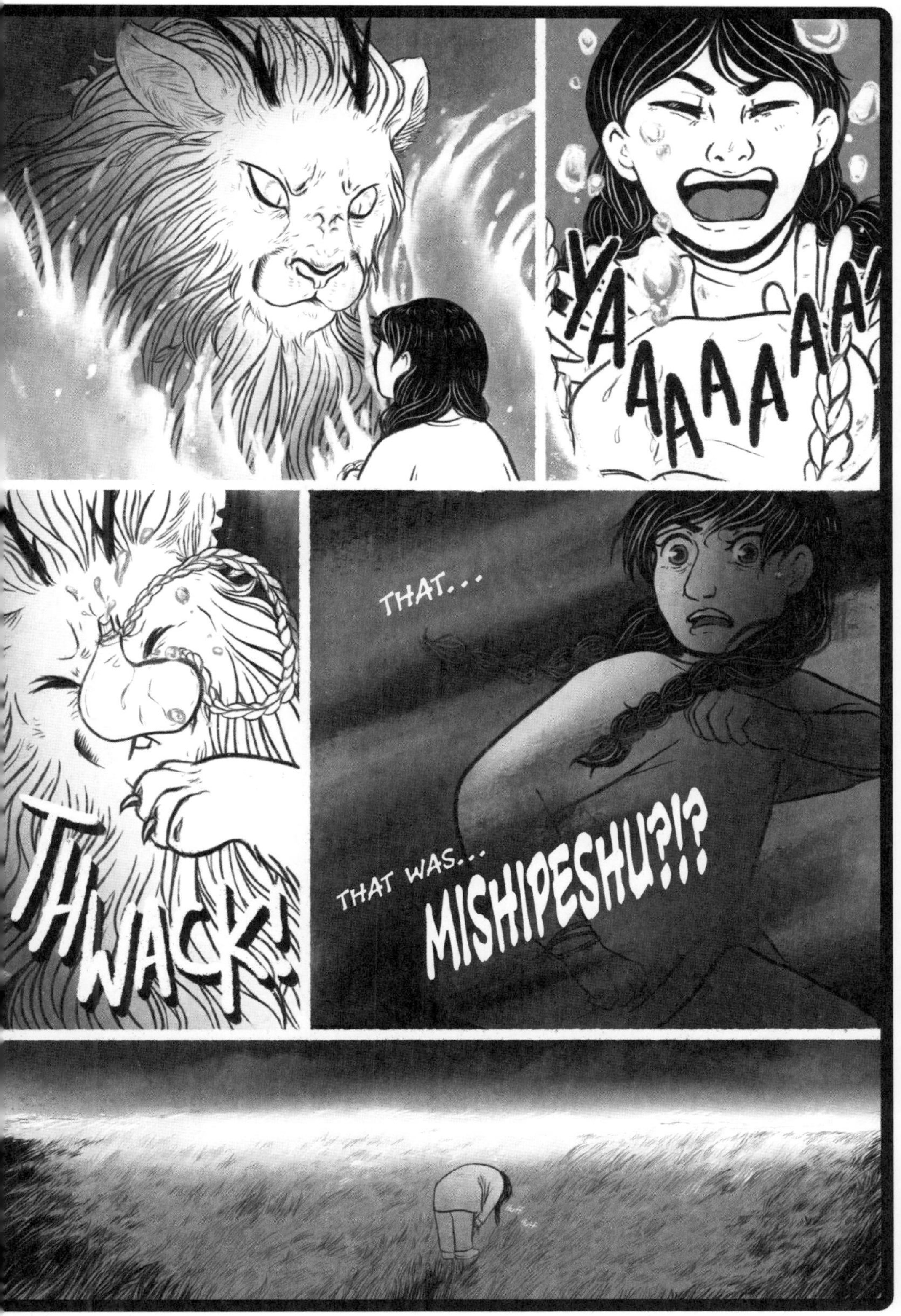
YAAAAAAAA
THWACK!!
THAT...
THAT WAS... MISHIPESHU?!?

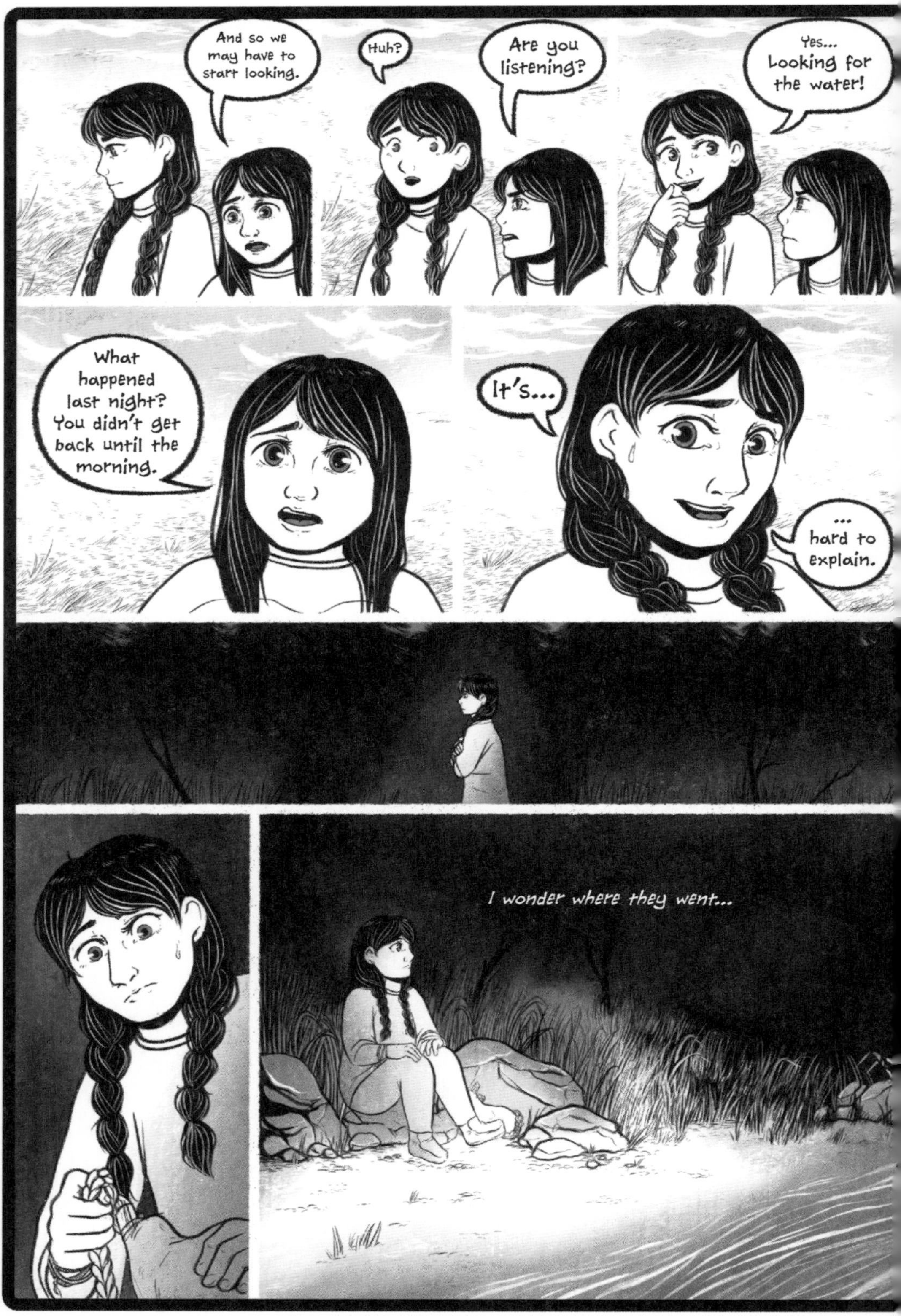

And so we may have to start looking.
Huh?
Are you listening?
Yes... Looking for the water!
What happened last night? You didn't get back until the morning.
It's...
... hard to explain.
I wonder where they went...

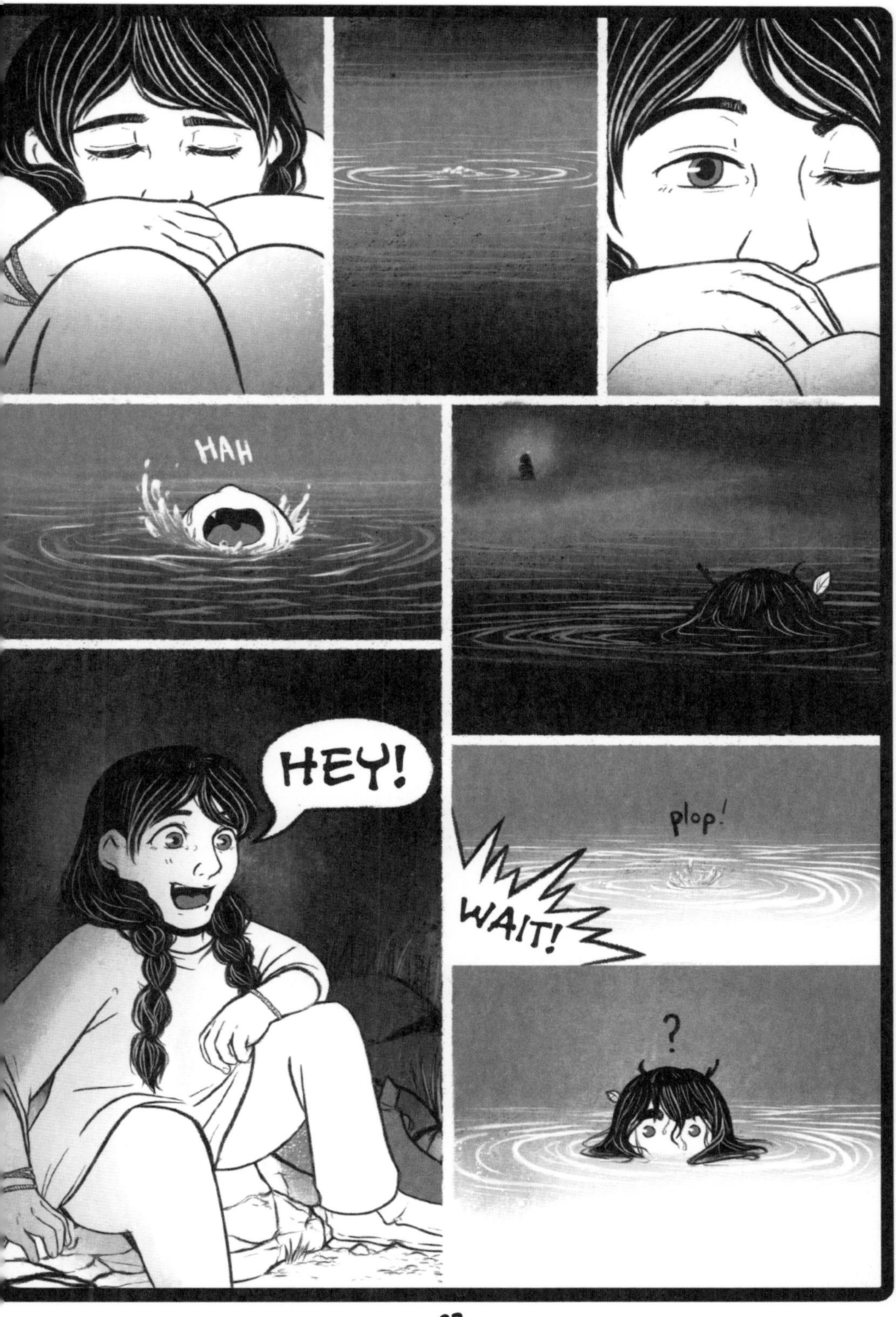
HAH
HEY!
WAIT!
plop!
?

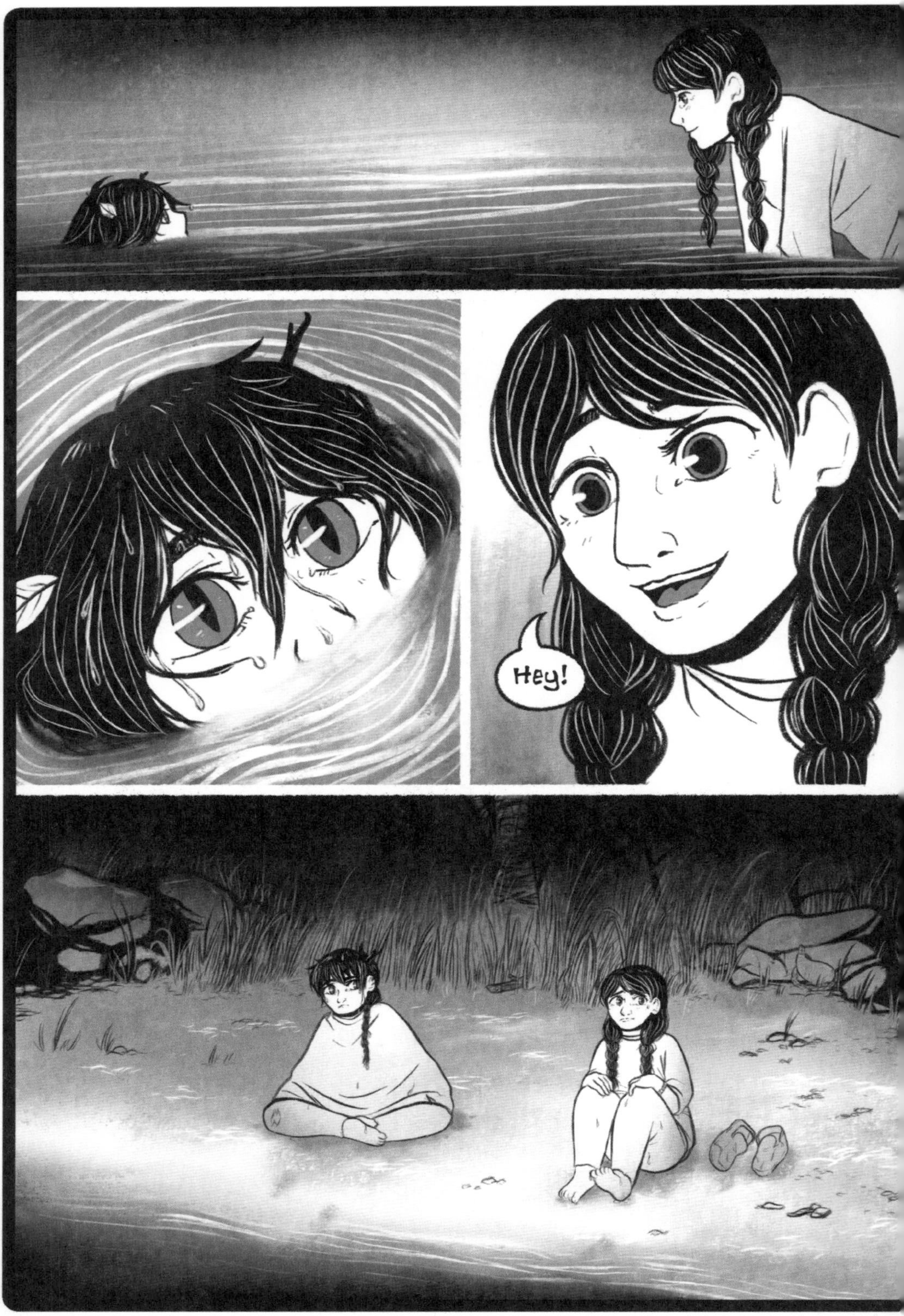
Hey!

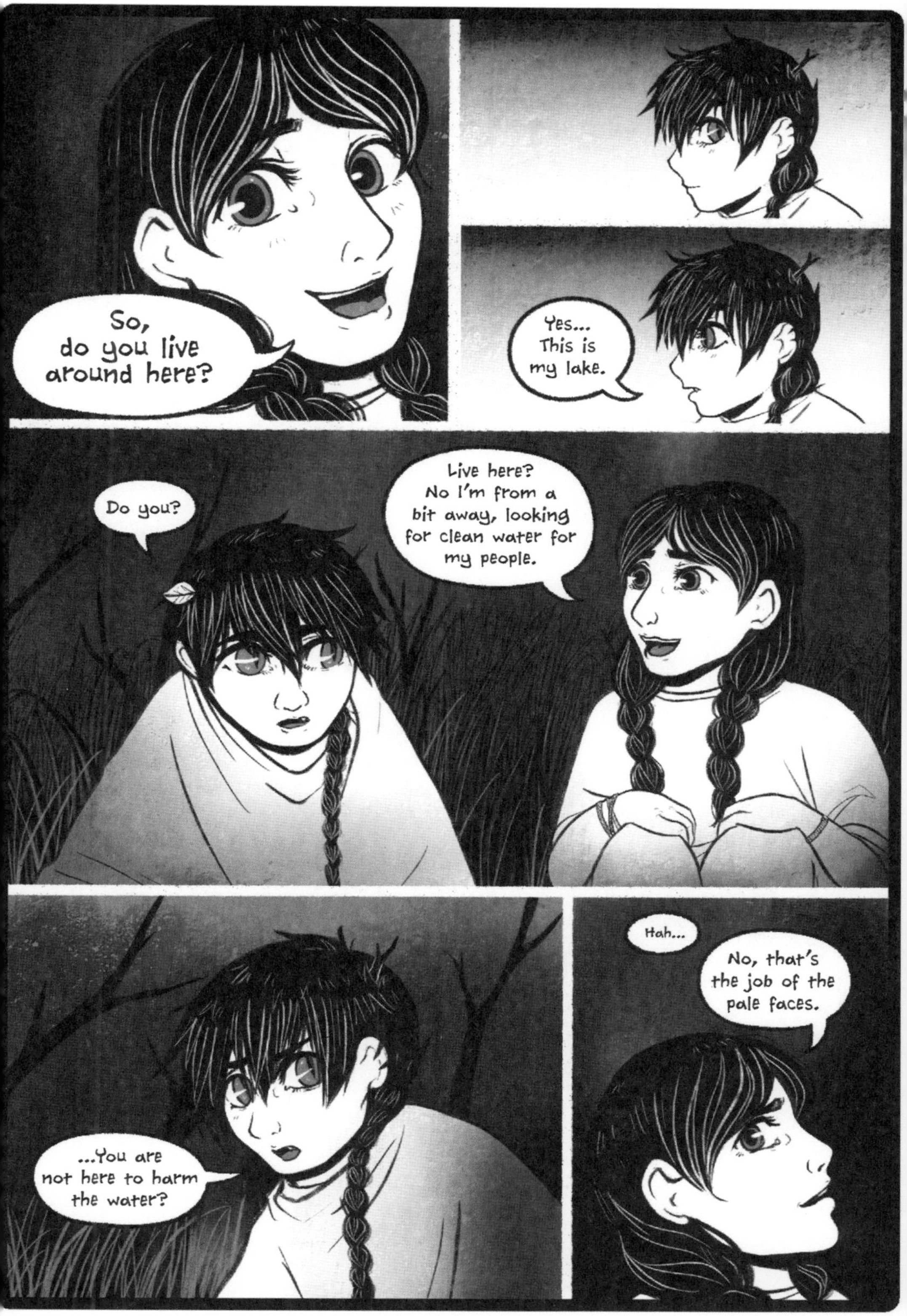
So, do you live around here?
Yes... This is my lake.
Do you?
Live here? No I'm from a bit away, looking for clean water for my people.
...You are not here to harm the water?
Hah...
No, that's the job of the pale faces.

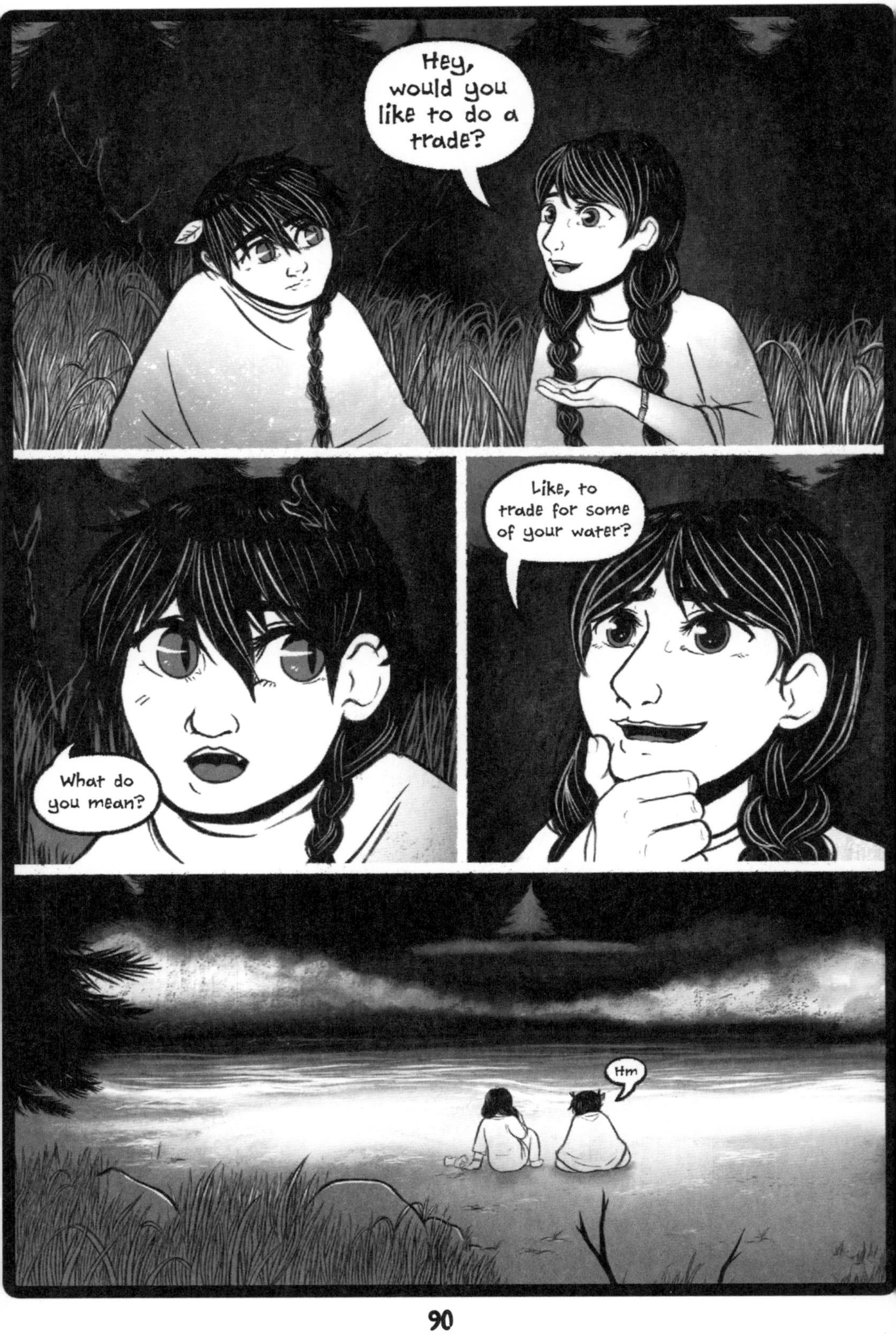
Hey, would you like to do a trade?
What do you mean?
Like, to trade for some of your water?
Hm

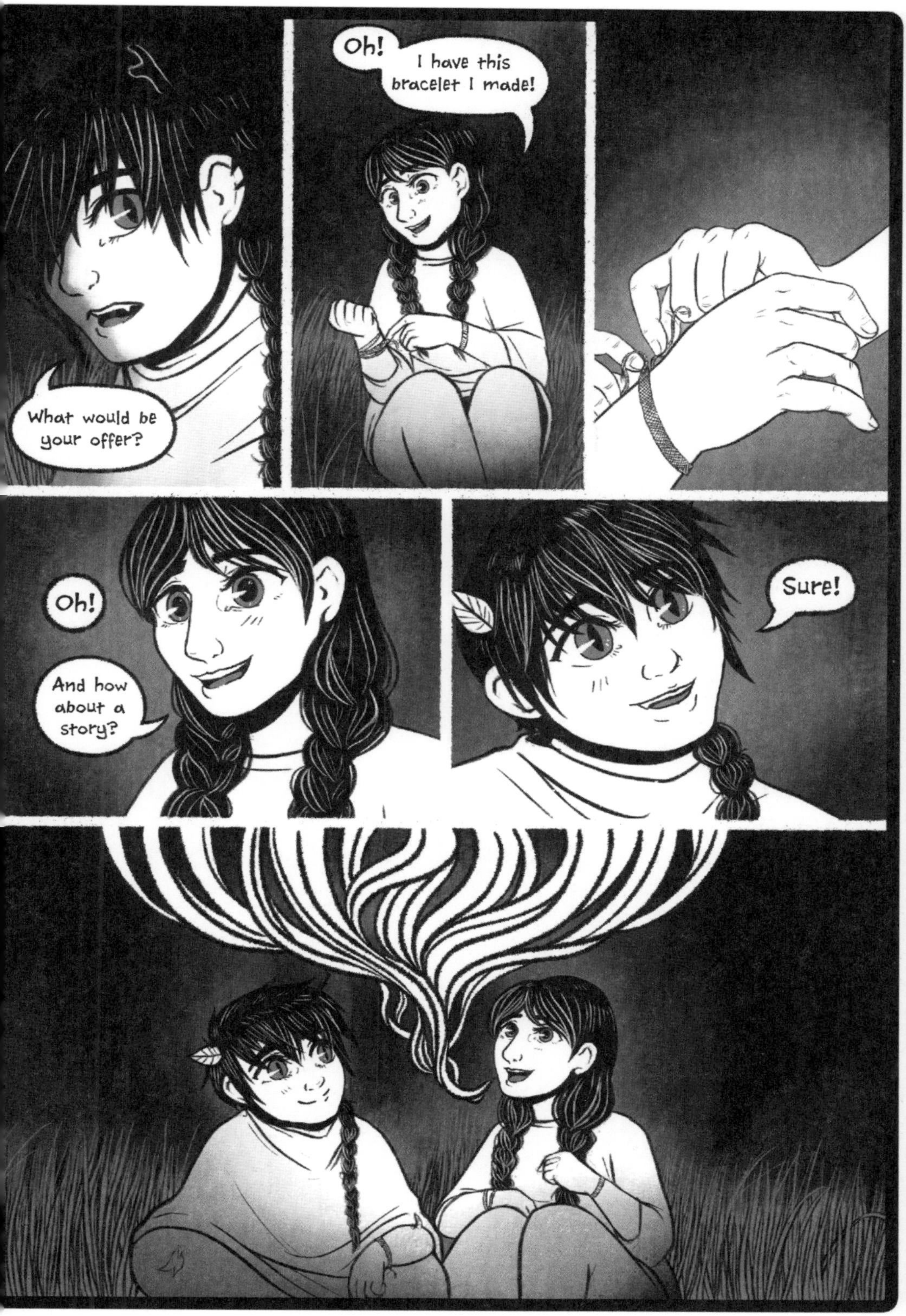
What would be your offer?
Oh!
I have this bracelet I made!
Oh!
And how about a story?
Sure!

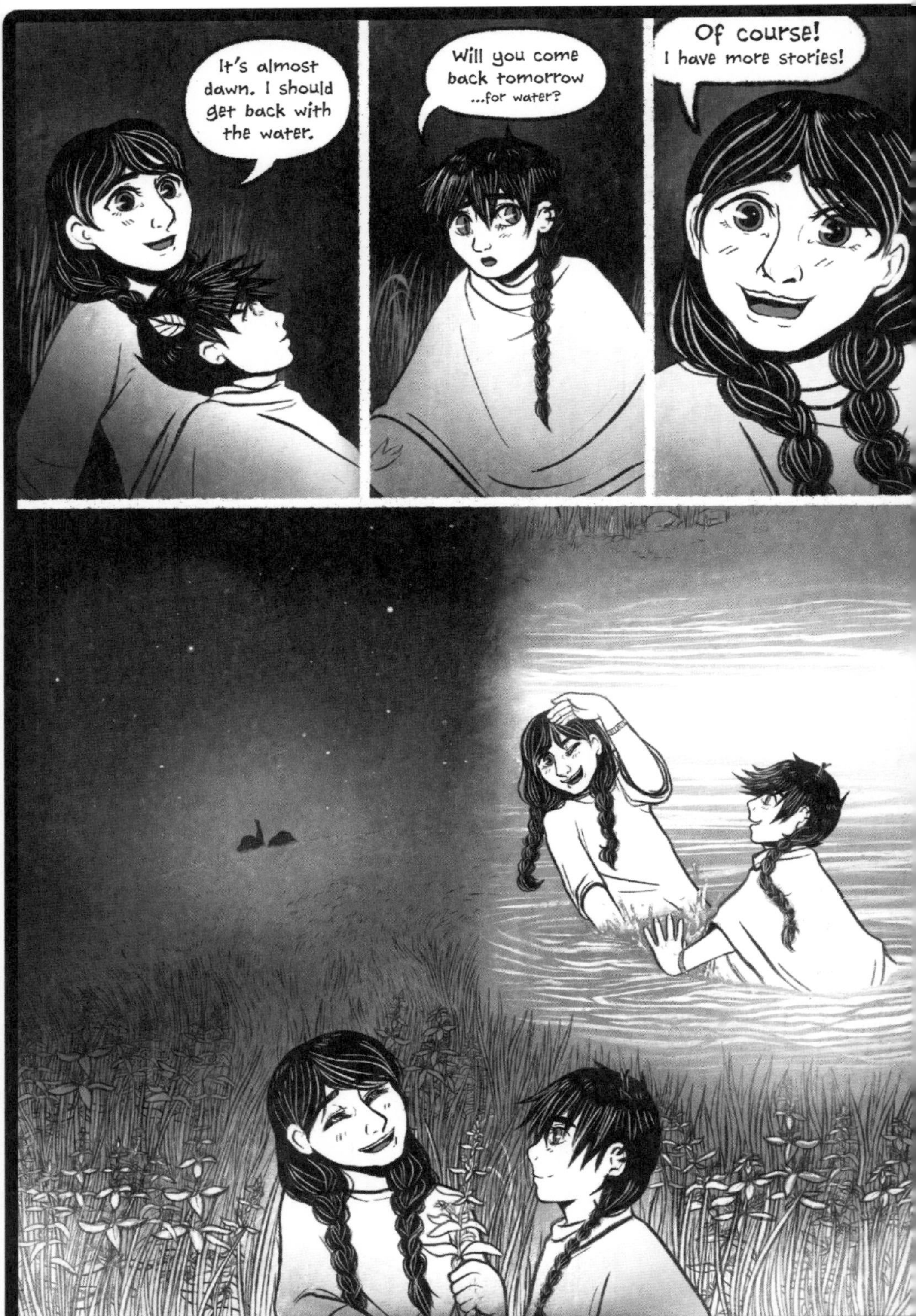
It's almost dawn. I should get back with the water.
Will you come back tomorrow ...for water?
Of course! I have more stories!

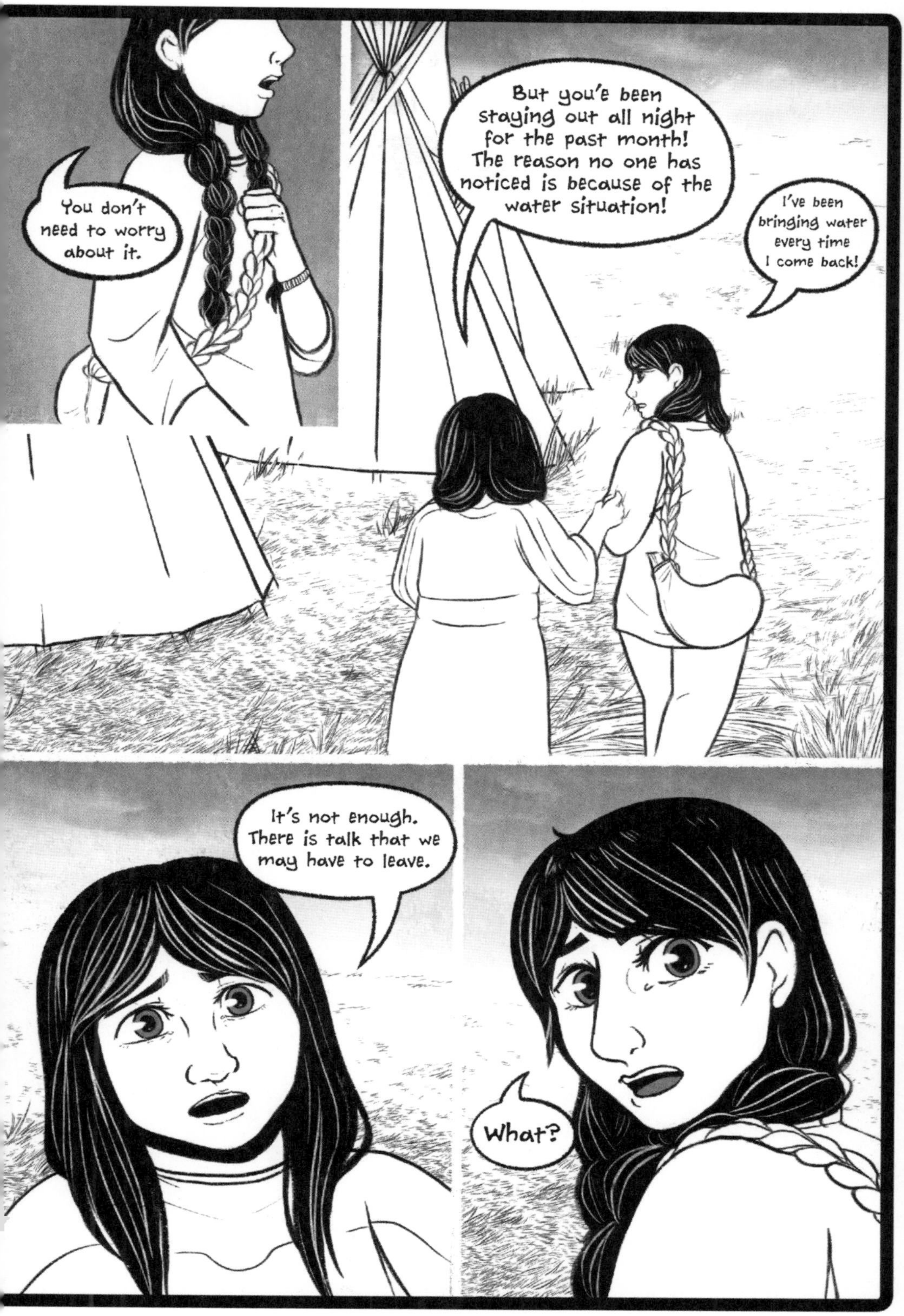
You don't need to worry about it.
But you've been staying out all night for the past month! The reason no one has noticed is because of the water situation!
I've been bringing water every time I come back!
It's not enough. There is talk that we may have to leave.
What?

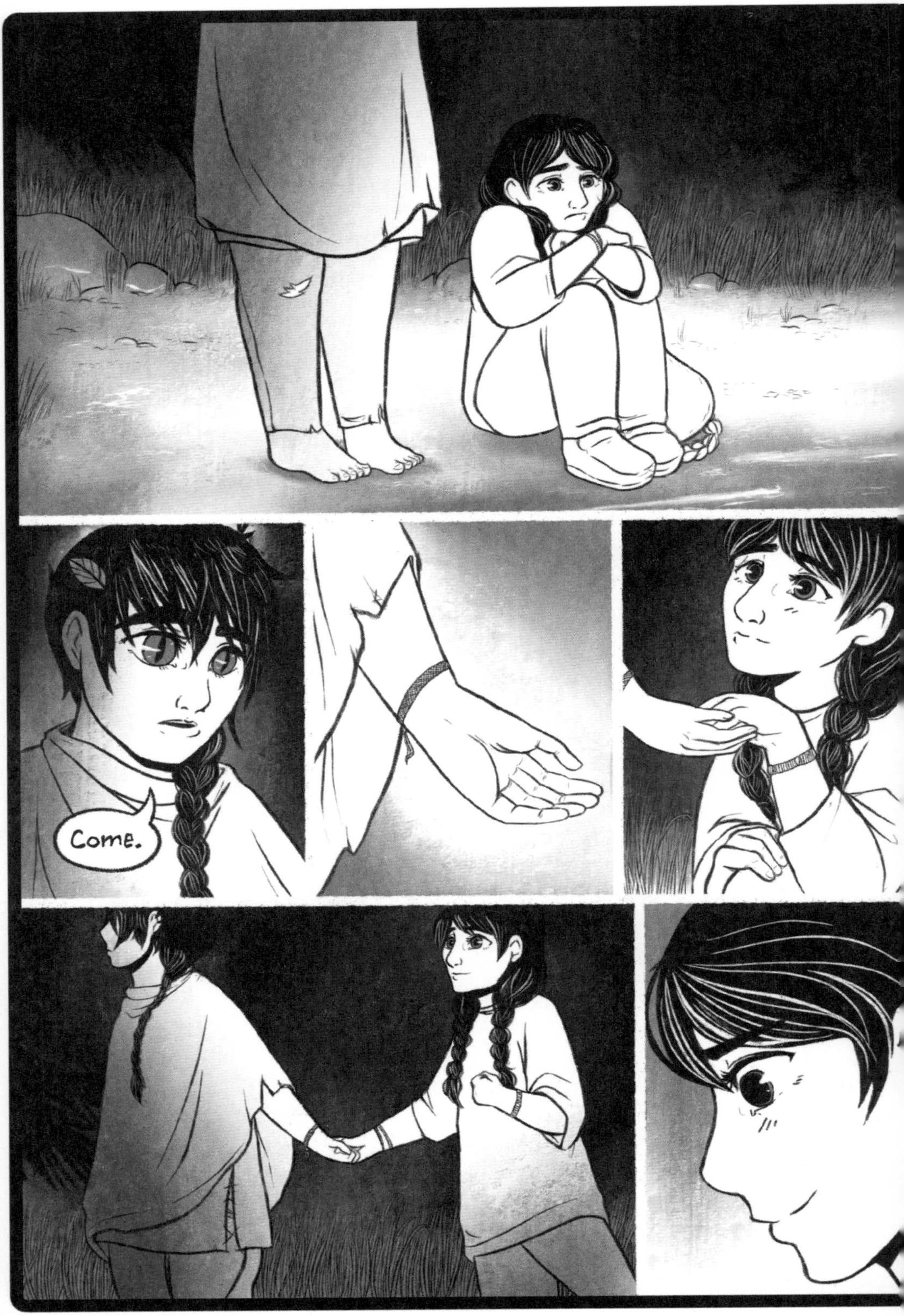
Come.

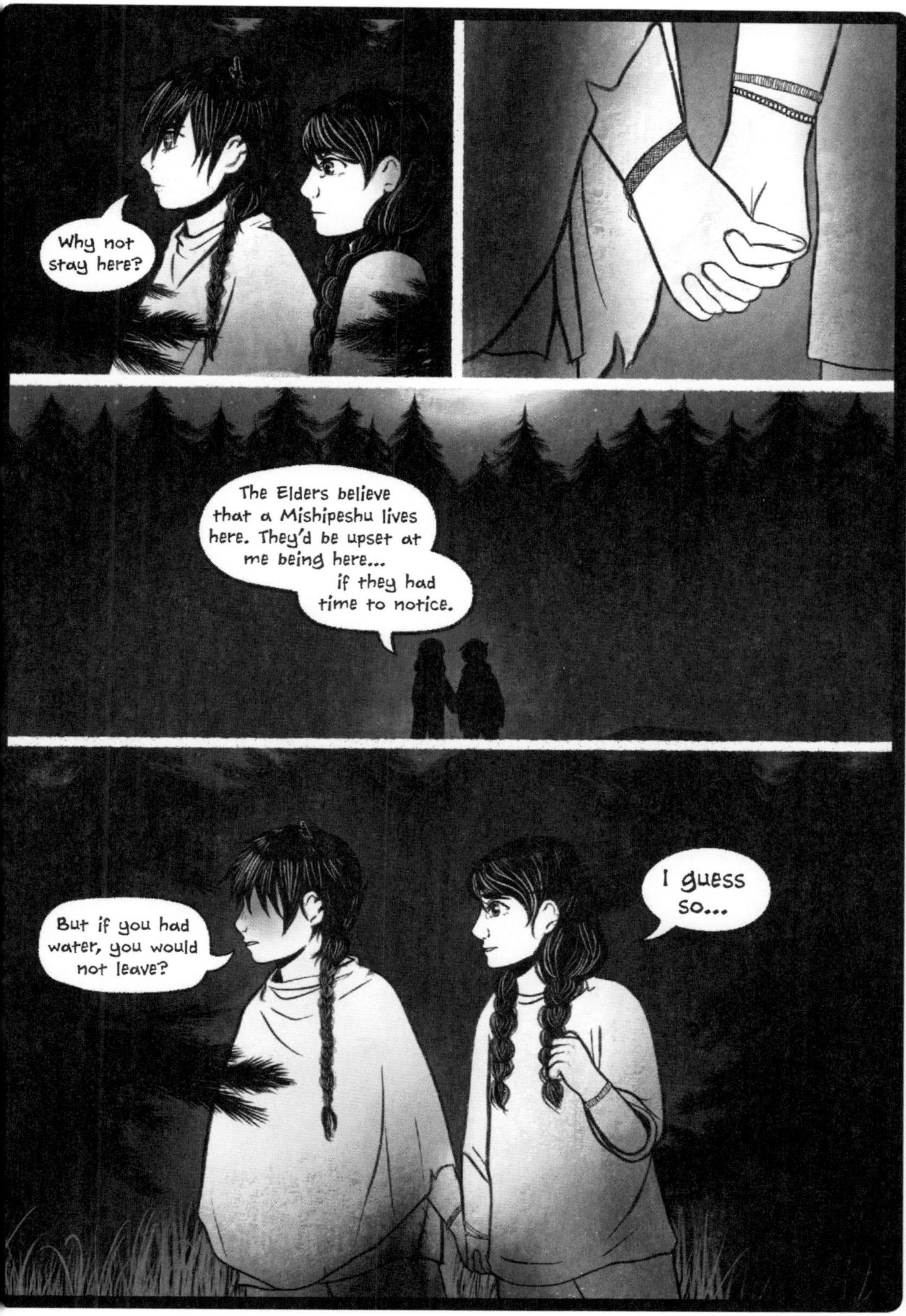
Why not stay here?
The Elders believe that a Mishipeshu lives here. They'd be upset at me being here...
if they had time to notice.
But if you had water, you would not leave?
I guess so...

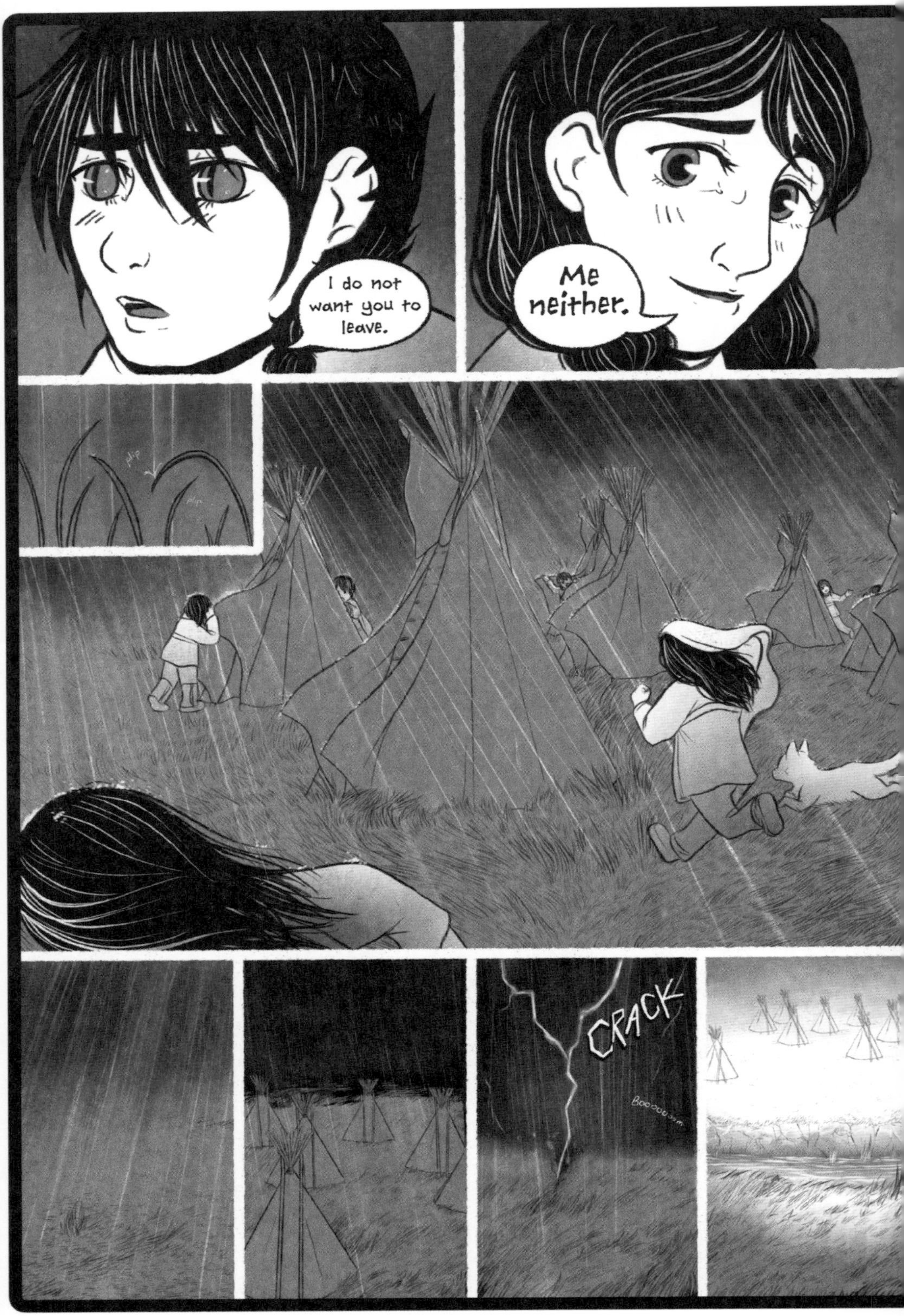
I do not want you to leave.
Me neither.
plip
plip
CRACK
Booooooom

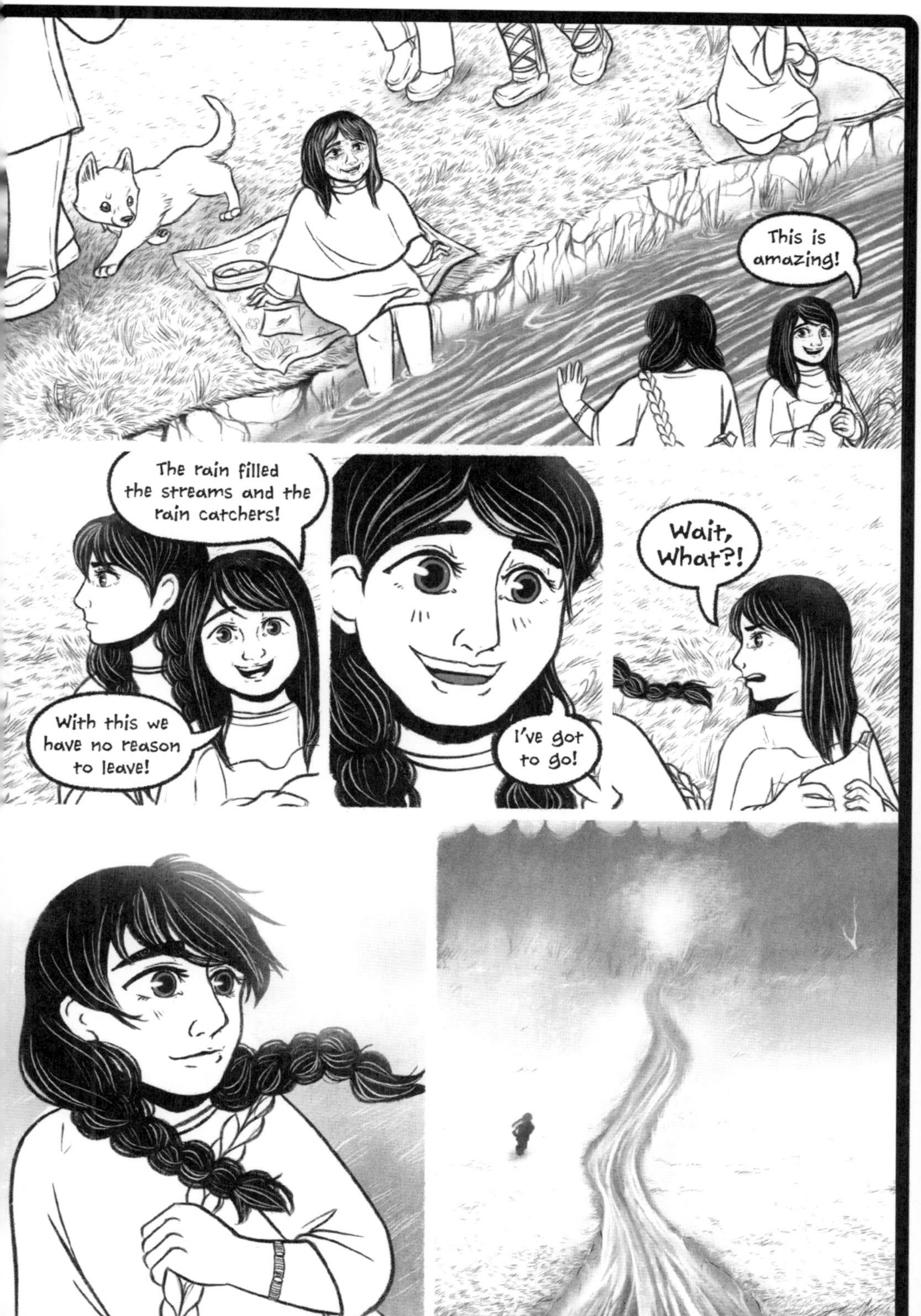
This is amazing!
The rain filled the streams and the rain catchers!
With this we have no reason to leave!
I've got to go!
Wait, What?!

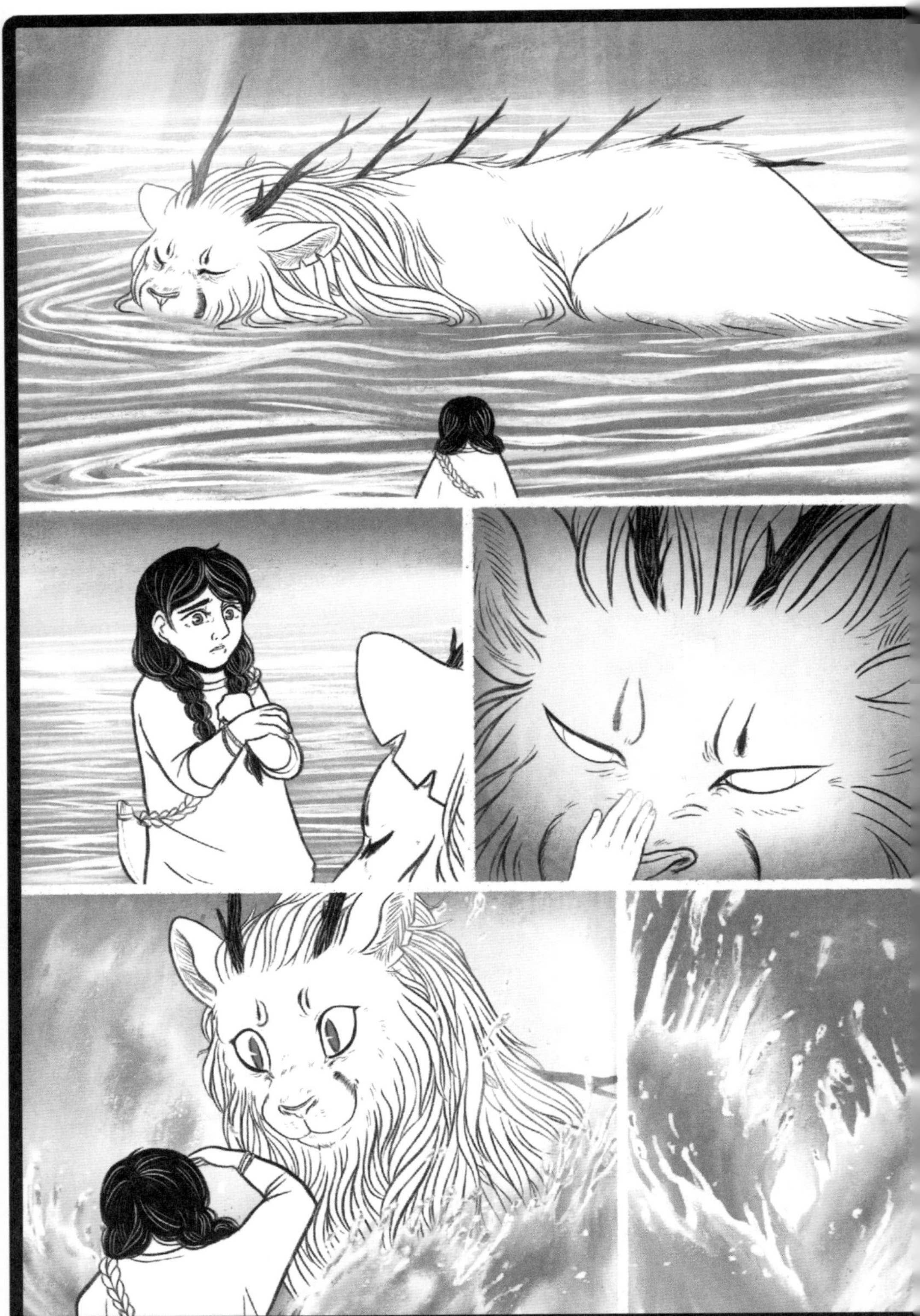

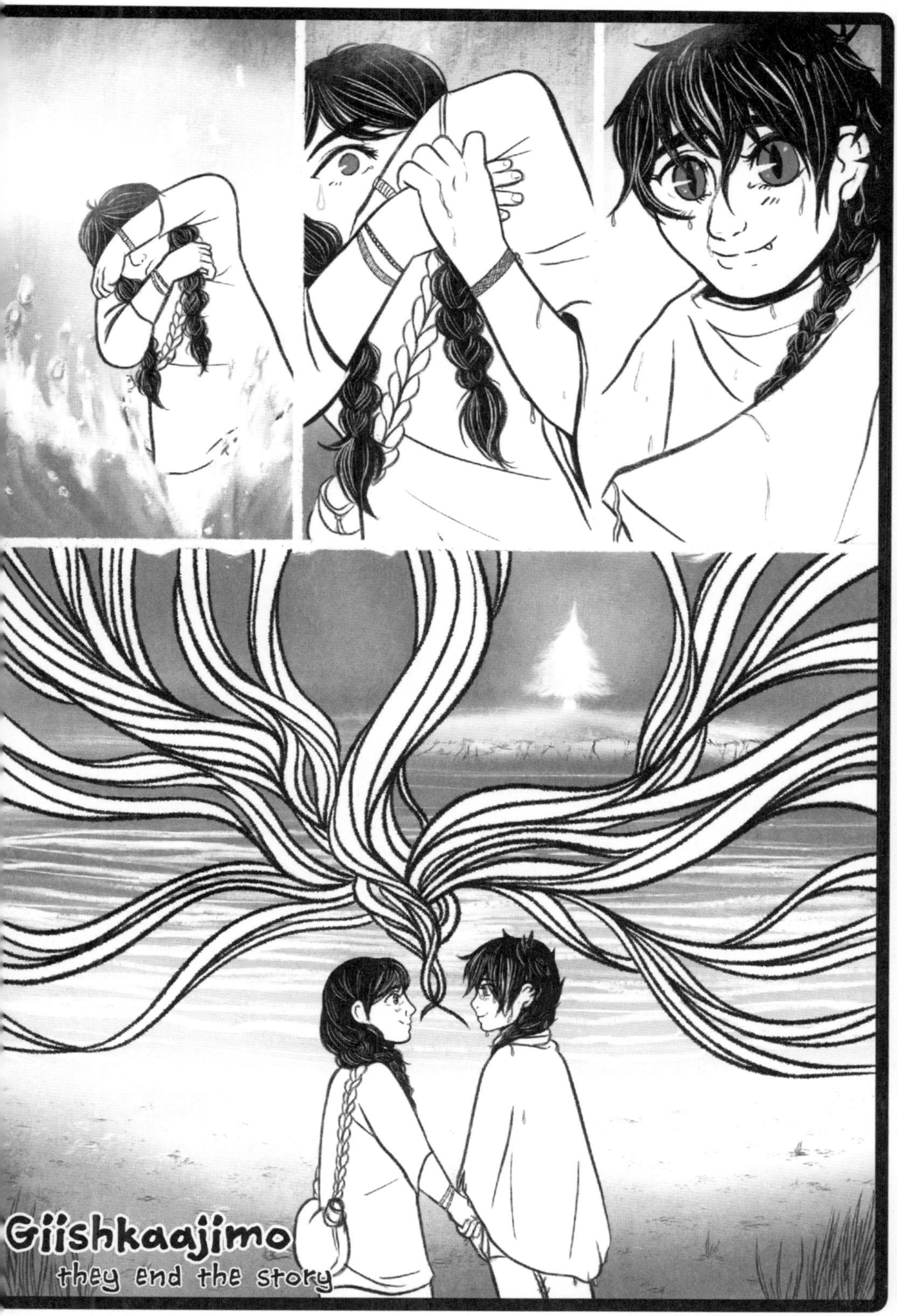
Giishkaajimo
they end the story

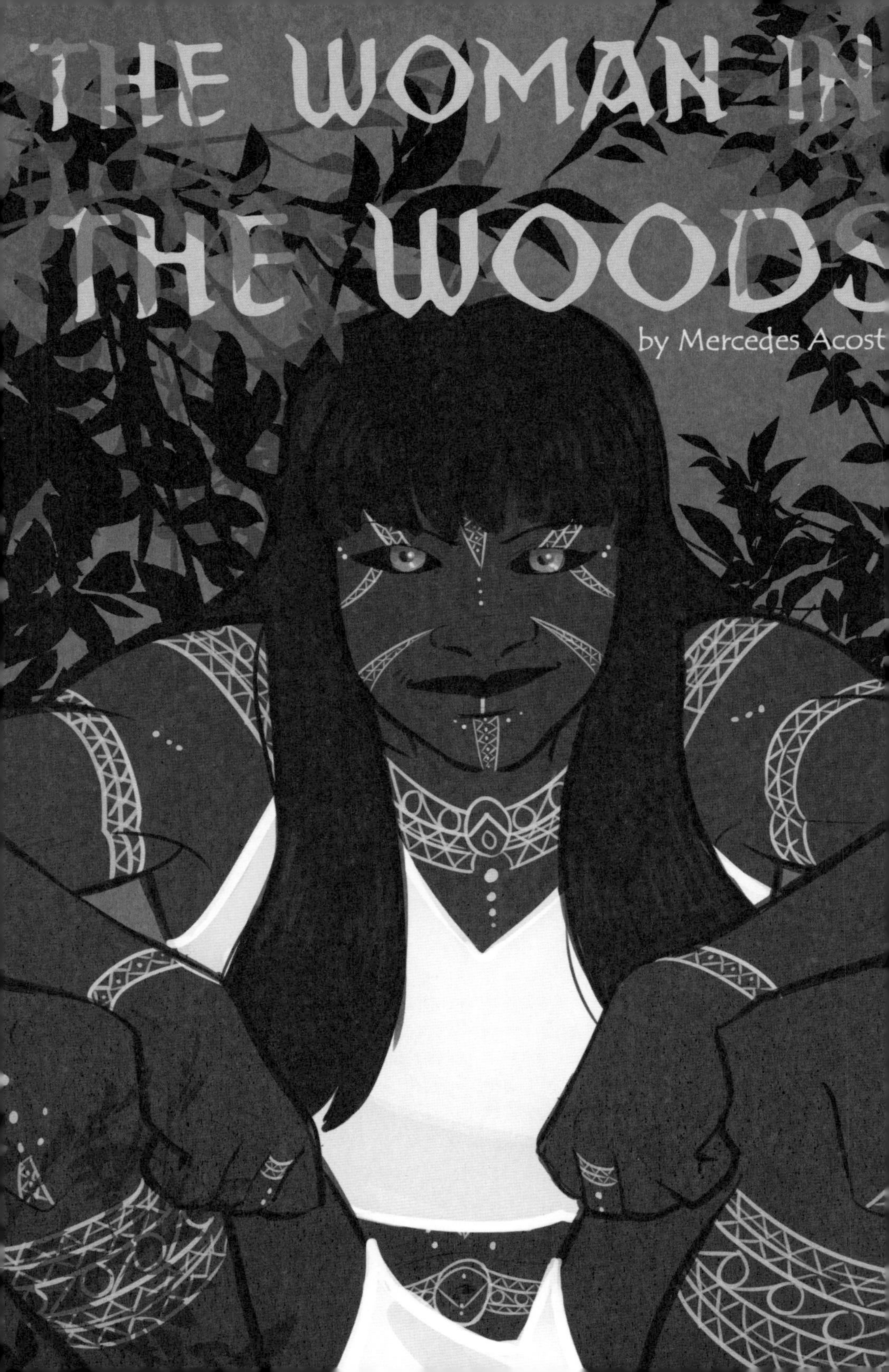
THE WOMAN IN
THE WOODS
by Mercedes Acost

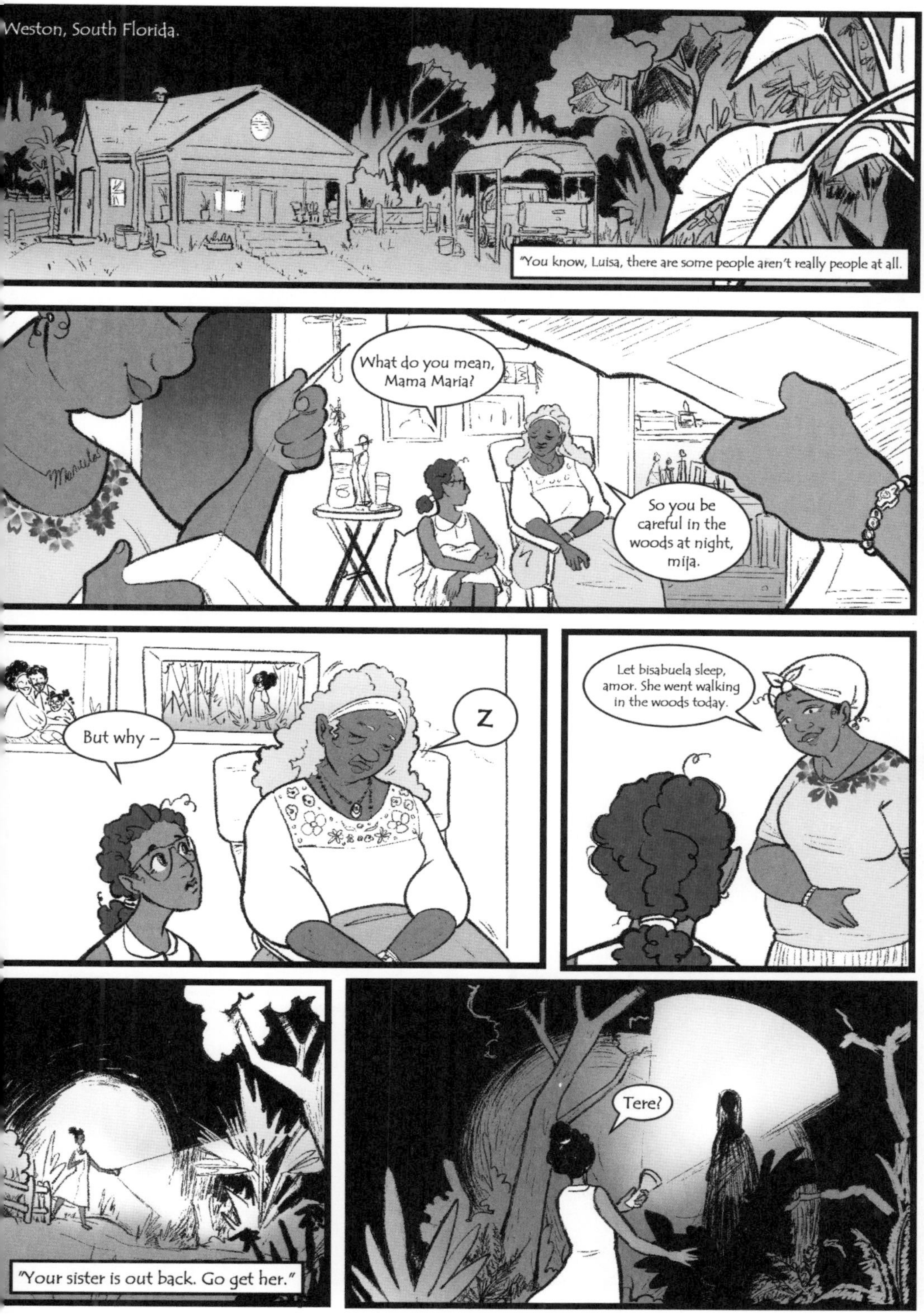
Weston, South Florida.
"You know, Luisa, there are some people aren't really people at all.
What do you mean, Mama Maria?
So you be careful in the woods at night, mija.
But why –
Z
Let bisabuela sleep, amor. She went walking in the woods today.
"Your sister is out back. Go get her."
Tere?

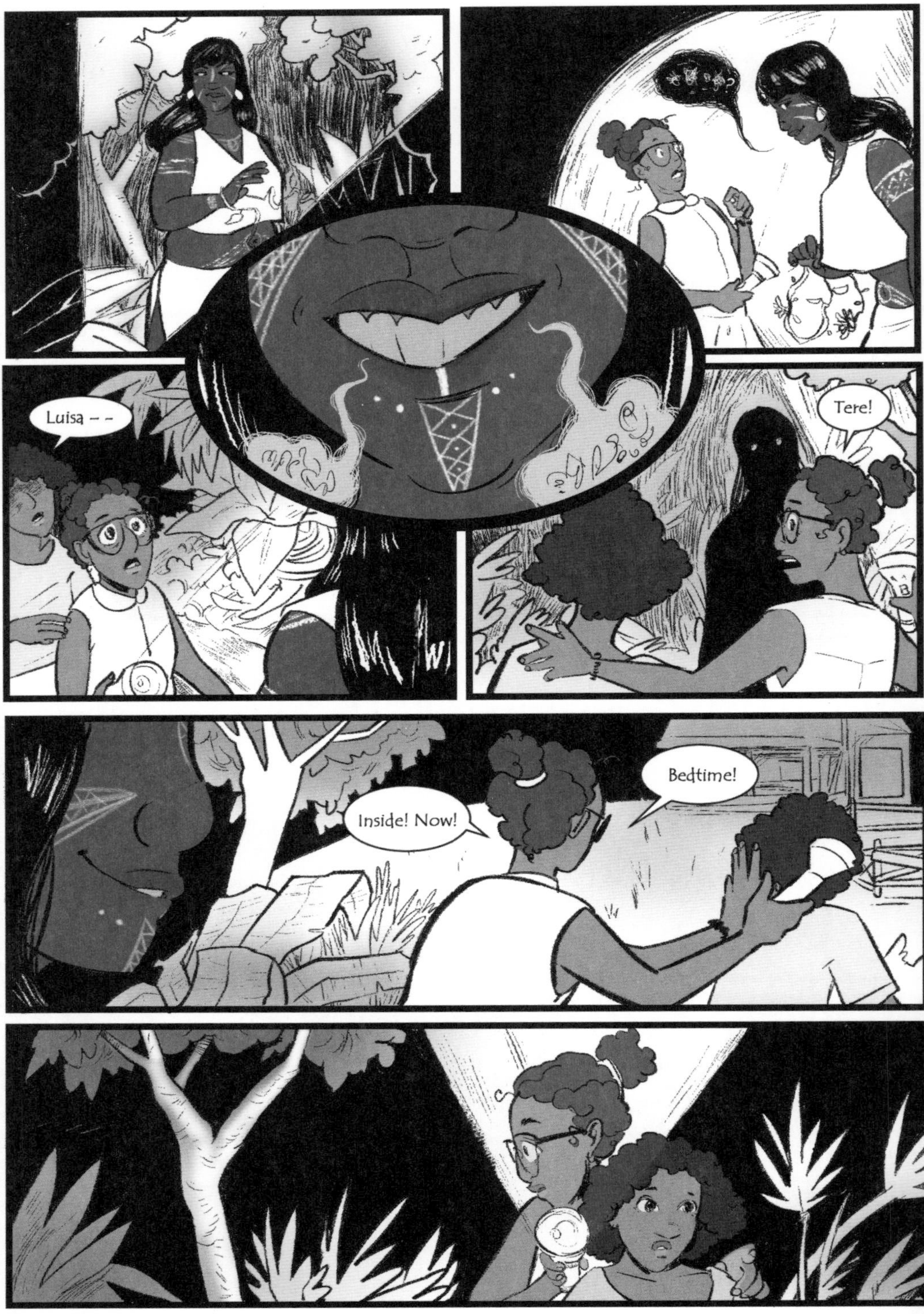
Luisa --
Tere!
Inside! Now!
Bedtime!

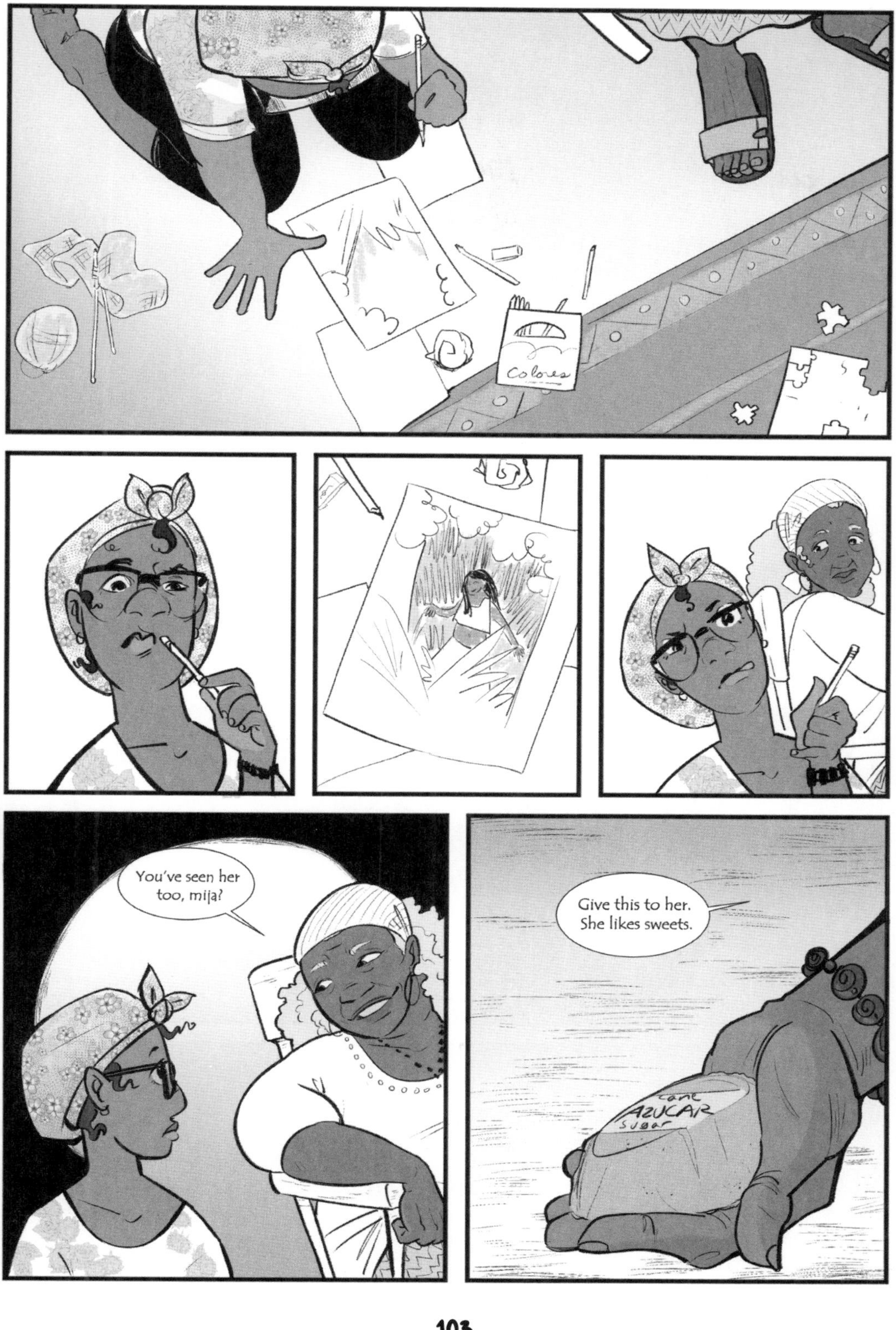
Colores
You've seen her too, mija?
Give this to her. She likes sweets.
cane AZUCAR Sugar

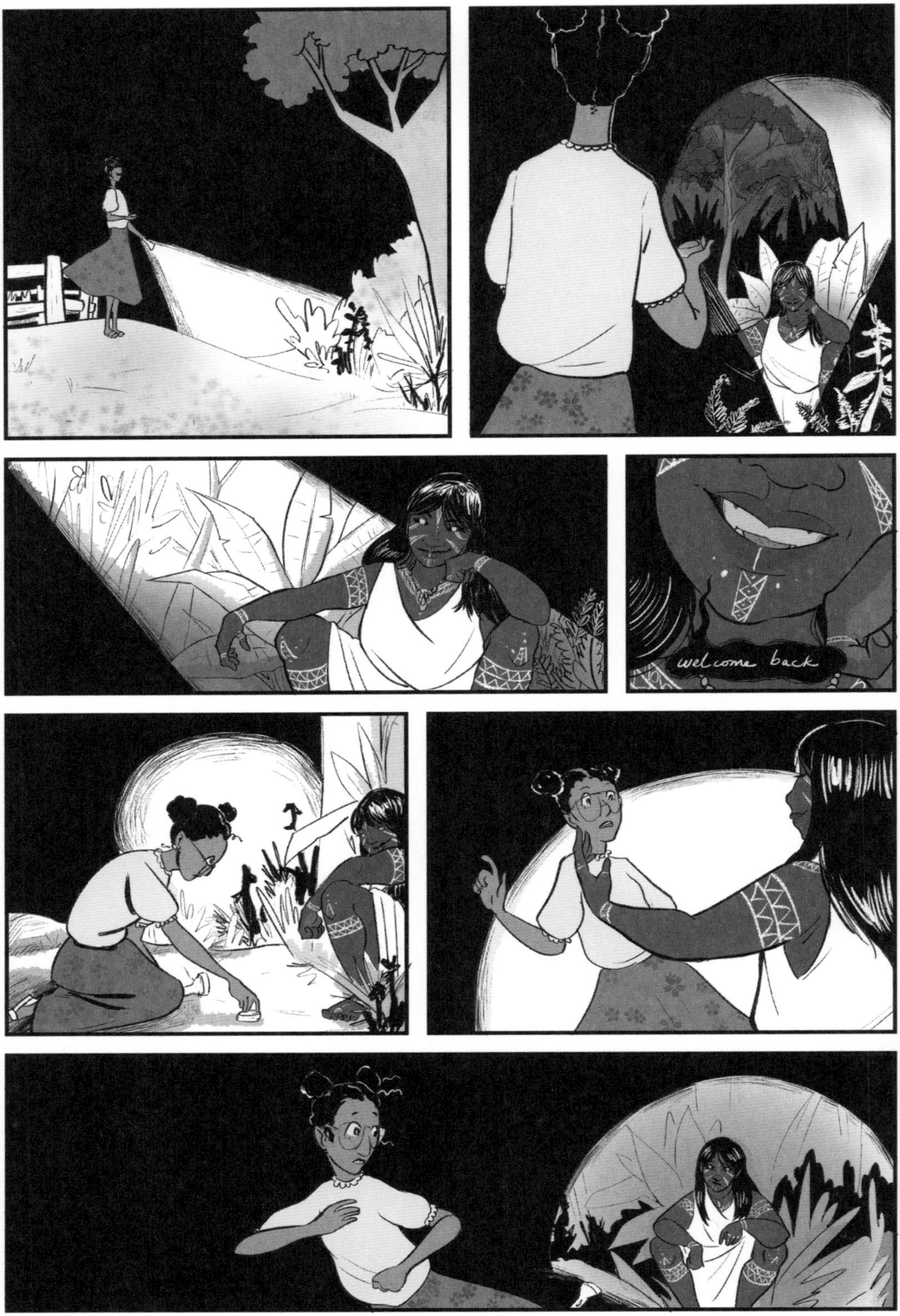
welcome back

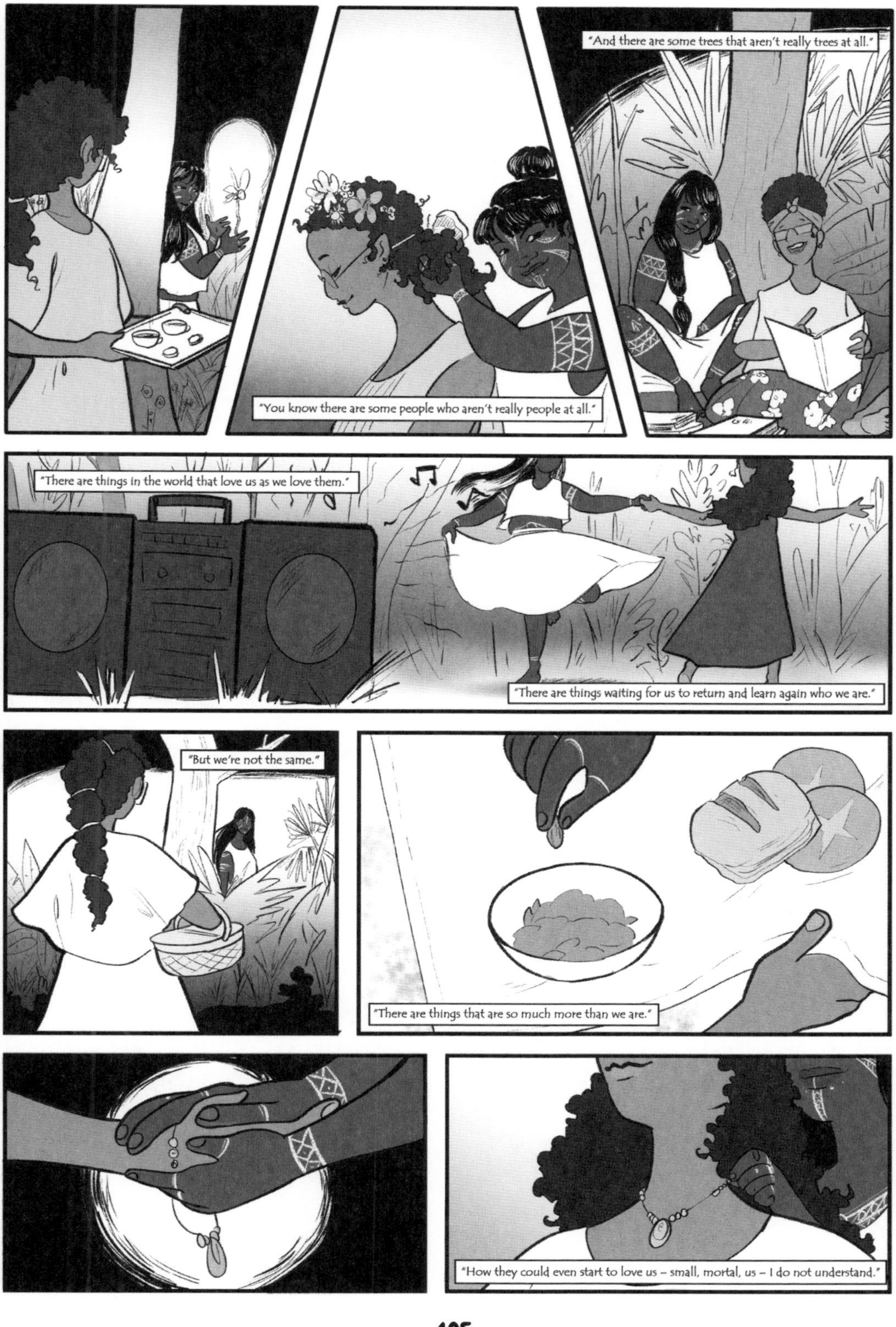
"You know there are some people who aren't really people at all."
"And there are some trees that aren't really trees at all."
"There are things in the world that love us as we love them."
"There are things waiting for us to return and learn again who we are."
"But we're not the same."
"There are things that are so much more than we are."
"How they could even start to love us – small, mortal, us – I do not understand."

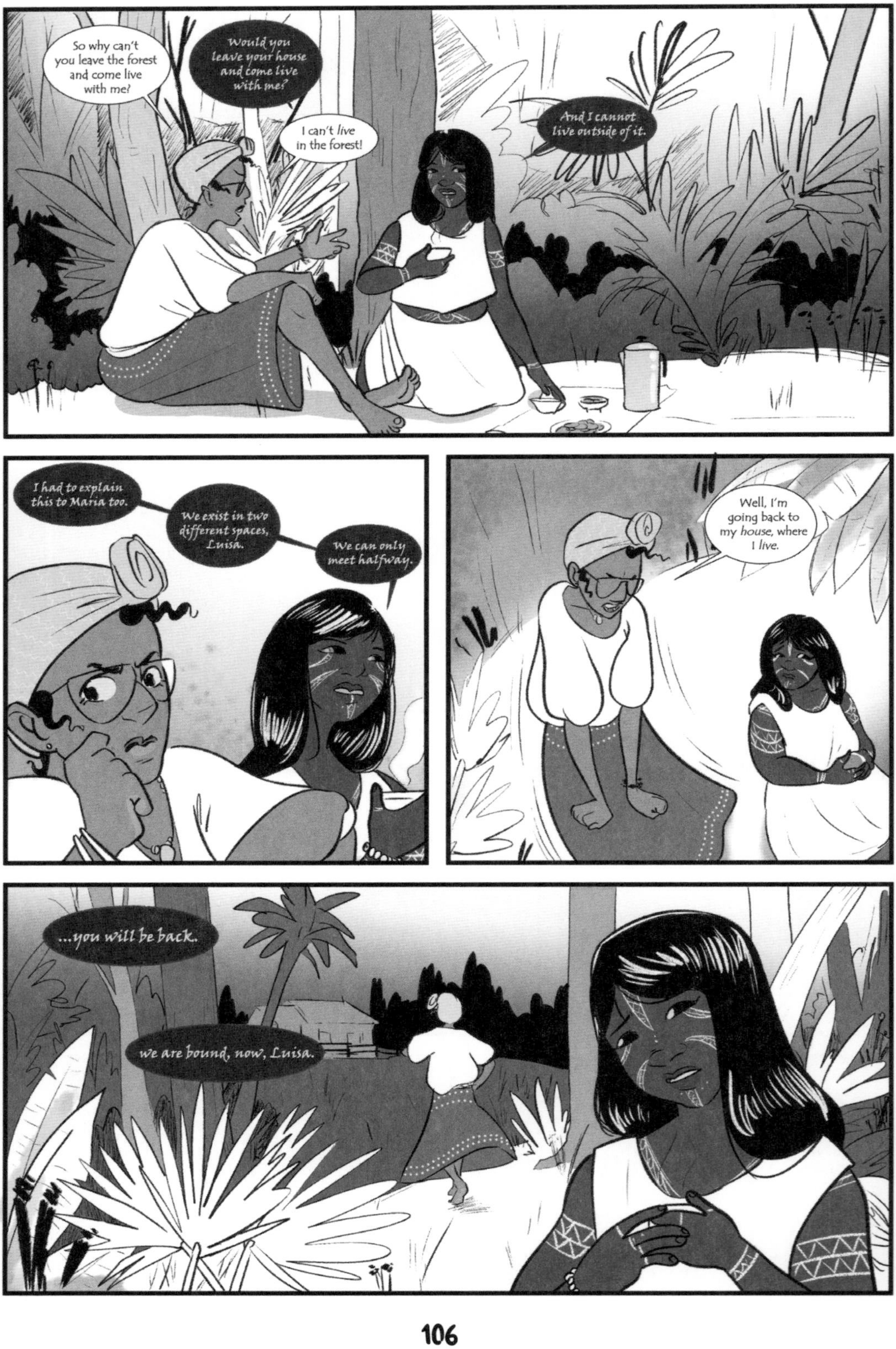
So why can't you leave the forest and come live with me?
Would you leave your house and come live with me?
I can't *live* in the forest!
And I cannot live outside of it.
I had to explain this to Maria too.
We exist in two different spaces, Luisa.
We can only meet halfway.
Well, I'm going back to my *house*, where I *live*.
...you will be back.
we are bound, now, Luisa.

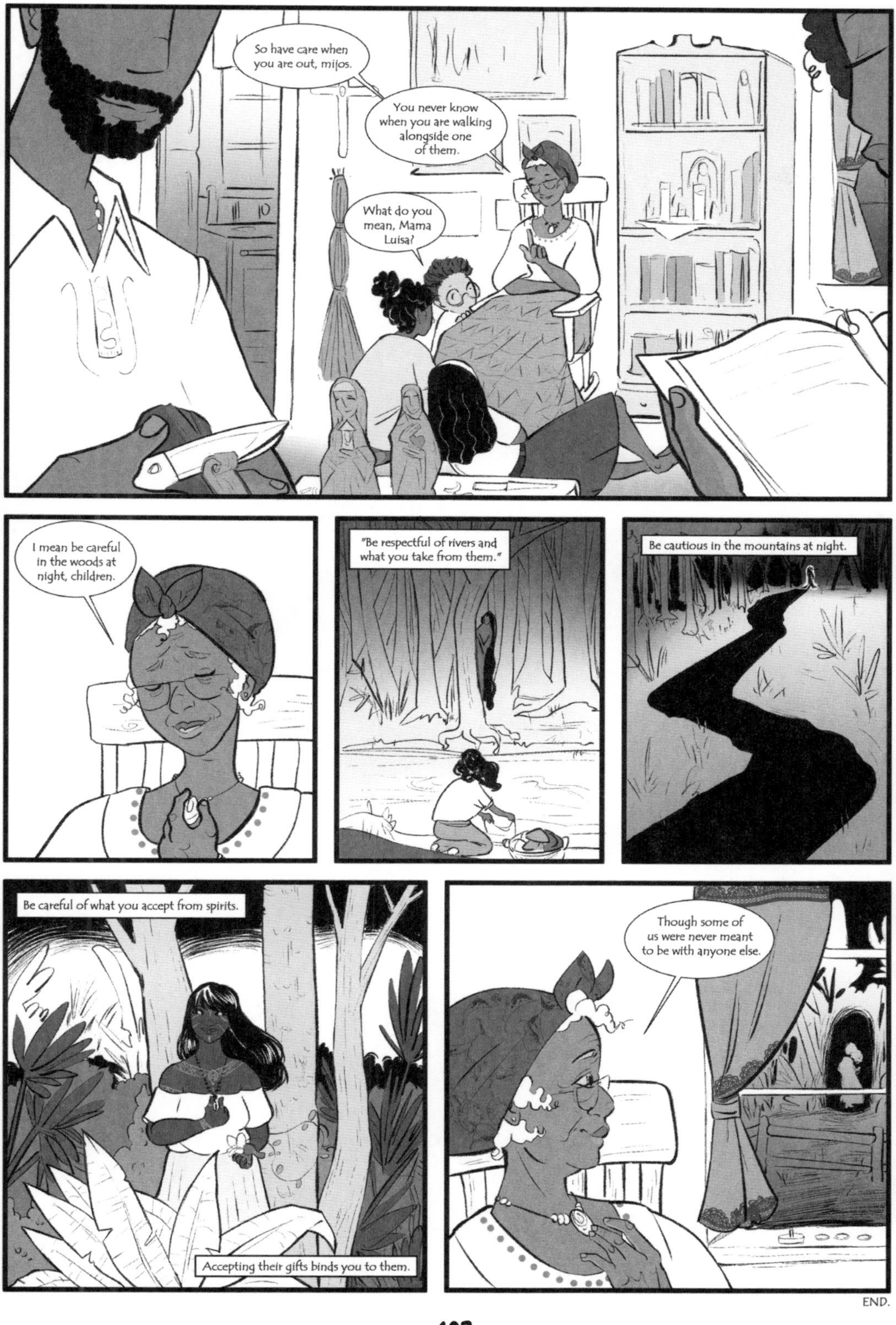
So have care when you are out, mijos.
You never know when you are walking alongside one of them.
What do you mean, Mama Luisa?
I mean be careful in the woods at night, children.
"Be respectful of rivers and what you take from them."
Be cautious in the mountains at night.
Be careful of what you accept from spirits.
Accepting their gifts binds you to them.
Though some of us were never meant to be with anyone else.

END.

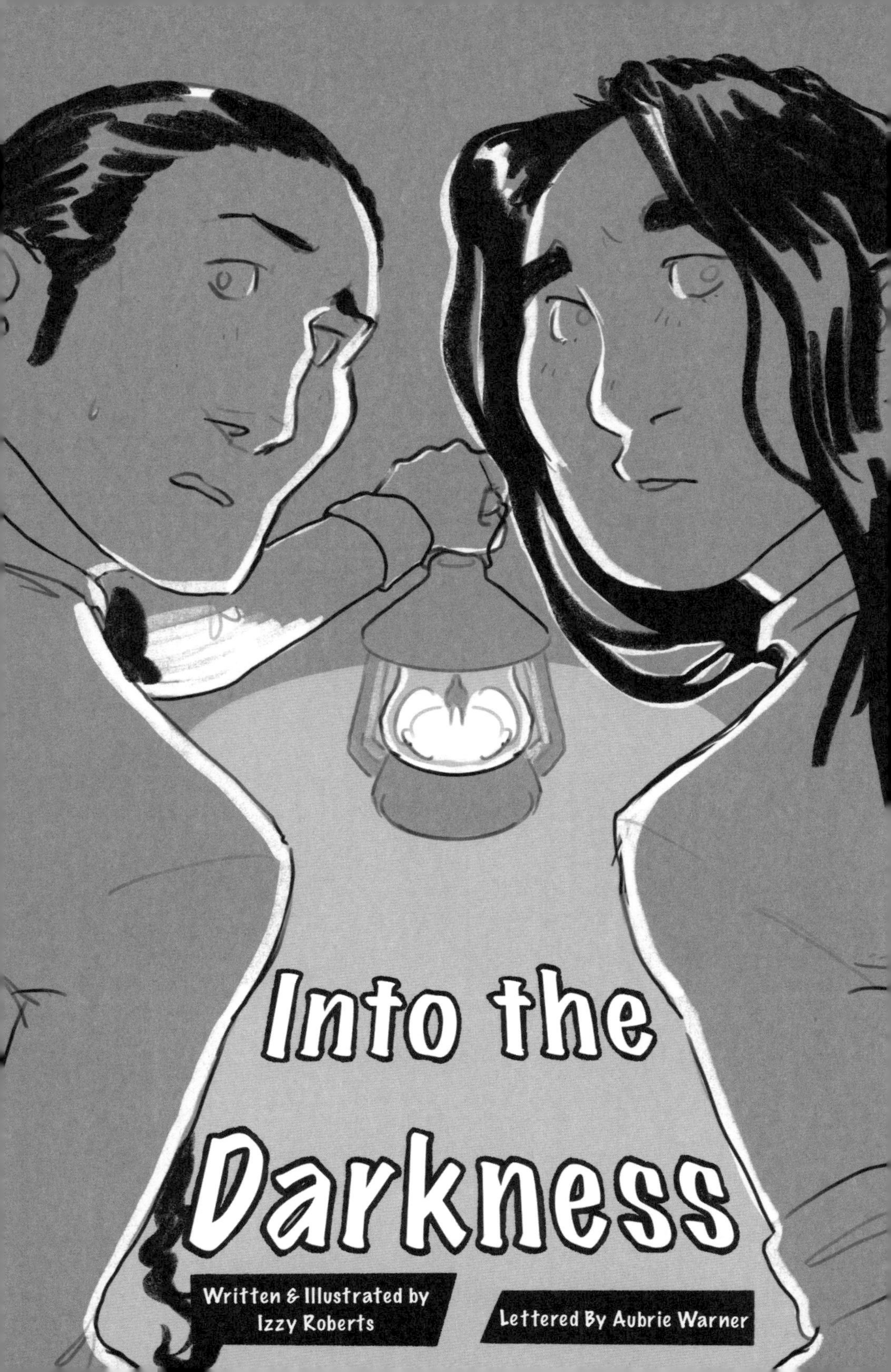

Into the Darkness
Written & Illustrated by Izzy Roberts
Lettered By Aubrie Warner

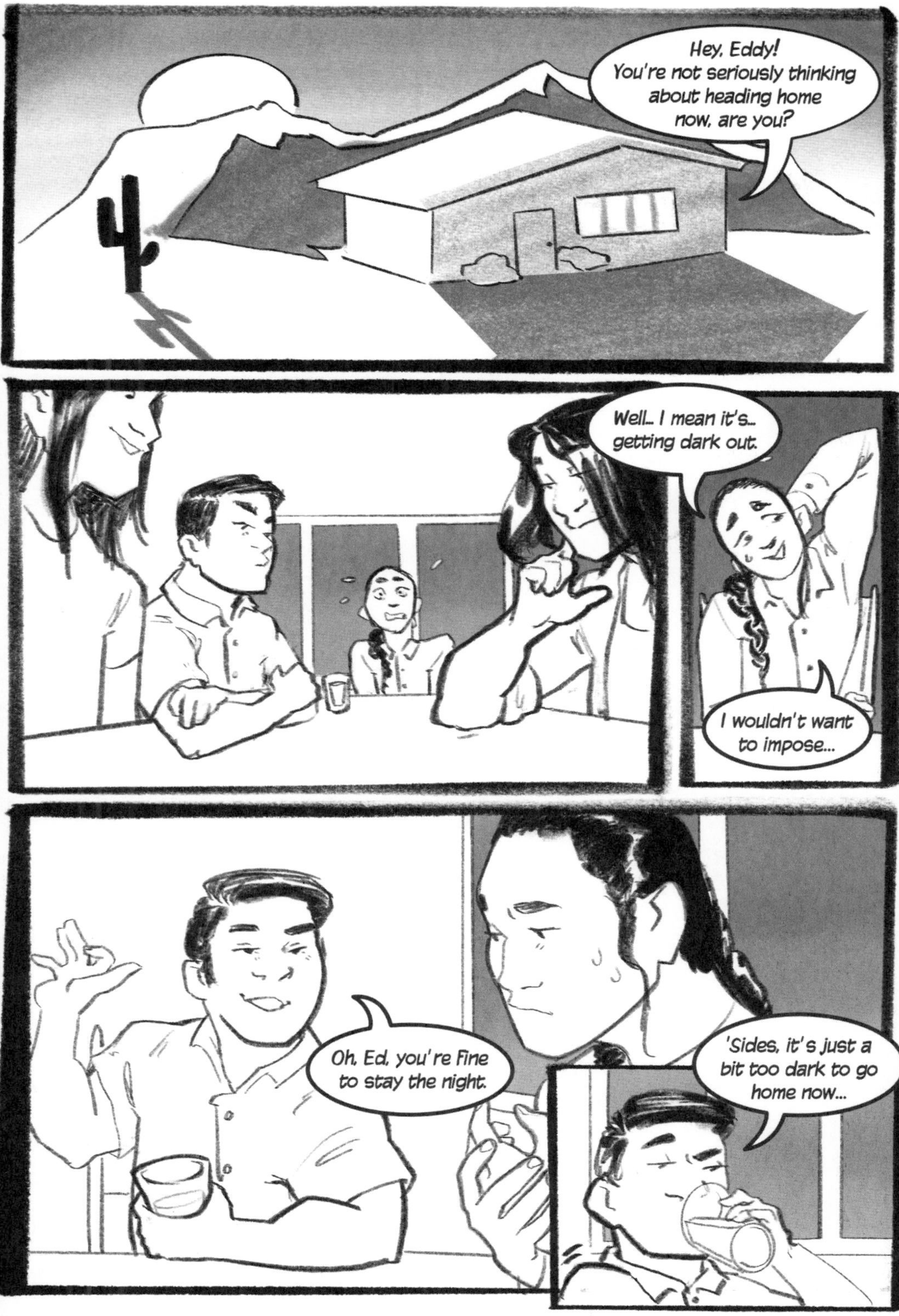
Hey, Eddy! You're not seriously thinking about heading home now, are you?
Well... I mean it's... getting dark out.
I wouldn't want to impose...
Oh, Ed, you're fine to stay the night.
'Sides, it's just a bit too dark to go home now...

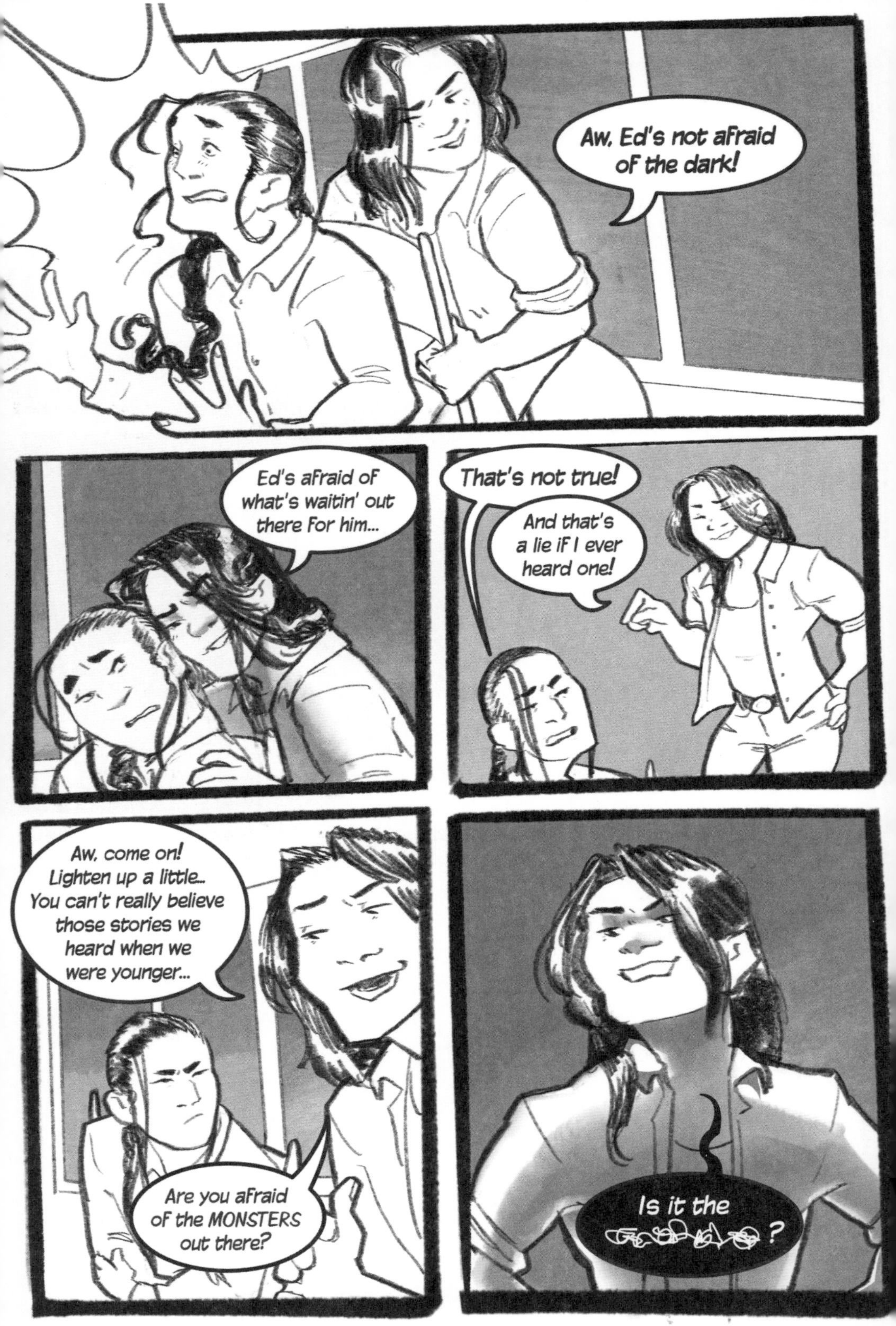
Aw, Ed's not afraid of the dark!
Ed's afraid of what's waitin' out there for him...
That's not true!
And that's a lie if I ever heard one!
Aw, come on! Lighten up a little... You can't really believe those stories we heard when we were younger...
Are you afraid of the MONSTERS out there?
Is it the

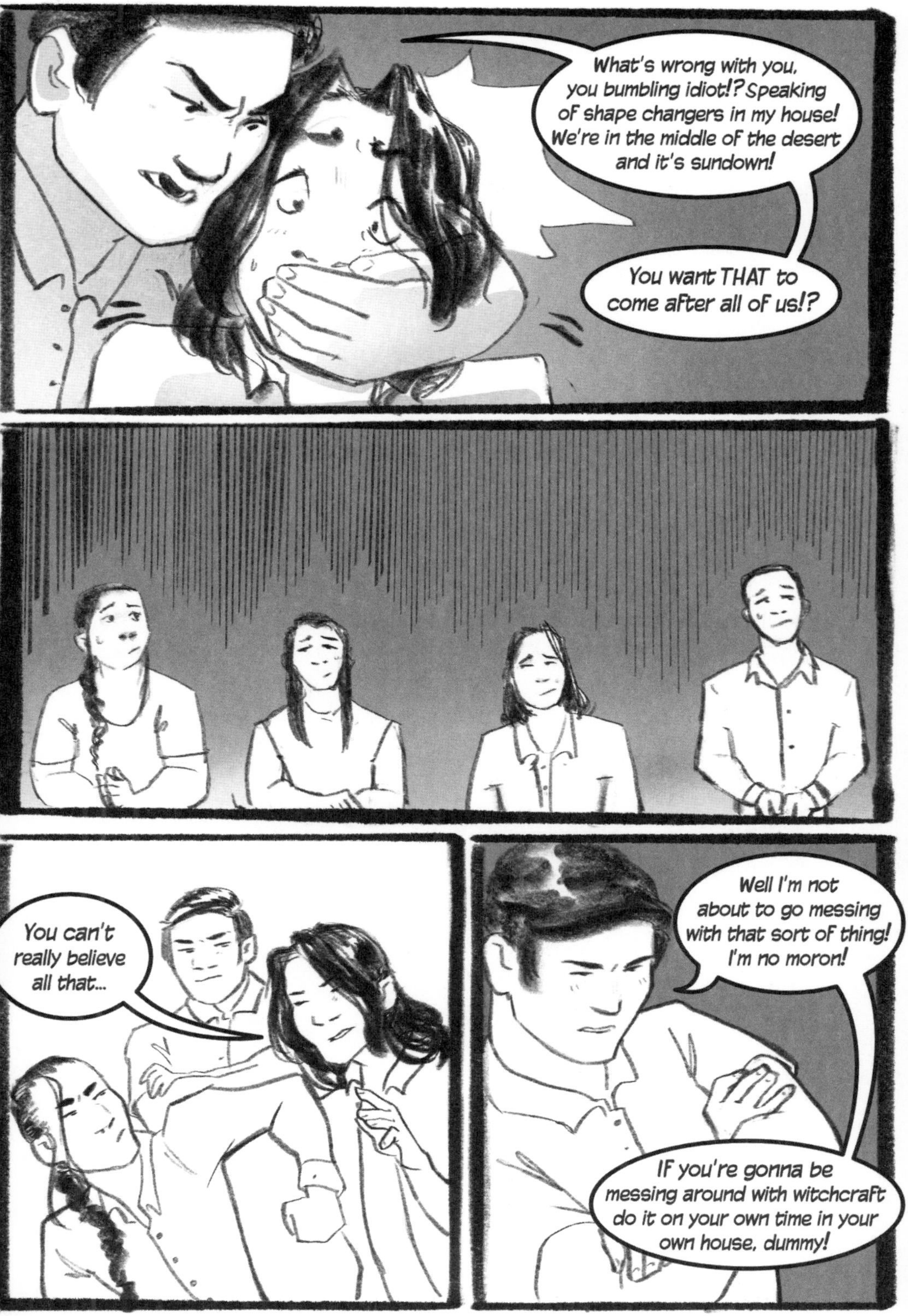
What's wrong with you, you bumbling idiot!? Speaking of shape changers in my house! We're in the middle of the desert and it's sundown!
You want THAT to come after all of us!?
You can't really believe all that...
Well I'm not about to go messing with that sort of thing! I'm no moron!
If you're gonna be messing around with witchcraft do it on your own time in your own house, dummy!

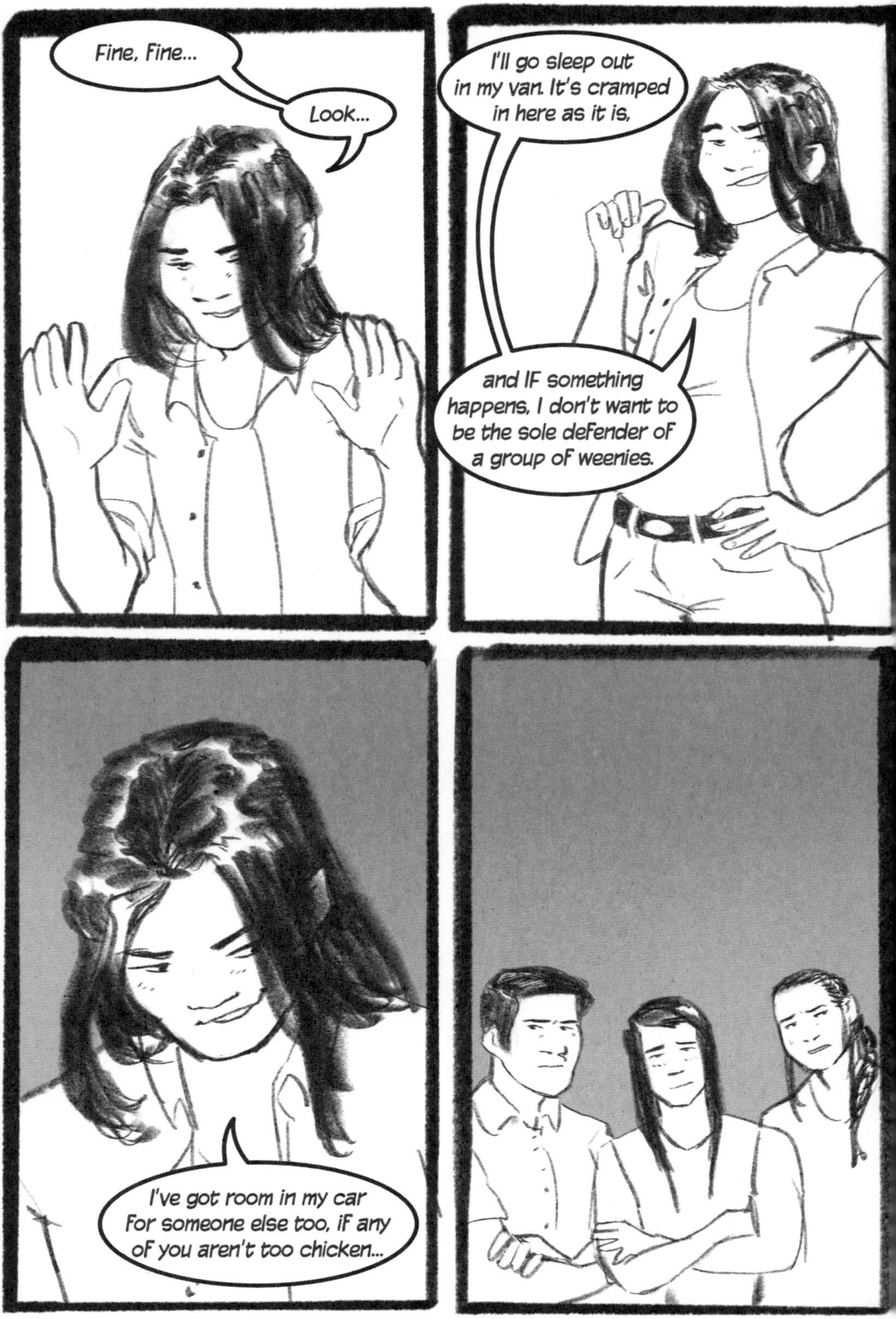
Fine, Fine...
Look...
I'll go sleep out in my van. It's cramped in here as it is,
and IF something happens, I don't want to be the sole defender of a group of weenies.
I've got room in my car For someone else too, iF any oF you aren't too chicken...

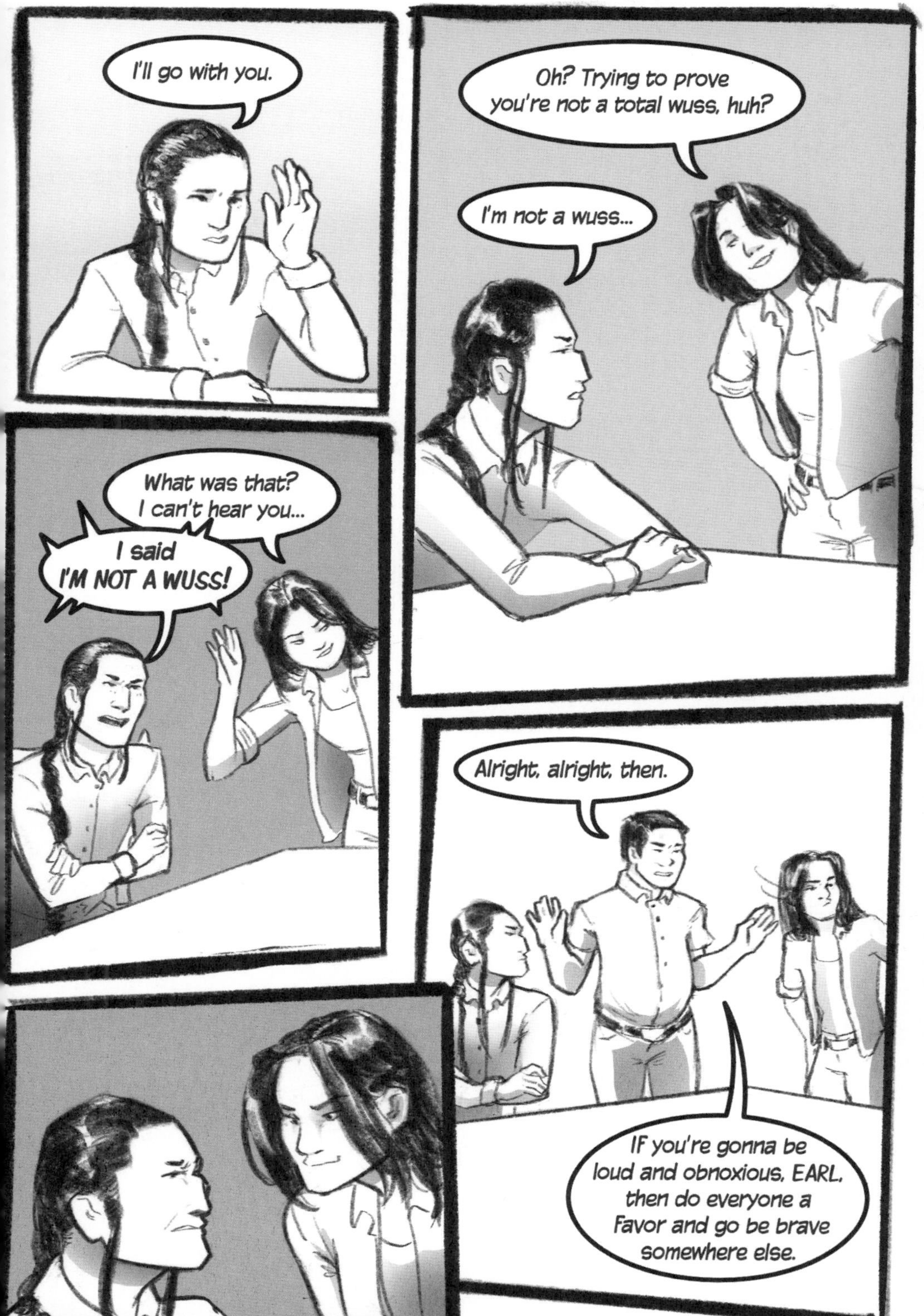
I'll go with you.
Oh? Trying to prove you're not a total wuss, huh?
I'm not a wuss...
What was that? I can't hear you...
I said I'M NOT A WUSS!
Alright, alright, then.
IF you're gonna be loud and obnoxious, EARL, then do everyone a Favor and go be brave somewhere else.

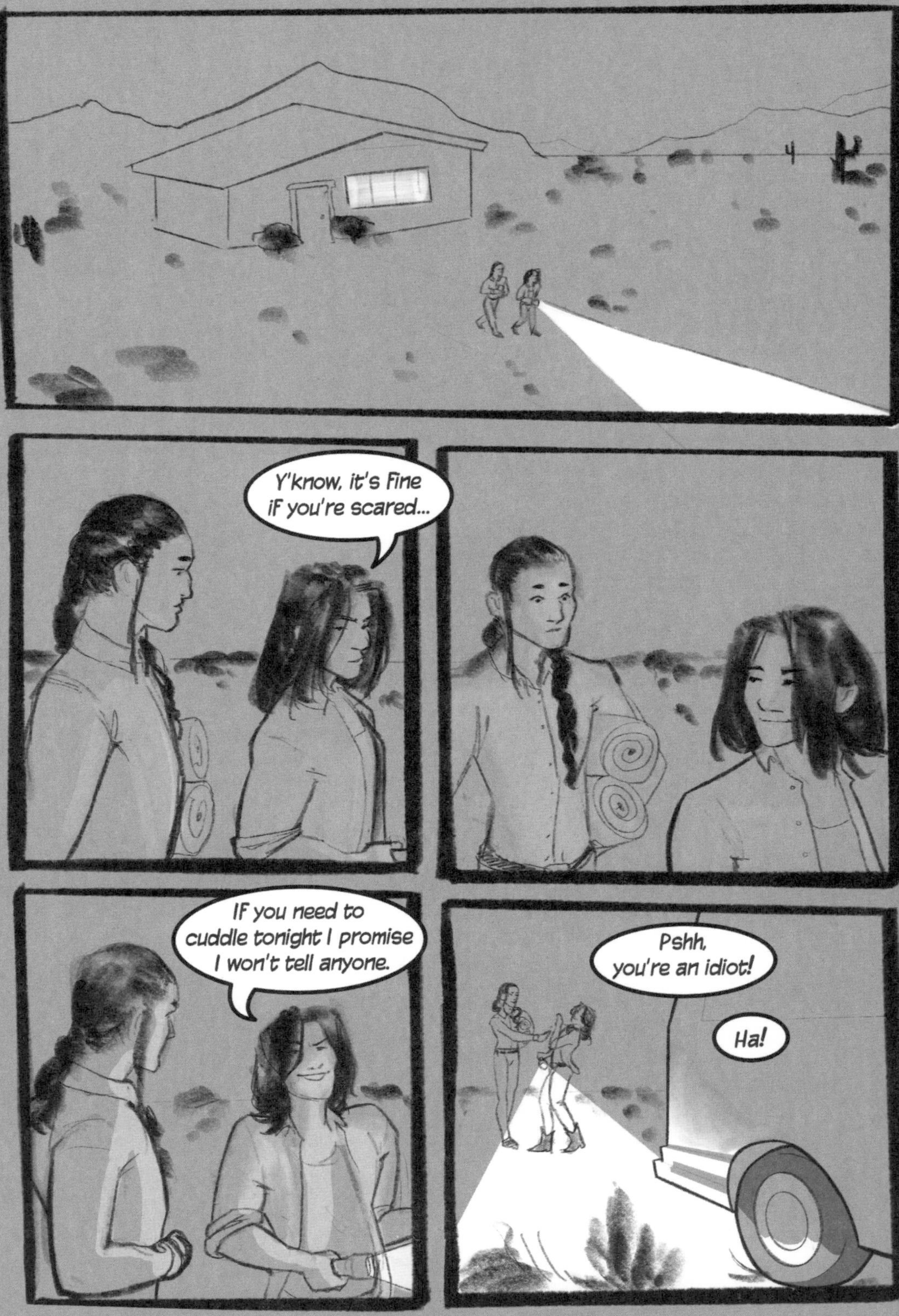
Y'know, it's Fine if you're scared...
IF you need to cuddle tonight I promise I won't tell anyone.
Pshh, you're an idiot!
Ha!

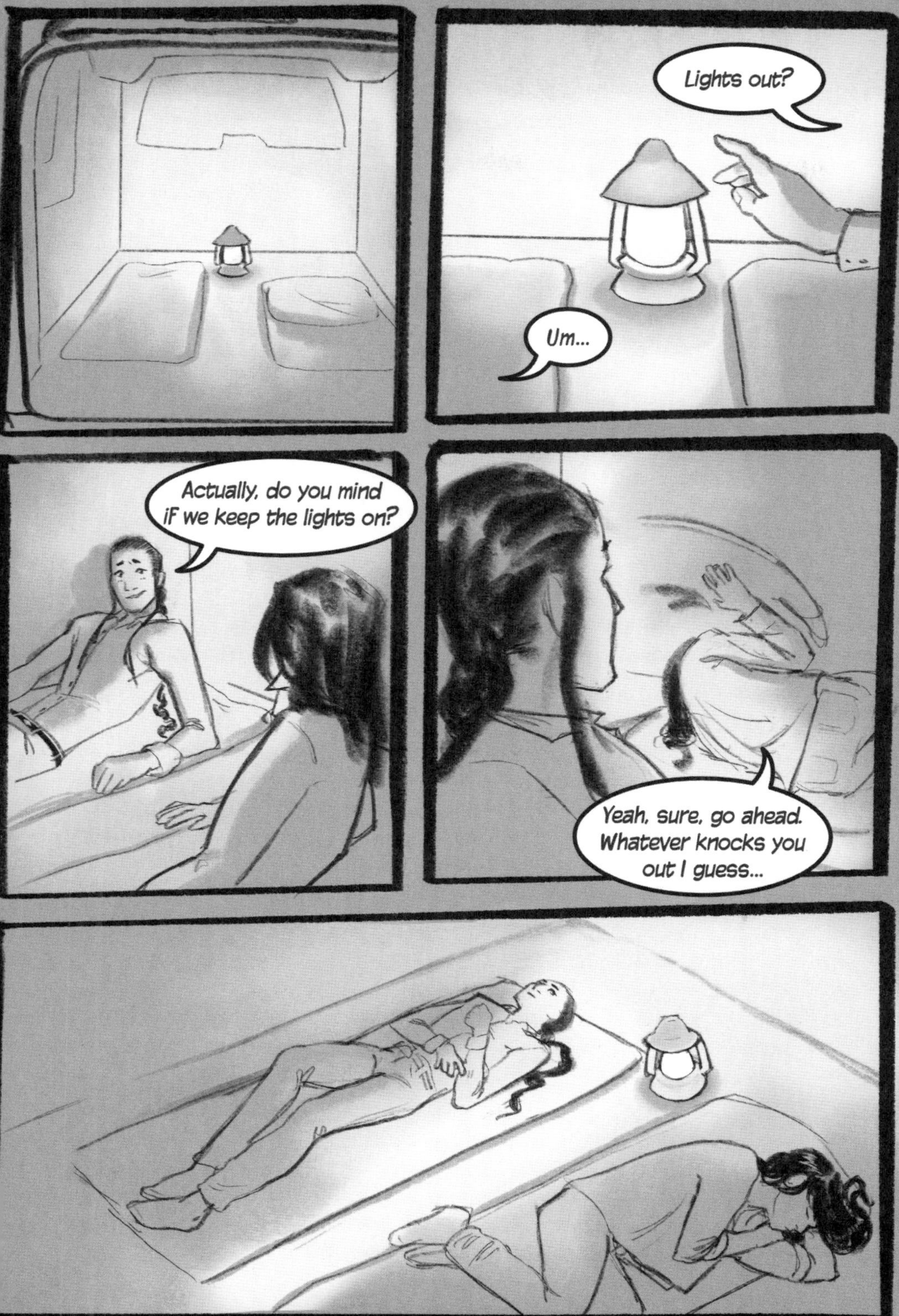
Lights out?
Um...
Actually, do you mind if we keep the lights on?
Yeah, sure, go ahead. Whatever knocks you out I guess...

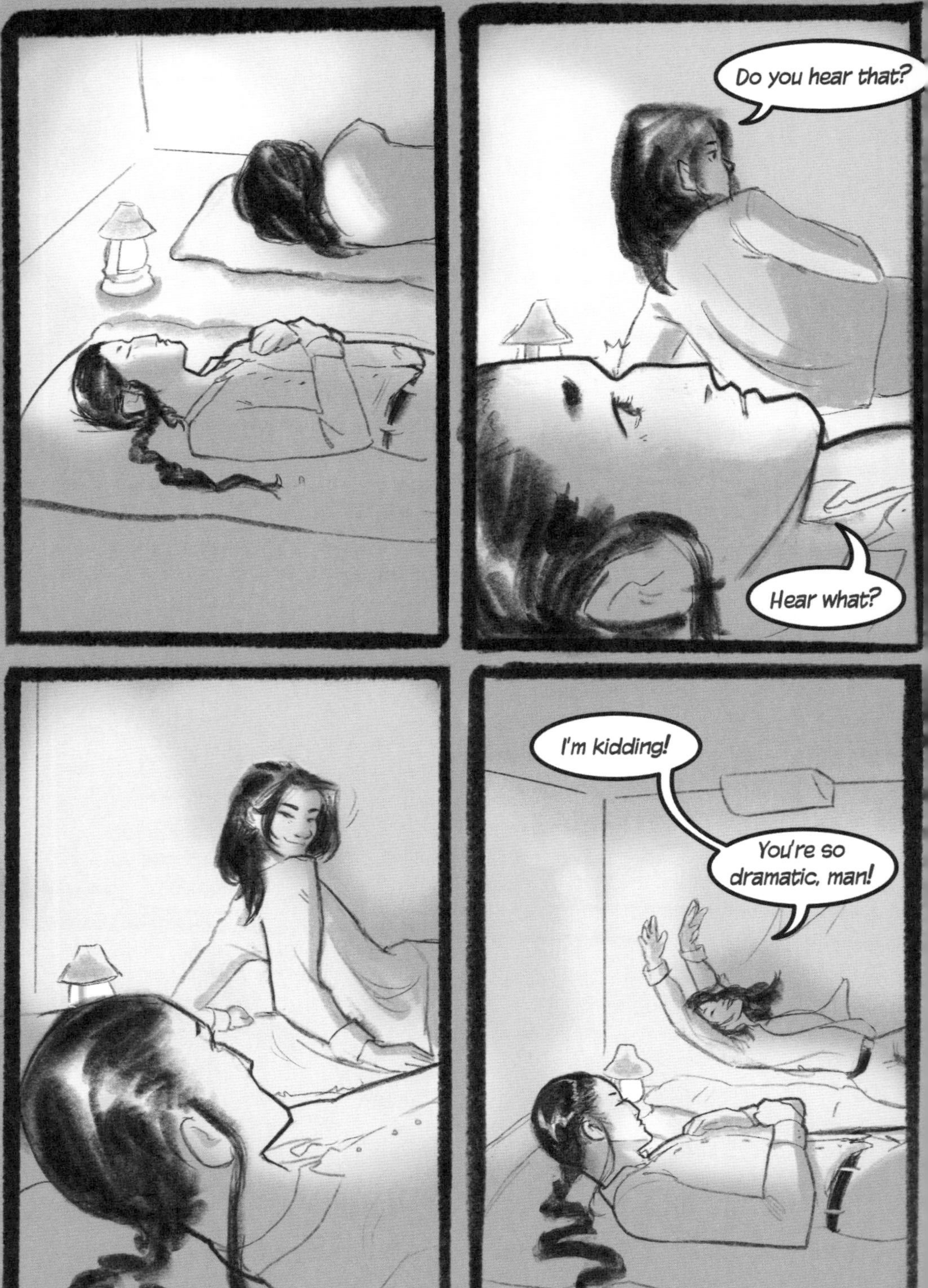
Do you hear that?
Hear what?
I'm kidding!
You're so dramatic, man!

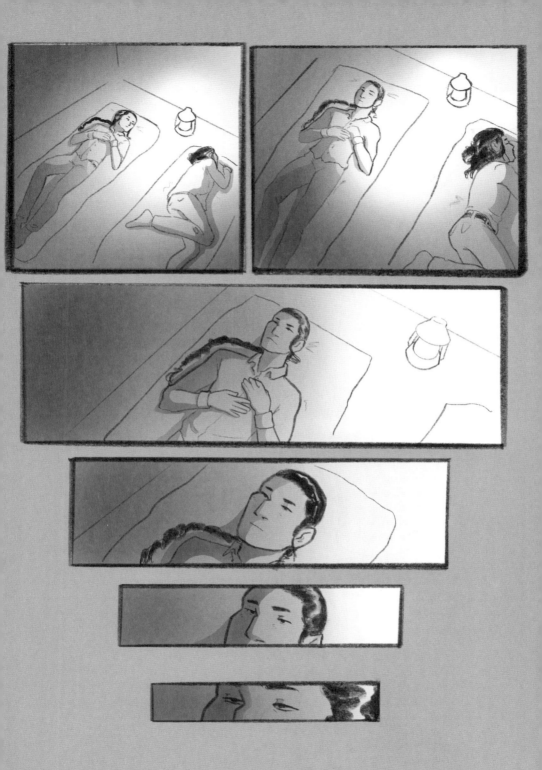

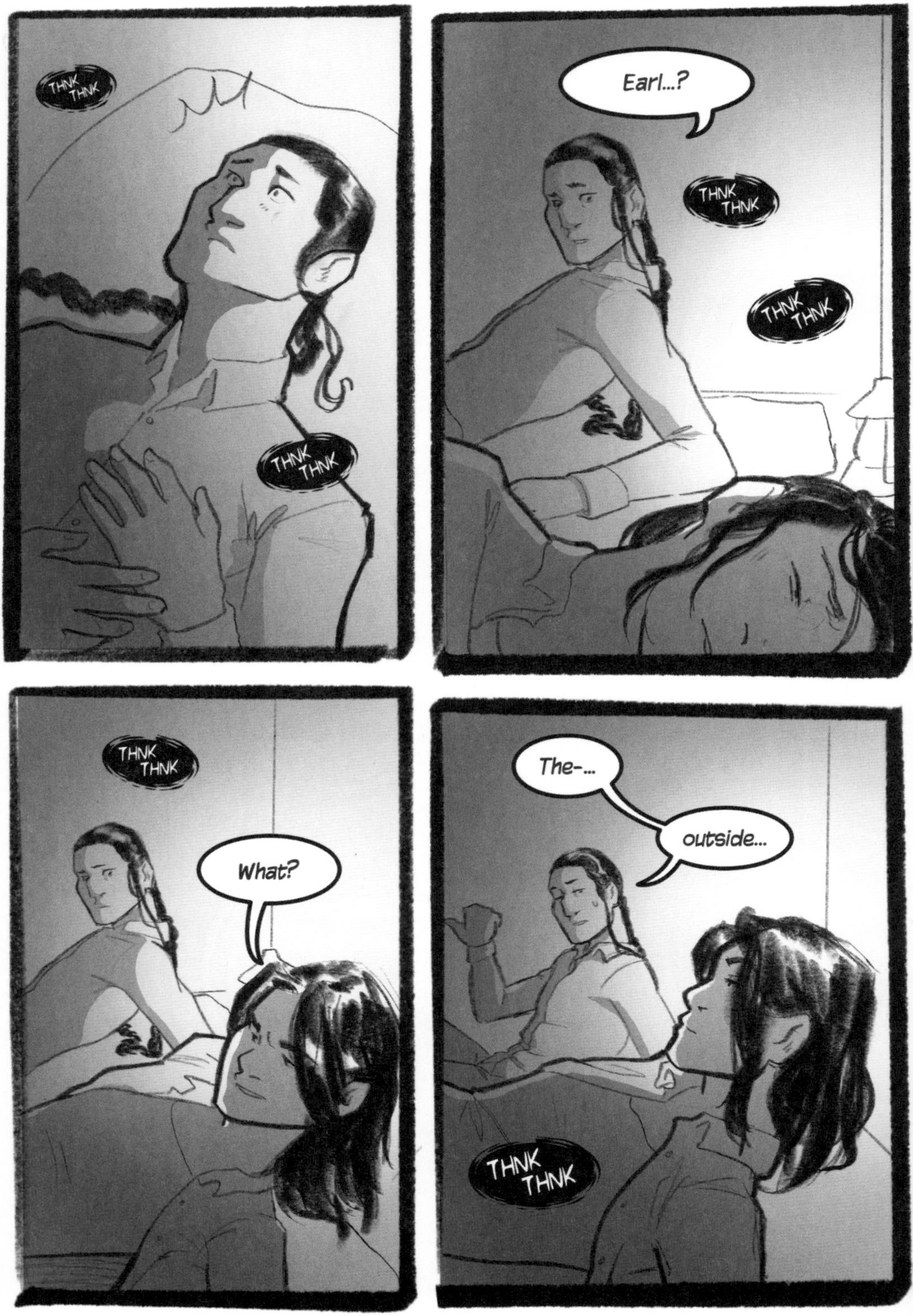
THNK THNK
THNK THNK
Earl...?
THNK THNK
THNK THNK
THNK THNK
What?
The-...
outside...
THNK THNK

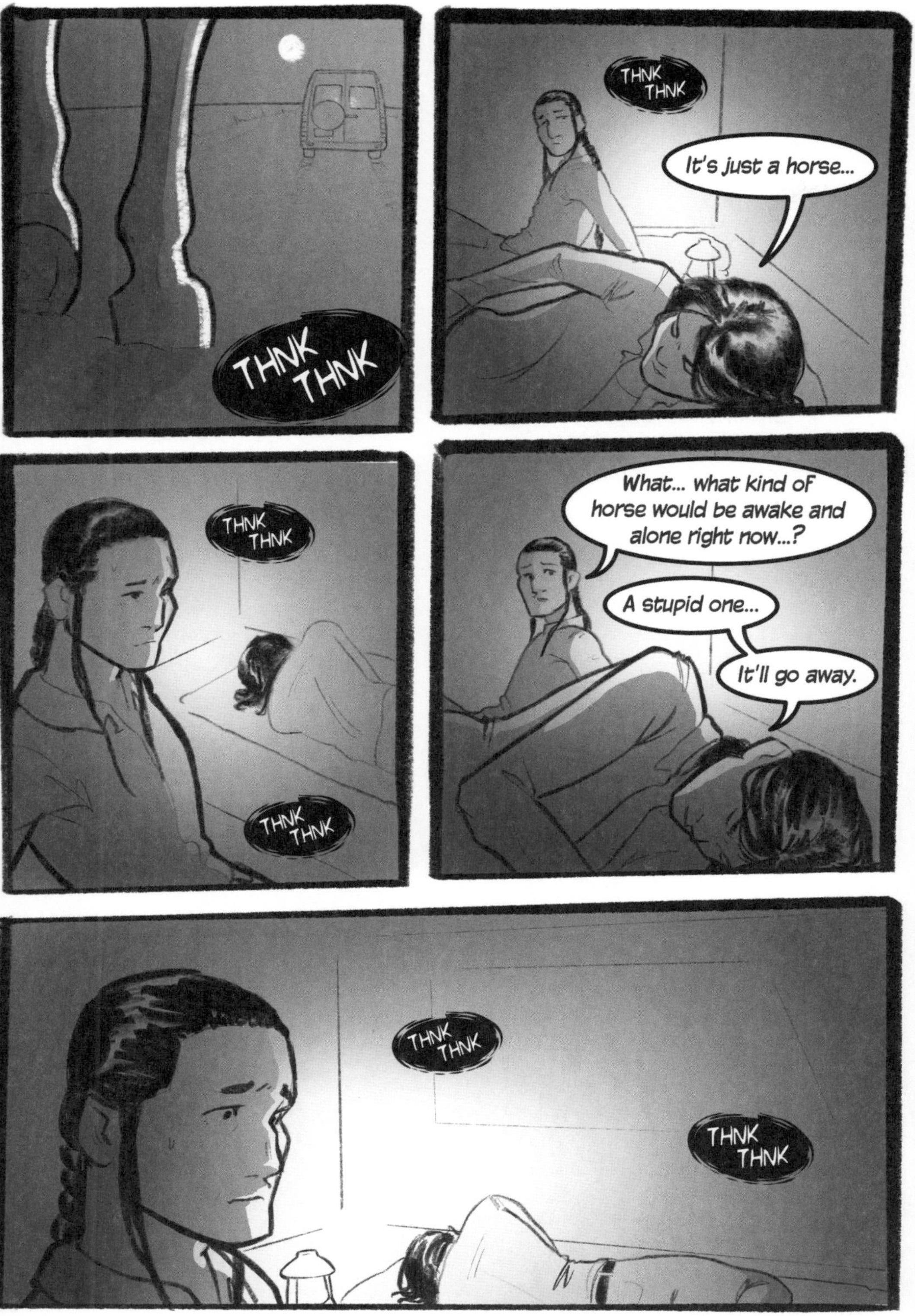
THNK THNK
THNK THNK
It's just a horse...
THNK THNK
THNK THNK
What... what kind of horse would be awake and alone right now...?
A stupid one...
It'll go away.
THNK THNK
THNK THNK

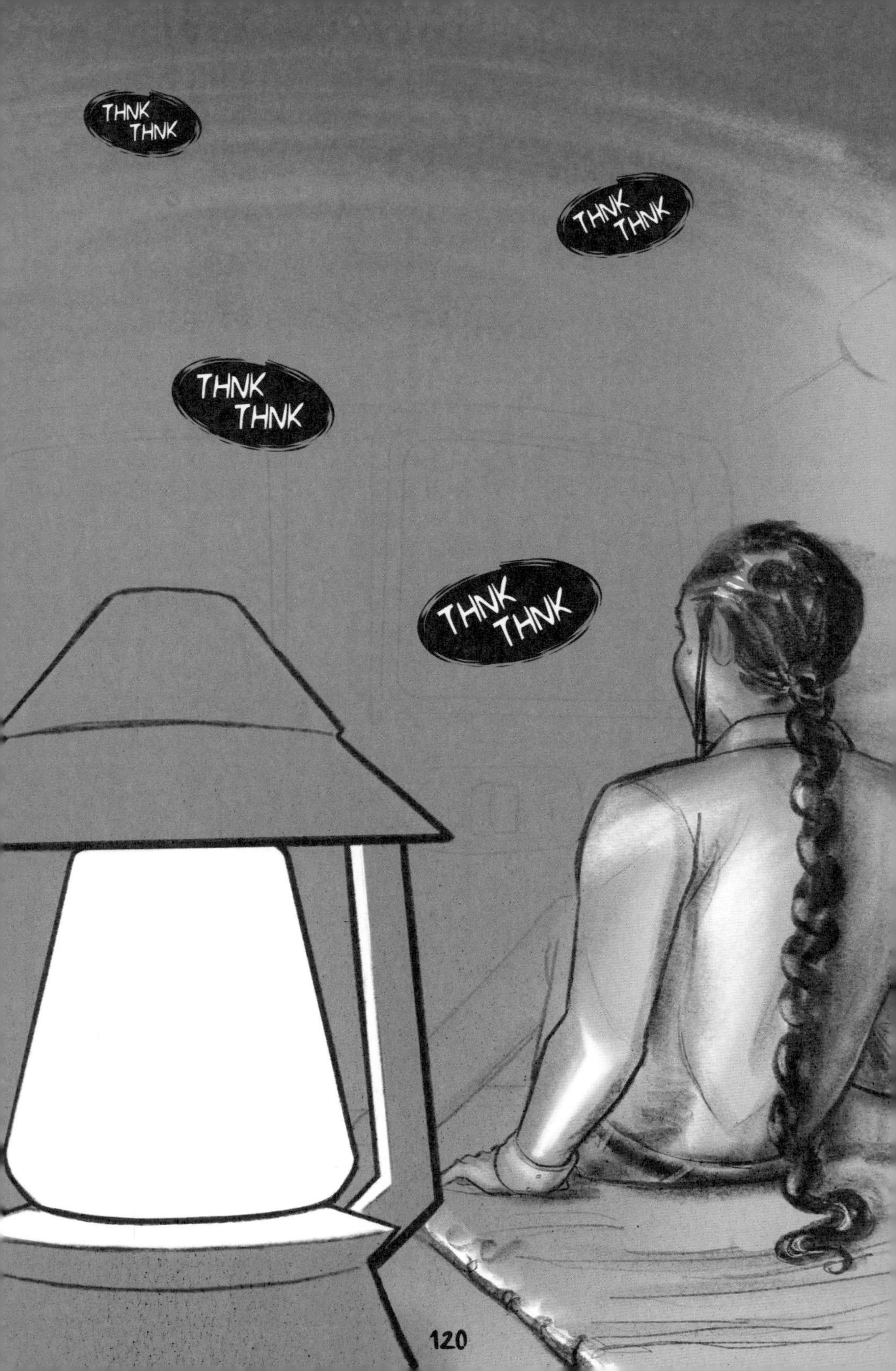
THNK THNK
THNK THNK
THNK THNK
THNK THNK

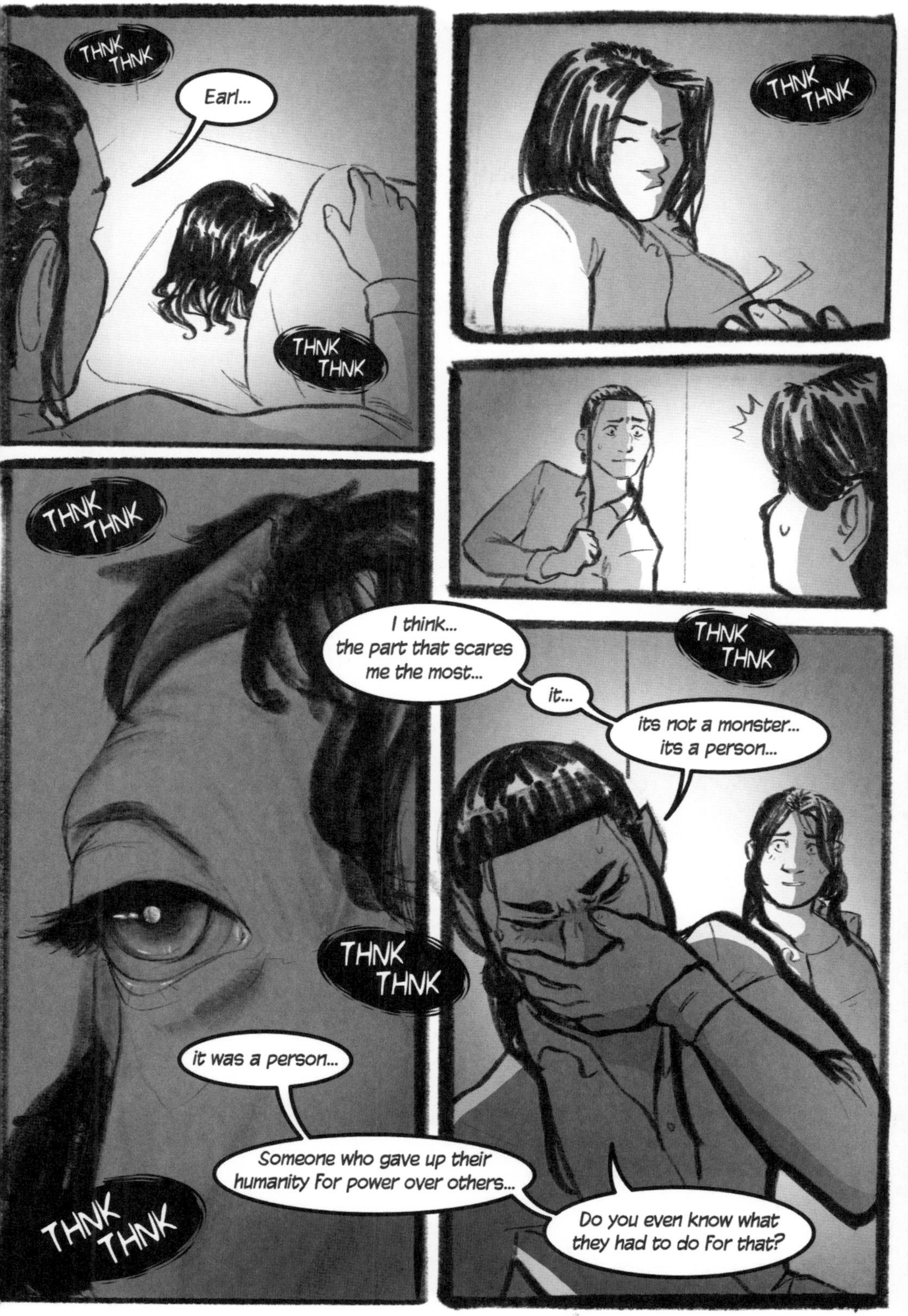
THNK THNK
Earl...
THNK THNK
THNK THNK
THNK THNK
I think... the part that scares me the most...
THNK THNK
it...
its not a monster... its a person...
THNK THNK
it was a person...
Someone who gave up their humanity For power over others...
THNK THNK
Do you even know what they had to do For that?

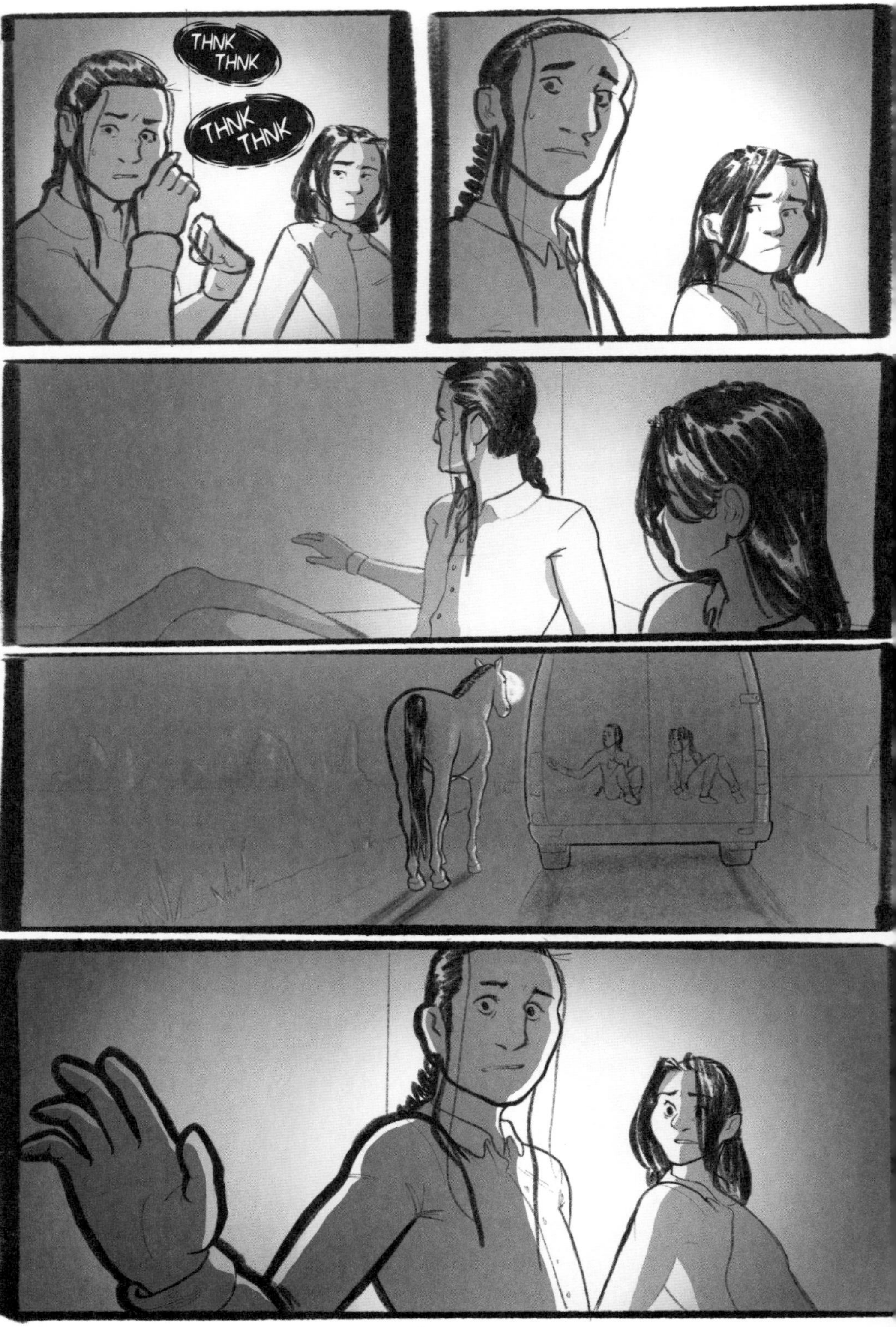
THNK THNK
THNK THNK

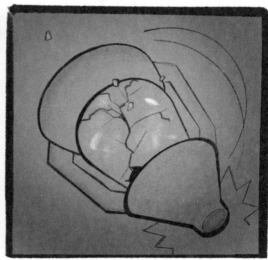

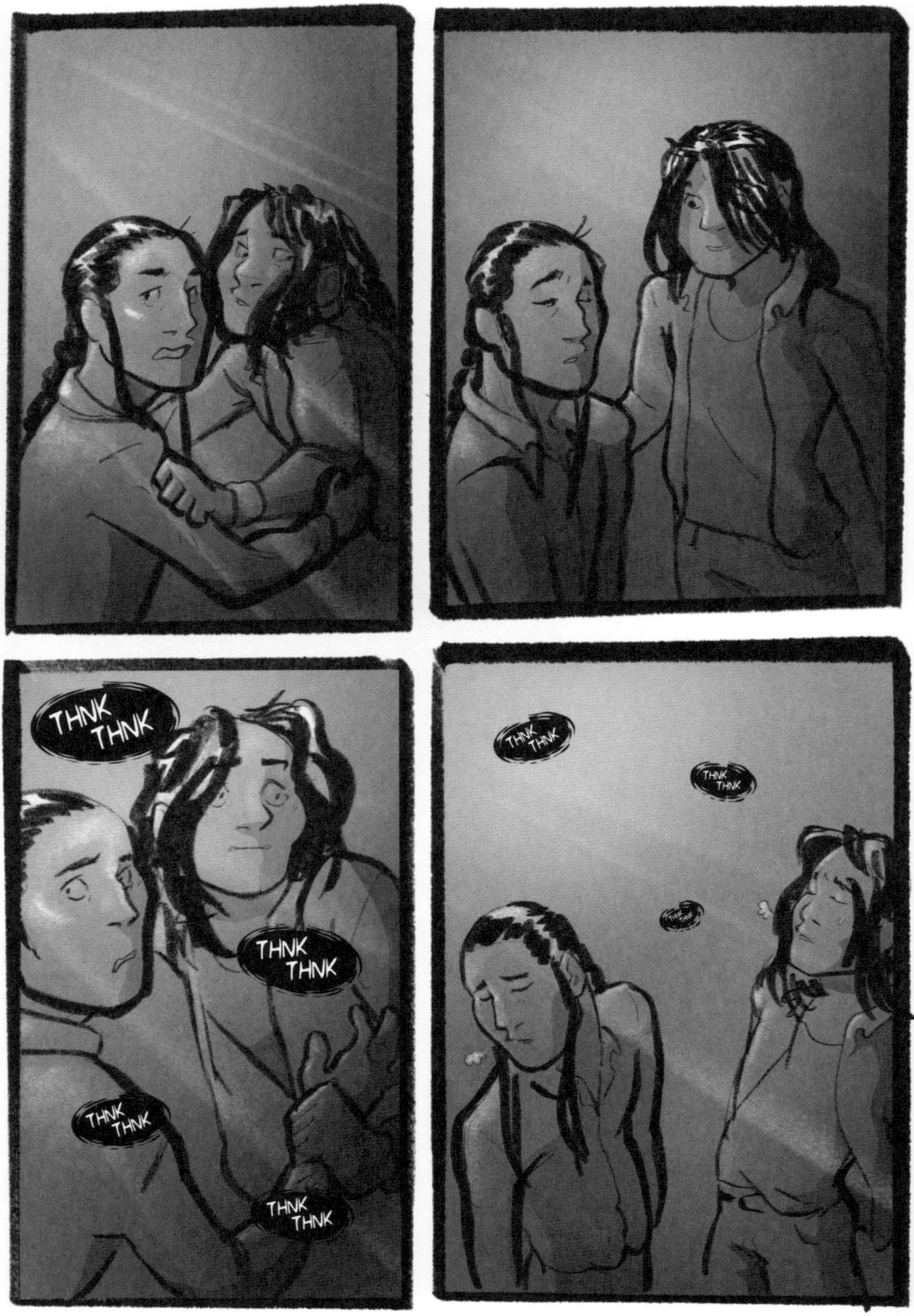
THNK THNK
THNK THNK
THNK THNK
THNK THNK
THNK THNK
THNK THNK

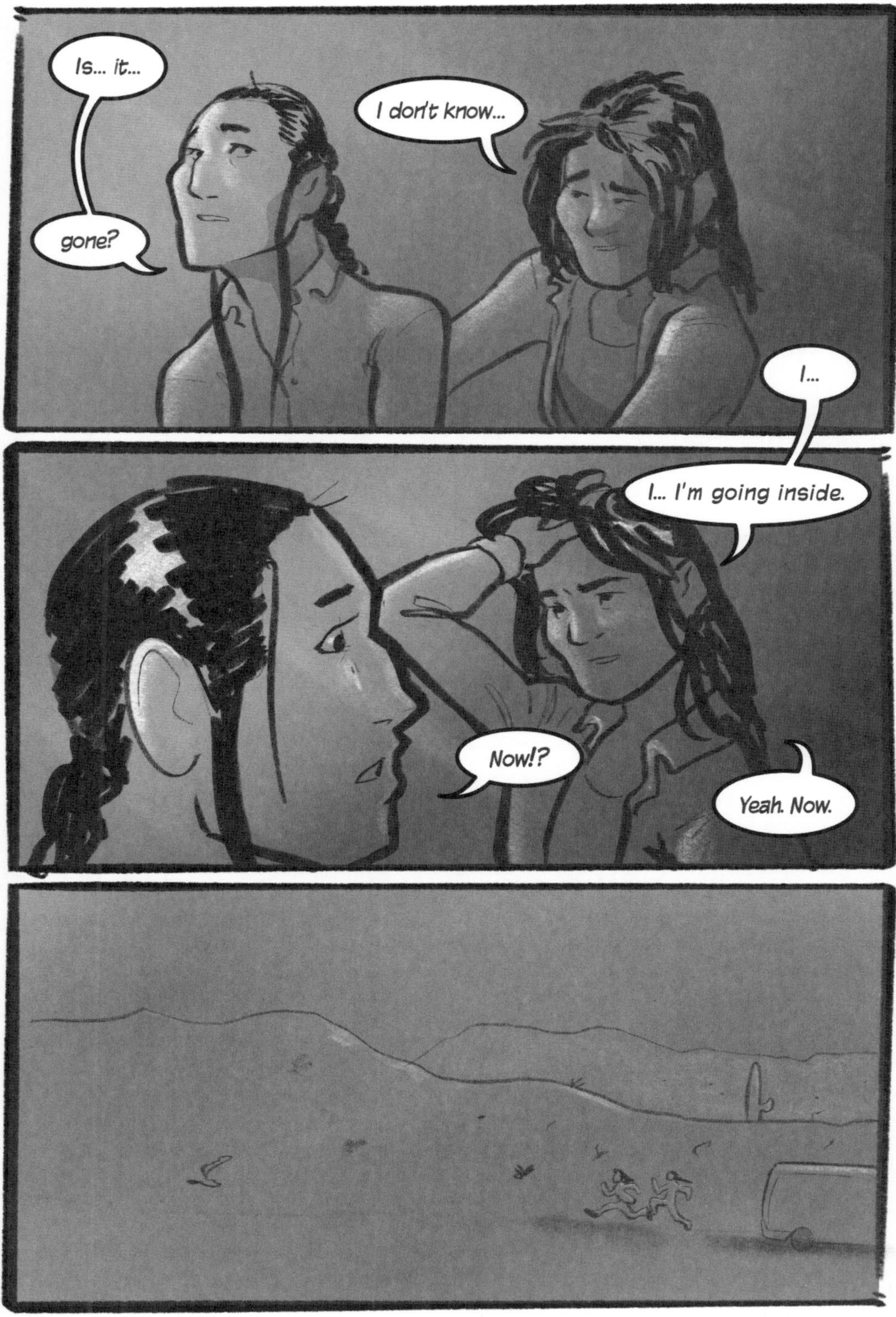
Is... it...
gone?
I don't know...
I...
I... I'm going inside.
Now!?
Yeah. Now.

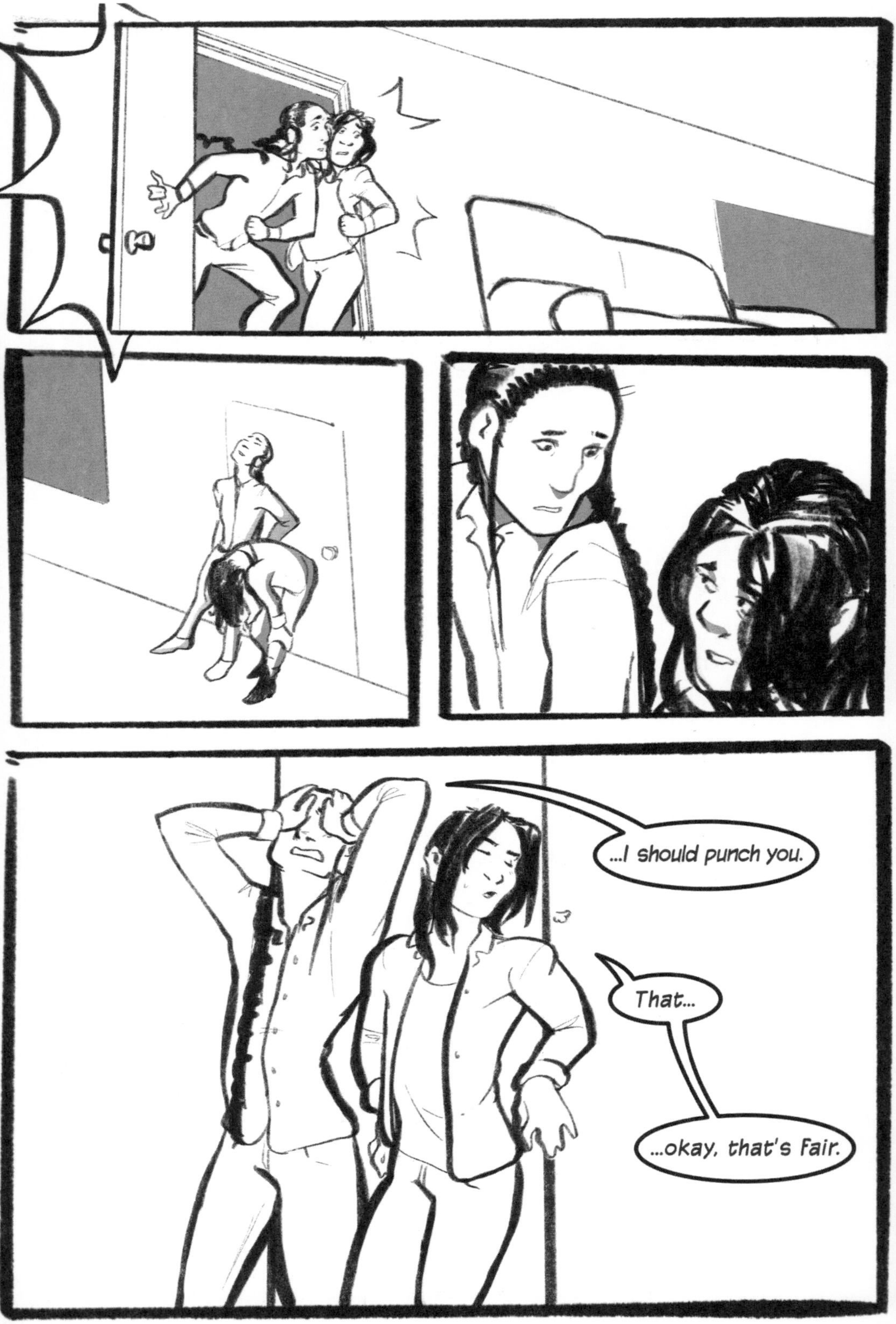
...I should punch you.
That...
...okay, that's fair.

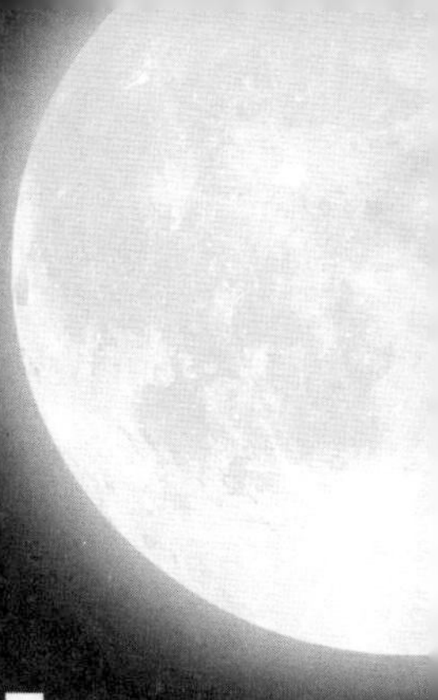

By the Light of the Moon

Written by Jeffrey Veregge
Art by Alina Pete

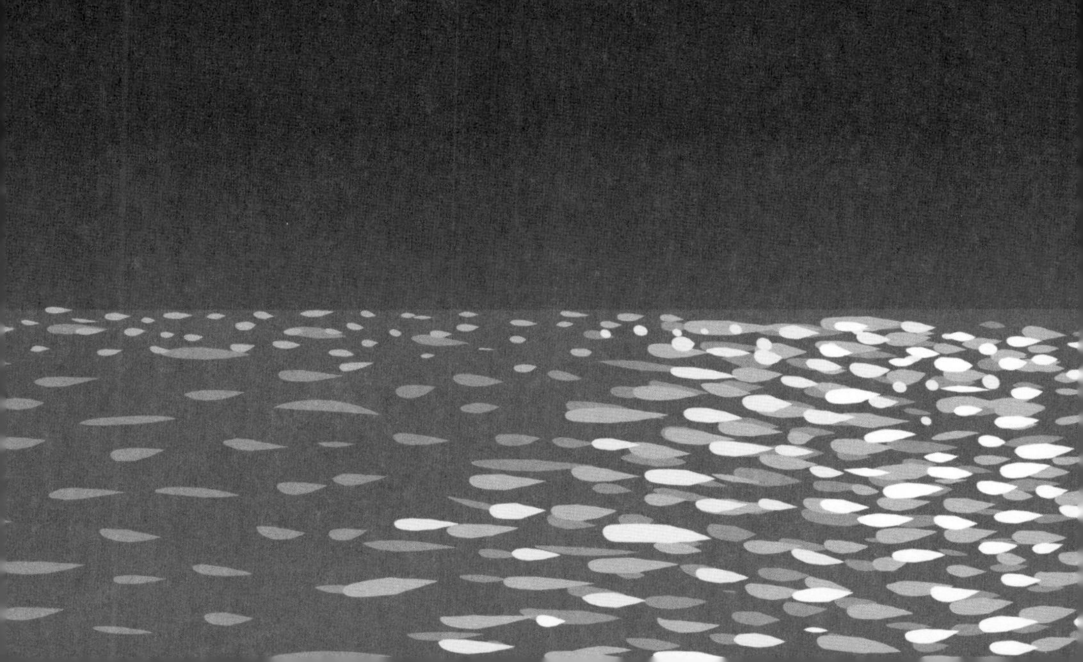

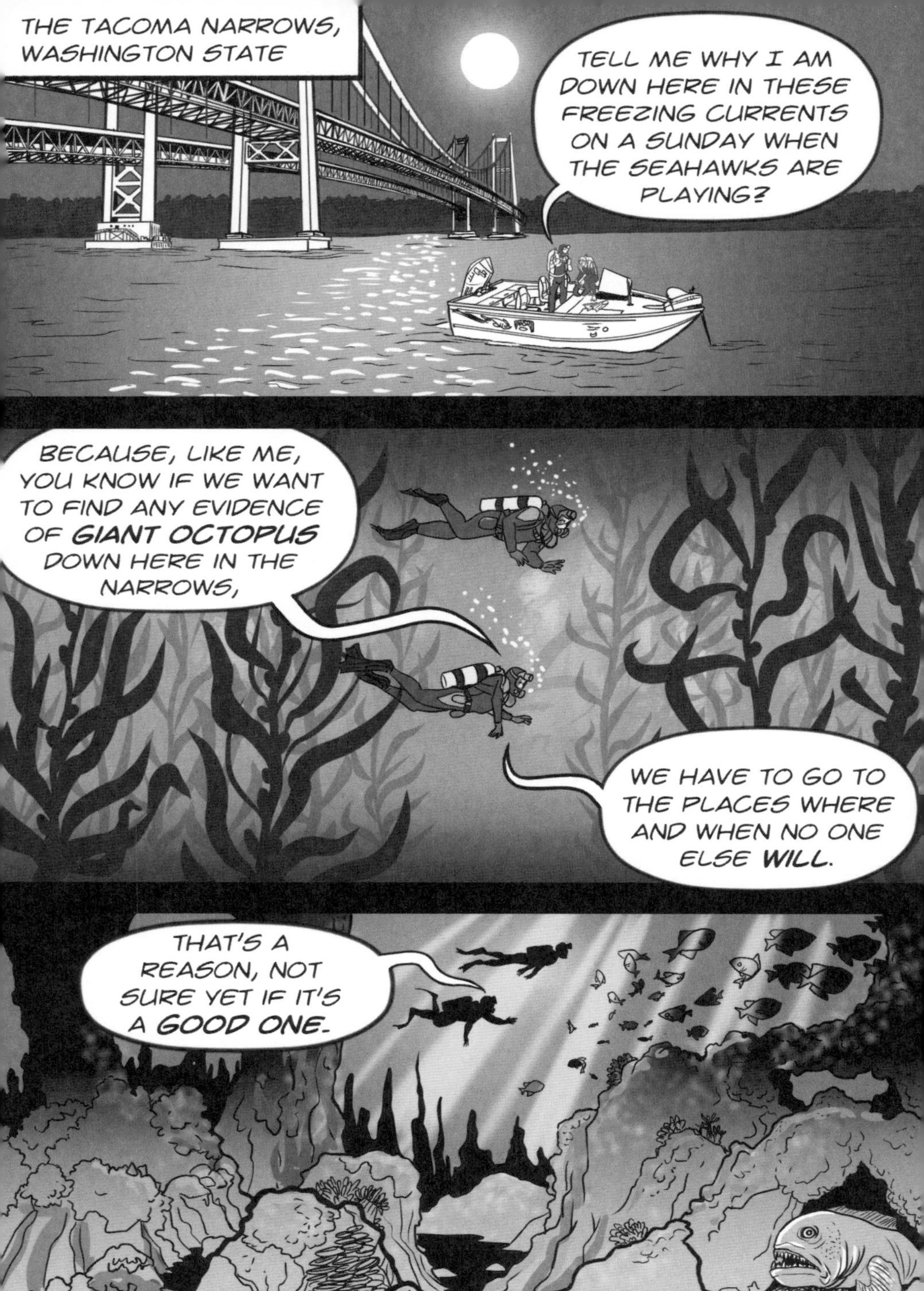
THE TACOMA NARROWS, WASHINGTON STATE
TELL ME WHY I AM DOWN HERE IN THESE FREEZING CURRENTS ON A SUNDAY WHEN THE SEAHAWKS ARE PLAYING?
BECAUSE, LIKE ME, YOU KNOW IF WE WANT TO FIND ANY EVIDENCE OF **GIANT OCTOPUS** DOWN HERE IN THE NARROWS,
WE HAVE TO GO TO THE PLACES WHERE AND WHEN NO ONE ELSE **WILL**.
THAT'S A REASON, NOT SURE YET IF IT'S A **GOOD ONE**.

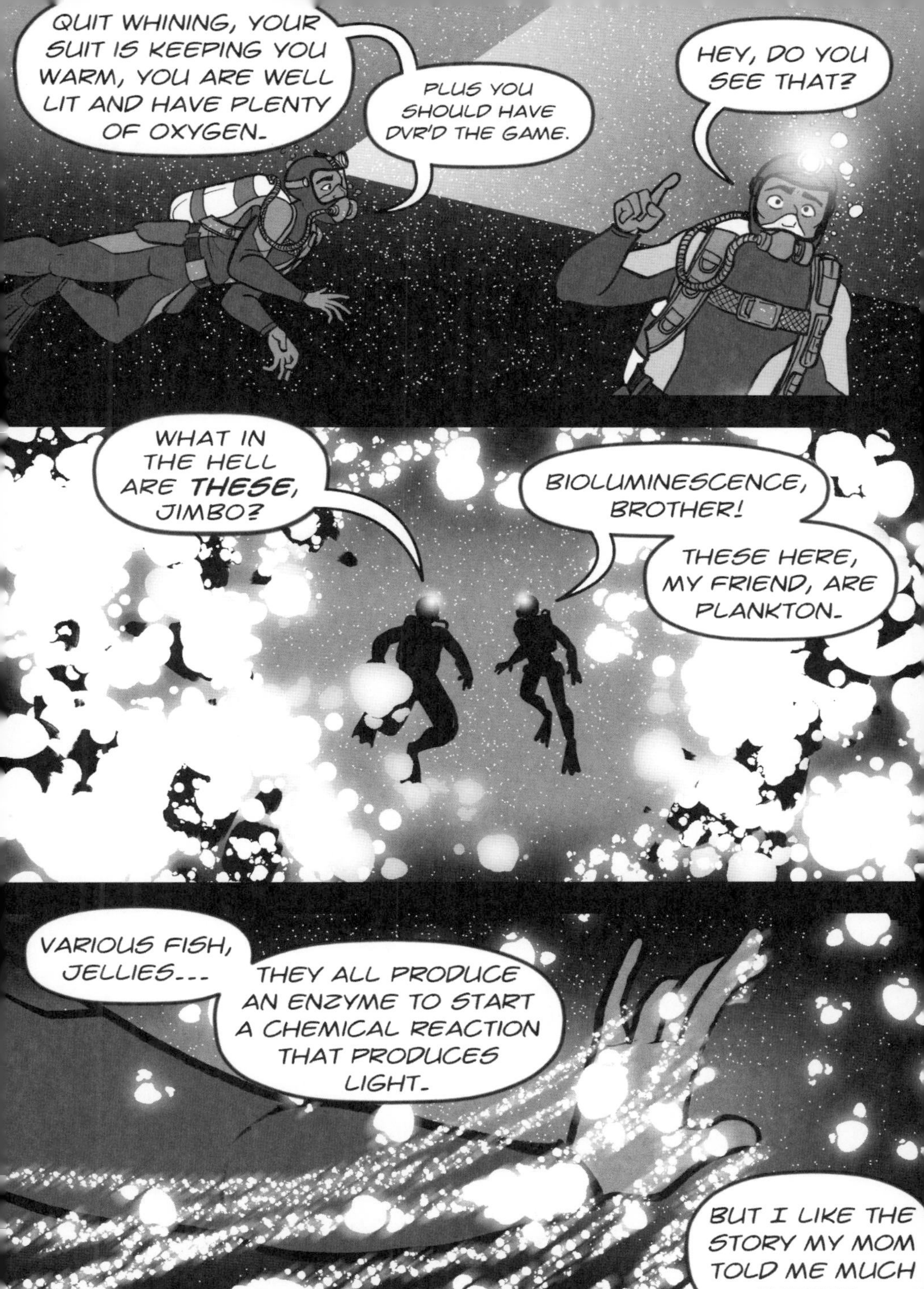
QUIT WHINING, YOUR SUIT IS KEEPING YOU WARM, YOU ARE WELL LIT AND HAVE PLENTY OF OXYGEN.
PLUS YOU SHOULD HAVE DVR'D THE GAME.
HEY, DO YOU SEE THAT?
WHAT IN THE HELL ARE **THESE**, JIMBO?
BIOLUMINESCENCE, BROTHER!
THESE HERE, MY FRIEND, ARE PLANKTON.
VARIOUS FISH, JELLIES...
THEY ALL PRODUCE AN ENZYME TO START A CHEMICAL REACTION THAT PRODUCES LIGHT.
BUT I LIKE THE STORY MY MOM TOLD ME MUCH BETTER.

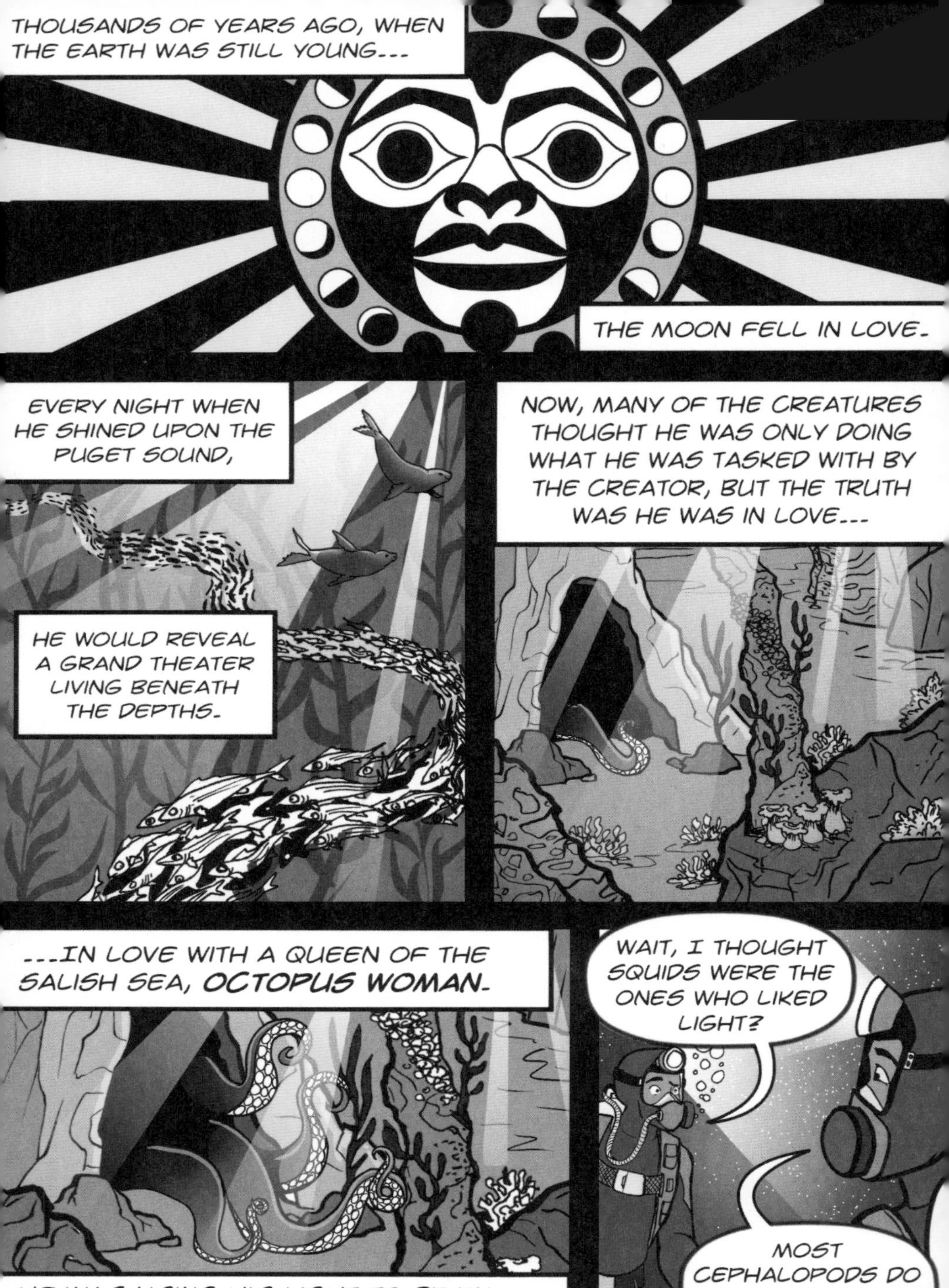
THOUSANDS OF YEARS AGO, WHEN THE EARTH WAS STILL YOUNG...
THE MOON FELL IN LOVE.
EVERY NIGHT WHEN HE SHINED UPON THE PUGET SOUND,
HE WOULD REVEAL A GRAND THEATER LIVING BENEATH THE DEPTHS.
NOW, MANY OF THE CREATURES THOUGHT HE WAS ONLY DOING WHAT HE WAS TASKED WITH BY THE CREATOR, BUT THE TRUTH WAS HE WAS IN LOVE...
...IN LOVE WITH A QUEEN OF THE SALISH SEA, OCTOPUS WOMAN.
HE WAS USING HIS LIGHT TO DRAW HER OUT OF THE SHADOWS.
WAIT, I THOUGHT SQUIDS WERE THE ONES WHO LIKED LIGHT?
MOST CEPHALOPODS DO ROB, INCLUDING OCTOPUS.

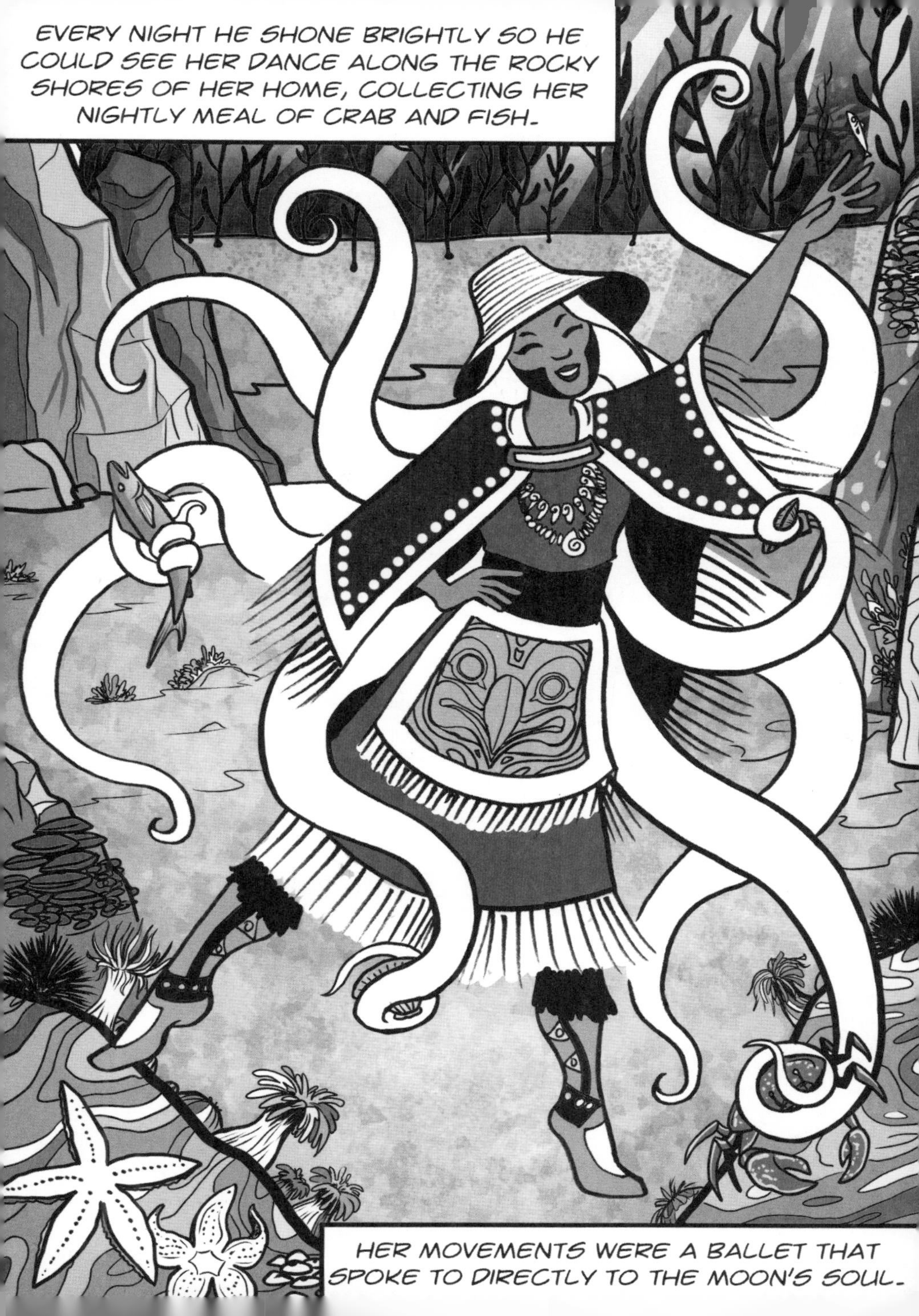
EVERY NIGHT HE SHONE BRIGHTLY SO HE COULD SEE HER DANCE ALONG THE ROCKY SHORES OF HER HOME, COLLECTING HER NIGHTLY MEAL OF CRAB AND FISH.
HER MOVEMENTS WERE A BALLET THAT SPOKE TO DIRECTLY TO THE MOON'S SOUL.

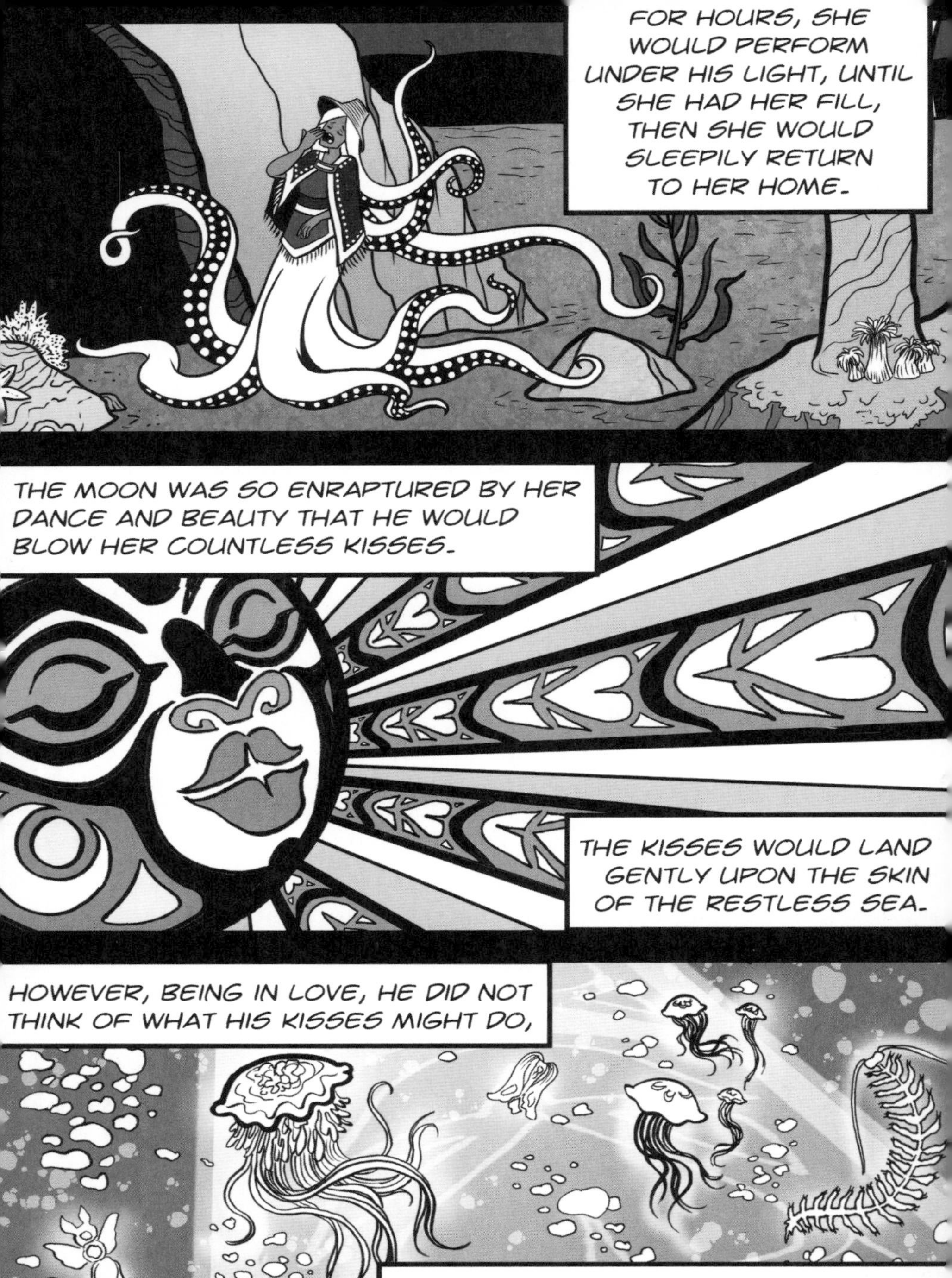
FOR HOURS, SHE WOULD PERFORM UNDER HIS LIGHT, UNTIL SHE HAD HER FILL, THEN SHE WOULD SLEEPILY RETURN TO HER HOME.
THE MOON WAS SO ENRAPTURED BY HER DANCE AND BEAUTY THAT HE WOULD BLOW HER COUNTLESS KISSES.
THE KISSES WOULD LAND GENTLY UPON THE SKIN OF THE RESTLESS SEA.
HOWEVER, BEING IN LOVE, HE DID NOT THINK OF WHAT HIS KISSES MIGHT DO,
AND DIDN'T REALIZE THAT SOME OF THE SEA CREATURES WOULD ABSORB THE LIGHT HE SENT FROM HIS HEART.

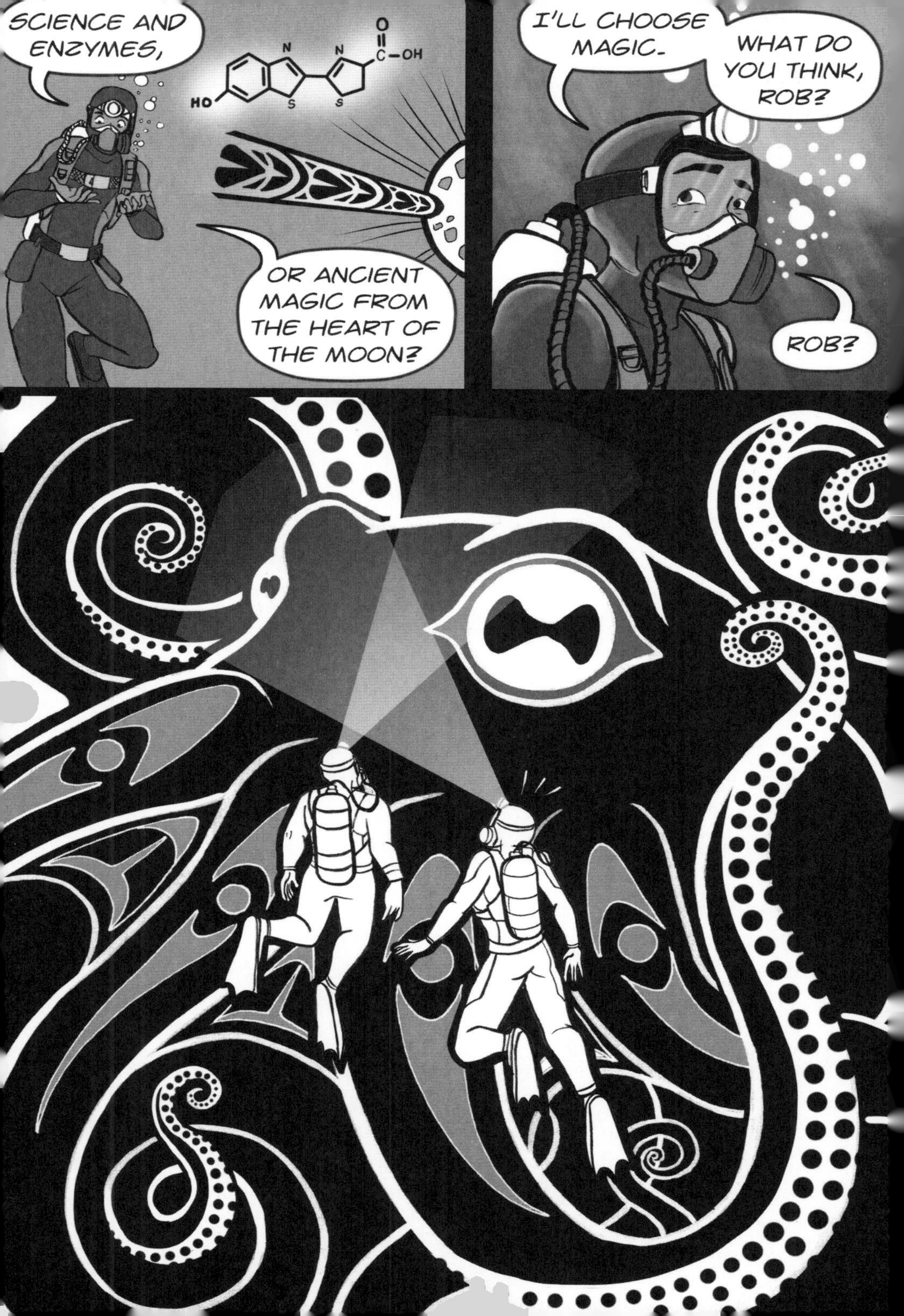
SCIENCE AND ENZYMES,
OR ANCIENT MAGIC FROM THE HEART OF THE MOON?
I'LL CHOOSE MAGIC.
WHAT DO YOU THINK, ROB?
ROB?

ABOUT THE CREATORS

Mercedes Acosta is a Cuban Taíno artist and storyteller who, as a child, was always warned to stay away from trees at night. She loves eerie and joyful things. Mercedes lives in the tropics of southern Florida with her Papí. mercedesdoesart.com

Milo Applejohn is an autistic illustrator of Métis and settler ancestry who resides in the unceded traditional territories of the səlilwətaʔɬ (Tsleil-Waututh), kʷikʷəʎəm (Kwikwetlem), Sḵwx̱wú7mesh Úxwumixw (Squamish) and xʷməθkʷəy̓əm (Musqueam) Nations. applejohnillustration.com

Jordaan Arledge is a trans, Chickasaw comic writer and founder of Arledge Comics. Jordaan's credits span from the award-winning *Alex Priest* series to all-ages titles like *Future Girl*. They graduated from Central Washington University with degrees in English—focusing in British literature—and in philosophy—specializing in religious studies and focusing in pre-Christian literature. When they're not reading or creating comic books, Jordaan can be found at your local comic book convention talking about indie press and queer representation in comics. twitter.com/itsyaboijordaan

Elijah Forbes (he/him) is a transgender Odawa illustrator who primarily works in the fields of graphic novels and children's literature. He has facilitated the creation of illustration projects such as the 2020 "Trans Awareness Week" through Twitter, as well as projects benefitting transgender rights groups, such as Sunshine House in Winnipeg, Manitoba. He seeks to create work that uplifts people of transgender and Indigenous backgrounds. paintedturtleco.com

Rhael McGregor is a non-binary/Two-Spirit Métis comic artist and animator from Winnipeg, Manitoba. They work primarily in writing LGBTQ2S+ imaginings of fantasy/sci-fi stories in hopes of making the world a little brighter! twitter.com/raysdrawlings1

Mekala Nava is a reconnecting Chicana designer/illustrator with a passion for storytelling. She likes to incorporate folktales, myths, legends, and history into her work and hopes to move into the realm of graphic novels. Mekala graduated from Cornish College of the arts with a degree in Visual Communications and a focus in animation and motion design. She likes to focus on the "human-ness" of storytelling and how it has inspired and connected people throughout our history. kdenlife.squarespace.com

Alina Pete is a Cree artist and writer from Little Pine First Nation in western Saskatchewan. They are best known for their Aurora award-winning webcomic, *Weregeek* (weregeek.com), and for their Shuster-nominated anthology, *Life Finds a Way*. Alina also writes short stories, poems and RPG supplements, and their work has been featured in several comic anthologies, including *Moonshot* Volumes 2 & 3.

Maija Ambrose Plamondon is a Métis writer currently living on treaty 6 territory. They spend their time writing music, comics, and being bad at rhythm games. Their current comics projects are two webcomics; one called *Mystery Solving Lesbians* which, surprisingly, is about two lesbians solving mysteries, and the other called *Coming of Age* which is an autobiographical story that seems to make people sad. maplamondon.carrd.co

Alice RL is a professional Illustrator and art teacher based in Winnipeg, Manitoba. The non-binary Ojibwe artist draws inspiration from their experiences and cultural teachings and melds it with a signature palette of bright, playful hues to create stunning juxtapositions of human brutality and emotion with hope and whimsy. Alice's range of projects include game and comic book art, digital and traditional illustration, and graphic design. Alice is a graduate of the University of Manitoba Fine Arts Program and Digital Media Design at Red River College. Alice is deeply involved in the local art community and strives to improve themself and others. Whether working in digital or traditional art, Alice brings a unique personal style and emotional impact into all their creations. behance.net/alicearel

Izzy Roberts is a Michigan-based illustrator and a member of the Navajo Nation and Kinyaa'áanii clan. They spend much of their time writing and illustrating comics or attending conventions around the Midwest. Most days they can be found working at home with their rescue dog, Pickles, close by their side. Armed with a love of seductive horror and a commitment to creating more Native representation in visual mediums, Izzy is a highly dedicated artist with a passion for storytelling. twitter.com/tsilghaah

Jeffrey Veregge is an award-winning Native American Artist & Writer from the Port Gamble S'Klallam Tribe near Kingston, Washington. He is best known for his use of form-line design with pop culture inspiration which his fans dub "Salish Geek." He has over 100 comic book covers working for Marvel, IDW, Valiant, Dynamite, Boom! & Darkhorse Comics. jeffreyveregge.com